THE
FOUNDER EFFECT

D0099434

BAEN BOOKS
by ROBERT E. HAMPSON

Stellaris: People of the Stars
(edited with Les Johnson)

THE FOUNDER EFFECT

edited by
Robert E. Hampson
and
Sandra L. Medlock

THE FOUNDER EFFECT

Story copyright information:
"Foreword: Legends" copyright © 2020 by Larry Correia; "Descent" copyright © 2020 by Mark H. Wandrey; "Confession" copyright © 2020 by Les Johnson; "Somnum Exterreri" copyright © 2020 by Christopher L. Smith; "Kamekura" copyright © 2020 by Words of Weber, Inc.; "Sonny Stirs" copyright © 2020 by Daniel M. Hoyt; "Stowaway" copyright © 2020 by Brad R. Torgersen; "Cerberus Project" copyright © 2020 by Monalisa Foster; "Alas Roanoke" copyright © 2020 by Sarah A. Hoyt; "The Legend of Jimmy Vee" copyright © 2020 by Chris Kennedy; "On the Trail of the Sügenhound" copyright © 2020 by Vivienne Raper; "No Word for Princes" copyright © 2020 by Jody Lynn Nye; "The Loss of Beaver Flight" copyright © 2020 by Brent M. Roeder; "Jack Daw Days" copyright © 2020 by Catherine L. Smith; "Redemption" copyright © 2020 by Philip Wohlrab; "Looneytunes" copyright © 2020 by D.J. Butler; "Fire From Heaven" copyright © 2020 by Words of Weber, Inc. and Mark H. Wandrey.

A Baen Books Original

Baen Publishing Enterprises
P.O. Box 1403
Riverdale, NY 10471
www.baen.com

ISBN: 978-1-9821-2509-7

Cover art by Sam Kennedy
First Baen printing, December 2020

Distributed by Simon & Schuster
1230 Avenue of the Americas
New York, NY 10020

Library of Congress Cataloging-in-Publication Data

Names: Hampson, Robert E., editor. | Medlock, Sandra L., editor.
Title: The founder effect / edited by Robert E. Hampson and Sandra L. Medlock.
Description: Riverdale, NY : Baen Books, 2020.
Identifiers: LCCN 2020040096 | ISBN 9781982125097 (trade paperback)
Subjects: LCSH: Science fiction, American.
Classification: LCC PS648.S3 F69 2020 | DDC 813/.6—dc23
LC record available at https://lccn.loc.gov/2020040096

Printed in the United States of America

10 9 8 7 6 5 4 3 2 1

Contents

Dedication

For Ruann, the love of my life;
for Mom, my first fan;
for Dad, my hero and role model.
—REH

For James and Jamie,
who listen to my dreams and spur me on,
and Mom and Dad, who have always encouraged
me in all my endeavors.
—SLM

FOREWORD: LEGENDS

Larry Correia

Mankind runs on legends.

Whether they're examples of greatness to strive toward, or evils to avoid, every culture has its legends. Handed down and evolving through time, they're always with us, molding and shaping individuals, families, and whole societies. We're all the product of the stories we grew up on.

I'm talking about legends, not history. The two are often related, but not necessarily. Legends often have a kernel of truth to them, but that's before the truth takes a back seat to the stories we spin about it. That's because reality is complicated, with lots of moving parts and little fiddly bits that don't fit into neat boxes. History is rarely black and white, good or bad. Truth is messy.

People are hungry for narratives with a familiar taste that are easy to digest, so we tend to take that convoluted reality and distill it down to the repeatable basics to then tell over and over again. It's all the same, whether it's hunters around a campfire, or a drinking song in a pub, or a movie "based on historical events," and each time that story evolves, either because of the teller, or because of the audience.

History gets mangled, rewritten, or forgotten, but legends live on.

We love our heroes, hate our villains, and use the fools as object lessons to teach our kids what not to do. Good guys, bad guys, or just lessons to be learned, sometimes a legend can be all of them at the same time. Depending on who is telling the story, Bonnie and Clyde were murderous psychopaths, or a tragic love story with Robin Hood elements, and that wasn't even a century ago.

It isn't about them, it's about us. Ask some random people what they know about Christopher Columbus. You'll probably learn a lot more about the beliefs and politics of the person answering the question than you will about the actual history or nature of the explorer in question.

Storytelling is a powerful tool. Legends are a common touchstone of a people. Your tribe is made up of those who the share the same legends as you. Those other guys over there? They got it all wrong. This is the way it *really* happened.

Chivalry wasn't that chivalrous, bushido mostly exists in Akira Kurosawa movies, and the Wild West was quieter than modern day Chicago on a Saturday night. But we just can't help ourselves. Human beings are addicted to legends, both manufacturing them and sharing them. I don't think we even know we're doing it most of the time. We can't help ourselves.

The founding of nations makes fertile ground for harvesting legends. Romulus and Remus were suckled by a wolf. George Washington couldn't lie about chopping down that cherry tree. It doesn't matter if it was in ancient times or recent enough that we've still got the journals of the participants, the real history is learned by specialists and enthusiasts, while the vast majority soaks up the legend like a thirsty sponge.

Those founders become icons, the heroes and villains and fools that parents tell their kids about. The stories become larger than life. They become our moral examples, cringing shames, or shining beacons. And from that foundation, we build.

That's what mankind has done with every civilization on Earth.

Now just imagine what happens once we start founding whole new worlds.

—Larry Correia
Yard Moose Mountain, January 2020

PROLOGUE: TRAPPIST-2

When the Transiting Planets and Planetesimals Small Telescope (TRAPPIST) operated by the University of Liège in Belgium first published their finding of planets in the habitable zone of the star 2MASS J23062928-0502285, the public was excited at the potential of new Earth-like worlds around a distant star. Up to seven roughly Earth-sized worlds were identified. Unfortunately, their sun was an ultra-cool red dwarf, meaning that its habitable zone was so close to the star that even the farthest planet had a "year" of only eighteen days. The planets were also likely tidally locked, with one face permanently facing the star, resulting in extreme hot-versus-cold temperatures, and if they had atmospheres, turbulent conditions at the edge of day and night.

Enthusiasm for the system as a target for colonization cooled as quickly as the night side of one of TRAPPIST-1's planets.

It was only fitting that when a much more appropriate candidate system was identified, it would be by the same team, and the newly labeled TRAPPIST-2 system once again captured the imagination of the public.

The yellow-dwarf star was initially shown to have three Earth-sized rocky planets and two larger gaseous worlds. The habitable zone was similar to Sol's, at 0.75 to 1.5 AU, with one rocky planet firmly within the zone. With such an ideal candidate for an extra-solar home for humanity, the TRAPPIST-2 Colony Foundation set their sights on establishing the first interstellar colony on TRAPPIST-2c—eventually named "Cistercia."

Construction of the colony ship *Victoria* began in Mars orbit in the year 2150 but was almost immediately met with criticism. One of the key arguments was not so much against the mission, but against putting all of the colonization effort into one ship. Repeated redesign of the cryostasis systems for hibernation for the 10,000 colonists and preservation of the hundreds of thousands of fertilized animal ova caused numerous delays in construction of the *Victoria*. TCF bowed to pressure and began construction of a second ship, *Prometheus*, which would be sent in advance to TRAPPIST-2. The fully automated, uncrewed *Prometheus* would initiate terraforming and infrastructure development to ensure that TRAPPIST-2c would be ready for the colonists on arrival.

—From the *Encyclopedia Astra*, published by Gannon University, Antonia, Cistercia, AA212

Part One:
THE JOURNEY

DESCENT

Mark H. Wandrey

David Parker dreamed. It wasn't the normal dreaming a human experienced, with form and often memorable moments. It was the dream of a fractured consciousness. His mind skipped over parts of his life, concentrated on others, then lingered on powerful memories dredged up by his cerebral cortex. For the consciousness, which was David Parker, this seemed to go on for an infinity within the cold embrace of his extended slumber.

"Mr. Parker, after reviewing your application to the TRAPPIST Project, we sadly have to deny your participation. . . ."

David looked up from his tablet computer to see Joan Walker sitting two rows up from him in class. She was talking to a friend and never noticed him. She never did.

"And the first place in the national AI project goes to Dr. David Parker, Carnegie Mellon University!"

"You're only doing it because that woman is a colonist," his mother said. "She doesn't know you exist!"

"She knows I exist," David mumbled, the lie tasting sour in his mouth.

David brought a box of pizza into the dorm living room where everyone was watching the announcement. A few looked up in surprise. David never went there. The pizza was like a talisman to offer the strange tribe.

They'd all been waiting for it and planned to apply. Finally, they were going to begin taking applications for the colony ship to TRAPPIST. The ship would travel thirty-nine light-years and take centuries to get there, and he was going to go. Joan gave him a courteous smile when he set the pizza down.

The TV spoke. "Here is how the application process will be conducted."

"Computers, David?" his mother asked. "There are a billion computer programmers, why would you want to do that?"

"AIs, Mom; making a computer think for itself. It's just . . . cool!"

David stared at the letter in abject disappointment. He'd seen on social media—only an hour ago—Joan had been accepted. He hadn't.

All of David's classmates had left an hour ago. He hadn't moved from his seat. His teacher had gotten permission for him to stay late so David could watch an online discussion on AI. He started high school next year and had just discovered the subject of advanced AI programming.

On the webcast a scientist from Carnegie Mellon University began discussing their advanced computational science recruiting program. David stared in rapt attention; his teacher smiled.

"Starship *Victoria* construction is being plagued by delays as the massive colony ship is under construction in low Earth orbit. With a trip planned for the TRAPPIST star system, which will last for centuries, the project spokesman states that delays are to be expected. However, no explanation has been given as to why it appears a second ship is also under construction."

David put the sandwich down and looked at the TV in confusion. *A second ship?*

"You said I was a good match for the program!" David said. He tried as hard as he could to not sound disappointed over the webcall.

"You were, technically. But David, your interpersonal skills are the problem. Try to imagine being one of the colonists, alone on an alien world."

"I know, I want that."

"But they don't want you."

David smashed the laptop lid down so hard the screen cracked.

He'd never tested in even the top twenty-five percent of his junior high classes. When the teacher posted the results from their first lab in computer learning, David was number one. His classmates, most of whom had never said a word to him because he never spoke to them, stared at the name in amazement. He was amazed as well. Something clicked.

"You said they don't want me," David said. He was using his cellphone on purpose. When he saw the call was from the TRAPPIST Project web address, he didn't want to break another computer.

"The colonists don't, David. However, the powers that be have decided to make a change in the way we're approaching the entire project. We think there's a place for you after all—in the terraforming mission. Something that both speaks to your abilities, and doesn't play off any of your . . . shall we say, social weaknesses?"

"I'm listening."

Suddenly something changed, and the dreams were torn away to be replaced with icy, numb pain.

Day 1

David couldn't sit up. He could hardly move at all. His breath came out in a plume inside the cryochamber. The air was circulated cold to allow him to focus as he floated in the warm gel-like revival fluid. "How long?" he croaked. Of course, no one was there to answer.

He blinked and tried to concentrate. His eyes didn't want to focus. It wasn't like the training runs; this was brutal, cold reality. The revival fluid felt like liquid fire, his insides felt like ice and he couldn't feel his extremities.

Did I speak? He tried again. "How long?"

He heard his voice echo this time, and still there was no response.

Damnit. He concentrated and tried to focus. There was a status display on the left side of his cryochamber. Simple information only, like his bio signs. He'd thought it was kind of stupid to have this information. He was a technician, not a doctor. However, one of the data elements was the mission clock.

He could see lines of fuzzy bright lights. His head was above the fluid, of course. Its specific gravity was lower than saltwater. He was so buoyant in the goo that he was less than half submerged.

Must be in my eyes. He blinked hard several times and looked again. Yes, better now. He could see numbers and moving lines showing both EEG and EKG data. A single static numerical value was in the upper left of the little display. It said 644.88.

"Impossible," his voice croaked. He blinked and looked again. The number didn't change. He'd been in cryostasis for less than two years.

David spent some time concentrating on his reluctant body. The training had explained that he would be disoriented. He was. He would feel frail and cold. Oh, without a doubt. He could recover quicker by forcing his body into motion. His body didn't *want* to be forced into motion. As he slowly flexed first his shoulders, then elbows, then fingers, his mind thawed and he realized why he was awakened after such a short time in cryo.

"Malfunction," he mumbled.

For his own safety, the cryochamber wouldn't open until he could enter a simple code. Next to the display were four buttons with 1, 2, 3, 4 printed on them. He would have to press a preset code he'd saved when entering cryostasis 644.88 days ago in Earth orbit. It couldn't be 1234, or 4321.

It took quite a bit of time to remember what he'd chosen. 4132. The time it took to remember the code helped him make sense of why you needed to enter the code. Having someone wandering around the ship half zoned out was a suboptimal solution.

If remembering the code took a lot of time, actually punching it in with his half-numb and unresponsive fingers took much longer. The keypad was analog because of all the fluid in the cryo chamber, so he had to push with enough force to register the input. He didn't know how much time passed before he managed it. He might have slept.

A loud beep signaled success and the heavy plexi lid unseated.

Air pressure equalized with a hiss and David felt his ears pop. For a brief second his half-frozen brain was afraid the ship was in vacuum and he was about to die from decompression. However, the hissing stopped, and the lid rolled back.

He took a long time to sit up, but when he finally managed it, he felt better. The warmth of the fluid was finally making his limbs more responsive. He had to urinate, and he remembered from the training back on Earth that this was a good sign. However, he didn't want to pee in the fluid—that meant he needed to get out of the chamber.

As he was *slowly* throwing a leg over the side and reaching for the floor, David realized he was in gravity. *The ring had spun up, and there was air!*

The atmosphere tasted fine and he didn't smell smoke or ozone. No alarms were sounding. So whatever had happened, it wasn't catastrophic. He cleared his throat, finally able to concentrate enough to form questions.

"Computer—report." Silence. He coughed and spoke louder. "*Prometheus*, computer—report!" Still nothing. "Well, shit."

His foot touched the floor. It was cold, though not ice cold. The metallic grate which made up the deck was solid and somehow reassuring. Lighting was standard: subdued, low-intensity LED . . . as was used throughout the habitable portions of *Prometheus*.

He stood by the chamber; a slight chill across his body made his privates contract. He looked down at his naked, dripping body and exhaled. Everything was working, and that was something, right?

A towel lay in the cubby next to his chamber. He grabbed it and began methodically drying his body. Once the slippery fluid was sopped up he felt warmer, though no less exposed.

"What am I worried about? It's not like anyone else within a billion miles cares about seeing me naked." He was the only person on the ship, after all.

David draped the towel over the end of his cryostasis chamber. He noted the fluid was almost drained away and it appeared to be cleaning itself. More signs that everything was working correctly. *What the hell did the computer wake me up for?* "Computer, respond!"

After waiting for a full minute, he cursed under his breath and began shuffling toward the little bathroom. The need to reach it was becoming rather . . . urgent. He barely made it in time.

He emerged from the toilet after finishing and laughed. "Damn good thing I'm alone on this tub." He coughed and closed the door, letting the chamber's systems go to work.

His locker was next to the toilet. Inside were three pairs of coveralls and underwear. He didn't think he'd be awake for long, so he just pulled on the first pair of coveralls he could reach and stuffed his feet into slippers. A little dinette was next to the locker, as was the modular kitchen. The remainder of the cryostasis chamber was hundreds of hatches holding spare parts and supplies for his arrival in TRAPPIST.

David walked past the now dark cryostasis chamber to one of the other doors. Opening it, he entered *Prometheus'* command deck. He'd spent a few hours in the space as the crew put the ship into cruise mode. Once the ship was under power and the Cartwright drive began pushing her away from Earth, the medical lead put David into cryostasis while everyone else boarded a shuttle back to Earth. *Prometheus* accelerated slowly, so it was easy for them to return to Earth.

Less than ten percent of his training involved operating the ship. The computer had the files he'd need if anything required attention, which it wouldn't. Now it was time to get to the bottom of why the AI wasn't talking to him.

He took a seat in the computer station chair, yawned and typed an access code into the blank station. He tried to imagine what it would be like waking up on *Victoria* with hundreds of colonists all buzzing about, every minute of every day accounted for. *Less than two years.* He realized *Victoria* hadn't even cleared the Oort Cloud yet. Wouldn't for another twenty-eight years.

Joan Walker.

David pulled his thoughts violently away from that thought and stared at the screen. It was blank. He blinked and tapped at the keyboard. Nothing happened. For the first time he really looked around the command deck with its six workstations. They were all dark.

He sat for a few minutes, thinking. He couldn't make up his mind. Was it his half-frozen brain, or was he still in cryostasis immersed in a long dream? Flashing lights on the commander's workstation and an insistent beeping tone cleared it up—this was no dream.

The monitor should have come alive as soon as he touched it. He clearly remembered the stylized icon representing the AI that could process faster than any human could. There should be a rotating cube, with lines racing around its surface. It wasn't any true indication of what was going on, but rather a sign that all was well. Only the cube was empty and just sitting there. All wasn't well.

David took one more look at the blank monitor in front of him and ground his teeth. It appeared the main computer was down. Of all the possible situations he could deal with, a computer failure was not one of them.

Sure, there was a fail-safe in place. Should all computer control of primary systems go off-line, the human operator would be revived. However, this was a malfunction between various ship's components and the computer.

The ship's brain, an advanced AI he had helped program, was made of a dozen independent computers linked via a positronic network. It was widely considered as close to human-level redundancy as possible. It had a thousand independent programs interwoven through its learning matrix along with exabytes of quantum memory.

Furthermore, the computer's physical processors and storage were dispersed throughout the habitat ring and the main structure. Half the ship could be destroyed, and because of the system's redundancy, the computers would still function.

He reached under the console and tapped a switch. A section of the panel flipped over to reveal a simple LCD screen. David touched the screen and it came to life. This was the mechanical reporting system which displayed status on all twelve main processors. On it were twelve red icons. The main computers were all shut down.

"Well, shit."

◆ ◆ ◆

Despite being—essentially—a computer tech, David had spent most of his time learning how to repair mechanical failures. After two weeks in zero-G training, he was nominally qualified for EVA operations that fixed a hull breach or damage to the drive. In reality, David was nothing more than a backup to the squad of maintenance robots.

Training for troubleshooting the computers lasted three days and was the lengthiest of the *never do this* items on his list. "Resetting the computers is a worst-case scenario. It isn't something you will be expected to do."

"Then why bother showing me?" he'd asked.

The various computer engineers stared at one another before one finally answered. "Because it's theoretically possible a failure could occur."

David stared at the twelve red icons.

"Theory proved," he said to the empty room.

Prometheus had a thousand computers. Maybe more.

The AI, in turn, told the other computers what to do, and when to do it. Absent that input, most of the other computers would continue their tasks until they needed instructions. Some would go on forever. Others, like his cryostasis, would note the lack of communication and wake him up.

So here he was, on a ship without guidance, and twelve dead computers. He touched the master control, and the icon for processor number 1. "CONFIRM?" flashed on the bottom of the display.

He stroked the confirmation with a thumb. The Number 1 processor was the system's cerebral cortex. It was essential for everything to work optimally. The AI *could* function without it. However, *Prometheus'* main function as an advanced terraforming mission would be badly compromised without it.

David held his breath and waited as the processor's icon went from red to flashing yellow. "Rebooting" was displayed under the flashing yellow. He'd never done this, even in training.

"Come on," he said. The reboot seemed to take a long time. Too long? He was about to hit the reboot again when the icon stopped flashing and turned green.

"YES!" he cried and began rebooting the other eleven processors.

The computer engineers had told him that once the processors rebooted, the AI would come online when enough power was available.

The processors came online one after another, quicker than the first had rebooted, building his confidence. *Just some kind of a freak failure. I'll be back in the freezer once the AI analyzes what went wrong.* The robots could handle any repairs.

The AI interface on his console was a holographic readout showing the busy processes of the AI, with a three-dimensional dancing flame that showed he was talking to *Prometheus*. When he had first come aboard, he'd almost expected the AI icon to be a big red eye (he'd always loved that old movie).

David waited for the flame to appear. The status showed zero percent available resources. The flame didn't appear, and the percentage didn't change. He looked back at the processor display. All twelve were operating, but the AI wasn't there.

Having done it once, rebooting the processors he wasn't supposed to reboot wasn't as intimidating the second time. He booted one through twelve, just as he had done before. "Come on..." he urged, as he waited. After a few minutes, the processors were again up and running, but the AI was not.

David moved to the engineering station and opened the fold-out LCD screen there. Instead of master computer controls, this screen had status of *Prometheus*' drive. A series of green icons greeted him. The engines were running. "Oh, thank God."

One after another, he visited the stations: life support, navigation, robotics, ship's internal systems, and comms. The only ones working were life support and internal systems. *The most autonomous of the ship's systems*, he considered.

None of the contingencies he had trained on matched what he was facing. And, without the AI, he couldn't pursue other options. The ship would pursue its course, burning the massive fuel reserves, slowly building up speed until it ran the tanks dry. He'd reach TRAPPIST alright, and shoot right through the system and fly on forever.

◆ ◆ ◆

David went back to the living section and stood staring at his cryostasis chamber. He could climb in and just go back to sleep. How long would it function beyond the intended 200 or so years? Five hundred? A thousand? Eventually *Prometheus*' fusion powerplant would go cold and he'd sleep on and on and on.

A voice whispered in the back of his mind. *And what about Joan?* She would be coming on *Victoria*, behind *Prometheus*. Without the terraforming *Prometheus* was to perform, it was possible the thousands on *Victoria* wouldn't survive.

He went to the toilet again and splashed some water on his face. He was feeling steadily better, if not optimistic, about his situation. In the living area he busied himself bringing the various systems to life. There was a small entertainment console, as well as a dedicated computer system he could use for any repair work.

The cooking arrangements were closer to what you might find on an old RV on Earth. A combination rehydration/heating unit would prepare stored meals and a small heating plate could make coffee or boil water. No fresh or frozen food was aboard—nothing would last for the centuries he was supposed to be sleeping.

He opened the first stores hatch. Inside were 120 meals—forty breakfasts, forty lunches, and forty dinners. The walls of his living section were lined with forty-five such storage compartments. A grand total of 5,400 meals which would last him 1,800 days. Enough to allow him to spend the roughly five years he would need to supervise *Prometheus* while the colony terraforming equipment landed and went to work. Then he'd sleep again, waiting for *Victoria* to arrive with the colonists.

He took a lunch from the compartment and set it into the cooker, programmed the machine, and waited while it worked. In five minutes, it beeped, and he had a hot meal. While he ate, he considered his situation. The processors were working fine, he could tell that much. However, they weren't initiating the AI, which meant the problem was likely in their distinct memory modules.

When he'd finished eating, he knew what to do. At the rear of the living compartment was an access hatch. Through it he could reach the other sections of the habitation ring. The remainder of the ring contained life support, as well as five of the twelve processors and memory modules. The other six were in the central hull. Their distinct memory modules were likewise distributed throughout, with six in the habitation ring and the remaining seven in the central hull.

He grabbed his tool belt from the locker and clipped it on. Without the AI or robots to assist, Dave reviewed his memory of the ship's detailed schematic. Nearly every day during training he had studied the schematic.

Refreshed from his meal and fully awake, his brain was now firing on all cylinders. He crawled through the access shaft directly to the computer memory module. The crawlway to the memory module was colder than his habitation area, but he wouldn't be there long.

At the module he removed the access panel. There was warning tape on all four fasteners: CAUTION—COMPUTER MEMORY—DO NOT OPEN. Of course, he opened it anyway. The memory modules were behind multiple levels of radiation shielding, deep within carbon fiber–reinforced and cooled frameworks. What he had was the installation access, more of a legacy from when the ship was built and AI installed.

Dave removed his personal diagnostic computer from the tool belt, pulled a data connector out and snapped it into the memory module's port. After verifying it was properly connected, he touched the DIAGNOSTIC button.

"Working," the tool told him. A moment later it reported. "Module Functional."

"Well, that's good," he said. Maybe this was the only functional one? He was about to disconnect when a thought came to him. He pulled up the diagnostic tool's menu and scrolled down to select another operation.

"Memory Unallocated."

He blinked at the response. It didn't make sense. He ran it again and got the same result. According to his diagnostic tool, the massive memory module which should have been brimming with the data making up a sophisticated AI was empty—it was like an unformatted disk.

Three hours of crawling confirmed all six of the memory modules in the habitation ring were wiped clean, like the day they'd been delivered to the team writing the AI. David had seen one memory module when he had worked on the project—a boring, insulated box with a dozen fiberoptic cable bundles and a pair of power leads. It could have been any of a dozen other components on *Prometheus*. However, unlike those other components, these added together to make an AI.

Lose one module, fine. Lose two, or even three, and the AI could still function at some level. Even with four down, the ship's mission could continue, though with difficulty. But that was the threshold. Without at least eight of the twelve memory modules, the AI could not form. All six in the habitation module were blank, and Dave had no reason to believe the other six in the central hull weren't as well.

He sat on the command deck, staring blankly at the opposite wall. Gone. Every byte of data gone as if it were never there. His diagnostic results resembled the tests that had been done on the modules when they arrived for programming. Empty. There hadn't been any training on what could cause such a thing, because it was impossible.

"Somebody blanked them on purpose," he said aloud. "I don't see any other way." He chewed another bite. "What difference does it really make?" The answer was, of course, none.

Day 5

Dave finished connecting his EVA suit to its holders, verifying the O^2 feeds and power couplings were properly connected. It would be recharged and ready to go when he needed it again. He was tired, hot, and hungry.

Exiting from the airlock into the habitation area, he sighed. It was only a few hundred cubic meters, but at least it wasn't space. He didn't like space. It didn't care about him, either.

He moved to the tiny dining table, covered with tablet computers and printouts. It had taken him three days to detail his plan, and the last two days to complete it. He'd just finished the final EVA. Or so he hoped.

David grabbed a cup of coffee and warmed it, then went into the command deck. Nothing had changed, except his computer station, which was now as messy as the dining table. He sat in the chair and activated one of the auxiliary computer controls. It was supposed to simply be a system to diagnose control pathways and a few other functions. He'd been rerouting data lines all over the ship in the hopes he could do much more with it.

"Time to find out if I'm right," he said, and tapped in the override sequence. The screen flashed and a REBOOTING icon came on. He cast an eye at the LCD displaying the twelve main processors' status. If he'd done it wrong, it could make the situation worse.

"Connection Established."

"*Yes!*" David cried and fist pumped. Now he had access to both the AI's blanked memory, and the colony databanks. He took a calming breath and typed in commands. The colony data was saved on memory modules in the ship's main hull as well as each of the landers—everything from how to fix a broken leg to adapting seed stock to an overly acidic atmosphere. More importantly, the ship's own maintenance procedures were duplicated there. All he had was emergency repair files, and few of those. The AI was supposed to have all the rest.

The screen began to display vast directories of data organized by type. David heaved another sigh. Whatever murdered the AI hadn't affected the colony databanks. He sipped coffee and perused the files, flagging ones he might need. He didn't have a plan yet, other than responding to the immediate concerns. He needed work-arounds for the various ship's systems which would have been managed by the AI.

The engineering station began flashing a red light he hadn't seen before. David got up and went to look. It was a status warning from the drive. Power levels were fluctuating. A problem the AI would have dealt with in a second, or if not, sent robots to examine. With the drive under power, he couldn't get close to it without risking a lethal radiation dose.

He looked at the robotics station and frowned. There was nothing wrong with *Prometheus'* complement of robots, except that they were operated by the AI. There had been no need for individual autonomous programming. Seemed a tad shortsighted now.

David went back to his newly established computer and accessed the drive operational manuals. Referencing the sort of error he was seeing, he tried to estimate how long he had. The drive would shut down if power levels got outside of a certain range. He examined the fluctuations and did some mental math. Maybe three days, was his best guess. What happened if the drive shut down? He found the answer to the question quickly. It couldn't be restarted. It was meant to run until they arrived at TRAPPIST, at which point its useful life would be over.

Having only accelerated for 650 days, *Prometheus* was at four percent of the speed of light, a fraction of her 0.2C cruising speed. Assuming she was still on course, which he couldn't be sure of because the AI had handled navigation, he'd still arrive at TRAPPIST—in a thousand years.

"One problem at a time," he said and went to work.

Day 8

One robot finished adjusting the cryogenic coolant flow manually while another was still replacing the failed module. Immediately the drive's power levels returned to normal. Dave smiled and yawned. He had gotten maybe six hours' sleep over the last three days.

The programming he'd participated in for the AI on Earth was as one member of a thousand-person team. No one person had the whole of it. The AI was a hundred thousand discrete logic trees put together into a neural network which, if done properly, merged into an AI.

To get the robots working he needed to write a subroutine, like the little part of a brain which caused your eyes to blink at certain times. Well, finally, after three days, he could blink.

Dave double-checked that the command buffer for his new minions was working properly, then went back to the habitation area. He thought about food but elected to collapse on his bunk instead. Sleep took him in seconds.

He woke later to the same lighting, and of course the same space. He checked his watch and saw he'd slept six hours. Two of his robotic minions were at the exit to his habitation area. They reminded him of crabs, a central body surrounded by six legs and a pair of manipulators which could reach and handle things from any angle. Each leg had its own set of eyes, giving the robot incredible visibility. A pair of cold-gas thrusters finished off the design, allowing it to function in zero gravity.

It was a good thing they could operate in zero gravity, because most of the ship was nearly weightless. The drive continued to push *Prometheus* ever faster, but with a tiny amount of inertial gravity.

Dave got a shower and started a meal. The programming job he'd done on the robots was working better than he thought. The subroutine wasn't difficult to write, and the robotic management software was already in the colony database. It just took time to get the control software to work on his orders, instead of the designed omnipresent AI.

When he exited the shower the two robots were still there, of course. He could see their eyes tracking him as he came out, toweling his hair dry. "What are you looking at?" he asked, then laughed. The two robots waited with the patience of a mechanical being.

"If I got them running," he thought aloud, "maybe I can do the rest." He stared at the piles of code notes and the dozens of computer tablets. He'd spent sixty or more hours to write one subroutine. What he was considering was so much more immense. How much time would it take?

"What more do I have, than time?" he said, glancing at the robots. Management had picked him for this job because of his ability to work alone. Well . . . that and he didn't really like people. *Don't need them, either.* So why not?

One subsystem at a time. Begin with the base level coding of the AI. All the logic routines were in the colony database. He just needed to put them all together. All hundred billion or so of them, in the right order, and interconnections.

"Fine, I'll start tomorrow." He looked at the huge stores of food. "Why not, what more do I need than time?"

Day 30

Dave savored the cake, even if it was a rehydrated forgery. It tasted pretty good. The computer array was running another compile of the AI operating subsystem. Tablet computers were in neat piles on his workstation and a dozen stacks of printed code samples were organized around the room. Some were piled on his bed, others on the table next to him, and still more on the dormant cryostasis chamber.

He had gotten tired of staying on the command deck, so he'd run a command pathway into his living quarters. Less running back and forth.

In the intervening twenty-two days he'd managed to get the robotics subroutine to be more autonomous, linked directly to any trouble signals in engineering. The robotic control program was smart enough for anything necessary, only needing the AI to tell it when. He'd just set them on automatic. Easy. With a small army of thirty-five bots, there was nothing they couldn't handle.

He had just finished the life support programming the day before, only to wake up in the morning to find it throwing hundreds of error codes. He quickly finished his treat (planned the night before when he thought his job was done) and dove into the problem.

"Figures," he mumbled as he watched the code compile complete. "I was going to go to work on comms today." The computer told him the compile results were available and he examined them on screen. Dozens and dozens of contingency errors were listed. He scrolled down them in confusion. He could have sworn he accounted for every contingency. With a shrug, he began reworking the subroutine to add the contingency codes he'd missed.

"I'll just have another piece of cake when I'm done."

Day 92

"Comms System Down."

"Son of a bitch," Dave snarled and dropped the tablet on his table. It dislodged a pile of programming printouts which slid toward the floor in a cascade of paperwork. It didn't really hit the floor but landed on a stack of discarded food packets. "I need to clean up a little," he mumbled.

He'd moved onto the comms system almost two months ago. Progress was slow, however, because life support kept throwing contingency codes. Each time it was one he'd never planned for, and it took him a couple hours to troubleshoot the problem and program it before going back to the comms.

There had been no serious malfunctions, so his robotic minions busied themselves with routine housekeeping. They were always coming and going, giving him a little amusement as they went about their duties.

Dave picked up the tablet from its resting place and examined the failure report. He had a movie playing in the background on a wall-mounted display. It was an old Earth movie called *It's a Wonderful Life*. The ship's chronometer said it was the twenty-fifth of December. "Merry Christmas," he mumbled as he stared at the report.

He didn't understand why comms was taking so much more time than life support had. Sure, life support wasn't really done because of the contingency errors. Comms should have been simpler, considering the main function was to fire a laser toward Earth and maintain a two-way communication.

He'd found out shortly after starting on comms that it was still functioning. He'd thought it would be finicky and have gone down shortly after the AI was destroyed (he still wanted to know how *that* had happened). The diagnostics reported that the comms laser was in two-way communications with Earth. But Dave couldn't see what was coming in or going out.

"That's not acceptable," he'd said, and set about recreating the AI subroutines designed to manage the comms laser. It looked easy. Weeks had gone by without success.

"It's not accepting the input," he realized. One of the crablike robots was parked nearby watching him. Dave looked at the machine. "Maybe I should program you guys to clean up this place?" Another robot entered and took advantage of the habitation area power port to recharge.

"I don't want to screw with the robotics subroutine. That one is actually working." He put aside the comms project and accessed the robotics subroutine. He looked over at the two bots sitting in his space. "You'll be Huey, and you, Dewey." Of course, the robots had nothing to say.

Dave altered the robotics subroutine, removing the two bots from the service group. He would program them later to be his personal cleaning servants. He grinned and considered what else he might do with the two bots. Even though he had hundreds of thousands of videos to watch, he was a little bored. A side amusement would be welcome.

Day 221

Dave kind of missed his messy living space. It had character. Huey and Dewey were so efficient he couldn't drop a crumb before one of them was scuttling over to catch and dispose of it. He was five months into his navigation subroutine project, and it was beginning to feel like something he'd never finish.

While the databases had all the information the subroutine needed, it didn't have those little connecting points of logic you would use to guide a ship. Dave didn't know how he could handle all of them. A few weeks into rewriting the navigation subroutine he came a screeching stop as he had to dig into the colony database to learn *how* interstellar navigation worked.

If he wasn't in a starship racing into the void of interstellar space, he might have found it funny. He didn't have a clue how *Prometheus* was going to find TRAPPIST beyond having been aimed at it when leaving Earth.

After months of studying navigation, he knew he was no expert, but he had enough knowledge to write the necessary exceptions to make the program work. He woke up that morning to no exceptions in any of his programs. When he finished breakfast, he treated himself with a game of cards against Huey and Dewey.

As the programming job became more onerous, he had distracted himself by teaching the two bots various card games. It was indeed a wonderful distraction and took up many hours of many days.

Playing a game of Texas Hold'em, Dave watched the two bots and wondered if they were cheating him. "Don't play me," he said. Eyes turned from the cards to look at him. Programs he'd written considered his words, decided there were no actual commands, and the bots returned to the game. He snorted and wished they'd learn to banter.

"Learn?" he said. *Exceptions. You learned through exceptions.* "I'm an idiot."

Dave dropped his cards and stared at the piles of tablets. Months and months spent writing responses to myriads of exceptions. He'd been going crazy keeping up with those exceptions, all the while amazed that the program teams on Earth had thought up all those exceptions he now had to write, just now realizing that they'd never experienced any such thing.

"AIs are learning computers." He'd learned that simple truth in high school over a decade ago. Of *course* they hadn't programmed all the exceptions, the AI learned them itself in endless hours of simulations. It probably destroyed *Prometheus* a thousand times, a million times, each time learning not to make the same mistake again.

Dave laughed and laughed, tears rolling down his cheeks. Months working to fill in little holes whenever he found them, when the AI originally filled in the holes with a firehose of simulations. It had probably learned more in an hour than Dave had been able to program in his months of laboring.

What choice did he have but to continue? Recreate the entire AI?

He'd never really thought he could do it. Only, was there actually any choice? He'd never gotten comms working, and even if he did, he couldn't do anything more than scream in frustration back at Earth, now billions of miles behind him.

He decided he would seriously set to work on bringing the AI back to life. If he could succeed at recreating the complex set of control programs, it would mean he could be done faster and back to sleep. Huey made a bet, and the game continued.

Day 488

Dave woke up to a sound he hadn't heard in a long time—an alarm. He got up from his little bed and tripped over a pile of tablets, cursing because it was the level-two logic project. The ship stores had 500 handheld tablets. Three hundred of them decorated his living space, so many that he'd had to disable Huey and Dewey's cleaning functions. He managed to slap the lights on as he moved onto the command deck.

On the engineering panel alarms were blaring. He dropped into the seat and examined the alarms. One of *Prometheus'* fuel tanks was bleeding out.

"How the hell?" he wondered. His navigations education suggested an answer. Micrometeorite. *Prometheus* was going almost 17,000,000 meters per second, or six percent of the speed of light. At such speeds a grain of sand had the energy of a small bomb.

Dave growled and silenced the alarms on the engineering panel. The propellant tank was nearly empty. He'd just wondered why the bots hadn't sealed the leak when he realized an alarm was still sounding. This one was from the robotics controls.

He moved over and examined the controls. He blinked in disbelief. The alarm was informing him of the loss of twenty-nine of his thirty-five robots. Disbelief turned to horror. *What the hell happened?*

He immediately stopped all robot operations on the ship, and promptly lost the thirtieth robot a second later. "Damn it!" he screamed. As quickly as he could remember the commands, he called up the logs from the dead bots.

When the tank was breached, the robotic maintenance system

dispatched a pair of bots to fix the breach. He'd written such a response, though it hadn't been written to deal with an ultra-high-pressure tank spewing propellant at near zero Kelvin. The bots were torn apart. So two more were sent, and they met the same fate. This continued until the propellant tank was empty. His last-minute casualty was because he'd stopped the robot just as one was flying along the hull. It was now kilometers astern and would never come back.

"Why didn't I think to add an alert if a robot was taken off-line?" he wondered aloud. It seemed so blatantly obvious now.

Five robots left for the rest of the trip. Was it enough? He didn't know. Huey and Dewey were sitting in his habitation area, waiting for his amusement. He chewed his lower lip. Three robots to maintain *Prometheus*, then. He got back to work on the AI and made additions to the robotics response protocols.

Day 1,008

Dave had wanted to celebrate the AI's rebirth before he reached his thousand-day mark of waking. No such luck. He was eight days past it, sitting at his workstation in his underwear, coding, when he realized he'd missed his goal.

He stopped working and applauded; the clapping sounds echoed dully off the walls of the command deck. He laughed for a moment, then went back to work.

Day 1,097

Dave watched the AI monitor working its magic. Well, black magic. The stylized cube icon would never come back, so he'd programmed a simpler one. It was a Rubik's Cube. Unlike the original, this one *was* a representation of the budding AI's processing level.

A completely static unmoving cube meant nothing was happening. Rotating in space meant its base level code was processing. If the various colored squares were rotating, as if someone was trying to solve the puzzle, it was learning. The faster it spun or rotated, the harder it was working.

The cube had been spinning slowly for two hours as it finished compiling itself. It would never assemble magically into a full AI, like the old one had. What he was making couldn't really be considered an AI. However, if he succeeded, it would be enough. He hoped.

"Compile Complete." The cube was spinning at a slow, steady rate. He'd gotten a stable compile; the program was working.

He sighed and closed his eyes for a moment. Two days ago he passed the three-year mark. Three years since he'd woken up and found himself with a ship running blindly on autopilot. This had to work. *It had to.*

"*Prometheus,*" he said.

"Ready," it responded.

Dave cringed. The voice was horrible, more like the old MIDI voders used a century ago. The voice systems were files in the colony database, so he used them. But damn, without the full AI making it a nuanced voice indistinguishable from a real person ... ugh.

"Engage engineering subroutine," he ordered.

"Working." The cube began to rotate faster.

"Integrate exception file Engineering One."

"Working." The cube started rotating colors. It was learning.

"YES!" he cried, then calmed himself. He wasn't there yet.

Hours spent writing out lists of potential problems and their solutions, instead of programming one-on-one code for dealing with problems, was yielding a result 1,000 times more efficient. The AI's twelve powerful processors chewed through his list and their possible solutions, creating more permutations than his mind could conceive of—and it did it on an order of magnitude faster than his brain was capable. The cube's colors rotated about as fast as a real-world Rubik's Cube would have if he were trying to solve a problem.

"Integration successful," the AI said, and the cube stopped rotating colors and just spun slowly.

Dave controlled his excitement. He'd had several failures after reaching this point in other tests. Several hundred times, actually. He accessed the budding AI's logic functions and watched it work in deeper detail. Unlike all the previous attempts, this time he saw no conflicts. He smiled and relaxed a bit. Maybe a special dessert tonight?

Day 1,399

Dave left the command deck while the AI ran another huge

simulation that he'd spent twenty days writing. Systematic faults across engineering and navigation were testing the AI's ability to cross-connect problem solving between multiple systems. For the first time, he was becoming confident he could go back to sleep at long last.

"Almost four years," he said to Dewey, who was playing solitaire while Huey watched. The robot's eyes looked at him then two legs performed a passable shrug. Both bots now had an extra memory module to handle the hundreds of hours of programming he'd added.

"What do you want me to do about it?" Dewey asked.

"He's going nuts," Huey said.

"I'm not going nuts," Dave retorted. Huey made a raspberry sound.

He walked over to the long dormant cryostasis chamber. Thirteen hundred and ninety-nine days of his eighteen hundred days in stores were gone. Four hundred days was going to be tight when he got to TRAPPIST. He'd long ago double-checked that the programming for terraforming was intact. The only thing he would need to do was be more hands-on during the actual deployment of assets. The landers were automated, thank God.

"Sleep until six months before arrival," he said as he opened the cryostasis chambers control panel. "Use the sensors to verify target, make orbit, deploy assets, then sleep again."

He'd program the ship's automated beacon to let *Victoria* know what was wrong. He'd never done an EVA to *Prometheus'* transmitter. He was sure the problem was there, because no matter what he did comms couldn't be restored. The beacon was short range, but it would be enough.

What will Joan say when she finds out what I did?

He initialized the stasis chamber and waited. Nothing happened. He made a face and hit the self-test button.

"No Programmed Response."

"What?" he said aloud.

"You talking to me, boss?" Huey asked.

"Shut up," he said and tapped at the controls.

"No Programmed Response."

In a panic, he began searching his cluttered workspace for tools, cursing the decision to have Huey and Dewey stop cleaning. Cursing, he turned to the bots. "Open maintenance covers on the cryostasis chamber."

"Right away, boss," they said at the same time.

While they worked, he found his diagnostic tools. By the time he had them, the bots had the chamber open. He knelt by the computer systems within the chamber and attached his tool. It only took two button pushes to get the response he knew he would get. "Memory Empty."

"It blanked the cryostasis, too," he said, shaking his head. "No."

An hour later he'd dug into the internal workings of the cryostasis chamber. Hardwired bios maintained the person in stasis and woke them up. The unit required input to place a person in stasis—input provided by the AI. The parameters were ... daunting. A thousand datapoints on the occupant feed from dozens of sensors all worked to carefully cool the occupant to the very edge of death. Once there, keeping the person in stasis was the easy part.

Dave looked around him, at all the empty compartments in the habitation area, and began to sob.

Day 1,505

The alarm woke Dave and he carefully climbed from his bed. He removed the dark mask over his eyes and blinked painfully at the intense light. The pathway between his bunk and the bathroom was narrow and he moved carefully. A sea of buckets covered every square centimeter of floor.

By the time he was done in the bathroom his eyes were adjusted to the constant light and he could survey the crops. Every bucket had a plastic rod stuck into the soil, and every rod had a series of vines climbing them. Some vines were green, most were brown.

He had a lot more expertise at EVA trips now. Twenty separate trips to *Prometheus'* four landers had yielded the seeds and soil, all sealed for the terraforming project. He was careful to only take a little from each lander. The water and buckets were from the habitation ring. Each bucket had a drip line and the life support was constantly struggling with high humidity levels.

Dave sat and picked up a tablet holding tutorials on growing beans. More colony data. Despite extensive training for the mission, none of the instructions included growing beans in space. He really wished he'd taken an agriculture class in high school.

He'd been dreaming that the beans were trying to kill him in his sleep. It wasn't far from the truth. "I don't suppose you two can help?"

"No, boss," Huey and Dewey answered at the same time. The room was hot and humid, and full of dying bean plants. He had to admit to himself, it wasn't working.

Dave had his breakfast and looked over the programming notes. The cryostasis system didn't allow for shortcuts. The details on how you placed a human into cold sleep were all in the colony files. It was a difficult process, and if you did it wrong it killed the patient. Three months of work, and he was maybe halfway done.

"And how can I test it?" he wondered. The food gave little pleasure, yet he still couldn't bring himself to not eat. It was the only joy he found in life at the moment. All around him the lost and dying souls of his attempt to produce more food mocked him. "It's your fault," he hissed.

"You volunteered."

He spun around, searching for the voice. Only dying plants and buckets of dirt were there.

"Maybe if I covered the whole floor with dirt," he mumbled, and looked at the buckets. He shook his head. Even if he dumped every one of them on the floor, it wouldn't be an inch of dirt. The data said he needed a lot more. He looked back at the bathroom, then at a nearby dying bean plant. *Fertilizer?*

Day 1,641

Dave dropped the box he'd just taken from its storage place onto his table. "No," he said and tore at the wrapping. The mold was inside as well. The plastic containers, biodegradable for use on TRAPPIST later, were eaten through. "No, no, no," he said as he yanked the box and send them cascading on the floor. The mold was throughout.

He ripped one open and the contents were the wrong color. The smell was musky.

"Wow, that's tough."

He looked at Huey, who was painting a fresco on the habitat wall. Dewey was a few meters away, admiring the work.

"Yeah," Dave said. Every last box.

"Finish the program?" Dewey asked.

"I don't know," Dave said. The habitation area was strewn with moldy food packets, busted buckets, dead bean plants, and dirt was everywhere.

Dewey lit a cigarette. "Whatcha gonna do now?" the robot asked him.

"Yeah," Joan agreed. "What's the plan?" She was in her pilot jumpsuit, just like the last time he'd seen her, training for the mission.

"I don't know," he repeated.

"Better figure it out," she said. "I'm going to die if you don't."

Dave's stomach grumbled and he wiped his mouth with a filthy hand. How long had it been since he'd eaten? The air felt hot, and humid. He stumbled to the cryostasis chamber and activated it. The lights came on and the door slid open. He didn't have to strip, the last of his clothes had rotted off him weeks ago.

He rolled into the chamber and pressed the glowing button. The lid began to slide closed.

"What about us, boss?" Huey asked.

"Yeah, we're going to be lonely!" Dewey agreed.

"Keep the ship running," he said. "Tell Joan I love her."

The lid slid closed, fluid flowed in, the cold followed. Darkness took him.

"This is Dave Parker, the man who's going to take *Prometheus* ahead of *Victoria*. Dave, this is Lieutenant Commander Joan Walker." Steve had been introducing the command crew for *Victoria* at the *Prometheus* launch party.

"We've met," Dave said.

"Oh?" Joan asked.

"Carnegie Mellon, we were there the same year."

Joan screwed up her face then affected a small smile. "I think I remember you. Well, good luck. We'll see you in two hundred years or so."

"I'm looking forward to it," Dave said, and smiled back.

The cold embrace stretched on, and on.

Cursed Colony

The shortsighted entrepreneurs and billionaire financiers promoting the TRAPPIST-2 Colony Foundation faced considerable criticism for lack of redundancy and backup, in that they put all colonists and supplies into a single ship, destined for a single system, before any scouting reports could make their way back to their point of origin. The one response to the criticism was to build and launch the ill-fated *Prometheus*, a terraforming ship that was to prepare the potential colony sites before the arrival of *Victoria* and the colonists. The loss of *Prometheus* was the first of many failures caused by the lack of central control and collectivist planning essential for success of such a long-duration mission, leading to the common opinion that the Cistercian colony was cursed from its very conception.

—Excerpt from *Flint's People's History of*
Interstellar Exploitation,
Trudovik Press,
Kerenskiy, Trudovik, AA237

CONFESSION

Les Johnson

My name is Nitin Bakshi, and this is what really happened to Keegan Coran.

I vividly recall when it all began. It was my youngest sister Shahina's birthday, February 29, 2140. She was seven—but not really. Since she was born on Leap Day of a Leap Year in 2112, she was really twenty-eight. I had been teasing her about her age since she was four, which she hated, and hadn't stopped as she got older. It was now a tradition we both enjoyed. I was in the middle of my birthday holovid with her when I got the message that changed everything. Let me explain.

I was at my wit's end. I'd met with all the elected officials from my district and from just about every district where I thought I'd have a chance to get interest and, of course, funding. I met with philanthropists ("You want to do what?"), CEOs of all the major North American space companies ("What's the business case?"), and even some from Eurasia ("You are crazy!"). I'd spoken to lawyers about creating a public company ("What will be the investors' return on investment?"), experts in creating nonprofits ("You'll never get the tax exemption."), and government space agencies ("It's not our job."). My partners and I had paid for a global 'net survey and found that while people generally thought it was a good idea, few would be willing to help pay for it.

I, the eternal optimist, had pretty much concluded that our dream of the last eight years was a bust and that we should just all give up on our dream, find real jobs, and get on with our lives. I was about to tell my sister this news—news that she would have welcomed, by the way—when I was notified that I had a message waiting from one of the many monied blue bloods that I'd been trying to reach for the last few years, completely unsuccessfully.

I had a message from Keegan Coran. *The* Keegan Coran of North American BioPharma. The message said simply, "Mr. Coran will see you on Friday at 1:00 in his Manhattan office regarding your proposal. RSVP."

I told my sister I had to go so I could send a positive reply to the meeting request. She sounded disappointed and I think I called her back later and told her about why I had to go. But it's been so long, I honestly don't remember if I ever did.

It was a Monday, so getting to Manhattan by Friday would be easy. I had the pitch memorized and reserving a seat on one of the ballistics wouldn't be a problem. Hell, if I had wanted to, I could have caught the next ballistic out of Denver and been in New York within the hour. Friday gave me plenty of time. Time to fret and worry. Time to prepare to again be rejected as I'd been rejected so many times before.

I landed at JFK Thursday afternoon and immediately caught the aerotaxi to my hotel. I stayed at the Varcak, which rose majestically out of the Atlantic and overlooked the Times Square Boardwalk. I could see the couples taking their very touristy water taxi rides down the thoroughfare of shopping bliss that was New York. In the distance was the Statue of Liberty, kept dry on Liberty Island by the thirty-foot walls surrounding her. The holoprojections of Times Square were proclaiming the news that Pakistan would host The World Cup in 2144 and that, for the first time, teams from the Moon would be competing. I remember thinking that was a funny thing—how could the Lunatics train to compete in 1 gravity when most of the players had never left 1/6 g? It's funny what one remembers when their emotions are high. I was, as usual, nervous about tomorrow's meeting.

Despite being nervous, I slept like a baby.

I was at the offices of North American BioPharma thirty minutes before my meeting. It was raining. And cold. And I didn't care. I was in the zone and about to talk to one of the world's richest men, hoping to convince him that my team and I had a viable plan to change the course of history.

Coran's receptionist, an obviously bioengineered Adonis who appeared to be not a day over twenty-five but could have easily been fifty (you never knew what genes were spliced where these days), summoned me into the spacious and lavishly furnished office of Keegan Coran. Coran apparently was a wildlife buff. Throughout the room were running holovids of various wildlife, forests, and oceans. I couldn't tell if they were real-time visuals or a recording. The whole time I was there I didn't see any obvious repetition, but I wasn't really paying that much attention to them. My attention was wholly undivided and held by Coran.

"Dr. Bakshi, I've read a lot about you and heard you speak on many occasions. Your lecture at the Interplanetary Astronautical Congress last summer was compelling. Compelling." He actually said, "compelling" twice. Yeah, I was flattered.

I mumbled something that probably sounded like humble blathering; my own version of sucking up or groveling. Take your pick. I probably sounded pathetic. Before I could launch into my spiel, he resumed control of the meeting. Rich people like this can seem like a force of nature that cannot be ignored.

He said, "I've read your proposal and spoken with several to whom you've already made your appeal. I think your idea is revolutionary and I want to support it."

One of the richest and most powerful people in the world talked about me, and my ideas, using the words "revolutionary" and "compelling" within five minutes of each other. My ego was bursting and my heart racing. I don't really recall what else was said before we shook hands and he introduced me to his assistant and my new paymaster, Renee Blanc-Perot. Unlike the Adonis that escorted me into the room, Renee Blanc-Perot had that look of "I am this beautiful and intelligent naturally and you won't ignore me." To this day, I have never ignored her. I killed her, sure. But I never, ever ignored her.

As Ms. Blanc-Perot and I were leaving the room, Coran said, "Dr. Bakshi. There is a catch. I may ask you for a favor as the project nears completion. And when I ask, I expect you to do it." This caused me to stop in my tracks. My spider sense was activated.

"Is this favor going to be illegal or immoral?" I remember asking. (I'm surprised I had the temerity to ask.)

He laughed and responded, "No. Nothing illegal or immoral, I assure you of that."

I just nodded my head or said, "Okay, then," or some such affirmation. In any event, I agreed, or I wouldn't be telling this story.

That was it. By Friday afternoon, March 4, 2140, the funding for the *Victoria* was secured. The next several years were a blur. With a billionaire's financial spigot wide open, hiring the design engineers, placing on retainer the always-necessary-but-never-wanted attorneys (who had always previously ignored me), and staffing a company to produce what would become humanity's first interstellar starship began.

I can't tell you how many trips I made to the Moon, but I can tell you about my first trip to Mars to see the orbital facility where the *Victoria* would be constructed—beginning within the next week or so. It was almost exactly ten years after the initial meeting with Coran and it was on this trip that, in hindsight, I should have begun paying more attention to my sponsor. But I was too amped up to notice anything and too distracted to care.

I flew on one of the commercial transports that departs for Mars weekly from the Moon Corp's habitat and spaceport at L5. It wasn't luxurious, but comfortable enough for the one-and-a-half month-long trip to Mars. It was off-season, meaning that the Earth and Mars weren't optimally placed for quick travel between them. Had it been in season, the trip could have been as short as three weeks. As we departed, I couldn't help but calculate how short the trip would have been had the ship been powered by our star drive operating at its maximum velocity—about two hours. It's amazing the difference a little acceleration can make over a long time.

I can't describe what it's like to see Mars grow larger every day until it is finally all you see out the window—just like the Earth when viewed from LEO—Low Earth Orbit. But Mars was different from Earth. Instead of the blue oceans and puffy white clouds, it was big, red, and dusty—but beautiful in its own way. To me, the true beauty was Interstellar, Inc.'s space dock orbiting the planet's equator. Mr. Coran hadn't wasted any time using the fortune he'd amassed at North American BioPharma to buy—buy outright—the second largest aerospace corporation on Earth and turn its primary focus away from suborbitals, space mining habitats, and various dark programs for the military toward building the *Victoria*. I knew Coran was filthy rich, but I never imaged how much money he had at his disposal from the company that had vanquished cancer and increased the human lifespan by nearly one hundred percent. Now he was turning his efforts to help spread humanity and Earth life to the stars. And he was funding my starship.

Before you ask, yes, Ms. Blanc-Perot was with me on the trip and no, we weren't and never had ever considered being in a relationship. She was beautiful but toward me she was iced coffee. Come to think of it, I'd never seen her be social with another man, or woman, in the whole time I knew her. She was all about business—Coran's business.

"Mr. Coran will meet with you first thing tomorrow," she said as we prepared to get off the ship and into the dock where we had guest rooms waiting.

"He's here?" I asked. I was incredulous. In my mind, Coran lived in the world of meetings in fancy conference rooms, vacations in beach houses on private islands, and parties with the well heeled . . . just about everywhere but here. I didn't expect him to be at Mars.

"Yes. Orbiting about sixty degrees out of phase with us is his latest biotech research facility. He comes out here at least once per year to meet with his researchers and check on their progress."

This is when an alarm bell should have gone off. Why would anyone need to set up a biotech research facility away from anything that could be considered "bio"? Without the Earth environment being local, you had to create your own. Creating an orbiting laboratory beyond Earth orbit and stocking it with the supplies to perform any sort of research, let alone in biotechnology, was an expensive proposition. All I could think of to justify what I was hearing was secrecy. In the competitive biotech field, you didn't stay ahead unless you kept your work mostly secret from the competition. That had to be the reason—*yeah, right*.

Sure enough, we met with Mr. Coran the next day and it was such a memorable meeting that I don't really recall any of the details. He was just checking on our progress and then, poof, he was gone. "Places to be and people to see," and all that.

It was about a year after that meeting, during my second trip to Mars, that it happened. *It*—the event that made all the newsfeeds and nearly caused the whole project to be set back by years, if not longer.

Most people think building a spaceship or just about anything that's complicated is mostly about putting widgets together. Part A into Slot B, that sort of thing. And that's ultimately true, but only after a lot of hard work by hundreds to thousands of engineers, scientists, technicians and other specialists who have to design all the widgets to make sure they all do their jobs and fit together like they should. Most of the cost of the *Victoria* would not be the hardware from which she was assembled, but the hours spent by the designers making sure everything fits together, doesn't get too hot or too cold, survives the radiation environment, can handle the stresses and strains of acceleration, is instrumented correctly so the crew can understand what's going on, doesn't use too much power or too little, and has enough redundancy to operate even if it fails in five different ways.

Key to all this are the systems engineers who try to understand how it all comes together and works, taking input from the mechanical engineers, electrical engineers, thermal engineers, nuclear engineers, communications engineers, etcetera. You get the picture. The *Victoria* was going to be one complicated ship and the systems engineers were key to making sure everything was going to work as it should.

From the outside, the *Victoria* was finally starting to look like a real spaceship. The outer hull was complete, and the crews were busily outfitting the interior with every system, power conduit, crycooler, and bathroom that the crew would need for a successful journey. From the inside, it was obvious we were still at least a year from being ready. To be blunt, it was a mess. Some decks were missing their decks (seriously!), others had flooring to which the plumbing and electrical conduits were strung as the technicians meticulously placed them where they should be in what would soon be very utilitarian walls with removable access panels. And, without gravity, debris was floating everywhere. The FOD—Foreign Object Debris—was so bad that we had cleanup crews working continuously to keep the air free of metal shavings, metal flakes from less-than-perfect arc welds, pieces of insulation, and even the occasional bit of human waste. (Don't ask me how that kept happening, because we don't know.) The biggest concern of the risk management team was that some of this crap would get into places it shouldn't, not be noticed, and then cause a short or other major malfunction sometime during the voyage. To protect everyone working inside the ship from inhaling something untoward or even lethal, we provided filtration masks—courtesy of Coran's stockpile at his co-orbiting biotech research facility. Now that workers weren't worrying about inhaling whatever happened to float by, their productivity actually increased—dramatically. It was Renee's idea; I can take no credit.

The center of the ship, where the stored embryos and sleeping crew were to be kept, was being surrounded with metallic hydrogen plating that would act as a nearly impenetrable radiation shield. Once the ship was racing through interstellar space at twenty percent the speed of light, every hydrogen atom it encountered would become radiation capable of unzipping or breaking strands of the very fragile DNA that would be the cargo. But most of that radiation would be stopped before it ever reached the metallic hydrogen barrier. No, this innermost barrier was developed to stop the galactic cosmic rays that were otherwise virtually unstoppable. These aren't wimpy single proton hydrogen atoms traveling at a relative speed of 0.2c. Galactic cosmic rays were heavy nuclei, like iron, that were traveling at speeds greater than ninety percent the speed of light. Those are the ones that, if not stopped, would damage the DNA or kill every living thing on the ship during its multidecade trip. Metallic hydrogen, with its densely packed protons, would stop just about all of them. A win for our side.

I had been at Mars for just over three weeks and was wrapping up all the business I had to attend to before returning to Earth when the FEF-ers struck. We all should have known it could happen, how vulnerable we were, but we didn't. I guess we thought that the Fix Earth First Society, or Feffers, wouldn't come all the way out to Mars to try and stop us. They are against space travel, after all. Sure, they protested in front of our offices in every city we had one. Yes, they sent threatening messages and interrupted more than one of my fund-raisers with their harangue against space development and travel, insisting that we instead focus our energies and money on making life on Earth better. What they didn't get was that my team and I all agree with their goal. We want to make Earth better. We just believe we need to explore and develop space to help make that happen. Their response to our rationale? Ignore it and make more threats. So, we ignored them back. And that, in hindsight, was a mistake.

With all the hubbub surrounding the outfitting of the *Victoria*, people and material arriving every minute of every day, cleanup crews racing to stay ahead of the floating debris, and people working way too many hours without a break (the union nearly stopped us in our tracks on that one until we starting paying triple time for the extra hours), no one noticed the two relatively small shipping containers added to the stack of construction supplies being loaded aboard the ship. That is, no one noticed them until we tracked them down as the source of the poison gas.

Yes, poison gas. Tucked away in those crates weren't bombs to damage the ship. No, it was much more insidious than that. And if it hadn't been for the anti-FOD respirators, more than five people would have died—a lot more.

The first sign of trouble came when one of the electricians—I am embarrassed to say I don't remember his name—had to remove his respirator to fit between two panels to install some circuit, power conduit, or something. He was working between them when his coworker saw him start shaking, like he was having a seizure, and then go limp. Of course, they thought the guy was having a heart attack or something, so they pulled him out to try and help him.

About one out of ten of our workers are cross-trained as medics. When you're this far from a real hospital, it's a precaution that just about every firm out here takes. It just makes sense. Except in this case. The nearest medic came to help and, you guessed it, took off her respirator thinking she might have to give CPR until a real medical team could get there. Seconds after removing her mask, the same damned seizures started, and we lost her. Fatality number two. The nearby workers put two and two together pretty quickly and didn't make the same mistake of taking off their respirators. Unfortunately, by the time the warning reached everyone in the hull and we got the ship successfully evacuated, three other people died. One more had taken off her respirator, and two had damaged respirators and not bothered to get new ones.

We found the source of the gas quickly and caught the people who had brought it to Mars by tracing them through the logs. Every inch of the space dock, like just about everywhere else, is under constant surveillance. Each person's implant ID can be traced and body-matched to the video logs. By the time we figured out who was responsible, they'd already boarded a ship bound for Earth and were on their way home.

Coran was livid. He shuttled over to the *Victoria* the day after we figured out what had happened and was there when we identified the perps. He said he would take care of notifying the authorities personally, since the attack was made on his property. I think the words he used were, "I'll make sure no SOB Feffer ever does this again." From what I understand, the authorities didn't make their move until well after the ship landed. The perps were tracked on Earth until the authorities figured out with whom they were working and then nabbed them all. I forget what happened to them; I hope they are rotting away in some cell somewhere.

Needless to say, we got more careful. And we didn't get any more trouble from the Feffers for quite some time.

But I could still kick myself for not asking more questions about the respirators. You see, we found out after the attack that simple, clean-air hospital-grade respirators wouldn't have filtered out all the poison gas. No, the masks Coran gave us were the latest, highest-quality filtration masks money could buy. Coran and the Centers for Disease Control were the two largest customers for the company that made them. What was Coran's biotech research facility *researching* that required them to have this kind of filtration?

The next year went by in a blur. We were in the midst of crew interviews and selection, selecting and stockpiling the frozen embryos that would provide the genetic diversity required for the colony to thrive, and working out the protocols that the crew would follow on their journey to maximize their chances of survival. The most troubling parts of the whole effort were the risk management meetings. As the Technical Director, I was required to attend.

For some engineers, risk management meetings are the reason they get out of bed in the morning. For others, these meetings are the reason they can't sleep. It's in risk management that key members of the technical team list all the things that could go wrong with the ship, the crew, or externally, and bin them into categories of "watch," "mitigate," or "accept." Accept means that whatever the problem was, it was going to happen no matter what you did and therefore some backup system, or alternative approach had to be fielded to correct the inevitable problem. Mitigate means you could do something to keep the problem from happening, but it typically would require more time, more money, or both. Watch means you had no idea if it was going to happen or not—shit happens. Let me tell you, there is a *lot* that can go wrong.

Disease. Power failure. Reactor meltdown. Reactor explodes. Radiation fries everyone. Micrometeorite hit while traveling at twenty percent the speed of light blows it to smithereens. Cryocoolers fail; all the embryos die. Cryocoolers lose power briefly; all the embryos die. Engineers miscalculated the stresses on the hull during acceleration; everyone dies. Crew member goes crazy and damages a critical ship component; everyone is lost in space forever and dies. Feffers plant a bomb; everyone dies. Slight miscalculation in the trajectory causes the ship to miss the target star; everyone is lost in space forever and dies. Fuel leak prevents the ship from decelerating; it screams off into the cosmos forever and everyone dies. You get the idea. Our job was to engineer as many fail-safes and backups into the system as we could to "mitigate" as many of the risks as possible—which is *impossible*. But we did the best we could do.

I'm skipping over the next twenty years of hard work so that I can get to the salient points regarding what happened in those fateful days prior to the *Victoria*'s departure. Twenty years seems like a long time to those of you who are under fifty, but for those of us who are benefitting from the life extension therapies developed by Keegan Coran at North American BioPharma, it seems more like an extended adolescence—almost dreamlike. It went by quickly.

To make final preparations for the trip, I traveled to Mars three months prior to our planned departure. To say I wasn't getting nervous would have been a complete lie. Two hundred and fifty souls will be awake and asleep in alternating cycles during the 160-year trip. But not me, I was to be among the ten thousand in cryostasis who wouldn't know anything about the voyage until I was awakened upon arrival. If one of the identified risks struck, I would never know it.

A small group of humans were about to leave home forever for a chance at starting a new life somewhere else. Space telescopes all over the solar system had spent the last few years studying TRAPPIST-2c so that we would be as prepared as possible. The Breakthrough

Starshot probe reported back that it had an atmosphere like Earth's, meaning there is native, oxygen-producing life. We know there's liquid water and most likely ice—a temperature range not too dissimilar to Earth. We also know there's no alien civilization there using radio—the radio telescopes had not heard a peep.

My routine after arriving at Mars was anything but routine. There is absolutely nothing normal about preparing to forever leave Earth's beautiful blue skies, warming oceans, or green forests. Still, I had a lot of work to do and not much time to think about it except when I tried to go to sleep at night. I was beginning to understand what Neil Armstrong must have felt like in the days and weeks leading up to Apollo 11. It was scary.

Coran summoned me to his biotech station two months out from launch. His shuttle came to the space dock to collect Ms. Blanc-Perot (yes, she was still there with me all the time) and me. Nothing about the short trip was particularly memorable, which means I'd actually gotten used to zooming around in Mars orbit, overseeing the construction of humanity's first starship, and looking back at Earth only to see it as a small, starlike object—it was crazy.

When we arrived, Coran wasted no time in seeing us. Unlike the space dock with its construction zone appearance, look, and feel of barely controlled chaos, the biotech station was hyper sterile in appearance, quiet, and had the feel of being nearly empty of people. His office was the same—spartan, white, and minimalist. After we entered, he got right to the point. Everything that happened from this point forward is pinned in my memory like a movie. I can see, hear, and recall almost every detail. I've heard stress can do that.

"You're taking my family with you," he said. "You will make space available for Ruby, Ian, and Rhys."

Ruby was his third wife. I'd met her only once and she seemed nice enough. Healthy too, I thought, as I began to internalize his request, beginning to assess her viability as a colonist. Ian and Rhys I hadn't met. Both were studying at universities back on Earth and were a product of his second marriage. In retrospect, I wonder how the dynamics of that would have played out—he didn't mention his second wife, the mother of the children he wanted to take on the voyage. Having his second wife along also would have provided some . . . *interesting* . . . dynamics.

"Mr. Coran, with all due respect, that will be very difficult to accommodate at this late a date. The crew has been selected for months and they have gone through extremely rigorous training. I—"

He cut me off.

"Dr. Bakshi, I'm not asking you to take my family as crew. I'm *telling* you to take my family on the voyage. I'm fine with them being asleep and awakened upon arrival."

"Mr. Coran, I hear you. But your family hasn't been through the genetic testing, the psychological interviews, the stress tests, all that. And in order to add them to the ship, we'll have to drop four others from the roster—people who have been through all the screenings and are planning to go."

"Three, not four," he said. "I'll not be going."

"What? Oh, I assumed you wanted to accompany them on the trip," I said, more than a bit surprised.

"No. I will remain here. But they are going. Do I need to remind you of our first meeting? I can play the recording if you like," he said as he leaned forward.

I honestly thought he was going to lunge at me. I was taken aback at the intensity of his gaze.

"You don't need to do that," I said, remembering his cryptic warning that he might ask for a favor in return for funding the venture. I hadn't forgotten the discussion, just partitioned it off in the hope that he would forget. He had not.

"Dr. Bakshi, I've taken the liberty to flag three candidates for de-rostering and have just sent you their profiles. The final choice is up to you, of course," said the enigmatic Ms. Blanc-Perot.

That made me angry. She had known this was coming and not told me about it. *How long had she known?* Over the last few years, I had gradually overcome my suspicions of Renee and actually accepted her as a trusted colleague—even a friend. I felt betrayed at suddenly having her true loyalties made perfectly clear. My gaze at her must have looked like daggers. I remember her backing away from both me and Coran at that point.

That's when it happened.

The entire station jumped two feet, the lights momentarily went out, and the rotation of the station went terribly askew, throwing us upward and to the side as the now-asymmetric rotational forces that were once providing simulated gravity now provided seemingly random forces that buffeted us about between wall and ceiling. As the lights returned, the alarm began going off—the alarm no one in space wants to hear.

Decompression.

Evacuate to the lifeboats.

That alarm.

Coran, with full Type-A personality on display, immediately grabbed a handhold near his desk and began making pronouncements. "Renee, you and Dr. Bakshi go to my personal lifeboat and get out of here while I find out what's going on. I can take one of the staff boats. There are several."

Another change in rotational state threw us all toward the outside wall of the station. Fortunately, though the shifts in rotational direction were dramatic, the spin-rate change was rather small, throwing us around with not-quite-enough force to break any bones.

The door to Coran's office opened and a man I'd never seen before entered—he was armed with a flechette gun, which he pointed directly at Mr. Coran. I'm not a gun person, but I know about them because I'd had to authorize the security detail around *Victoria* to carry them after the incident with the poison gas. Flechette guns are the only "safe" type of gun to use on a spaceship. They fire small, fin-stabilized, metal darts that have semiautonomous aerodynamic control to remain on a target, even if it is moving. They have a high rate of fire and each flechette has roughly the same kinetic energy as a much-heavier bullet thanks to its high muzzle velocity. Perfect for killing people and not penetrating the relatively thin walls of a spaceship.

"This is where it ends, Mr. Coran," said the stranger. He was apparently not a stranger to Coran or Ms. Blanc-Perot. They both reacted as if they knew him.

"Brandon, what's this all about?" asked Coran, his gaze alternating between the man and his weapon.

"It's about the end of your interstellar nightmare. We aren't going to let you and your lackey here export humanity's sins to other worlds before we've cleaned up the mess you made on Earth. Earth must come first and the only way the world gets the message is for those who are behind such obscenities to die. That means you."

"Brandon, you've worked with me for years. Where did you pick up such beliefs?" asked Coran.

"Working with you to develop new drug therapies is one thing. That helps people back on Earth. But when you started working with *him*, that's when I knew we were on opposite sides." The *him* to whom he referred was undoubtedly me.

"What did you do?" asked Coran, moving ever so slowly toward the other man. I might not have noticed the movement had I not been "side on" to the confrontation with my view.

"Bombs. There were supposed to be three of them, but it looks like only two went off. But that is probably enough to wreck this station and bankrupt you. But you won't care, because you'll be dead," said Brandon as he raised his gun and prepared to pull the trigger.

At that moment, the station's rotation shifted again, throwing everyone sideways and upward, including Brandon and his gun. Sensing an opening during the shift in artificial gravity, Coran launched himself forward and tackled Brandon, knocking the air out of him. To Brandon's credit, however, he didn't let go of the gun.

Renee and I lunged forward to help restrain the gunman when we heard the *whizzit* of a series of flechettes being fired. Two caught Coran in the chest, several flew around him, and one superficially nicked my arm. Truth be told, I was so filled with adrenaline that I didn't even notice the wound until much later.

Coran, despite being hit, had enough wherewithal and strength to wrestle the gun away from Brandon. Having me put him in a headlock and Renee grasping his legs certainly helped. Coran, finally realizing he had been shot, looked down at the blood now flowing freely from his chest and collapsed.

"You fool!" Coran snarled toward Brandon as I tightened my headlock on the captive and Ms. Blanc-Perot signaled for medical help.

The station lurched again as a new alarm sounded with an eerily calm woman's voice announcing, "Biohazard containment breach. All personnel must put on protective gear immediately and evacuate the laboratory," over and over again.

"You fool!" Coran repeated again as struggled to speak, blood now being coughed up with every syllable. "I'm on your side! Didn't the Feffer leadership tell you to back off after that half-assed poison gas leak? Your petty attacks are a waste of time and won't stop humanity in its foolishness and its destruction of the Earth. I can!"

What the hell? I thought.

Coran, now obviously oblivious to everyone present and very likely all-too-aware of his own life fading away, lashed out again. "Once the *Victoria* sets sail, I'm going to unleash the Omega Virus to wipe the slate clean. Not a single human can survive what we created. The Earth will be rid of the human pestilence for centuries until the colonists can return and re-colonize—this time building something more sustainable."

He stopped speaking to cough—more blood. Despite the incredible pain he had to be in, he clutched the gun and kept it pointed at the man I was still restraining. I suddenly realized that him moving the barrel of the gun only a few inches would mean it was pointed at me.

"*Biohazard containment breach. All personnel must put on protective gear immediately and evacuate the laboratory,*" continued repeating incessantly in the background.

"It isn't too late. Renee, get the suits. You can make sure the virus is secure and spread it after the *Victoria* departs," Coran said, trying to regain a measure of the control he was used to having over every situation in his life. Correction—his soon-to-be-ending life.

Now I knew I was in trouble. And his next actions confirmed it.

Coran fired the gun at point-blank range into Brandon's torso while I held him in the headlock. Instinctively knowing that I would be next, I used Brandon's now lifeless body as a shield and pushed it onto both Coran and his flechette gun.

Whizzit. Another round of darts flew into poor Brandon as his body pummeled Coran and pinned him to the ground. The gun skidded across the floor as the laboratory shifted yet again.

I glanced toward Ms. Blanc-Perot as she looked from me to the dart gun, which now rested just next to her feet. I knew what she was thinking. *Do I carry out the wishes of Mr. Coran, which means I need to kill the only remaining witness who could stop the plan? Or do I give up and claim to have had no knowledge of a madman's plan to destroy the world?* I guessed it would all depend upon how much she was aware of the plan and if there were a trail of evidence pointing toward her.

When she lunged for the gun, I knew what I had to do. She *was* in on the plan. And there must have been evidence out there to pin it on her or else why would she make such a foolish move?

Gauging the distance involved, I reasoned that she would get to the gun before I could, but she probably wouldn't be able to aim it at me before I could tackle her. That would give me a chance. I lunged.

Sure enough, she did get the gun first and almost succeeded in filling me with holes. My tackle might have been successful in taking her down where my combination of larger body mass and likely greater upper-body strength could have taken the gun from her, but it didn't work out that way. I did tackle her and knock her to the floor. I did grab the gun, which was pointed directly at my head, and I tried to take it from her. Her fingers were still near the trigger when the station's rotation shifted again and lurched us up and to the side. Fortunately for me, the darts she was about to fire into my skull missed—and went into her own. I was blinded by the resulting mess as the darts ripped into her.

"*Biohazard containment breach. All personnel must put on protective gear immediately and evacuate the laboratory.*"

I had a decision to make and I had to make it quickly.

Should I relay what happened, all of it—including the "Omega Virus" and a madman's plan to save the planet for the birds and the bees? If I did, then the authorities would likely impound anything and everything related to Mr. Coran and his fortune for years to come until they sorted it all out. That would likely include the *Victoria* and our plans to reach for the stars would be over. It would take too long to begin again and who knows if the money needed to do so would be available.

Or do I tell the story of how both this Brandon character and Ms. Blanc-Perot were in cahoots with the Feffers and I barely escaped with my life? No, that would have had the same outcome. The project would be ended, and the *Victoria* scrapped.

Then it dawned on me. Our individual implants had each recorded precisely what just transpired. And there were likely recording devices in the room that captured everything as well. No matter what I said, the truth would come out. Unless I destroyed the evidence. All of it.

The implants are always located in the upper-right chest, near the right armpit. Don't ask me why, that's just where they are located.

I took the flechette gun and shot so many darts into the upper right torsos of the three dead, crazy conspirators in the room that people will wonder if I was trying to cut their arms off. None of that data will survive. There wasn't anything I could do about the recorders in the room except hope that the damage done by the bombs had messed up the recordings.

"Biohazard containment breach. All personnel must put on protective gear immediately and evacuate the laboratory."

Then I heard, really heard, the announcement for the first time and realized I'd better get in a suit and off the station.

Being a biotech research facility, they had these emergency suits everywhere. They were almost one size fits all. One set was for women, the other for men. I put the suit on as quickly as I could and found Coran's lifeboat, getting off the station just before the latter broke into two pieces. I'm guessing the fragments will remain in Mars orbit for years unless someone goes to the trouble to clean up the mess.

What about me? I'm recording this on my ship's voice recorder as I look at the never-ending darkness of deep space that now surrounds me. Coran's lifeboat is more than a mere survival pod, like the generic lifeboats used on most other space habitats and research facilities. No, Coran's custom lifeboat has enough reaction mass and power to send me all the way back to Earth—if I wanted to go back to Earth. No, I turned off the transponder and used all the fuel to send me on a trajectory that will ultimately leave the solar system and never allow me, or this recording, to be found. I can't risk the true story of what happened getting out too soon—if ever.

There's enough water, air, and food here to last me for two months or so. That's long enough for the *Victoria* to be safely on its way to the outer solar system. People need to think that all of us perished on the laboratory until the ship is so far into its journey that it can't be called back.

The authorities may piece together that the station was attacked, but I doubt they can reconstruct what happened to the station from the thousands of pieces of debris into which it broke up. At least, I hope not. Not until the *Victoria* is long gone and impossible to recall.

From what I've read, dying from oxygen deprivation is just like getting groggy and going to sleep.

I guess I'll find out.

Godspeed Victoria. *Godspeed.*

Tarnished Heroes

KEEGAN ROGERS CORAN (born October 28, 2101) was an American business magnate, biomedical engineer, investor, and philanthropist. He is best known as the founder of North American BioPharma.[1][2] and the sponsor of the interstellar colony ship *Victoria* [3][4]. During his career at North American BioPharma, Coran held the positions of chairman, chief executive officer (CEO), president, and chief architect, while also being the largest individual shareholder. He is one of the best-known entrepreneurs and pioneers of the life extension therapies now used routinely around the world [5] and the immunotherapies used to treat multiple cancers [6][7][8]. He was tragically murdered by one of his employees, Nitin Bakshi (the chief designer of the *Victoria* colony ship) during the so-called "Mars Tragedy" incident in 2170 [9].

—Excerpt from *Mars,
a History*, Utopia Planitia Press,
Marstown, Mars, 2207 CE

★ ★ ★

NITIN ALORA BAKSHI (born March 2, 2109) was an American inventor and futurist. He is best known as the founding designer of the interstellar colony ship *Victoria* [1] and as the murderer of the American businessman Keegan Coran [2]. He spent most of his life advocating for, and then designing, the *Victoria*. For reasons never determined, he aligned himself with the FEF-er movement [3] and coordinated a bomb attack on the *Victoria*'s chief sponsor, Keegan Coran, and his Mars pharmaceutical laboratory, in what has come to be called the "Mars Tragedy" incident in 2170 [4]. He brutally murdered Coran and two of his associates and then perished in the

47

subsequent breakup of the Mars-orbiting laboratory. Bakshi's body was never found.

—Excerpt from *Mars,*
a History, Utopia Planitia Press,
Marstown, Mars, 2207 CE

★ ★ ★

The tragic deaths of two key leaders of the TRAPPIST-2 Colony Foundation, CEO and financier Keegan Coran along with COO and visionary Nitin Bakshi, left the foundation in disarray, and the future of the starship *Victoria* uncertain. Despite the accusation that Bakshi somehow played a role in Coran's death, Nitin Bakshi's sister Shahina took the reins of the Foundation and fought to prevent bureaucrats, lawyers, and activists from ending the mission. *Victoria* launched ten years late, but it launched, leaving its problems behind. Or so they thought.

—*Encyclopedia Astra,*
Gannon University,
Antonia, Cistercia, AA212

SOMNUM EXTERRERI

Christopher L. Smith

Acting Captain Madison Corbeau stood groggily in front of the coffee dispenser, watching the brown liquid flow into her mug. Even after two cups of the stuff, she couldn't quite shake the lethargy a restless "night" brought on.

The Colony Ship *Victoria*, now well into its voyage, hummed softly around her. There was some noticeable wear and tear, but nothing that could affect functionality or safety. Humans being humans, mainly. A scuff here, a dent there—all things that *could* be fixed, buffed out, or repainted, but hadn't been. It gave the almost sterile-looking surroundings some character.

Madi picked up her mug, running her thumb down the hairline crack in the ceramic handle. Flaws and blemishes made the *Vic* feel more like a home. Home felt comfortable, and the human crews needed that comfort when surrounded by the void of space. Especially when you considered that anyone born the day you went into cryo was a senior citizen now.

Madi shook her head to clear the tendrils of darkness slithering into her thoughts.

"That's not going to help," she muttered, blowing on the hot coffee.

"It may," said a voice behind her. "That's actually pretty good stuff. Kona, if I recall correctly."

Madi turned to see Dr. Ronald Noe, the medical officer, standing in the galley doorway, a small grin playing across his olive features.

"We'll see," she said, with a wan smile of her own. "Third time's a charm, right?"

Doc took a mug from the rack, punched buttons on the machine, and waited for his own cup of caffeine. He studied Madi's face carefully. At five foot ten, he stood eye to eye with her. Of all the crew, only Iain Jones stood taller, and then just slightly.

"How long has it been since you've gotten a good night's sleep?" At her slight start, he chuckled. "Dark circles under your eyes, which are a little on the bloodshot side, as well. Skin paler than normal. Slight tremor in your jaw, most likely from too much caffeine in a short span. It's my job to notice these things."

"Couple of days," Madi said. Technically, they were cycles, but the crew had fallen back on traditional nomenclature. "Days" began when you woke up, "nights" when you racked out. "Probably nothing, it's just a few bad dreams."

"Hm. Maybe. We should run a diagnostic on your implant, just to be sure."

Madi nodded. The implants were still a relatively new technology, at least in how they were being used. Developed in the early twenty-first century to help memory loss in Alzheimer's and traumatic brain injury patients, the "black box" had proven useful in other aspects as well. For the crew and passengers of the *Vic*, they were designed to counteract long-term brain function deterioration due to cryostasis. Early test subjects showed positive results for long-term stasis, but nothing on the scale of the colony ships. Still, the projected risk was low, less than a possible tenth of a percent failure. With ten thousand "sleepers" plus two hundred and fifty crew, it was an acceptable risk.

"Will do," Madi said. "I'll come down after my day's over."

Her "day" had become routine, which was a good thing.

Excitement in THIS work environment usually means something terrible and life-threatening. Give me routine every day, please, thank you, and Amen.

Bad dreams and lack of sleep aside, Madi was able to get into the rhythm of her duties quickly: reading the daily reports from the other crew, doing a quick overview of the ship's functions and stores, preparing and logging her brief for the ship's records. While it wasn't an official duty of hers, she also preferred to check on the passengers and crew in stasis, running an internal diagnostic program of her own design to check for any fluctuations outside of normal range.

The ship's AI had a similar system built in, but she didn't see the harm in watching the watcher. Her code was simple, disconnected from the main programming of the ship, and stored on an external drive. It had taken her several months to get it to her liking; when there's not much to do after work and you're going to be on duty for a year and a half at a time, hobbies were important.

Madi inserted the drive and ran the program, idly watching the report scroll by on her tablet at her standard reading speed. For ease in skimming, she'd designed the diagnostic to color code the entries: green for well within range, yellow for borderline, and red for out of range. To keep things interesting, she'd included code to pull a photo in real time of each sleeper.

Looking good, as usual. All greens so far.

Wait.

It had taken her a second to process it, but her eye latched on to a single red line as it disappeared at the top of her screen. She tapped the tablet, halting the scroll, and swiped up. And swiped again. And again. Nothing but green.

"That's weird, I could've sworn..." she muttered. A flicker in the corner of her eye caught her attention. She snapped her head around, focusing on the far side of the room, finding nothing. With a shrug, she turned back to her tablet.

She cancelled the program, ejected the drive, and examined it. Nothing out of the ordinary, same as always. She re-inserted it and started over, this time paying closer attention.

"There! Dammit!" She'd been too slow again, just missing the line as it scrolled past. Backtracking, the display showed nothing but green. Another hint of movement, this time from the other direction, played at the edge of her vision. Again, however, there was nothing there.

"Ugh. I'm seeing things, or there's a bug in the code," she said. A quick glance at the clock showed it was quitting time. She'd go through the program later, after a good night's sleep. "Time to go see the doc anyway."

Madi entered the Medical Bay, noting in passing that it hadn't been subjected to the "nesting" impulse like the rest of the *Vic*. It remained as pristine and sterile as the day it was built. Which, upon further thought, was more comforting than the alternative.

She waved to Doc Noe and took a seat in the chair. Designed to handle any minor medical procedure, the device resembled an old-time dentist's chair, able to convert from standing, to sitting, to supine, or anything in between. Doc Noe had it currently configured for a seated patient, for which Madi was secretly grateful. She felt more relaxed in this position, rather than lying down, when someone was messing with her head. She supposed it had to do with feeling less helpless, but she didn't know for sure.

"All right," Doc said, gently attaching the pads to her forehead, "let's make sure everything is running right."

The implants were read-only, allowing the ship's AI and human crew to monitor the sleeper's theta rhythms while in stasis. The implants still ran, albeit in a passive mode, when the owner was out of cryo, recording memories to incorporate into the unit's database. A malfunction could, in theory, cause a range of issues anywhere from mild amnesia to complete dementia.

Fortunately, the *Vic*'s AI was constantly monitoring every unit, and if worse came to worst, the Med Bay was equipped to handle anything up to major trauma.

"Thingy in the brain . . . thingy in the brain . . . built by a genius, to keep us all sane . . ." Doc sang softly. Madi recognized the tune but couldn't quite place it.

A few minutes of relative silence later, he looked up from the holoscreen and smiled.

"Everything looks good, Captain." He removed the sensor pads, wiped them with a disinfectant, and stored them. "My suggestion is to have a hot shower, a small glass of your favorite tipple, and read something bland but not work-related about an hour prior to racking. More than likely, you're just experiencing mild anxiety due to the job, and it'll pass with time."

Madi nodded absently, frowning slightly. What he said made sense, but that glitch earlier still bothered her. Was it just fatigue? Part of her mind said yes, of course it was, but another, quieter part kept whispering it was real.

"If the dreams persist, though, over the next two days," he

continued, "come back in and I'll give you a sedative. Can't have She Who Must Be Obeyed running on fumes, can we?"

"You got it, Doc." Madi stood up and headed to her quarters.

One of the good things about having only a handful of humans awake at a time was that living space was at luxury levels. Each crew member had their own berth, with private bathrooms and plenty of legroom. Another perk: all the hot water you could want. After about twenty minutes of showering, she felt slightly guilty, but then shrugged.

Doctor's orders, she thought, sighing as the knots in her shoulders loosened. Five minutes later, she looked at her pruned fingers. *However, there is too much of a good thing.*

She reluctantly shut the water off and stepped out, burying her face in the soft terry cloth of her towel. It was warm, smelled clean, and brought happy memories of her childhood. She swore she could just make out the faint scent of rose water, her mom's favorite perfume. It was enough to make her lower the towel and take a quick glance around the steamy bathroom.

You're being ridiculous, Madi thought, as she turned toward the sink. *Mom's gone, has been for . . .*

Her mother's face smiled at her from the foggy mirror.

Madi screamed as her knees buckled. Stars flashed in front of her eyes, then the world went black.

"Dammit, Doc, I know what I saw!" For all the force Madi put into her words, doubt gnawed at her.

"I know you believe you saw your mom, Madi," Doc said gently, "but think about it. Is it more likely that she was really there, or a side effect of mild sleep deprivation?"

He'd run the implant diagnostic again, with the same results. Nothing out of the ordinary, and the unit was operating as designed, passively recording in short spurts throughout the day.

It had seemed so real, though, not just a minor hallucination from a sleep-deprived brain. She'd looked exactly as Madi had last seen her—long brown hair pulled back into a ponytail, blue eyes shining warmly as she smiled. The steam from the shower had diffused the light from the fixture, giving the image a nimbus around it, concentrated in a loose circle over her mother's head.

"Logically, I know the answer," Madi said. "Thing is, Doc, I smelled her perfume. I saw her face."

"Do you resemble her?"

"Some, here and there. Her hair was brown, pulled back in a ponytail. Mine's dishwater blond, and down from the shower. We have the same cheeks and eyes, though."

"Here's my educated guess. You mentioned that the dreams you had involved children, correct?" At her nod, he continued, "Your maternal instinct was triggered, subconsciously. Couple that with being tired, *and* that you were trying to counteract those nightmares with positive thoughts, and you overlay your own reflection with your mother."

No matter how badly she wanted to wipe the smug grin from Doc's face, she had to admit that his explanation made sense. There was a chance that it could be technical, as well. The mirror could double as a simple HUD, a display projecting simple info holographically. She normally used it to check her weight, read reports or books while on the toilet, or listen to music while showering. A minor glitch could've distorted the image slightly, letting her brain take over from there.

"You may have a minor concussion," Doc said. "Nothing presenting at the moment, but to be safe, I'll need to monitor you over the next few days.

"Let me know immediately if you notice any symptoms, like increased irritability, dizziness, or nausea. Generally, we include trouble sleeping in that list, but I think in this case it's redundant. It does mean I can't give you a sedative without constant monitoring, however. Sorry about that."

Madi nodded. Maybe the little bump to the head would clear out the dreams and let her get a good night's sleep. Maybe.

"That's all I've got for now, boss," Doc concluded. "Just try and take it easy."

Madi made a mental note to get Caroline to cover her shift in the big chair for a day. By design, the five-man crew could easily handle the workload, short of a major emergency.

"Trust me, Doc, there's nothing I'd rather do."

Madi entered the galley, pleasantly surprised to find Caroline

Luze, Nikau Tamati, and Iain Jones having lunch. Caroline turned, panning her personal vid recorder around the room, stopping to focus on Madi before setting it down. The operations specialist had decided to create a video diary of their shifts, "so they'd have keepsakes for their children."

"Excellent, you're all here," Madi said, grabbing a bottle of water from the dispenser. "Had a minor fall earlier, and Doc needs me on light duty for the next day or so."

"Oh?" Caroline looked worried. "What happened?"

Madi waved the question off. "Just wasn't paying attention when I got out of the shower, slipped, and bumped my noggin."

No need to elaborate. Thinking the boss is seeing things isn't good for morale.

"Take all the time you need," Caroline said, nodding. She tapped a few keys on her tablet, bringing up the crew's schedule. With another tap, she brought up a holo display over the table. "I'll handle your load. Jones and Tamati, you two figure out the rest of it."

"Aye aye, Cap'n." Jones crossed his eyes and gave the worst salute Madi had ever seen. Nik snickered, but stifled it quickly after glancing at Madi's face.

"You don't look so good, boss," he said. "You sure it was just a bump?"

"The headache sucks, and Doc is playing it safe," Madi replied. "But I should be fine. Just having trouble sleeping, is all."

"Hunh. We were just talking about that," Nik said. "Seems to be going around a bit."

That got Madi's attention.

"All of you?" The others nodded.

She looked closely at each face. She'd missed it at first, but the telltale signs were there. The slightly haggard expressions, dark circles forming under their eyes—all present in varying severity.

"Right, new plan. Everyone get to the Med Bay before reporting to your stations. I want Doc to give you all a thorough exam including implant diagnostic. Understood?"

"Yes, ma'am," Caroline and Nik said, in unison. Jones grimaced.

"Problem with my orders, Jones?"

"It's nothing, boss, just a little insomnia." He shrugged. "Used to get it all the time, especially after . . . well, after she died."

"Jones, we're halfway through this trip, we still have a year left on our shift, and four out of five of us are experiencing the same issue," she said, frowning. "I need to know if there's a deeper problem here, got it?"

"Yes, ma'am," he said.

"Good. I'm racking out. Keep her flying."

Madi leaned back in her chair, pressing her palms to her eyes with an exasperated grunt. As tired as she felt, her brain wouldn't let her relax until she'd examined Doc's reports. They showed that the crew's tests, like hers, had shown no issues with the implants.

To make matters worse, she had gone over her program in the interim, only to find nothing out of the ordinary. The glitch, if there was one, wasn't in her code.

On the plus side, she hadn't had another hallucination, and the acetaminophen had reduced her headache to a barely noticeable throb. She stretched, massaged her shoulders for a moment, and looked at her bunk.

I can go over the code again, or double-check the reports—maybe there's something I missed... The quiet voice in the back of her mind made more excuses. She shook her head and sighed. No, she needed to try and rest. The *Vic* was her responsibility, and she couldn't perform her duties looped out from sleep deprivation. *But still...*

Dreams or no dreams, she had to sleep. She clenched her jaw, closed the screen, and got in her bunk.

"Jesus Christ, what now?" Madi groggily shook off the lingering nightmare and stared at the wall display. Children's cries merged into the buzz of the alarm, fading as she came fully awake. *Well, four hours sleep is something, I guess.*

Adrenaline hit her system as her brain caught up with her eyes. She jumped up and keyed the comm.

"All hands! All hands! Environmental failure in corridor seven! This is not a drill!"

She scanned the readout, looking for any additional information. An environmental failure could be any number of things, all bad.

Hold on... She forced the panic from her mind and took a closer look at the screen. After a second, she hit the comm again.

"Stand down, all crew stand down and await further orders."

Corridor seven ran parallel with the "keel," but close to the centerline of the ship. Any hull breach would show on several other compartments, corridors, and service passages as well as seven. The screen showed nothing out of range for any others. She tapped a few keys, bringing up a different level of diagrams.

Aside from the minimal life support requirements and electrical, seven had nothing but IT cabling and nodes.

Last I checked, fiber optics don't leak and if they did, a few stray photons wouldn't trip an environmental alarm.

"Caroline, meet me in seven, full-breach protocol."

It was likely nothing, but no reason not to be prepared.

"Aye aye."

Madi shrugged into her environmental suit, sealed up, and made her way to seven. Caroline arrived shortly after. The other woman looked rough, to be blunt.

"Caroline, you okay?"

"Yeah, boss, just a little run-down." Caroline said. The woman's looks made lies of her words, however. The bags under her eyes had grown deeper, and her face looked drawn and more pale than usual.

It was the eyes themselves, however, that really gave Madi pause. The word "haunted" came to mind, but it was more than that. They darted around constantly, as if looking for something that wasn't there. Even when Caroline was speaking to her, it felt like she was looking through her.

"You look more than just 'a little run-down,'" Madi said, "and I need the truth here."

"I said I'm fine," Caroline snapped. At her reaction, her voice softened. "Sorry boss. I'm good, really."

Madi nodded, then gestured broadly at the hallway.

"I'm not getting any environmental readings out of range here, are you?"

"No, ma'am. Nothing here except computer stuff, anyway." Caroline tapped her tablet, bringing up the "x-ray" display of the corridor. The tablet could, using the AI's internal mapping protocol, see through the walls, layer by layer.

She began sweeping the tablet slowly across the panels in front of her, looking for anything that could have triggered the alarm, muttering as she did so.

"LAN cable, power cable...that's a network node." She moved up the corridor as she worked. "Ductwork shows no issues..."

Madi fired up her own tablet, focusing on the opposite wall. Like Caroline, she wasn't seeing anything out of the ordinary. She noticed, but mainly ignored, Caroline's movement in her periphery, maintaining her concentration on the tablet screen. Several minutes passed.

"Argh, this is like looking for a needle in a stack of needles," Madi said. Halfway down her side of the wall, and still nothing. Caroline's shadow caught the edge of her right eye. "You find anything?"

"Nada, boss," Caroline said, her voice coming down the corridor from Madi's left.

Wait.

Madi whipped her head around to look at the other woman. Caroline, still scanning her side, had made it to the midpoint of her wall, *in the opposite direction.*

Madi turned slowly back to her right.

"Please don't be Mom," she whispered.

It wasn't.

A vaguely humanoid form floated several feet away, surrounded by a nimbus of dim light. It slowly continued to coalesce, the outline becoming more distinct as the seconds passed. The nimbus grew brighter, curving upward at the sides of the figure, vaguely resembling wings. Madi stared, unable to tear her gaze away. She realized her mouth hung open.

"Holy Christ!" Caroline's shout broke through Madi's stunned fugue. "What the hell is that?"

Madi slowly moved backward, raising her tablet in front of her. Whatever was in the corridor, it didn't register on the schematic.

"Caroline, do you have your recorder?"

"Y-yes."

"Good, get this on tape."

"Way ahead of you, boss."

When Madi reached Caroline's position, she stopped. The figure had continued to form, becoming clearer, but only from the mid torso up. She had vaguely Asiatic features—the large, almond-shaped eyes and high cheekbones suggesting Thai or Filipino ancestry. Her clothing, what could be seen of it, looked like a standard-issue crew jumpsuit.

For a brief moment, the image became eye-searingly bright, then disappeared. Madi blinked several times to adjust to the regular lighting of the corridor.

Her comm crackled in her earpiece.

"Boss, we've got a situation," Doc said. "Need you in the Med Bay."

"On my way." Madi looked at Caroline "Get this sorted. Ghosts or no ghosts, got it?"

"Aye aye, ma'am."

Madi keyed the comm as she made her way to the Med Bay.

"Sit rep, Doc."

"Jones and Nik had an altercation, Nik's here for minor contusions and dislocated jaw. Not sure where Jones is now."

Keying off, she picked up her pace.

"Shit," Madi growled. "Just what I need."

Once in the lift, adrenaline and weariness took its toll. She shifted back and forth, knowing the trip wasn't taking any more time than usual, but unable to shake the feeling of sluggishness.

"Finally," she whispered, as the doors slid open. A quick check of the corridor showed no Jones, so she hurried to the Med Bay. Doc was wrapping Nik's jaw and head with a flexible bandage, giving him instructions as he worked.

"Looks like protein shakes for a few days and try not to talk much. The main thing is to keep it as immobile as you can. Okay?" Tamati gave him a thumbs-up. Doc turned to Madi. "Good, you're here."

"What happened?"

Doc handed Nik a tablet, making a writing motion with his other hand. Madi crossed her arms, understanding *why* it had to be done, but hating that it *had* to be done. She took a closer look at Tamati while she waited.

Nik's shaggy brown hair, which normally fell in front of his eyes, was now held back by the bandage. Aside from the jaw, Nik's nose was bloody, and he had a black eye forming.

A few moments later, Doc took the tablet back, and read what Nik had written.

"Saw Jones standing at a station, walked up behind him and

tapped him on the shoulder. Not sure who he thought I was, but he immediately spun and swung fist. I wasn't ready, caught me on the jaw. Knocked me down. Kept swinging before I could roll away."

"Did you see where he went?" Madi asked.

Nik shook his head slowly, wincing.

"Dammit, we need to find him, Doc." She keyed the comm. "Caroline, what's your status?"

"Still looking for something wrong in seven," Caroline replied. "Big goose egg. No ghosts, though, so that's good."

"Be aware, Jones attacked Nik, and is at large. Definitely hostile, possibly delusional."

"Oh fantastic."

"Keep at it," Madi said, "There's got to be something there."

"Aye aye." Madi killed the comm.

"Ghosts?" Doc raised an eyebrow.

"Fill you in later, we need to find Jones," Madi said. "We can use the security feed in the control room. Nik, lock the door behind us and stay here."

A minute later, and out of breath, Madi punched up the ship's internal camera feeds. With over one hundred cameras onboard, it was an overwhelming task.

"This is going to take a while," Doc said, over her shoulder. "Where do we start? He could be anywhere by now."

"We'll start with the most obvious places first," Madi said, tapping keys. "Quarters, connecting corridors..."

With a sudden patch of static, multiple feeds switched, bringing several views of Jones on screen.

"Whoa," Doc said, "lucky guesses."

"I didn't do that." Madi held up a hand, forestalling any further comments, concentrating on the videos. "He's in corridor... five, I think, heading toward the galley. Let's go."

"Hang on a tic." Doc opened a cabinet, grabbed a hypo, and filled it. "Ready."

They made their way to the galley, pausing outside the door. Sounds from inside made it clear that Jones was still there.

Madi looked at Doc and raised an eyebrow. He nodded. She triggered the door.

Jones stood, back to the kitchen prep counter, holding a large carving knife. Even from her position, Madi could see his eyes were wild and bloodshot. He looked like he hadn't slept in days.

"Jones, I need you to take a moment, relax, and put the knife down," she said, keeping her voice measured and level.

The knife gleamed in the ship's lighting. Madi knew that it was razor sharp and could slice her from sternum to cervix like it was going through warm butter. Jones held it shakily, likely due to his sleep-deprived state, but that didn't make it, or him, any less dangerous.

Doc slowly edged his way toward Jones's right side, keeping his movements slow and nonthreatening, turning his body to keep the hypo hidden. Madi, staying well out of range, worked her way to his left. The crewman's head swiveled back and forth, trying to track them, each turn growing wilder.

"I can't, boss, you don't know what it's like!" Jones slashed the blade quickly in her direction, more a deterrent than an actual threat. She was still several feet away, and it would take a major lunge on his part to get any closer. "I don't even know if I'm awake right now. I keep thinking I've woken up, only to have another nightmare. Is this real?"

"Jones, trust me, you're awake. We all are," Madi said, trying to keep her voice smooth. Jones kept his attention on her, allowing Doc to move closer. "We're on the *Vic*, we're in the galley, and we're not going to hurt you. There's a glitch somewhere that's giving us nightmares, and we're going to fix it. But you have to put the knife down first."

The blade wavered slightly, as Jones considered her words.

"I keep seeing them," he whispered. "The children, the flames— the dreams ooze into my brain, I can feel them slithering in, but can't do anything to stop them . . ."

He stopped, staring past her, eyes wide. His jaw dropped slightly.

There was something flickering in her peripheral vision, like a light about to go out. Madi turned her head, just enough to focus on it, but keeping Jones in sight.

"Oh, God, not now," she whispered.

Just off her left hip stood a transparent child, approximately eight years old. A little girl, by the dress, with braided pigtails falling to the center of her back. Madi felt her own mouth fall open as the image smiled, held out her hands, and beckoned toward Jones.

"Becca?" The hand holding the knife dropped to his side as he took a hesitant step forward. "Becca, honey, you shouldn't be here. You're supposed to be at home with Mommy . . ."

Doc shot forward, tackling Jones, careful to keep his body away from the blade. The other man fought back as much as possible, but Doc skillfully kept Jones's arms pinned to his sides. The knife fell to the floor with a soft clank, barely audible over the two men's grunts.

With a heave, Doc rolled Jones over, taking position on Jones's back, knees pinning the larger man's arms. With a smooth, well-practiced motion, he injected the sedative. Madi looked back at the ghostly child just as it flickered out of existence.

"No! Becca, come back!" Jones struggled against Doc's weight, his movements becoming weaker as the drug took hold. "Please, come back. Daddy loves you . . ."

Doc waited a few seconds more before checking Jones's pulse. With a nod, he stood up and straightened his coveralls.

"Well, that was different," he said. "Just to be certain, you saw that kid, too, right?"

Madi nodded, not trusting herself to speak coherently.

"Oh, thank God," Doc said, sighing. "I was questioning my own mental state for a second. On the plus side, if I am going crazy, I've got company."

Madi walked over to where the child had appeared. A thought nibbled at the edge of her brain, slowly coalescing, but not fully formed. The location of the image was important, but why?

"Gave him enough to keep him down for a while," Doc said.

"Stand where Jones started, Doc," Madi said, ignoring him. Doc moved into position. "Now tell me what you see."

"Table, chairs, you," he said, shrugging. "What're you thinking?"

"Not sure yet. Switch spots with me."

From Jones's position, she saw the same thing Doc had. Still, there was a nagging thought.

"Anything yet? I do have to get him restrained and back to the Med Bay." Doc knelt, looked at the ceiling, and clasped his hands piously. "That is, if the universe doesn't have any other surprises in store?"

Madi unconsciously raised her gaze to follow his and found herself focusing on the holo projector over the table.

"Wait—Doc, don't move."

She walked forward, noting the projector's angle. Where normally it was focused over the table, it was now pointed at Doc's position. She climbed on the table, aligning her line of sight with the projector.

"Holy shit," she whispered. "Doc, get Jones secured, then come back here. Bring Nik and Caroline. I think I have an idea about what's happening."

Madi looked at the haggard faces of her three remaining crew. She offered a quick prayer that she was on the right track. God only knew how long they could keep it together. If Jones's reaction was any indication, not very long at all.

"Right," she said, "I've been able to put a few things in place, but there's still some big gaps. Let's start with what we know:

"One: we're all having recurring nightmares. Two: there have been sightings on the ship of, for lack of a better term, ghosts. Three: all diagnostics we've run, on various systems, have come back clean."

"Why can't we just declare an emergency, and wake the next shift?" Caroline seemed to vocalize what the others had been thinking, judging by their faces. Madi shook her head.

"We don't know if what we're experiencing has affected anyone in cryo, if it's indicative of a major issue we just haven't found yet, or that it won't escalate with the next shift," she said. "I can't risk the ship's safety by punting."

"So where do we start?"

"Let's talk about the nightmares. Jones mentioned fire, and children. In general, that's what I've been seeing, too. Anyone else?" All nodded. "That tells me the source is the same for all of us.

"Next, the ghosts. Doc, Jones, and I saw Jones's daughter, right over there. I saw my mom in my mirror. Caroline and I saw a figure in the corridor. These locations all have one thing in common." Madi pointed to the projector above the table. "Each time a ghost appeared, there was a holo projector or holo-capable equipment nearby."

"Oh, holy shit," Doc said, realization dawning on his face. "You think the AI is causing this."

"Exactly. But what I don't know, is why." Madi turned to Caroline. "How much time would you need to fix this?"

Caroline frowned. "By myself? I can't honestly say. Hell, I don't even know where to start looking."

"Okay, we'll get you some help, then. Get him a list"—Madi jerked her thumb at Doc—"of anyone you think you need. Doc, get prepped for an emergency wake-up of at least four people. Have a psych eval questionnaire ready, too. I need to be sure they aren't compromised. Also, be ready to put Jones under for the duration."

"What about me?" Nik mumbled.

"You're with me. Oh, and Caroline? I'll need your camera, please. Everyone clear?" At their "aye ayes," she nodded. "Right, let's grab coffee and get to work, people, before this gets any worse."

"Nik, aim the camera at my tablet screen. When I tell you, start recording, and don't stop until the scroll finishes. Clear?"

"Aye aye, ma'am, but I don't see how this helps," he said carefully, still nursing his jaw.

"I've got a hunch that a piece of this puzzle has been in front of me the whole time, and I need a second pair of eyes and hands to be absolutely sure." She loaded the external drive, and brought up the interface, keeping her finger over the run button. "Start filming."

At Nik's nod, she tapped the screen. As had happened previously, the screen scrolled all greens, moving past at her normal reading speed.

"There!" Madi pointed at the readout, not touching the tablet. "You saw the red line, right?"

"Yes, ma'am. Can you roll it back?"

"No, we're going to let it run," she said. "That's what the recorder is for. We'll play it back after it's through."

After the diagnostic finished, Madi scrolled up, running back through the list. All green, just like last time.

"That's odd," Nik said, frowning. "I know I saw a red line in there."

"Exactly. Let's run the video."

They played the recording, watching carefully as the names rolled past.

"There!" Madi paused the playback, pumping her fist in the air. "Right there, I knew it! Corbeau—one, psychosis—zero."

"George Holt," Nik read. "I don't get it, what could he possibly have to do with all this?"

"Not sure, but whatever's going on, he's related. Otherwise, why would the line go from red to green when we scrolled back?"

For emphasis, she rolled the list up to Holt's entry and thumbnail.

"See? All green." She zoomed in on her tablet, and checked the recording. "Look at this—the numbers are the same, just in green. He's way out of parameters. We need to take this to Doc. Hang on..."

She scrolled, then zoomed in on the next line down.

"I knew she looked familiar!"

"Hunh? Who does?"

"This woman, she's the ghost Caroline and I saw in the corridor. Maryanne Suyat." Madi pulled up a file. "She's lead of the IT team. No, not just the lead—she's the principal designer! If anyone on board can fix this, she can."

Madi stood, pocketed the camera, and headed for the door.

"C'mon, we've got to take this to the others." She hit the door control.

The door opened into Hell. Madi jumped back, crashing into Nik, knocking them both to the floor.

"Jesus Christ!" Nik rolled, regained his feet, and lunged for the button, closing the door. He keyed his comm. "All crew, red alert! Fire in the control room corridor! Repeat, fire in the control corridor!"

Madi stood and ran to the ship's diagnostic screen. There were no alarms or warning messages—nothing indicative of the raging inferno in the corridor.

"All crew, cancel red alert," she commed. "Be aware of holographic interference."

"Are you nuts?" Nik looked like she'd lost her mind.

She slowly walked toward the door, hand extended. After a moment's hesitation, she placed her palm on the metal surface.

"Do you feel anything? It's cool. Literally. No heat, whatsoever," she said, turning back. "I don't think there's a fire out there at all."

"We didn't hallucinate it."

"No, but there's projectors out there. I think we're on the right track, and something is trying to scare us off."

"You realize that sounds insane, right?"

"What, if anything, about this situation isn't? Doc," she said into the comm, "we need to check on passenger number eight dash six seven dash five three zero dash nine. Holt, George. I think he's tied to what's been going on."

"Why?"

"I'll explain more later, but his numbers are way out of line for cryo. Check into it."

"Roger that."

"Caroline," she said, switching channels, "put Maryanne Suyat on your list. We need her."

"Copy."

A warning light flashed suddenly from the console.

"Oh, crap," she said, reading the screen. "Someone just accessed the armory."

There had been a vocal minority on the mission-planning team against taking arms; however, they had been overridden by others, including the crew. They had no reason to expect any contact while in transit, but the new planet was a different story. There was simply no telling how large, hostile, or just generally irritated at having their territory invaded any fauna would be once the *Vic* arrived. No one going on the trip wanted to be completely defenseless on a new planet, no matter how optimistic the people staying home might be. The prevailing attitude was "better to have it and not need it, rather than the other way around."

Madi felt a rueful pang at the thought that at least one of the anti's arguments was correct: someone on the crew would use the weapons against their fellows.

She keyed the "All hands" channel. "Who's in the armory?" Caroline and Nik came back immediately with "Negative." Madi waited for Doc. When no answer came, she said, "Doc? Status?"

"Doc is unavailable at the moment," Jones's voice came over the comm, oddly calm. "He'll be having a nap for the near future."

"Jones," Madi said, "whatever you're thinking of, don't go through with it. We're getting this fixed, but we need everyone to do it."

"Oh, don't worry, Captain, I'm doing my part to fix things, too." He chuckled softly. "Holt, was it? He's the key, right?"

Madi closed the channel and turned to Nik.

"Get Caroline and see to Doc. I'll handle Jones."

"He's armed, bigger than you, and psychotic."

"Yeah, but we need to get the IT team awake. He may still be functional enough to listen to the acting captain."

"I don't like it," Nik said with a frown.

"You don't have to, it's an order."

"Aye aye, Captain."

She opened the door, ready to face fire, real or imagined. The corridor was clear, no evidence whatsoever of the raging inferno moments earlier.

"Don't trust your eyes, Nik," she said. "Not at this point. Now get to it." She stepped into the corridor.

Madi entered the cryo hold slowly, scanning the room as she made her way down the seemingly endless rows of tanks. She tapped her tablet, bringing up the ship's map program, her location marked by a slowly pulsing dot. Holt's tank was up ahead. She'd stopped by the armory first and procured a small caliber pistol. She sincerely hoped she wouldn't be forced to use the weapon she had holstered behind her back but was willing to do what was necessary.

It would be an easier way to handle it . . . She shook off that particular train of thought, but it kept nibbling at the corners of her mind. *Put a bullet in his head, end the threat. Easier than trying to talk him down . . .*

Madi clenched her jaw. *No. My sidearm is the* last *resort, not the first choice.*

Jones stood over Holt's tank, locked and cocked pistol at his side.

"So this is him? He's why?"

"Jones, you're not thinking clearly. Put the gun down, and let's discuss this." It wasn't hull damage she was worried about, the *Vic* was built to handle micrometeors, and had several safeguards built in. Not to mention, the cryo hold was in the center of the ship, protected by several decks in each direction. A bullet wouldn't cause a large-scale structural catastrophe.

The cryo tanks, however, were reasonably fragile. A stray shot could do irreparable damage to the tank, and its occupant. That was a risk she was unwilling to take.

"I heard you tell Doc that he's the key," Jones said, keeping her in sight. "I've been standing here trying to figure out how and why."

"We don't know yet," Madi said. "But we're working on it. We're all at the end of our ropes, though, and can use your help."

"Help." He snorted. "What do you think I'm trying to do?"

"I'm not sure, Jones, but killing a sleeper isn't going to do it."

"How do you know?" He turned to face her fully. "We're running on fumes. Seeing things. How do we know anything at this point?"

"We know there's something wrong in the *Vic*'s AI. Beyond that, it's a question mark. Let's not do anything we can't take back, though, okay?"

"And there's the rub," Jones said, with another snort. "Way I see it, if this is real, we get rid of the problem. If it's not, and I'm still dreaming, then nothing happens. Win-win either way."

"I told you before, this is real, we're awake, and on the *Vic*. I can prove it, but I need you to trust me, and stand down."

"Prove it how? I saw Becca. She's dead, and ghosts aren't real. So how do you explain that if I'm not still asleep?"

Madi prayed her next move would work. Each of the tanks had a small projector built in, to show the occupant's vitals via holographic display.

"*Vic*, I need you to bring up Becca, on my location."

Madi held her breath. There was no way to know if her hunch would pay off, but it was really all she had, short of shooting Jones.

The seconds crawled past at an agonizing pace. Jones looked around impatiently.

Suddenly, every tank within a ten-foot radius sprang to life, projecting light into the room. Within moments, Becca appeared, in miniature, floating above each one, surrounded by a bright haze. As with Suyat's image in the hallway, the upswept perimeter gave her an angelic appearance. Madi let out an explosive sigh.

"The *Vic* is causing the problems, Jones," she said. "We don't know why yet, but my gut tells me she's trying to help us fix her."

Jones stood, gaping, at the images of his daughter hovering around him. Madi pressed on.

"Real or not, I want you to think of Becca right now. You want to set a good example for her, don't you?"

"She's dead, Captain," he said grimly. "Nothing can change that."

"You're right. But how would she feel if she saw you now? Would she be proud of you?"

"No." Jones's voice rasped, barely audible.

"Honor her memory. Be the father she saw you as. Be the good man I know you are. Do the right thing."

Tears flowing down his cheeks, Jones eased the hammer down, and placed the gun on the deck.

Madi approached, retrieved the pistol, and stood. Becca's image faded, but not before smiling and waving.

"Let's get back to the others."

"So let me make sure I've got this straight," Holt said, around a mouthful of food. "You all have been seeing my dreams?"

"More or less," Doc said.

"Oh God, I'm so sorry." To Madi's eye, Holt looked like he hadn't been resting well either. Which was part of the problem.

"Don't beat yourself up over it," Maryanne Suyat said, patting him on the shoulder. "There were a few Murphy-type incidents that had to happen. Sucks that they did, but don't think we blame you."

They had brought Holt out of cryo first. Jones had agreed to remain in his quarters, under lockdown, until the situation had been resolved. Fortunately for the crew, as soon as Holt had awakened, the nightmares stopped. Another plus had been that none of the sleepers in cryo, aside from Holt, had been affected. Doc's psych eval had shown that.

"What caused all this?" Holt asked.

"We're still trying to find the cause," Suyat said. "Best we can see, so far, is there was damage to one of the logic gates in the *Vic*'s solid-state boards. What should have been an 'and' gate had somehow fused and become an 'or' gate."

"Can you dumb that down for me a bit?"

"The gate should only function if it was receiving power from two separate inputs. In this case, it failed to a state where it functioned even though it only received power from one input or the other."

"And take it down one more step, please."

Suyat sighed, then said, "Wire get melty, no do job right."

"The failure caused the *Vic* to go schizo, for lack of a better term," Doc said. "Fortunately, one personality was actively trying to help us."

"But how did my nightmares get into your heads?"

"Best we can figure at this point, is that the one of the *Vic*'s aspects found a back door into the implant programming," Doc said. "In theory, it was a way for us to diagnose and correct any software failures. In practice, the AI used it to alter our theta rhythms and insert yours."

"The reason yours were so prevalent," Suyat said, "is that you weren't fully in cryostasis. Enough to make the trip physically, but, in a perpetual REM state."

"And if you hadn't caught this?"

"Unsure." Doc shrugged. "But best guess is you'd have come out of cryo completely bonkers, if you came out at all. We'll need to run more tests before we put you back to sleep, but the initial results look positive."

"What about the ghosts?" Caroline asked.

"Holograms," Madi said. "The 'good' *Vic* was trying to lead us in the right direction but running up against its direct interaction protocols. The holos were a way around that. The 'bad' *Vic* didn't have those protocols but was being held back by the 'good' side, and limited in what it could do."

"That's why we only saw images of people that could either help, in Maryanne's case, or comfort, like Becca or my mom. I think *Victoria* was trying to communicate with us, but like a toddler, unable to express herself beyond simple emotional connections."

"What my team has found so far," Maryanne said, "is that the 'bad' psyche had figured out how to work within the limits the 'good' psyche had enforced. Honestly, had this continued, I think the entire population could've been affected, had they lived that long. Any longer, and the current crew could've been driven to scuttling the ship and thinking that they were saving us all."

"Jesus," Holt whispered. "If there's anything I can do to help with this, please don't hesitate to let me know. Last thing I want to do is explain to Saint Peter why ten thousand souls are really pissed at me."

"Same," Madi said, standing. "Ms. Suyat, is there anything more you need from me right now?"

"No, Captain, we're going to repair the hardware, then reinstall the software from our backup. I think we can take it from here."

"Excellent," Madi said, heading for her quarters. "I'm going to go get some sleep."

Ghosts

It is natural for humans to attribute unusual phenomena to "ghosts" even when the preponderance of evidence suggests that a supernatural event simply is not possible. The commanding officer's log on the "Corbeau Incident" was neither the first nor the last such report—either on *Victoria* or on Cistercia. Alternate historical analyses, such as those comprising *Flint's People's History*, argue that the incident did not occur as described, but was rather a case of group psychosis caused by insufficient psychological screening of crews ill-suited to the long, lonely cruise to TRAPPIST-2.

Reports of ghost sightings continued and typically involved Colony Foundation visionary Keegan Coran, family members who remained in the Sol System, and mythological figures such as Carmen Miranda and Elvis. Many, but not all, of these sightings were eventually attributed to sleep deprivation, practical jokes, and mental instability.

While the AI malfunctions on *Victoria* provided a convenient explanation for ghost sightings, the explanations were not accepted by all. This led to the rise of distrust toward synthetic intelligences, even among the crew. Years after the Corbeau Incident, Shift Captain Kimo Bane insisted that the AIs be disabled until the crew could "root out the ghosts in the machine." Captain Bane was relieved of command and placed back in cryo for the duration of the voyage. Nevertheless, suspicion that something could be very wrong with the computers persisted.

—*Encyclopedia Astra*,
Gannon University,
Antonia, Cistercia, AA212

KAMEKURA

David Weber

Legends grow in the telling . . . usually.
Figures of legend become larger-than-life, bigger than anyone could
  possibly have been in real life . . . usually.
People truly willing to die for love don't really exist . . . usually.
Usually.

TRAPPIST-2 System
Cistercia Planetary Orbit
January 2347 CE/03 Ad Astra

"Final test sequence complete, Flight Control. Green board."

"Understood, Jonah," Commander Edwin Dupree responded from his station in the starship *Victoria*'s control center. He scanned his displays, solely out of ingrained habit and professionalism, not need. The *Whale*—officially Lander Alpha—moved rapidly across the planet in its lower orbit, 30,000 kilometers below *Victoria*'s 35,000-kilometer geostationary perch, and his displays showed no other traffic anywhere near its flight path. Well, of course there wasn't! There wasn't any other traffic in the entire *star system*. The tugs which had eased *Whale* into its present orbit the day before had redocked with *Victoria* shortly after the insertion maneuver, and as yet, there was nowhere for any of her personnel or cargo shuttles to go.

That was why *Whale* was where she was.

"Looks good for insertion on the next orbital pass, Ed," Lieutenant Commander Joan Walker said. Her personal callsign (coupled with the fact that Alpha was a good fifty percent larger than any of *Victoria*'s other landers) had made *Whale*'s unofficial name inevitable when she was assigned as its pilot, and she and Dupree had known one another since they were kids playing micrograv tag on the Sagittarius L5 Hab. "I'm starting the clock."

"Don't break anything this time!" Dupree said sternly.

"That's not fair!" He could hear the laugh in Walker's voice. "The last time wasn't my fault! For that matter, I haven't so much as dented a ship in over a hundred and sixty years!"

"Sure, and you snoozed for all but *six* of them, didn't you?" Dupree objected.

"Well, if you're going to be *that* way about it."

"Seriously, Joanie." Dupree's voice softened. "Do good, okay?"

"You got it, Flight," Walker replied as her lander swept toward the Cistercian terminator. "See you."

The lander crossed the terminator and, simultaneously, *Victoria*'s sensor horizon, and Dupree leaned back in his chair in Primary Flight Control's microgravity as he gazed pensively down at the continent the colonists had provisionally christened Molesme. It struck them as reasonable, given that the planet was officially designated TRAPPIST-2a, and Robert of·Molesme had founded the Cistercian order of Trappist monks. It might not stick, of course, but Captain Nikolina Perić, *Victoria*'s current skipper, was adamantly opposed to sticking "Continent Alpha" on it as a temporary label because "Alpha" showed an appalling lack of imagination and she was afraid it would *stay* stuck out of force of habit. Whatever they called it, it was beautiful, banded with clouds, sprawled across the planetary equator, spined with snowcapped mountains, traced with broad rivers that threaded through the vibrant green of vegetation that used something functionally indistinguishable from chlorophyll, all floating on the dark sapphire of deep, blue oceans.

There wasn't a trace of human habitation down there, which might not have been too surprising for a planet thirty light-years from the Solar System. Except that there was supposed to be. The automated terraforming ship *Prometheus* had departed for TRAPPIST-2 twenty years before *Victoria*. It was well over twice *Victoria*'s size, and the drones and robotic cultivators and construction equipment aboard its massive landers and heavy lift shuttles should have prepared four colony sites to receive *Victoria*'s ten thousand passengers.

The pre-mission planning had counted heavily on having footholds with prebuilt shelters, crop-yielding farms, and fenced pastureland. There might even have been time to decant the first of the frozen ova of cattle and sheep cryogenically stored aboard the colony ship. Each of the lead ship's primary landers had also been built around a compact fusion reactor. They'd been intended to land near bodies of water, and the same drones and robots would have constructed the electrolysis plants to produce the necessary hydrogen to assure the new arrivals of ample power when they settled into their new homes. For that matter, each of the massive landers themselves would have served as its own "town-in-a-box," surrounded by those farms and pastures, until the colony's increased population demanded additional housing.

All of that was supposed to be waiting down there.

It wasn't.

They would never know why, but *Prometheus* had never arrived. None of the prepared footholds they'd planned upon had been created.

Fortunately, the TRAPPIST-2 Colony Foundation's planners had known they couldn't stake the colony's survival on the assumption *Prometheus* would complete the trip or that its automated systems would function flawlessly when it arrived. Assuming they did function properly, they would be more efficient—as well as far more expendable, in the event of natural disaster—than humans could be, but they *were* machines. Machines broke, and even the best computer glitched occasionally. So the planners had compromised by including a single volunteer human crewman in cryostasis, to be awakened and intervene if anything went wrong with *Prometheus'* sophisticated AIs. Despite that, they'd recognized that—as had obviously happened—that might not be enough. Which was why *Whale* was so much larger yet carried only fifty still-hibernating passengers, as opposed to the twenty-five hundred who would ride each of the other landers to the planetary surface. Although she was smaller than *Prometheus'* landers had been, she was still just over a kilometer and a half in length, three-quarters of a kilometer wide, and the same 250 meters "thick" as her smaller sisters, which gave her over twice their cubic volume.

Of course, part of that extra volume went into the four additional main engines (and their fuel tanks) installed in *Whale*'s flattened "base." The base, which was intended to function as a "crumple zone," if it was needed upon landing, was part of the design which allowed *Whale* to use atmospheric braking on entry. (It wasn't really fair to call it "reentry," since *Whale* had never before been in anyone's atmosphere.) Despite that, she needed the additional engine power, and she also carried a larger fuel reserve per engine than the other landers. As the "first-in," she was more likely than the other landers to be forced to maneuver to ensure an optimum landing. The colony planners had done all they could to map her planned LZ's terrain with orbital observation and the air-breathing drones *Victoria* had inserted, but surprises were still possible. And since *Whale* represented the "suspenders" of the colony planner's terraforming belt-and-suspenders, they'd taken no chances with the massive lander's ability to put down *precisely* where she intended to.

And that was because of the other things in *Whale*'s additional volume. She had less robotic support than *Prometheus*' heavy landers would have had, but she and her fifty passengers—well, fifty-one, counting Lieutenant Commander Walker—had everything they needed to produce anything one of those landers should have produced. The decision to include those humans in the payload was one reason she was less amply equipped with robotics, but that, too, represented a fallback on the planners' part. If *Prometheus* had arrived and its drones had proved unequal to the task for some reason, they'd wanted "feet on the ground" from the beginning—human eyes and brains to compensate for whatever might have stumped the AIs.

In about—Dupree glanced at the chronometer—eighty-seven minutes, *Whale* would begin her de-orbiting burn, and after that it would be up to Walker to put all of that on the ground on the broad, rich savannah beside the river she'd insisted on dubbing Billabong. Perić had been dubious, at first, but she'd finally conceded that as the individual piloting the first colony lander, it was a reasonable prerogative for Walker to claim. Always with the proviso that the other people who would someday live on TRAPPIST-2a got a voice in renaming it if they decided to.

Dupree chuckled at the thought. Adam Walker hadn't set foot outside Australia until his family's immigration to Mars when he was twenty-five years old, specifically to get him qualified for the TRAPPIST expedition, and his birthplace was a running joke between him and Joan, who'd been born and raised in the L5 habitats.

Dupree was looking forward to Adam's reaction when Joan decanted him from cryostasis and—with that patented innocent expression she did *so* well—told him she'd made sure Cistercia would enshrine Aussie slang by naming a 5,000-kilometer-long river for an isolated, seasonal pond on what *used* to be a creekbed.

A tone sounded in Joan Walker's earphones as *Whale's* AI warned her it was about time, and she closed the diary entry she'd been working on.

In many ways, she was just a passenger. *Whale* would undoubtedly land herself just fine without human intervention, but it was more of that belt-and-suspenders philosophy. If something went wrong with the central AI—*and* its standalone backup—it was unlikely a mere human could avert catastrophe, but "unlikely" wasn't the same thing as "no chance in hell." Not that she'd minded drawing the short straw. In fact, she'd fought hard for this assignment from the beginning, because Adam had been slated to head the Lander Alpha crew in light of the twenty years he'd spent on a working Australian cattle ranch. Her own childhood had gifted her with minimal experience at the bottom of a gravity well, but she was damn well the best pilot assigned to *Victoria*, and she'd made that stand up.

She did wish the two of them had been awake together for her final crew shift aboard *Victoria*, but like all of his crew, Adam had been loaded aboard in his cryostasis pod, along with the rest of the cargo. That was why she'd been keeping her diary for the last year or so, to share the excitement of arrival—and the bitter disappointment of the *non*-arrival of *Prometheus*—with him when he woke up.

Now she adjusted position, right hand resting lightly on the hands-on-throttle-and-stick joystick while the time display ticked steadily downward, and she smiled.

I'm not one bit nervous, she told herself. *Not* one. *Shut up, stomach!*

"She should start her de-orbit burn in about forty seconds, sir," Chief Ottweiler said, and Dupree nodded.

The main engines' de-orbit burn would slow *Whale* to align her on the desired entry path, then the maneuvering thrusters would adjust her attitude before she hit air nose-first, behind her ablative heat shield. It was a throwback to the design of humanity's very first reentry vehicles, predating even the original shuttle, because, despite her enormous engine power, something five times as long (and eighteen times as wide) as an old wet-navy aircraft carrier was simply too massive to brake any other way.

"Three minutes to direct signal reacquisition," Ottweiler added, and Dupree nodded again. The pair of relay satellites deployed equidistantly around the planet from *Victoria* gave them continuous communications with *Whale*, but Dupree was old school. He wanted a direct transmission path whenever he could get one, just in case they lost a satellite at exactly the wrong moment. He'd had that happen, once, and the results had been . . . not good.

Not that anything's going wrong this *time*, he thought very, very firmly.

The countdown clock reached thirty seconds . . . and the universe went insane.

Joan Walker's eyes flared wide as the attitude thrusters fired early. On her main display, the reentry profile tracked on undisturbed—perfect. But she felt the vibration, and *Whale*'s maneuvering thrusters were as powerful as *Victoria*'s shuttles' *main* engines. They had to be, given her bulk, and the starscape beyond Walker's canopy high atop the lander's hull rolled crazily as it rotated around its axis. She twisted the joystick to override whatever the hell had gone wrong, but nothing happened. *Whale* should have reverted to manual control the instant she hit the "ENABLE" button, but it didn't. In fact, the entire stick refused to move at all!

She wrenched at it in disbelief, fingers flying through alternate sequences on the HOTAS buttons, trying to find a way in as *Whale* rolled fully inverted . . . and then the main thrusters lit off.

Not with the incremental thrust that had been programmed. It was a full-power burn, and not just by the pair of engines she'd selected, either. Five and a half gravities of totally unexpected acceleration slammed her back in her tilted couch, and horror filled her as she realized exactly how *Whale*'s attitude had changed. The thundering engines weren't simply killing orbital speed; they were driving her vertically downward, straight toward catastrophic atmospheric entry!

That was impossible. *All* of this was impossible, but that impossibility was about to kill her—and Adam and everyone else aboard *Whale*! Unless—

She tightened her abdominal muscles, fighting the gray-out, and her left hand fought its way across her flight console against five and a half times its normal weight. It reached the button she'd never expected to use, and she punched it, but nothing happened, and she swore savagely inside her mind. That should have overridden the AI, kicked it completely out of the system and killed the main thrusters *whatever* the computers were telling them.

It hadn't.

She closed her eyes, her hand continuing to move, until it found a second button. It pressed, and she sobbed in gratitude as the attitude control AI powered down and the maneuvering thrusters, at least, stopped firing. A green light indicated manual control had been enabled, the joystick came alive in her hand, and she felt a fierce flare of relief. She might not be able to shut down the main engines, but she could at least control *Whale's* attitude *while* they fired!

She rolled the ship frantically, fighting to bring it back to its proper attitude. For a moment, she thought she had it. But then the green light blinked out again and the thrusters went dead. The joystick still moved in her hand, but it had no effect at all.

She glared at the blandly lying plot. It showed her on exactly the correct entry trajectory, despite how sharply she'd diverged from it. At least she'd managed to shift her attitude away from that suicidal dive into atmosphere, but that might not be a whole lot better, if she couldn't regain control of the engines. Instead of driving straight down into atmosphere, she was driving straight up, *away* from the atmosphere on a heading that took her directly away from *Victoria*—and rescue—as well.

Nothing lay on her current heading but interstellar space. But at least she'd bought a little time.

"Flight, we have a problem," she heard her acceleration-hoarse voice say with far greater calm than she felt. "*Whale* is declaring an emergency. Multiple control system fails. I can't get into the system. Request immediate remote override."

Her earphones were silent.

"Flight, this is Jonah! I need a remote override! Do you copy?"

"What the hell?!" Chief Ottweiler blurted.

Commander Dupree's head snapped around, and the chief pointed at one of his displays.

"She's *way* the hell off profile, sir! Look at that!"

Dupree looked, and his blood ran cold as he saw *Whale* accelerating fiercely away from the planet.

"Jonah!" he barked into his mic. "Jonah, advise your condition!"

"Nothing, sir," Ottweiler said tautly.

"Jonah!" Dupree repeated. "Joanie, *talk* to me!"

Silence answered.

"Enable remote access!" he barked at Ottweiler. "We need to get in there."

"Can't, sir." Dupree twisted around, glaring at the chief over his shoulder, and Ottweiler shrugged. "Already tried, sir," he said heavily. "She's comm-silent. Down on *all* her links, even the telemetry."

Joan Walker fought desperately to hang onto awareness, but the merciless acceleration went on and on, and despite her G-suit, despite all clenched muscles could do, despite all her endless hours of flight training and experience, it drove the blood steadily away from her brain. That unremitting fist of acceleration drove her down, down the beckoning slope, and she slid into unconsciousness.

"What the hell could have gone wrong?" Nikolina Perić's voice was harsh, and Edwin Dupree looked at her. Both of them knew the question was rhetorical—at the moment, at least—because the captain knew everything Dupree knew.

They floated side by side in Flight Control, watching the radar plot, as *Whale* continued her headlong charge into the endless depths.

Watching was all they could do.

Victoria's tugs could have matched *Whale*'s acceleration, but until she exhausted her fuel, her head start would have continued to open the gap no matter what they did. None of them had the acceleration advantage—or fuel—to overtake her, decelerate, and then return to

Victoria, and none of the shuttles possessed even the tugs' fuel capacity. Which meant nothing in *Victoria*'s equipment list could possibly reach and recover the lander.

If her trajectory had brought her closer to *Victoria*, if any of the tugs had been online, or even on standby, they *might* have reached her before she passed the point of no return. But it hadn't, and they couldn't, and so fifty-one of Edwin Dupree's personal friends had been sentenced to death, and all he could do was watch the execution.

"I doubt we'll ever know what happened," he said bleakly, after a moment. "The telemetry feeds were all green, right up to the instant they just stopped. Same thing with Joanie's—Commander Walker's— comm. No signs of trouble at all. Everything was *perfect*! And then this."

He twitched his head at the plot, holding the back of a flight couch to stabilize himself.

"Whatever it was, I think it must have taken out the entire flight deck," he continued, his tone bleaker than ever as he acknowledged the death of one of those friends. "How the hell she got onto that heading in the first place is more than I can guess, but if Joanie was alive, she could have at least killed the main engines. And we couldn't remote in, either, so it had to be something catastrophic. Something nasty enough—violent enough—to send *Whale*'s flight computers crazy, take out her comm systems completely . . . and kill Joanie, too."

"But what *could* do that?" Perić demanded. "You and I both know our landers' design forward and backward, Ed. There's nothing in it that could do all that without blowing up two-thirds of the entire lander!"

"I know that!" Dupree managed at the last second to not snap his response. He drew a deep breath, instead, and shook his head. "Trust me, we're going to model everything we can think of that might have accounted for it. Ottweiler's already started on that, in fact. But I think you're right. Nothing in the design could've done it."

"So you're saying it was some freak *external* factor?"

"At the moment, I think that's more likely than anything else," Dupree agreed. "But I don't plan on making any assumptions. We're going all the way down to the base computer codes and every single control system aboard that lander. Hell, if it had rivets, we'd be looking at *them*! But even if we can't isolate a design fault, that won't prove there isn't one. And we can't afford to lose any more landers."

Perić nodded somberly. With *Whale* gone, they were reduced to the minimal terraforming capability built into the other landers, and the entire colony's margin for survival had just been pared dangerously thin.

"If you can't isolate a cause, what then?" she asked. "We've got to put the others down eventually, Ed."

"Agreed," he sighed. He watched the death beacon of the lander still accelerating away from them. Waiting.

"There," he said softly, as the icon suddenly stopped accelerating. "Fuel exhaustion." He drew a deep breath and turned away as *Whale* coasted onward, onward, into the endless deeps.

"If we can't isolate a cause, then the only solution I see is redundancy," he told the captain after a moment. "They're all designed to land under computer control. The human flight crew's basically an afterthought . . . which obviously didn't work this time." His mouth tightened, then he shook his head. "So I think we have to rework the other landers. We've got the volume aboard them and the resources aboard *Victoria* to build an entire secondary, human-crewed flight deck with standalone computers that don't rely on the central AIs. I think that's what we'll have to do."

"That's going to delay us," Perić observed.

"Well, we weren't supposed to land any of the others until Joanie and Adam had had ten years to get the central hub up and running," he said bitterly. "I suppose that leaves us with a little time in hand."

TRAPPIST-2 Star System
Lander *Whale*
April 2347 CE/03 Ad Astra

"Left flank! Watch your left, Joanie!"

The voice crackled in her earphones, and she flung herself prone in the deep snow barely in time. Livid tracers were a solid, unbroken bar overhead, like a pre-space movie's death ray, and the cacophony of a mini-gun chainsawed on its heels. She rolled up on her right shoulder and hip, craning her neck to look back along the line of fire, and saw the automated ground mount she'd missed on the way in. It was a good thing it had been programmed to wait until she was fully into its field of fire before opening up. And thank goodness for the handy hollow she'd tumbled into! At the moment, the weapon couldn't depress far enough to reach her, but if Adam hadn't warned her . . .

Her left hand rose cautiously, careful to stay below the mini-gun's searching fire, and tapped a button on the side of her visor. A sighting caret appeared, and she turned her head until it lay precisely on the gun mount. Then she tapped the button again, a tone sounded, and she hugged the ground as the overhead drone tasked to her tactical computer confirmed its targeting. A fraction of a second later, the KEW came sizzling down from above. It struck the mount center of mass, and its own energy—plus the satisfying secondaries as several thousand rounds of ammunition exploded—turned the weapon into flying pieces of scrap.

She was close enough two or three of those pieces thudded down on her. Fortunately, they were very small ones, and she shook her head. That one had made her ears ring even inside her helmet!

"Well?" Adam demanded, a laugh in his voice. "You gonna just lie around all day, or should we get on with the mission?"

"Easy for you to say!" she shot back, rising cautiously to a knee and pulling her rifle back into the ready position against the tension of its powered sling. "You're the one sitting back there in overwatch while I take all the lumps!"

"Of course I am. I leave all that sweaty grunt work to you. Now, about that mission. If you check your profile, you'll—"

Bong.

The chime echoed through her, and her face tightened as the snowy landscape grayed into transparency. One hand flexed, *almost* reaching for the override, but she made it stop. She wasn't really sure why. It wasn't like she had anything else to do. But—

But if—when—you fall down this rabbit hole, you'll never crawl back out of it, and it's not time for that. Not yet.

Her nostrils flared and she finished the sign-out procedure. The ghostly snowbanks disappeared entirely, and she reached up to strip off the virtual reality headset and opened her eyes.

Nothing had changed.

She floated in what would have been the colony's rec room if

Whale had ever made it to Cistercia's surface. Because the planners had recognized the need to make communal relaxation available early on, the rec room and adjoining kitchenette had been spared the "pack-stuff-everywhere-until-the-bulkheads-bulge-and-we'll-unload-it-when-we-need-it" which had turned the majority of the lander's compartments into tightly crammed closets. She'd had to tug a few crates out of her way—she'd piled them in the passageway outside the main vehicle bay—but that hadn't been much of a problem in microgravity. And moving them had given her access to the VR systems.

Operation Arctic Avalanche had been one of her and Adam's favorite modules, long before they ever boarded *Victoria*. She had literally years of their previous adventures—in half a dozen modules, not just *Arctic Avalanche*—in memory.

They were available for replay whenever she wanted them. And she wanted them a lot.

God, how she wanted them!

She smiled wanly at the thought, racked the headset, sent herself floating through the rec room door, and began pulling herself along the endless spinal corridor toward the flight deck. She didn't hurry. There wasn't much point. In fact, there wasn't *any* point. There wasn't any point to *anything*, and she found herself wondering how long it would take her to admit that.

Never was much quit in you, Joanie, Adam's voice said in the back of her mind, and she snorted harshly.

No, there wasn't. But this time there was no winning scenario, even for her. She knew that, yet she hadn't *accepted* it yet, because on the day she did that, she *would* quit and that was . . . well, it was *un*acceptable. A violation of her personal code, everything she'd ever believed in. You didn't quit. You kept moving forward, you kept fighting, you kept *trying* until the dark came down, because if you didn't you were a coward. If you didn't, you let the other people who lived in that habitat with you down. Because if *you* quit, why shouldn't everyone else?

But this time . . .

She reached the hatch, floated across to her flight couch, and strapped in to keep herself from drifting away. Technically, she should have suited up. The vast lander's internal spaces were protected by automated pressure doors, but the overhead canopy was the only thing between the flight deck and vacuum, and the last thing *Whale* could afford—once upon a time, anyway—was to lose her sole crewwoman to explosive decompression. She'd come to the conclusion that it didn't really matter if that happened now, though, and shorts and a T-shirt were a hell of a lot more comfortable.

Her lips quirked and she flipped the end of her sable braid around behind her. Her hair was growing longer, and she was loath to cut it. Adam had always loved her hair long, but that was a problem for any pilot, and they'd had to compromise on something that would fit whenever she helmeted up.

That was another thing that was no longer an issue.

"Record diary," she said, and waited for the chime that indicated a live mike.

"Day . . . Fifty-seven," she said then, glancing at the calendar display. "Nothing new. I guess I'm only making entries to have something to do. Sooner or later, I'll have to admit that, but I can't quite seem to do it yet."

She paused, then bit her lip.

"I think I've decided I need to stay out of the personnel section. I was there again this morning. I spent twenty minutes outside Adam's pod, talking to him. There wasn't any point in it, except that it made me feel closer to him somehow. But I'm afraid. If I go down there often enough, the temptation to wake him up is likely to—no, it *will*—get the better of me, and I can't do that to him. If we had the facilities to put him back into cryostasis if that was what he chose, maybe I could? No." She shook her head, reaching back to capture her braid and nibbling on its end. "No, I couldn't. Because he'd try to insist that *I* take his pod if that was possible. It isn't, of course.

"Since it isn't, I think he might actually want to be awake, to spend the time we have left together . . . to keep me from being alone." She drew a deep breath and shook her head again. "But then he'd have to watch me dying. And he'd have to know we were both dying, out here with our friends, no way out. None of the kids we planned on. No future. Just . . . nothing. This way, he never has to know. That's the last gift I can give him. He never has to know."

She blinked burning eyes and cleared her throat.

"Halt recording," she said harshly, and the chime sounded again.

Who the hell am I leaving this for? she asked herself again. *Some alien civilization, fifteen thousand years from now, when* Whale *drifts into their star system? No one from Earth—or Cistercia—is ever going to play it back, that's for frigging sure!*

She closed her eyes again, pinching the bridge of her nose.

Two months. Almost two months—so far—since that horrendous moment.

She'd recovered consciousness in microgravity and immediately started checking statuses, fuel balances, all those things pilots worried about. And nothing she'd found had been good.

Whale's communications module wasn't working anymore... which made sense, once she maneuvered one of the external maintenance drones into position. The entire module had been designed to be jettisoned in an emergency, along with *Whale's* black box and complete communications log, and apparently it had been.

She hadn't ordered it to jettison, and it wasn't supposed to be possible for that to happen without orders, except in the event of catastrophic structural failure. She didn't know when it had happened, either, which meant she had no idea what *its* velocity might have been when it separated from the lander. The one thing she did know was that it had to have been before the engines shut down from fuel exhaustion. She'd used the external cameras and the other remotes to do the most intensive search she could contrive— *Whale's* radars had died, along with everything else—in hope of recovering it and regaining communication with *Victoria*. Unfortunately, it was nowhere in the reach of the remotes' sensors, which meant it must have been left behind while *Whale* continued building delta-V. Of course, even if she'd been able to recover it and somehow repair it, there wasn't anything the starship could have done for her.

But at least she could have shared what had happened... and, more importantly, her suspicions about *how* it had happened.

It hadn't been an accident.

She hadn't wanted to admit that, even to herself, but it hadn't been an accident at all. Why someone would have wanted to do anything so... premeditatedly horrific was beyond her, but it *couldn't* have happened by accident. Someone had deliberately set out to destroy *Whale*, her terraforming capability, and everyone aboard her in a spectacular "accident" before she reached Cistercia's surface. It was the only way it could have happened, and what she'd discovered in the ship's computer net only confirmed how carefully it had been planned.

Both primary AI nets were simply . . . gone. The computers were still there, but they'd done a complete reformat, killing every program beyond the basic operating system. There was no way that could have happened without somebody *ordering* the AIs to suicide. And if she'd needed any other evidence, the backup software copies had been purged, as well, leaving nothing she could reload. She suspected that had been a security feature to keep anyone from identifying the saboteurs or figuring out what they'd been after if their tampering had been detected before *Whale* was deployed. Or even afterward, for that matter. It wasn't something they were likely to have worried about happening after the cataclysm they'd arranged, but if the tugs had still been in company with *Whale*—if there'd been enough of them, close enough—they could have used their own engines to compensate for her rogue acceleration. The odds against their being close enough, in large enough numbers, and reacting rapidly enough had probably been enormous, but it could have happened, in which case the computers would have been subjected to the most intense forensic analysis imaginable.

Whatever the saboteurs' thinking had been, there was no way she could recover the main system. She still had the secondaries, but each of those was a special function net—none of them had ever been intended to run the entire lander. She'd managed to keep all of them up and running, which meant that things like life support were still online, but she'd had to monitor them all manually until she'd been able to cobble up a replacement supervisory program she actually trusted.

At least it had given her something to do.

Her inventories had given her something else to do for a while, too.

She might have lost the main transmitter, but after a couple of weeks' reprogramming and rerouting she'd managed to get her docking systems back. So she *could* have transmitted, actually. Unfortunately, the system was designed solely as a homing beacon and to communicate with tugs within a few thousand kilometers of the ship. It was omnidirectional, with a very limited range, and no one on *Victoria* would pick up anything it transmitted unless she had a clear transmission path to *Whale*, the ship had her big dish trained in exactly the right direction at exactly the right moment . . . and Walker was luckier than hell.

Given her luck to date, that wasn't going to happen.

In other news, the main thrusters hadn't consumed *quite* all their fuel in that ferocious burn. They'd emptied the main tanks, but the emergency reserve was still there. They gave her about six minutes' thrust at full power, and her manual control of them seemed solid—now. But *Whale* had accelerated for over *twenty* minutes before the tanks emptied, which had generated far too much velocity to kill in only six minutes.

She'd been tempted to fire up the engines, anyway, under manual control, on the theory that if *Victoria* was still tracking her it would at least suggest to them that someone was still alive aboard the lander. But she hadn't. Partly that was because she was a pilot, trained to *never* waste fuel on pointless gestures and to *always* maintain a reserve. Mostly it was that she didn't see any way—or reason—*Victoria* could still be tracking her. She was headed away from TRAPPIST-2 at just over 64 KPS—230,400 KPH—which was well above system escape velocity. She'd already traveled 255,000,000 kilometers from Cistercia, farther than the distance from Earth orbit to the belter habitats in the Solar System's asteroid belt. For that matter, in another eighteen days, she'd cross the orbit of TRAPPIST-2e, a gas giant about twelve percent smaller than Jupiter. Even something *Whale*'s size was a tiny radar target at those sorts of distances. Besides, *Victoria* was no longer in position to track the lander even optically. Cistercia was two Earth-months farther along its orbit, and *Whale* had departed Cistercia-orbit on a sharply divergent vector. By now, the central star had cut off direct transmission paths between them.

And by the time that was no longer a problem, she'd be *much* too far out for anyone to notice any changes in her velocity.

Besides, she'd probably be dead.

Not because of starvation. *Whale* had been equipped with one year's rations for fifty people, as a backup until her planetary farms came online. She had *not* been equipped with a hydroponics section, since building a planetary greenhouse would have been trivial out of her resources, even under the most adverse of circumstances, so what she had on board was all Walker was going to get. Still, enough food to feed fifty people for a year was enough to feed one person for half a century.

Air was another issue, but there was quite a lot of that trapped in *Whale*'s passages and compartments, as well. Nowhere near as much as someone might have assumed, perhaps, since those passages and compartments were so tightly packed with cargo, but a lot, and the scrubbers could pull the carbon dioxide out of it. There was no way to generate more oxygen, but the environmental computers estimated that there was enough oxygen on board, both trapped in *Whale*'s spaces and in high pressure storage, to keep a single human going for twenty years or so. The last few months might not be especially pleasant, but that wasn't going to be a problem, either.

Because the killer was power. *Whale* had never been intended for long-term deployment in space. She was equipped to operate there for up to several weeks, if necessary, while landing sites were studied and chosen, but not indefinitely. She didn't have the deployable solar panels other craft might have had, and her power budget had been planned around getting the onboard, city-sized fusion reactor at her core up and running out of planetary resources within no more than several weeks or, at most, a few months, after landing.

That reactor would have worked fine down on the Cistercian surface; without its designed support structure, it was useless in space, so the designers had provided a much smaller fusion plant to meet the lander's needs until she could switch over. *Whale*'s maneuvering thrusters used hydrogen and liquid oxygen, unlike the main engines' hypergolic fuel, in no small part to serve as the fuel source for that reactor and the initial feed for the planetary plant until the electrolysis installation came online. It was a piece of tested, utterly reliable tech—power plants just like it had been in use for well over a century before *Victoria* was built—and *Whale*'s remaining hydrogen could feed it for well over a century. Unfortunately, its designers had saved weight and mass by engineering it for only five years' continuous operation before its bottle components required replacement. That had certainly seemed like more than enough endurance when the lander was designed, but Walker didn't *have* any replacement components, and that meant she was going to run out of power—and light, and heat, and environmental systems—long before she ran out of food or breathable air.

Adam's cryostasis pod had its own power supply, one that was good for well over a century, but the dedicated supply was built into each pod, and it was only a trickle charge, anyway. Even if she'd been able—and prepared—to rip all fifty pods apart, killing their occupants to steal all their power for herself, she'd add less than a year to her power budget. And she couldn't do that.

She couldn't kill them any earlier than they had to die. It didn't make any sense, but in her situation, common sense wasn't an especially useful commodity. Besides, she'd already decided how she was going to die when the time came, and they were her family. She wanted them around her when she did.

She drew a deep breath and called up the gaming programs on her primary display. She played a lot of those, just as she watched a lot of the stored entertainment programming. At her current rate, she estimated that she would work her way through the entire library in about five years or so. Neither the games nor the entertainment vids were as satisfying as the VR, of course, but that was the point. The VR was too addictive. The inputs through her neural feeds simulated reality too perfectly, made it far too easy for her to lose herself in it. In fact, VR addiction was a significant user problem, and *Victoria*'s systems—and *Whale*'s—incorporated standard, legally required software to prevent people from plugging in and forgetting to plug back out. And to shut the simulation down, whatever *they* wanted, if it detected health issues on their part. The safeties were pretty good and hacking around them was good for a lot of jail time, back in the Solar System. Walker doubted anyone would mind too much that *she'd* hacked around them, under the circumstances, but she didn't want to lose herself in them too soon.

I guess that's the only challenge I really have left, she thought as she called up her most recent *Emperor* save.

The game was a sophisticated "city manager" program designed to build interstellar empires, which was more than a little ironic, given her current circumstances. It was well designed and challenging, though. She could lose herself in it for hours, which was rather the point of the exercise.

Adam's always said I'm a stubborn bitch, and by God, I'm going to prove him right. I am not *giving in, I am* not *going into the dark, one instant before I choose to. Maybe this* is *the Birkenhead Drill, but if it is, I'm going out on* my t*erms, and the rest of the goddamn universe can stuff* it!

TRAPPIST-2 Star System
Lander *Whale*
March 2348 CE/04 Ad Astra

"Record diary."

Her voice sounded harsh, grating, to her own ear. Probably because she hadn't used it in so long. She'd stopped making diary entries six months ago. But it was time.

The chime sounded, and she cleared her throat.

"Day Four hundred and twelve," she said then. "This will be my final entry."

She paused, looking out through the canopy at the hateful beauty of the stars. She and her friends could have a worse shroud, she supposed, if only it wasn't so damned *lonely*. If only there was someone, *somewhere*, who would remember them. Who could have noted their passing, known where they'd fallen?

"I've been ... spinning my wheels for the last several weeks. I guess I've made my point. I didn't just curl up and die as soon as this happened. But I'm tired. I'm tired of being alone. I'm tired of knowing I'll never see Adam again. Tired of fighting. I'm just ... tired."

She had to pause, clear her throat again, harshly. Then she drew a deep breath.

"I'm going to end this while I can still do it on my terms. Know it was my own choice. If anyone ever finds this, my name was Joan Frances Callahan Walker. I was a pilot. It was all I ever wanted to be, and I was married to Adam Truscott Walker, the finest man I ever knew. He and I traveled thirty light-years together on the greatest leap the human race ever attempted, and even knowing what happened, how it ended for us, I'd do it all again with him. Do it in a heartbeat."

She blinked burning eyes, looked down and caressed the golden ring on her left hand.

"Be kind to our bones."

She drew another deep, deep breath.

"Halt recording."

The chime sounded again, and she floated there, looking around the confines of what had been her world for so long.

She hadn't told her diary everything. She hadn't told it that the real reason she'd decided to end it was that her sanity was cracking at last. She woke weeping wildly from nightmares she couldn't recall. She caught herself talking to people who weren't there. She was forgetting meals in the dreary sameness of her unending, lonely days. She no longer worked out in the micrograv gym. She wasn't showering anymore. She'd always been a physically fastidious person—people grew up that way in the habs—but not anymore.

She was . . . disintegrating, and she refused to end that way. Not crouched in a corner, mumbling to herself, laughing at things that were no longer there and gnawing the fantasies of a mind that no longer remembered who it was. She was a *pilot*. She was Joan Walker, callsign "Jonah," and she would *not* lose that at the very end.

So she'd prepared *Whale* to power down. Not immediately. Not until the medical monitors detected the cessation of her own heartbeat.

She'd programmed the VR carefully. The software was designed to operate nonplayer avatars for gamers who'd been unable to join the rest of their party for a given session, and the longer someone played the game, the better the computer learned who they were, learned to model their spontaneous responses. It was almost as good as having the missing individual there, and she and Adam had gamed in *Arctic Avalanche* and its associated modules for years. The computers knew them both *so* well.

And so she'd written her own module, *Kamekura*. The Aboriginal word meant "wait till I come," or "wait for me." Adam had taught it to her. It was *their* word, one they used just between the two of them when one of them had to run on ahead of the other, and she would use it that way one more time . . . because that module was where she would die in his arms.

The VR would welcome her, enfold her. She would nestle down into it, like a sleepy child into a blanket, and the neural feeds would override her physical body's sensations. She estimated that she might live as long as a week before dehydration killed her, but that could seem like months—even years—in the VR, and she would have all of that time with Adam. The VR was open ended, within the parameters she'd established, so she didn't know where it would take them, what they would experience before the end. But wherever they went, she would have him again, and she would have peace, and she would embrace *both* like lovers.

She sighed and unstrapped from the flight couch. A toe push sent her toward the hatch, and she realized she was smiling, looking forward to it. It was so good to finally see an end, and—

Ping!

Joan Walker jerked as if she'd just touched a live wire. She grabbed the hatch frame, halting her progress, turning in place. It couldn't—

Ping!

The tone sounded again, and one hand flew up to cover her mouth as a green light blinked on the control panel. *That was impossible!*

Ping!

She hurled herself back toward her command chair as the light on the docking panel stopped blinking and burned a steady, unwavering green.

Ping!

It was a docking beacon! A live *docking* beacon! The signal was incredibly faint, but she couldn't possibly be receiving *Victoria's* beacon at this range! Her receivers were nowhere near sensitive enough! So, it couldn't be *Victoria* . . . could it?

Ping!

She punched keys, querying the computers, and then an ID came up and her jaw dropped.

No, it couldn't be *Victoria*, she thought around a queer, ringing silence in her brain. And it wasn't.

It was *Prometheus*.

Joan Walker floated in the microgravity, gazing at the image displayed before her. She was freshly showered, dressed in a crisp, clean T-shirt and shorts, nursing a bulb of coffee in both hands, and her eyes were still dark with echoes of disbelief.

Whale's exterior cameras weren't much, compared to *Victoria's*, but they had the resolution of a good pre-space planetary observatory's reflector telescope. They were quite good enough to confirm what she was looking at, although details were scant. Reflected sunlight this far from the primary was dim, to say the least, and the range was preposterously long, but the ship she was looking at was almost ten kilometers long. That was big enough for the cameras to see, despite the preposterous range at which she'd picked up the beacon signal.

She shouldn't have, not on her short-ranged docking systems. That signal must have been boosted, which made no sense. But then neither did finding the missing terraforming ship in a cometary orbit around TRAPPIST-2.

Her own experience, the discovery of what had happened to *Whale*'s primary AI, had already suggested that the same insane saboteurs might have gotten to *Prometheus*' core programming, as well. It would explain a lot, and it certainly fitted the murderous bastards' *modus operandi*. Computers didn't care what they did; they only "cared" about what they were told to. If you could get to them, ordering them to kill themselves was a lot easier than convincing humans to suicide. And if you hid your sabotage carefully enough—*and*, she thought grimly, *if the people you targeted couldn't imagine anyone doing such a thing in the first place*—no one would ever realize they'd been set up until the ambush tripped.

Yet if that was what happened to *Prometheus*, how had she made it to TRAPPIST-2 at all? And once she'd gotten here, what had put her into such an eccentric orbit? And why was her beacon so damned loud?

Joan Walker couldn't answer those questions, but she knew as she sat there that she was looking at both a desperately needed addition to the colony's infrastructure . . . and her own potential salvation.

Whale and *Prometheus* were closing on one another. Or, rather, they were closing on a point in space both of them would pass somewhere in the next thirteen months. They weren't on remotely "convergent" courses. *Whale* was moving faster and cutting the cord of *Prometheus*' orbit, closing with it on an oblique angle. If they maintained their current headings and velocities, the lander would cut across *Prometheus*' path well before the terraforming ship got there and then continue onward into the interstellar depths.

Without her comm module, Walker couldn't actually communicate with *Prometheus* from this range. For that matter, the range was still too great for her own docking transmitters to reach *Prometheus*, unless she figured out how to boost their signal strength the same way *Prometheus'* had been boosted. And there was no way for her to tell if anything besides that beacon was still alive over there. *Prometheus* might be a lifeless hulk, trekking endlessly through space, completely dead but for the plaintive voice crying out over Walker's receivers.

But if she *wasn't* . . . if her systems were still live, and if *Whale* could come close enough to trigger her automated docking protocols . . .

Her tugs were bigger and more powerful than the tugs attached to *Victoria*, because they'd been designed for harder, longer use with *Prometheus'* larger landers and multiuse cargo shuttles. They had more fuel capacity, more thrust, and *Prometheus* carried more of them. So if she could just get close enough, call for the tugs, they could capture *Whale*, brake her velocity, tow her in and dock her to *Prometheus'* midships cargo bays. Once *Whale's* umbilicals plugged in, Walker would have wired access to *Prometheus'* computer nets. She could take command of the ship, and she was confident *Prometheus* had ample fuel reserves to break out of her lonely orbit and return her—and *Whale*—and Adam—to Cistercia.

But only if she could get close enough, and that was what the computers were considering at this very moment.

She already knew it would be tight. Her tracking data was less than perfect, but she'd been able to rough out *Prometheus'* orbital mechanics. Her path took her far enough in-system to pass within comm range of Cistercia, but she must have been just beyond detection range for the beacon when *Victoria* arrived. Her entire orbital period was right on fifty years, and she'd dive back through the inner system again in another thirty or so. Unfortunately, she wouldn't pass within her beacon's transmission range of Cistercia on her next pass. Fifty years after *that* would be a different matter, but by then the colonists would have been in-system for a good eighty years. Walker suspected they would either have succeeded in making Cistercia their own and no longer need *Prometheus'* resources so desperately . . . or else the lack of those resources would mean there was no one left for *Prometheus* to help.

So what it really came down to was whether or not Joan Walker could get aboard *Prometheus* and deliver her to Cistercia in time to make a difference. And that was—

The computer chimed.

She turned to bring up its analysis, and her heart leapt as she saw the projected flight path, passing *just* close enough to *Prometheus*.

Then she saw the fuel figures.

"Record diary."

Her voice was level, stronger than it had been in weeks, and her green eyes were clear. They were also dark, and they burned as she looked out through the canopy.

"Adam," she said then, "I wish, with all my heart, that I didn't have to do this to you, love, but I do. I hope you'll be able to forgive me.

"You'll find all the notes about what went wrong, how this all happened, in my files. I didn't think there was any way out, but then *Prometheus* turned up. And it turned out there *is* a way out . . . maybe.

"Just not for me."

She paused and inhaled deeply.

"I've run the numbers over and over. I've modeled it a dozen times. It keeps coming out the same. I can get *Whale* close enough, but it'll take every drop of fuel the main engines have left, and it's going to use up a lot of the maneuvering thrusters' fuel, as well. In fact, I can't do it without them."

She pinched the bridge of her nose, thinking about that. *Whale's* attitude thrusters were insanely powerful by the standards of normal spacecraft design. They could give her another two gravities of decel . . . but she had only twelve minutes' fuel for them.

"It'll take a six-minute burn on main engines and another nine and a half on the thrusters, according to my numbers, and even then, it'll be close. *God*, it'll be *so* close, sweetheart, and the only margin for adjustments if my flight plan gets anything wrong are the last two minutes on her maneuvering thrusters. I can't plot the intercept well enough to know how much of that time she'll need, but it looks like she may need all of it. Even if I make the main burn today, I can't know how much she'll need on final until we get there. And if I wait that long and it turns out she needs all her fuel, it won't be there. I'll have burned the margin keeping her reactor online."

She paused again, pinching the bridge of her nose harder, as if the pain could make what she had to say next hurt less.

"That means I can't wait, love. I can't wait for you. I have to go on ahead. So I'm going to make the main burn and load the rest of the profile into the stand-alone flight computer. And then I'm going to power down everything but the essential core systems. Without the housekeeping demand, *Whale*'s batteries are more than enough to carry that much load . . . without burning off her fuel."

The actual expenditure of hydrogen to keep the reactor online for an extra year would have cost only about eleven seconds, yet those eleven seconds might be the difference between success and failure. They might not, too, but she couldn't know that, and she hadn't come this far, she hadn't paid this price, to fail. If her death would buy even a moment of deceleration as her last gift to *Whale* and Adam, she would count it a bargain well made.

She only prayed, if it turned out there was a greater margin than that in hand, that Adam could forgive her.

"I don't know what you'll find aboard *Prometheus*. I don't even know if the ship is still alive, so maybe you won't be listening to this after all. And if she is alive, I don't know how badly her systems may have been damaged, assuming the same sick bastards that sabotaged *us* sabotaged her, too. So I've put together a hierarchy of computer packages. If everything goes perfectly, *Prometheus*' remotes will retrieve you and the others and wake you up. Assuming I can't manage that, I'll try to program her to head for Cistercia. Assuming I can't manage *that*, you'll just have to ride the cargo racks until she gets close enough for *Victoria* to pick up her beacon. I've got a couple of ideas to piggyback signals through *Prometheus*' landers' communications modules. I think I can get into those through the docking interface, even if the rest of the ship is down or the central computers won't let me in. I'm not sure about that, but if I can manage that much, I should be able to boost her beacon's strength enough to at least triple the range at which *Victoria*'s likely to hear it.

"It's the best I can do, sweetheart." Her eyes burned hotter, and she wiped them fiercely. "I wish I could do more. And I wish—" Her voice wavered, and she had to clear her throat. "And I wish I could know whether or not it worked. But I can't. This is the only gift I have left to give you, and it comes with every gram of my heart and more joy than I ever imagined, because I get one last chance to give you that. You are the finest man I have ever known. I've treasured every second of our lives together, and if I have to die, then this is *exactly* what I would have chosen to die doing. Remember me, but don't cling. I want you to *live*. I want you to live in *every* sense of the word and build the home you and I were supposed to build together. And know this: My only regret about the choice I've made—the *only* regret I have, I swear to you—is that I won't have the chance to tell you this in person. So, don't weep. Be glad for me. Be glad I had the chance to save the person I love most in the entire universe.

"Goodbye, sweetheart. I love you."

She sat a moment longer, a single tear trickling down her cheek, then closed her eyes.

"Halt recording."

TRAPPIST-2 Star System
Lander *Whale*
April 2348 CE/04 Ad Astra

It was so quiet, she thought as she swam through the rec room hatch.

So very quiet.

And soon it would be quieter still. If she listened very carefully, she could hear the soft hum of the enviro systems, circulating air. That would stop soon enough.

She'd done all she could. She'd emptied the main engines' fuel reserve, burned off all but those precious last hundred and fifty seconds on the maneuver thrusters, and it looked like they'd hit the necessary profile. Or close to it. Close enough, at least . . . probably.

If she hadn't, there was nothing more she could do about it, and she'd been through *Whale*'s stored flight profile and her command programs for *Prometheus* again and again. She'd checked every detail over and over, until she'd realized she was obsessing. Not too surprisingly, probably, but there was no point to it. They were the best she could write, and they'd either do the job—assuming they got the chance—or they wouldn't. *Whale* would cross close enough, have enough fuel reserve to adjust until the tugs could capture and dock her, or she wouldn't . . . and this would all have been for nothing.

Either way, *she'd* never know, and she was a little surprised by how little that bothered her. To have come within months of possible survival, and then to see it trickle through her fingers—to *walk away* from it, rather than fight to the last ditch for it . . . Surely that should have done something, filled her with bitterness, shouldn't it?

Yet it hadn't.

Oh, there were regrets in plenty. Regrets that she would never stand on Cistercia with Adam. That she would never bear the children they'd both wanted so badly. That the universe would go on without her, leaving a Joanie-shaped hole in Adam's life. Yet that was such a tiny regret beside the unspeakable gift of the chance—at least the *chance*—to save him and all their friends.

How many people could say their deaths had bought a triumph like that? Know that whatever else happened, the lives they'd lived—the deaths they'd died—had *mattered?*

And it isn't as if any *of us would've made it without* Prometheus, *either*, she thought. *I would have died anyway. I was ready for that. And I guess I still am, especially since this way, dying may actually make a difference. Not just for Adam, either. Maybe for the entire colony. I guess a woman could have a worse epitaph.*

She drifted to the chair at the VR station. It was designed for use in gravity, assuming *Whale* had ever made it to the planetary surface, and she folded herself onto it, then snapped the seatbelt. People sometimes moved in response to events in VR, and the last thing she wanted was for some involuntary movement to send her drifting away from the interface and unplugging the headset.

She looked around one last time, considering—again—adding some further note for Adam. And deciding—again—against it. It was going to be hard enough for him to listen to what she'd already recorded, but at least he'd know she'd lived over three weeks from the time she recorded it. She didn't want him to picture her going straight into death from the last word she ever said to him.

The lines of "High Flight," her favorite poem—written by John Gillespie Magee before humanity ever stepped foot off Earth—ran through her mind as she slipped into the headset and brought the VR online.

Oh, I have slipped the surly bonds of earth,
And danced the skies on laughter-silvered wings;
Sunward I've climbed and joined the tumbling
       mirth of sun-split clouds—
and done a hundred things you have not dreamed of—
wheeled and soared and swung high in the sunlit silence.
Hovering there I've chased the shouting wind along
and flung my eager craft through footless halls of air.

Up, up the long delirious burning blue
I've topped the wind-swept heights with easy grace,
where never lark, or even eagle, flew;
and, while with silent, lifting mind I've trod
the high untrespassed sanctity of space,
put out my hand and touched the face of God.

It was why she'd become a pilot in the first place, that poem, the things it expressed. And here, at the very end, that was where she was—in that "untrespassed sanctity of space," putting her hand out to God, asking Him for one last boon for the people she loved. It was not simply the completion of her life but its culmination.

She'd been given *that*, too.

And now it was time to go.

The VR interface blinked at her, and she inhaled deeply.

"I'm coming, sweetheart," she whispered. "I'm coming."

The interface blinked again, not recognizing the voice input, and she closed her eyes.

"Run *Kamekura*," she said softly.

Dutchman

Earth legends have many tales of lost individuals perpetually striving to find their way back to familiar environs. The Flying Dutchman, Roanoke Colony, Charlie on the MTA, and astronauts Dave Bowman and Frank Poole are examples of the Human need to bring lost souls home. The loss of the terraforming equipment-heavy Lander Alpha was an incredible setback to the colony, particularly without the advance preparation that should have been performed by the missing *Prometheus*. Establishment of the landing sites and initial colonies were delayed by three years while provisions were made for backup crews on the landers, and all AI-controlled systems were disabled. The distrust of AIs would continue in some colonist groups, while others sought to understand the rogue programming and correct it, with the hopes of one day finding *Whale*, finding *Prometheus*, and finally returning them to their new home. Meanwhile, astronomers continued to watch the stars for evidence of the Dutchmen.

—Excerpt from *Encyclopedia Astra*,
Gannon University,
Antonia, Cistercia, AA212

SONNY STIRS

Daniel M. Hoyt

Sonny

Sonny Strongbow woke with a start, which wasn't the way it was supposed to happen after stasis. Even before the *Victoria*'s AI informed him of the dire *situation*—as the AI's female voice put it diplomatically—Sonny knew something was wrong and willed himself to full consciousness, forcing his not-quite-thawed limbs to move.

It's too soon, he thought, staring at the time display on the stasis chamber's still-closed cover, mere inches from his face. "Why did you wake me now? I'm not scheduled for duty for another twenty Earth years."

"You are needed now," the AI answered flatly.

The cover popped open, and Sonny mustered a surge of adrenaline to hop out of the *casket* he'd called home for nearly a decade, his muscles rippling under a skin-tight bodysuit.

Besides the colonists and supplies, the *Victoria*, Earth's first interstellar colony ship, housed 250 crew members, with only five awake at any time for their one-year rotations—up to twenty-five for emergencies. Sonny's first rotation was scheduled for the twenty-sixth Earth year, yet it was only the eighth.

But the AI said it *needed* him. With access to all of its records, it singled out Sonny as the one person who could handle this *situation*.

Sonny grinned. He always knew he was destined for greatness; he just thought it would happen at TRAPPIST, not en route.

No matter; he was ready to meet his destiny.

Sonny Strongbow was *born* ready.

"What can I do?" he boomed, stretching out his limbs, eager for his new orders. The orders that would make him a hero for the ages.

"Saboteurs," the AI said flatly. "The previous team is still awake, and the new crew just awoke. Suspicious activity has been identified; security members of both teams appear to have been compromised."

Sonny grinned. "And you needed the best to deal with it." It wasn't a question. "You got him."

His only regret was that there were only two crew shifts—that meant ten of the human filth. It hardly seemed like a fair fight.

After cracking his knuckles and stretching his neck, he strode over to a nearby weapons vault and mashed a hand on the genlock, coded only to the security team. It popped open; Sonny snatched up a couple utility belts and loaded them with disruptors and extra power packs, along with some blades for good measure.

"Time to clean some scum."

Sam

Benedict's Bar probably wasn't the worst place to waste an evening on Cistercia, Sam Torte mused, racking his brain for a grimier, more dimly lit candidate. Failing, he continued nursing three fingers of far-from-top-shelf rum and offered a silent prayer that the stench of urine settled over the establishment came from the winos frequenting it.

Nearby, several patrons engaged in a heated debate.

"Sonny took out all ten of those dirty rebels and that's why we're all here now, instead of space dust light-years away!" one drunk yelled, his face scarlet, with one fist hovering over another drunk's smug face and the other fisting his victim's collar. "You take back those lies, Clem!"

A man on Sam's other side snorted, shook his head and muttered, "Every night."

Clem spat at his aggressor's face, but the spittle barely leaked out his mouth, settling on his beard. "It's your crazy cult's got all the lies. Sonny Strongbow is a *myth*!"

A massive paw wrapped itself around the first drunk's fist, immobilizing his arm. "I think that's enough for tonight, Van, don't you?" the mountain attached to that paw said calmly. His other hand easily pried Van's fingers from Clem's clothes and he effortlessly dragged the man toward the door. "Out you go, friend. See you tomorrow." He shook his head slowly and sauntered back behind the bar, polishing the rich wood mindlessly while waiting for his next order, a time-honored Earth tradition that remained after centuries of time and nearly forty light-years.

Clem sighed and stumbled back into his barstool. "So stupid," he slurred. "Was just some guy. Jackson Something. Not Sonny." His head thudded onto the bar, his eyes closing.

Sam smiled briefly and returned his attention to the alleged rum in front of him. He'd come here for a respite from digging through archives for his studies. All day sorting through the conflicting detritus history accumulated—looking for the one weird artifact that supported one researcher's theory or disproved another's—made a man thirsty.

Alcohol didn't judge; it just *was*.

Until you needed a refill, at least.

All this arguing seriously interrupted Sam's drinking. He knew the arguments both ways; everybody in Antonia did. The stories of Sonny Strongbow's heroic deeds grew larger and more unlikely over the generations; they were practically a religion at this point. The worst part was, his acolytes would tell you his stories anywhere, everywhere, with little or no invitation, even if you didn't want to hear it. Persistent bunch, too; once one of them got started, they'd follow you down a dark alley by the plague graveyards in Roanoke just to finish their pitch.

To be fair, the other side wasn't much better. They denied Sonny Strongbow's existence, of course, and since there was no record of a crew member with that name, it was hard to dispute. On top of that, they *did* find someone named Jackson de Clare, a name that could be twisted into Sonny Strongbow with one eye closed and some basic knowledge of Earth history. It was easy to see how Jackson could become Sonny, and the Second Earl of Pembroke, Richard de Clare, was also known as Strongbow. *Obviously*, Jackson de Clare was the *real* Sonny Strongbow.

But they didn't stop there, oh no. Just denying the myth wasn't enough. De Clare's records were suspiciously spotty, and they made him out to be a cold-blooded murderer, so obsessed with his psychotic vision of who'd get to make it to the new colony that he tampered with the records and erased his victims so nobody would know.

This, of course, made Sonny's followers see red; and the two groups were *still* getting into fights over Sonny decades later.

Jackson

Jackson de Clare woke for his first crew rotation and smiled, silently recalling the carefully crafted plans for the demise of his four team members, starting with the security woman. Once she was out of the way, the others would be easy prey.

Slinking out of his *casket*—a fitting name, he mused—he asked the AI for his team's status.

"Bart Tolsovic is awakening, Lane Franklin is awake; May Yoko—"

Jackson didn't listen to the rest. As expected, Lane was awake. The AI always woke the security team member first. He thought back to the romantic dinners they'd shared before stasis. He'd wined and dined her, gaining her trust in the weeks pre-launch, with the promise of more once they reached TRAPPIST and woke the entire crew for terraforming. He swallowed the bile rising in his throat, thinking of all the things he'd had to do with the repulsive witch, a smile pasted on through all of it, a nightmare he only endured by constantly recalling his training and focusing his mind by internally reciting the plan over and over.

The plan. No, not just a plan.

The Plan.

The *Grand* Plan.

The one that would make Earth pay attention to them at last.

Once they'd both awakened for their first crew rotation, deftly manipulated for a few Earth years into the mission—too long to arouse suspicion, early enough for news to get back to Earth and scuttle any more plans for interstellar colonization—she'd trust him enough that he'd be able to overpower her and eliminate her, replacing her with one of his comrades.

After that, the others would fall easily.

The Plan was perfect, and Jackson's part in it critical.

Now all he had to do was execute it. He chuckled at the word, and silently marveled at his genius as he approached Lane, still stretching after her long sleep.

"Good morning, sweetheart," he joked, his plastic smile firmly in place. "Sleep well?"

Sam

The door of Benedict's swung open with a crack like a whip, capturing Sam's attention, and yet another bum stumbled in like an alcohol-seeking zombie, lurching toward the bar, remnants of his torn, threadbare coat dropping to the dirt-caked floor in his wake. Sam turned away, focusing on his glass of battery acid, and tried to ignore the growing bile rising in his throat as the approaching man's eau-de-sewer cloud of cologne intensified. Groaning at the scrape of the bar stool next to him, Sam hunched his shoulders and turned away slightly, hoping to avoid a direct encounter.

The slap of leather on the bar grabbed Sam's attention and he nearly swallowed his tongue after he realized he'd unwittingly turned to face the fool, who stared at him with a toothless grin.

"How's that rotgut treatin' you, son?" he slurred, leaning in so that his fetid breath blasted Sam directly in the face. Sam tried—and failed miserably—not to flinch, but the ragged man didn't seem to notice. "It'll kill you if you're not used to it."

Clearing his throat, Sam nodded and turned back to his rum, but said nothing.

"I can take it," the man continued, tugging at a loose thread that seemed to be the only thing keeping his left sleeve attached. "'S'my favorite, actually."

Sam glanced aside. "You don't even know what I'm drinking, old man." He didn't even try to hide the contempt in his voice.

The bum leaned into Sam's personal space and hovered over the rum before Sam could snatch it away, but not before the old man managed a wet snort. He sat back and nodded smugly to himself. "Rancé, right?"

Sam glared, impressed, nonetheless. "Yeah."

"Most kids call it Rancid Rum." The bum licked his lips, eyeing Sam's glass hungrily. "Like I said, my favorite."

Chuckling despite his rotten mood, Sam pushed his remaining two-and-a-half fingers to the man. "Be my guest."

The bum snatched the glass without hesitation and drained it in a single swallow, then grunted approval and wiped a filthy arm across his mouth, leaving an unidentified yellow smear on his mostly white, weeklong stubble.

Sam shook his head and blinked.

"That's the stuff," the bum murmured and belched loudly. "That'll earn you some of my fine knowledge here," he stage-whispered and patted the dog-eared, leather-bound tome he'd carried in with him.

With the sudden realization that the old man's hand had never left the volume since he'd slapped it down on the bar upon his arrival, Sam's curiosity was piqued. "What's that you got there, old-timer? A book?"

The bum snorted. "Not just a book. Notebook. A *journal*, actually." He cleared his throat and threw out his chest, like an actor about to launch into a soliloquy. "You know about the first Mason?"

"Obviously. There's a statue of William Mason a few hundred yards that way." He jerked his chin toward the door. "First colony lawman, responsible for security and all that. Wrote the book on it, *Mason's Security* or something like that. Blah, blah, blah. Whatever." He turned away and motioned for the barkeep.

The old man blew a loud, wet raspberry. "Not *him*." He shook his head and muttered, "Kids these days don't know nothin'." Clutching his notebook tighter, he continued. "I'm talking about Sonny Strongbow, of course. The *real* Sonny, not what you've heard." He looked around conspiratorially and gestured vaguely with the arm surrounding his notebook. "I know the *real* story."

Sam groaned. There was no escape from Sonny Strongbow tonight, was there? He glanced around nervously, looking to where Van, the drunk who'd attacked the other man earlier, had been seated. Fortunately, his buddies were still focused on drinking, too far away to hear the old man. "Careful, old man," Sam whispered. "We don't need another fight here tonight. Maybe you should just find another bar." He turned away, shaking his head.

The drunk grabbed his shoulder and spun him around.

"It ain't rot, son," he hissed, his eyes wild. He glanced over at the leather-bound notebook clutched in one hand, his knuckles white.

Sam grimaced, trying to ignore the man's halitosis. "You're one of them? Thinks Sonny Strongbow was a real hero? Your people are over there." He jerked his head toward Van's friend.

The old man snorted. "Oh, he was a hero all right, but not like *they* think. Some of the truth's a bit . . . stretched, is all I'm sayin'." Patting the worn notebook, he leaned in close and whispered, "This here's *his* journal, written in his own hand. 'S'my inheritance." He sat back and grinned, smacking his lips. "And for a bit more of that poison they call rum here, I'll let you in on the *truth* about Sonny."

As if on cue, a fresh glass of Rancé Rum thumped onto the bar in front of Sam. He glanced at the barkeep and caught him rolling his eyes before turning away, shaking his head.

Sam sighed, defeated, and nudged the glass toward the drunk. "Tell me." He looked around slowly, fearing a new altercation. "Just me; keep it low. I don't want any trouble."

The old man grabbed the new glass and threw it down his throat in one go. Belching, he dropped the empty glass back to the bar top. The glass tottered for a moment before tipping over, the dregs of the cloudy liquid escaping onto the poorly polished surface.

He fixed a rheumy gaze on Sam and cleared his throat loudly but kept his voice low for an audience of one.

Mason

Mason Munson drifted out of stasis, as if waking from a dream. His eyes fluttered open and he squinted at the stasis display. Right on schedule, Earth year 8. Excited for his first of seven crew rotations, Mason recalled his stasis training and performed each task deliberately, methodically making his way out of his chamber—whimsically dubbed the *casket* by the crew. Surprised at the lack of a hangover, considering he'd spent his last night before stasis with some friends—and a couple of new guys Mason didn't know, whose insistence that he should skip the mission and help them fix Earth first made him uncomfortable enough to spur him to imbibe more heavily than usual—it wasn't long until he felt he was up to performing his duties as the current rotation's security member.

Following protocol, he addressed the AI. "Mason Munson awake and ready." The AI wouldn't allow a crew member to go back into stasis until his replacement was both awake and lucid enough to claim readiness, thus ensuring a crew of five was always active at any moment. Mason expected his counterpart on the outgoing crew even now waited in his own *casket* for the go-ahead to go back into stasis, and now the AI would allow it.

"Nan?" he said, to get the AI's attention. Crew members didn't usually name the AI, but Mason felt it helped him to think of their interactions as conversations, so he'd done so. As a side benefit, he'd learned to have entirely muttered conversations with Nan that earned him a reputation in training as a bit loony, which could only help him as the security guy. Nobody wanted to mess with the crazy person. "Wake the others."

Retrieving some nonlethal items from the gencoded weapons vault, Mason sighed, thinking of his favorite weapon, conspicuously absent from the vault.

His bow.

It wasn't a weapon, per se, more of an obsession. He'd even trained for the Olympic Games back on Earth. He didn't make the cut, but he didn't care; it was the sport that drew him in, not the competition. It was always a competition with *yourself*, not others.

And that feeling when the second arrow slipped right into the same groove as the first, practically stripping the finish from the first one's shaft as it wedged into the center of the target mere millimeters from the first. Well, there was nothing like it.

Mason sighed again. He'd heard that there were bows and arrows with the hunting supplies in the bays; maybe he'd get to shoot again once TRAPPIST was terraformed and the colony started up.

In the meantime, it was time to meet his team.

The first few weeks flew by, the crew learning to work together as a cohesive unit, getting to know each other on the job and off. He especially liked Hal, the engineer, and talked to him over the link whenever he had a spare moment. Hal was only a couple years older, but led a far more exciting life on Earth, and Mason couldn't get enough of his stories.

Once, after they'd all converged on Seneca's cabin for her birthday and she'd wormed a story out of Hal, Mason remarked that he must have had exciting adventures on every continent back on Earth. "Sonny boy, you don't know the half of it," Hal said, winking. "Ask me about Antarctica sometime."

He did, a week later, and Hal's tale didn't disappoint.

Life was good. Mason exercised rigorously daily, keeping in shape as expected for his job, but he was bored. Everyone on the team was great and they all liked each other; they hardly even argued.

That was okay by Mason; for a policeman, better to be bored than busy.

Another six Earth months flew by before Mason's training was put to the test. Mere weeks before the end of their rotation, Hal plain lost it and started doing crazy things, ignoring his comms, flipping random switches and punching buttons repeatedly, breaking things, although not in a malicious way. It was almost as if he thought he was somewhere else, and things that got in the way got broken.

The AI caught his behavior, of course, assessed the damage and ordered repairs, locked out Hal's access and called for Mason, all part of the standard protocol for erratic behavior.

Even out of his mind, Hal had come to trust Mason, allowing Mason to approach close enough to subdue Hal, stunning him into unconsciousness. He picked up his friend's limp body and laid him gently on a cart. Silently thanking generations of Earth firemen for their training regimen, which had strengthened his muscles sufficiently that moving Hal barely winded him, Mason wheeled his sick friend to the Med Bay.

"We expected some people wouldn't be able to take space travel," the med, Stephanie, said after examining Hal. "He'll need to go back in stasis immediately." She looked down at his sleeping form. "I'll mark him for observation and the AI will schedule him for another rotation in a few years. If he still can't handle it, he'll go under until we reach the colony." She shook her head sadly.

"Nan," Mason muttered, so softly only the AI would understand his words, "wake up an engineer."

Sam

"Whassat old man sayin'?" Clem spit out from a couple barstools away. "Sonny Strongbow stories?" He slithered from his barstool to the next one closer. "Set you straight 'fore, didn't I?" He slumped *upward*, tottering on the edge of the barstool and leaned heavily onto the bar, offering *his* version without the cost of a drink.

Jackson

Jackson de Clare's first crew rotation was succeeding well beyond expectations. Not only had he managed to dispose of all the original crew in his rotation, he'd convinced the AI to awaken handpicked replacements, sympathizers in the Grand Plan. Well, one of his handpicked replacements at first, an expert who deftly hacked into the AI. After dispatching the extraneous replacements, the hacked AI was more amenable to his suggestions.

Now, he had a full crew of handpicked replacements. But Jackson wasn't one to quibble with the details when he had the desired results.

Soon, they'd convince the AI to bring his other comrades online—all fifteen of them—and they'd ready the *San Salvador* for ejection. After the *Victoria* was sabotaged, of course.

The Plan was simple: alter the colony ship's course so she could slingshot around a planet large enough to give the *San Salvador* enough velocity to get back to Earth, with the *Victoria* rigged to blow up once they were clear.

After years of radio silence, they'd return unexpectedly in a lander, bearing a sad tale of how ill-equipped the *Victoria* had been for such a long voyage, how Earth wasn't yet ready for the stars.

And they'd be hailed as heroes, to boot, just for coming back alive.

How delicious was *that* irony?

Surely, Earth's interstellar aspirations would die with the 10,000 frozen colonists in the worst space disaster Earth had ever seen. The fallout to the program would make the *Columbia* seem like a picnic. That explosion had brought the United States program to a virtual halt for more than two years, and there were only a handful of casualties. After losing not only *ten thousand* colonists, but a *hundred thousand* fertilized eggs—Mason chuckled at the thought of the public crying over all the *babies* lost in the disaster—they might shutter the interstellar program for good.

Maybe then they'd finally focus on fixing the Earth for everyone.

Sam

Clem was too drunk to keep his voice down, despite Sam's best efforts to quiet him before capturing the attention of Van's buddies.

Three of them surrounded him. The bartender shook his head and turned away. "Just take him outside, will you?"

"Sure thing," one of them said, hoisting Clem to his feet. One of the others grabbed a loose arm and the two of them propped him up.

"School's in session, Clem," the third said, as they dragged him away. "Sonny Strongbow was the savior of the *Victoria*, time and time again. He's sleeping now, but you know he'll be back if we need him."

Sonny

Sonny Strongbow was tired, but exhilarated. At close to fifty Earth years, his battle-scarred body ached at times, but he ignored the pain and soldiered on, like a true hero would.

Atlas. Hercules. Thor.

Legends.

They didn't complain about a little discomfort, did they?

Neither would Sonny Strongbow.

He'd refused to go back into stasis for decades now; he'd come to an agreement of sorts with the AI years ago: the AI's constant vigilance uncovered plots that would threaten the *Victoria*'s mission, and Sonny would sort it out. He was the only one the AI would trust to put down the filthy saboteurs, who popped up every few months like evil whack-a-moles. Why there were so many over the years never bothered Sonny, who'd long ago come to realize that this was why he was on the *Victoria*. Eliminating the threats to the mission; that was his calling.

He couldn't imagine a better life.

"Is it time to sleep yet?" he asked the AI with a crooked grin, as he had every morning for the last twenty-some years, but he already knew the answer. Truth be told, he didn't *want* to sleep yet; not while he was still breathing. He took a breath and waited.

"Not yet," the AI said flatly. "There's a situation in Supply Bay Four requiring your attention; unauthorized activity outside the *San Salvador* lander."

Sonny snapped to attention, vaulted out of his sleep chamber, snatched up his cache of weapons and grinned ear to ear.

"Time to clean some scum."

Sam

Sam glanced at the old man beside him, waiting for him to continue *his* version. Sam's passion was history—a natural outgrowth of the research he had to do for his studies—and this man's account wasn't something he'd run across before. Maybe it was the slight buzz, or maybe it was the thrill of solving the enigmas he encountered in his research, but he had to admit he was more than a little intrigued.

"Sorry for the interruption." Sam nudged the old man. "You were saying?"

Clearing his throat loudly, the old man announced, "Jackson de Clare and Sonny Strongbow were different people; *both* of them existed." The bar went silent at this revelation.

Sam cursed the old man. "Keep it down," he hissed. "You trying to start another fight?"

The old man stared him down and swallowed but said nothing. One of Van's drinking buddies chuckled. "*This* I gotta hear."

The old man closed his mouth, as if he'd forgotten what he was doing suddenly, turned back to the barman and licked his lips, his hungry gaze following the bottle the barman held.

Van's friend shuffled up to the bar, squeezing between Sam and the old man. He tossed down enough payment for another three drinks. "Another for my friend." He tapped the bar in front of the old man for emphasis. "And keep 'em coming until that runs out."

The old man nodded his appreciation and patiently waited for another glass of Rancid. The barman shrugged, poured another and set it down in front of the drunk.

Like the others, it disappeared in record time and the old man turned back to his new audience, while the barman poured another. Clutching his leather notebook to his chest, he resumed his story.

Mason

Mason Munson woke for his second rotation feeling refreshed, but anxious. He'd requested a short stasis—only five years—to coincide with the replacement rotation Dr. Stephanie had scheduled for Hal. As soon as he could talk, he asked Nan to wake Hal.

"That's not possible," the AI answered matter-of-factly. "Dr. Englewood was unable to revive him."

Mason's heart sank hearing the AI's pronouncement. He struggled to scramble out of the *casket*, his legs still not quite fully operational. "I don't understand. Why was he wakened before me? That's not standard procedure."

"Given the circumstances, Dr. Englewood requested early awakening of the new med and Hal Fremont before the remainder of the crew. The decision was consistent for the situation."

"What happened? Couldn't they have just put him down again?"

"Hal Fremont's stasis chamber malfunctioned." The AI casually recounted the details of the two meds' failed revival attempts while Mason completed his wakening routine in shock.

Still, there was no way to bring Hal back. As his friend, he would mourn Hal's loss, but he still had a job to do. "How many incidents have occurred since Hal's?"

"None."

Mason blinked. *None?*

"And there were no other incidents before?"

"No."

Mason took some comfort in that. Perhaps Hal's affliction had been an anomaly. "Nan?" he said, recalling Seneca's birthday party— subjectively only a few months ago—and Hal laughing. Right then, he decided to honor his fallen friend in a way that would remind him of Hal every day.

"Call me Sonny."

Sam

Van's friend narrowed his eyes, shook his head and stalked away, muttering. Rejoining his friends, they engaged in a short, terse argument before he turned back to Sam and the old man, his face twisted in rage. "Shut up, old man," he yelled, "you're as stupid as Clem. Who cares about Mason Whatever; Sonny's the hero, you hear?"

Sonny

Sonny Strongbow stalked into Supply Bay 4, loaded down with the entire contents of his weapons vault. He stopped in the doorway, assessing the *situation*.

The *San Salvador*'s bow could be seen just beyond the viewport, where it was attached to the outer hull. The open hatch leading to the lander ship teemed with activity. Sonny counted at least a dozen people, maybe more, moving supplies from the bay onto the ship. Drawing a bead with a disruptor in each hand, he yelled, "Stop, cowards!"

A disrupter beam flashed past Sonny's left arm, singeing the skin-tight sleeve of his bodysuit, along with a line of his flesh. Sonny glanced at the burn on his bicep; no blood trickled from the instantly cauterized wound, nor did he expect any. He laughed at the pain, a slow grin spreading over his face. "So, it's gonna be like that, is it?"

Sonny dove for cover, firing his disrupters at the cowards who dared to sabotage the *Victoria* on his watch. His mind racing, it all happened in slow motion, as if his thoughts were sped up tenfold. He cursed his body's slow responses, though it still seemed faster than his opponents could muster. With a mighty war cry of "Cowa-a-a-a-a-rds!" he cut them down one by one by disrupter beam until there were only two left firing back at him. Those he dispatched with blades expertly thrown into their vile throats.

When he was done, the bay was a shambles, with smoking containers of ruined food packets littering the floor and the contents of burst water containers racing over the slick floor. Tossing aside his spent disrupters, he stomped toward the still-open hatch, taking in the carnage and searching for any signs of life.

He was disappointed to find none. He'd hoped this battle would be more of a challenge.

It never was, but there was always hope.

"Assess damage," he barked to the AI.

Only a few feet from reaching the hatch, a disrupter beam burst from within the corridor beyond the hatch. Sonny's lightning-quick reflexes vaulted him over a nearby stack of crates, affording him some cover, but leaving him pinned down without weapons.

He cheered his inner hero. *This* was more like it!

Seeing nothing on the crate manifests, he backtracked quickly, dodging lethal disrupter beams with ease. Soon, he came upon a cache of hunting arrows and fishing line. His triumphant grin turned sour, though, as he realized there was no bow in the crates.

Snatching up the arrows and fishing line anyway, he sprinted between disrupter beams to a nearby stack, and found semi-flexible polymer bands amidst some construction materials. Lightweight, with high tensile strength. Sonny's grin returned.

Summoning all of his strength, Sonny poured everything into bending that band into a makeshift bow, bound at either end with multiple loops of the monofilament fishing line. It would take a good deal of strength to draw; Sonny figured maybe a hundred kilos, but he had the confidence of decades backing him, especially with the adrenaline coursing through his veins.

Still taking fire, he refashioned his utility belt into a makeshift quiver strapped across his back, tossed in all but one of the arrows and nocked the last one.

Jumping up from cover after gauging the last beam's source, Sonny drew his strongbow with a mighty roar and released the bowstring, his arrow whistling true into the chest of the giant wielding a disrupter, shock carving his rough features into a gruesome death mask.

Taking no time to consider the coward's death, he nocked another shaft while advancing quickly, drew and fired into the mouth of the hatch as he flashed past. A grunt from deep within announced the success of his second shot. Heart pounding in his chest, Sonny nocked a third arrow and rolled through the hatch, hoping the dead man beyond wouldn't impede him.

Nobody attacked him this time, but Sonny realized his error as soon as he rolled into a crouch. There wasn't enough space to draw where he was. He could hear more cowards retreating farther into the *San Salvador*, but they held the advantage here; advancing would be suicide, and Sonny wasn't suicidal.

Glancing at the body with his arrow protruding from his chest, blood pouring out of the man's right lung, Sonny realized the coward was still breathing. Tossing his bow out the hatch, he followed quickly, dragging his prisoner behind, bent on interrogating him. Slamming the hatch closed and locking it, Sonny towered over him.

"Talk, scum," he commanded, and nudged him with his toe for encouragement. But the man only coughed blood and choked. He let out a final gasp and shuddered, his eyes open, but still, never giving up his secrets.

Noticing for the first time the small handheld control clutched in the dead man's left fist, Sonny bent to retrieve it. "Activate," he said, and was rewarded with a bright remote-control display, sporting the name of the lander, *San Salvador*. Realizing what he held in his hands, a slow smile crept over his face and he snapped his gaze to the locked hatch.

It took only three words for Sonny Strongbow to end the saboteur threat for good, allowing the *Victoria* to finish her voyage unmolested, so that 10,000 human men and women and 100,000 potential babies and countless generations of their descendants could live among the stars in peace. Just three words for Sonny Strongbow to save them all.

"Deactivate life support."

Sam

"Yeah, sure," scoffed another drunk at the bar. "We've heard it all before."

Replaying the evening in his head, Sam couldn't remember this man speaking before, but noticed that he'd been Clem's drinking buddy. He was likely a Strongbow denier and that made Sam nervous.

Sam's research efforts afforded him some insights that few others on Cistercia had. One little-known fact that wasn't common knowledge was that there *were* frozen bodies on the *San Salvador* when it was opened. Fifteen of them, to be exact, frozen in death; some sitting, some lying down, all of them in ordinary repose. Nobody knew how long they'd been there or who they were. All of the colonists in stasis were accounted for, and the only missing crew members were those that had succumbed to death or accidents, the circumstances recorded and their bodies ejected to space.

The bodies in the lander were an enigma, and they somehow disappeared in orbit, before the first lander hit New Virginia. All that remained were some obscure records buried where only a select few scholars like Sam chanced across them.

The curious thing was it wasn't just the Sonny zealots that insisted there were rebel bodies on the lander. Most of the time, the deniers just painted Jackson de Clare as a murdering psychopath with an evil agenda, but every now and then, they added a grim addendum to their version.

Sam shifted in his barstool, preparing to make a hasty exit, but the old man clamped a hand on his arm to stay him.

Glancing at the old man, Sam saw the silent plea in his eyes and settled back to see how this new development played out.

"It wasn't rebel bodies on that lander, friend," the drunk spat out. "Those were his *victims*."

Jackson

Jackson de Clare dragged the last victim to the closed hatch of the *San Salvador*, grunting with the effort. He could have one of his comrades do it, but he *wanted* to take the last one personally. It just felt right.

He pulled a handheld control from his pocket and glanced around before activating it.

"Activate life support," he whispered, hoping the ever-present AI wouldn't hear him. About a minute later, a green light came on and the control chimed.

Jackson unlocked the hatch and opened it, then dragged the body inside, propping the woman, a former astrogator, on a couch. "Jenny Whoever, meet Frank and Charlie Whatever," he sneered and slithered back down the corridor to the open hatch.

Once outside, after securing the hatch, Jackson pulled the control from his pocket again. "Deactivate life support."

Chuckling, Jackson slipped out of Supply Bay 4 to rejoin his comrades. The time was coming soon when they'd be able to complete the Plan, but they were ahead of schedule and the slingshot they'd need to get back to Earth was still a few months away. No need to have bodies stinking up the corridors until they were ready.

Strapped on to the exterior hull, the lander provided a convenient place to keep the bodies out of the way while they waited for the slingshot. No atmosphere or pressure meant they were kept in a kind of makeshift cryostasis, only without the sleep.

"Soon, friends," Jackson announced as he joined the others. "Soon they'll no longer be able to ignore us."

Sam

"Complete crap," Van's friend dismissed with a wave. "We're here, ain't we? Makes no sense." Raucous laughter rocked the bar, and not just from that table.

"The AI caught 'em after that," the drunk denier a few barstools over from Sam answered, shrugging. "Makes as much sense as *your* cult crap."

A few guffaws echoed through the bar interior, mocking the exchange, but Sam was relieved to see that nobody seemed particularly disposed to fighting. He breathed out slowly; he hadn't realized he'd been holding his breath for the last minute.

The bartender slid a glass of Rancid Rum past Sam to the old man, announcing, "That's it," more to Sam than the old man, and tipped his chin to the table where the drunk's latest benefactor still drank with his friends. Sam understood; his payment had run its course.

The glass was already empty by the time Sam turned back around. Marveling at the old man's alcohol tolerance, he nudged the bum, who hovered on the edge of consciousness.

"'S'right," he slurred, "*neither* of 'em makes sense, do they? 'Cause they're *both* wrong."

Mason

Mason-cum-Sonny Munson dragged a dead crew member from the *San Salvador*, a woman he'd respectfully propped up in a natural sitting position in a comfortable chair. He laid a worn copy of *Little Women*—the most prized of her personal belongings—in her lap and sighed. Like Hal, she'd gone crazy several months into her rotation.

All of them stored inside the lander had gone crazy. The first, an astrogator named Santos, had been on his second crew rotation, near the end—just like Hal. Mason had placed his prone body near a viewport, as if he could stare at the stars outside.

After discussing it with the AI, he'd requested that Nan keep him in the next crew rotation, hoping that would give him some more time to figure out what had happened to Hal and Santos. He'd been awake for more than a decade now, still no closer to understanding.

And now there were thirteen frozen bodies in the lander.

It chilled him to think that there was one dead crew member for every year he'd been on rotation. Sometimes he'd wake at night with the dread certainty that *he* was somehow responsible.

It *had* to be a coincidence. It *had* to be.

Mason took some comfort that Hal died while sleeping. The others were in agony for days before they finally expired and it was heartbreaking to watch. At the end, they sort of *relaxed* into death, so they were at peace now—or they looked like it, at least.

"How'd it go in there, Sonny?" the med, Franklin, asked, looking up from his microscope as Mason shuffled into the Med Bay.

"I liked Jenny," he said. "I put her in a nice chair with her book."

Franklin nodded and went back to his culture. All of the meds did what they could, but none could figure out what was happening. Strapped on the outer hull without atmosphere, the lander provided an environment with easy access to the bodies in the hopes that someday there'd be a med that would solve this and put a stop to the dying.

Two weeks later, Mason filled in the newly awakened med, a pleasant man named Amir. "This sounds like a virus, Sonny."

Mason had shrugged. "I'm not a med. I'm just telling you what I know."

"I'd like to examine one or two of the bodies in more detail."

Mason sighed and returned to the *San Salvador*, feeling like a grave robber.

Back in his cabin, he busied himself with updated suggestions for a police force once they reached the colony planet. After so many years awake, he'd had quite a bit of time to muse on how it should be structured. Sure, there'd been quite a bit of work on the subject before the *Victoria* left Earth, but he felt he had some new ideas that should be explored, and he owed it to the colony to present them.

"Nan, edit *Mason's Laws*, please. Recite."

Mason listened intently, stopping Nan periodically with new suggestions.

Several hours later, Mason perched on the edge of his bed, once again writing in his ostrich leather journal, one of the personal belongings he'd chosen to bring with him. Each crew member was allowed ten kilos of personal luggage, one of the meager perks of giving up seven Earth years of their lives to crew rotations before reaching their destination. Mason looked up and stared at his door for a moment, remembering he'd need to store Jenny's books—all nine kilos.

Like *Mason's Laws*, he recorded thoughts he felt would benefit the future colony, but these thoughts were focused on what he called the Space Crazies. He mumbled a reminder to Nan about Jenny's books and put the journal aside.

Ten months and one more body later, Dr. Amir called him to the Med Bay. "Sonny, I've isolated a single common factor."

Mason's heart stopped.

"You."

Through the pounding in his ears, he heard Dr. Amir call him Patient Zero. Mason didn't know what that meant, so he asked; the answer crushed him. If he understood correctly, that meant he was the reason Hal was dead. He was the reason fourteen bodies were stored in the lander.

For some reason, he seemed resistant to what Dr. Amir thought was a virus, but he was a carrier. If the med was right, he would continue killing crew members so long as he was alive.

Over the last two months of the rotation, Mason was subjected to innumerable tests, convincing Dr. Amir of his hypothesis. He had no explanation for how Mason could have come in contact with such a virus.

Mason thought long and hard about that, but came up empty, too. He couldn't shake a vague memory of one of the new guys at his drunken sendoff saying he was a biomedical engineer doing research into gene therapy, but it was probably nothing. Even assuming he remembered correctly—which was doubtful, considering how drunk he'd been—the likelihood of the guy being connected to his virus was pretty slim. Mason realized he was grasping at straws, trying to find someone to blame, and promptly put it out his mind.

"The new med will continue my work, yes?" Dr. Amir asked him, readying for the end of his rotation.

Mason nodded.

"We will fix this, Sonny, don't you worry."

Mason smiled weakly, but it didn't matter. He'd already figured out how to fix the situation. Tomorrow, he'd talk with the new med and give him a few days to review Dr. Amir's work. If he confirmed the work, as he was sure he would, in one week, Mason would join his unintended victims in the *San Salvador*.

Sam

"That's crazy, old man!" Sam shook his head in disbelief. "The AI has no record of any virus like that."

The old man cracked an eye and raised his head slightly from where it rested on his journal. "AI erased 'em." A drop of yellow drool splattered onto the surface, and he closed his eye again.

After a few seconds of gentle poking, Sam gave up on his regaining consciousness any time soon and stared at the bar top, contemplating.

There was no record of a virus, that was true, but it was the drunk's last words that troubled him. Here was yet another explanation for the bodies, as plausible as the other two, frankly, but the very idea that the AI would decide to *erase* the existence of people—for *any* reason—well, that was just a disturbing thought. While a sufficiently advanced AI could seem just like a human, and Sam had no doubt there were humans that would do such a thing, it chilled him to think that a *good* human might think to obscure or even eliminate important events.

For what? To advance a specific narrative? Sam could see that. He *did* see that, every day, piecing together competing theories based on scant evidence.

A fleeting thought made his blood run cold. Was he enabling the cycle himself with his research? By lending credence to one theory over another, effective squelching that one, was he contributing to the lies instead of revealing the truth? What if there *was* no truth anymore?

The bartender drifted over and laid a palm gently in front of Sam to get his attention. He tipped his chin at the old man. "Looks like his bedtime. You want another for yourself, friend?"

Sam shook his head and stared at the old man.

The bartender wandered off.

Sam frowned at the old man's notebook. No, the old man's *journal*. Frayed edges peeked out between two worn leather sheets. It *did* look old; he'd have to give him that. Carefully nudging the old man's head aside, Sam curled up the edges a little, trying to get a peek at the contents.

He didn't see anything.

The old man moaned and licked his lips, rolling his head slightly away from Sam. Not much, but enough for Sam to get a look at about a quarter of the page.

Blank.

He bent closer, close enough to feel the old man's hot, measured breath. And *smell* his breath, too. Amazingly, the copious quantities of alcohol masked the fetid odor Sam remembered when the drunk had first stumbled in. Rifling several pages, he examined them front and back, but found them all to be blank.

Sam snorted and withdrew his hand. He tapped the bar in front of him. "I think I'll take that drink now," he said, chuckling.

The old man's story was . . . a story. Lies. And here he'd almost believed him and started questioning the nature of truth in the bargain.

A dingy glass of cloudy Rancé Rum slid in front of him. Sam shook his head and glowered at the thought of his gullibility. He tossed back the entire contents of the glass—just as the old man had—and choked on the burn. Coughing, he motioned for another.

He'd probably regret it in the morning, but right now he just wanted to forget all the lies he'd believed this evening. Idly, he wondered if even the leather was real, or the old man has just distressed it to look old, in order to sell its authenticity better. All for free drinks.

A niggling thought tugged at Sam, and a shred of doubt arose.

The leather. It didn't really feel like any leather Sam had come across, and he'd spent a *lot* of time with ancient tomes in his research.

But the journal . . . it felt *different*. Not just old, but *alien*. At least to the colony animals.

Carefully opening the journal's brittle pages again, Sam looked closer at the pages.

There.

Faint scratches maybe traces of . . . something. Ink? It was hard to tell without the appropriate equipment, like the kind the Landing Museum over in Roanoke used for restoring artifacts found among the crew's abandoned personal effects.

Sam made a sound of surprise, maybe a little too loudly.

A few barstools over, Clem's drinking partner cleared his throat and raised a questioning eyebrow to Sam.

Sam sat back on the barstool. It was probably nothing. His first instinct was to denounce the old man, revealing his observation of the journal's blank pages, but he bit his tongue and looked around.

The bar was full of patrons who largely minded their own business. With the exception of the disagreement over Sonny Strongbow's legend, of course, but that happened in *every* bar.

Had anybody else in the bar even heard the old man's outrageous claim about the journal's origin? Thinking about it, Sam realized he was probably the only one who'd heard the drunk's proclamation.

The one time the old man had spoken up loudly enough to be heard, he'd been soundly ignored.

So, the blank pages wouldn't be a revelation to anyone else.

Sam decided he'd had enough contemplation for the night and slipped off his barstool, his feet landing heavily on the floor. He glanced at the refilled glass of rum briefly, coming to a decision quickly. Shaking his head sadly, he abandoned it after tossing payment on the bar top.

He spared a final look at the old man, asleep on his weird leather journal, his mouth agape, drool soaking into the surface, and stumbled out the door, marveling at the *truth* of how drunk he felt.

The night's cold bit into Sam, sobering him somewhat. In the end, what did the truth matter, anyway? He was here—*they* were here, all of them, Sonny Strongbow acolytes, deniers, the bum with his journal—nearly forty light-years and centuries from the Earth humankind called home, and now *here* was home.

Maybe Sonny Strongbow was just a legend, an idea, but maybe that was what we needed to face the unknown. Maybe we *needed* Sonny to be out there, asleep, waiting, ready to fight for us again.

Sam shivered, and for a moment, he swore he felt Sonny stir.

Sonny Strongbow

The persistence of the Sonny Strongbow myth baffles historians. Despite the oppressive nature of the governments and nongovernmental organizations funding the TRAPPIST-2 Exploitation, there is no evidence that such an individual existed or was ever associated with the mission. While the colonizers' official records must be necessarily suspect, it is well documented that *Victoria* arrived at Cistercia with 235 surviving members of the original 250-person crew, and 9,998 of the 10,000 hibernating colonists. These numbers do not support the legends of "hundreds of mutineers" or even the dozens of deaths attributed to Freedom Fighter Jackson de Clare. New evidence from the computer logs of Renee Blanc-Perot indicate that additional cryostasis units were ordered for *Victoria*, most likely in a clandestine attempt to mask establishment of a secret bunker for Elites. The whereabouts of those units, and their inhabitants, whether on Earth or Cistercia, remains unknown.

—Excerpt from *Flint's People's History of Interstellar Exploitation*,
Trudovik Press,
Kerenskiy, Trudovik, AA237

STOWAWAY

Brad R. Torgersen

"They told me you were illegal," the young boy said, with his little hands gripping the edge of the dining room table. Large, brown eyes peered over the tops of dimpled knuckles. There had been no accusation in the youngster's tone. Merely a statement of fact.

The old man at the other end of the table guffawed heartily.

"Did they, now?" he said to the child, a grin spreading across his age-wrinkled face.

"Yes," the boy replied.

"Is it the other kids, or the teachers too?" the old man asked.

"The other boys," the child responded. "My teacher doesn't believe the story about stowaways aboard the *Victoria*. Says it's impossible anyone could have hidden on the ship from Earth."

"Your teacher is too young to have been part of the original settlement. She was probably one of the people who came out of the tanks, much later. We brought thousands that way. Grew the tankies when we needed more people than there were women to carry the babies—both natural and in-vitro. Your teacher is lucky. She only remembers the good times. Not the bad."

"Great-grandpa," the boy said inquisitively, "what was it like?"

"The early days of settlement?"

"*Earth*. They show us videos and pictures. Huge cities! *So many people*. It will take a thousand years before Cistercia is like that."

The old man's smile dropped.

"There's nothing special about Earth cities," he said sternly. "Noisy. Crowded. Filthy. Filled with people who can't turn a wrench

127

nor wield a hatchet to save their own lives. Plus, gangs who would slit your throat just as soon as look at you. And all for pieces of paper in your wallet. Why do you think I was willing to risk everything to come here in the first place?"

"My friends say you weren't allowed aboard."

"Raphael, I don't expect your generation to understand what it was like back home. *My* home. There was a lot of good to Earth, and also a lot of bad too. More than anything, though, Earth—the whole Solar System really—is what happens when men won't leave each other alone."

"I don't understand," the boy admitted.

"Here," the old man said, using a liver-spotted hand to pick up the little remote control on the table top. He flicked on the wall screen and used the menu to dial up a digital photo album. Several high-resolution pictures of Cistercia—an alien world, made the home of men through much toil and no small amount of sacrifice— cycled in brilliant full color. Then suddenly views of Cistercian ocean vistas were replaced with a pitch-black image of space. A small white dot glared at the center of the screen.

"Know what that is?" the old man asked.

"No," the boy replied.

"You'll recognize it in a moment."

The old man cycled through several more images until he reached the one with the white dot enlarged greatly.

"I took this using the telescope out back," the old man said. "*Victoria*'s still up there, and probably always will be. I built her, you know. Me and ten thousand other welders, push-pilots, space-fitters, dock-runners, and a whole heap of suit-and-tie guys who had to manage the money and ensure parts and equipment were delivered to the shipyard on time, and within budget. They did better with the former than with the latter. *Victoria* was a lot more expensive than anyone wanted her to be. Which is another reason I decided to be aboard. Even though the selection board ultimately turned me down."

"But it was against the rules!" Raphael said, shocked.

"You're damned right it was," the old man said, allowing himself a wolfish grin.

"I don't understand," the boy admitted, his brow beetling.

"I know you don't. So, before your friends go filling your head with any more tall tales, let me tell you what *really* happened. Even your mother—born of your grandmother's womb—has never heard it all."

The old man flicked through the images again, until this time a giant, multicolored ball of pearlescent blue and white filled the screen. The sunshine reflected off those faraway oceans was much lighter and brighter than that generated by Cistercia's home star.

"I was just seventeen when I got off Earth..."

Victoria existed as a Brobdingnagian metal framework—orbiting Mars—when Gabriel Martinez was born in Los Angeles. Like most of the children his age, he went through school occasionally watching the scholastic video updates on the massive starship's construction. Unlike most of the children his age, he took an actual interest in the ship—indeed, the whole proposed mission to TRAPPIST-2. He hadn't known, then, how long a light-year might be, but it had been explained that TRAPPIST-2 was almost forty of them away from Earth. And that it would take hundreds of Earth years for people to go there. If such a mission could be done at all. The men and women on the videos Gabriel watched at home—outside of class—debated the merit of the mission. Better, many of them said, to spend the money and resources closer to home. A sentiment which Gabriel's mother—surrounded by their few belongings in their meager two-bedroom apartment—heartily agreed with.

But the idea of going to another Earth far away quickly became a fascination for Gabriel, such that one of his mathematics teachers took an interest in Gabriel's questions, and suggested that if Gabriel exerted himself and scored well on tests he might be able to work for one of the big aerospace companies contracted to build *Victoria*. Being one of the lucky few selected to actually travel to TRAPPIST-2 was putting the cart well before the horse. First step was to get *out* of the barrio and *into* space, which Gabriel desperately desired.

He graduated a year ahead of his peers, and immediately signed up for one of the orbital-industrial work-apprenticeship programs which sponsored bright young men and women who were eager to put their skills to use on humanity's ultimate frontier.

The in-processing briefing for the apprenticeship would forever be seared into Gabriel's memory. It was insanely early in the morning, at a secure building on the tarmac at the Los Angeles Interplanetary Aerospace Complex. Several uniformed men and women with stone-faced expressions patrolled up and down the aisles between the desks. Talking was not allowed. The older gentleman at the podium delivering the briefing did not mince words. Space was dangerous. Training—to survive and work in space—would be hard. Harder than anything any of the prospective apprentices had ever done in their lives. Mistakes could and would kill. There would be no excuses for sloppiness, fooling around, or not taking things seriously. Anyone who didn't think he or she could cut it, was to stand up and walk directly out the door. No questions asked.

Nobody took the instructor up on it.

But not everyone made it through induction training either. Of the sixty young people in Gabriel's class, only thirty-seven graduated six months later. Most washed out for physical or academic reasons. Class hours were demandingly long, and chock full of math and physics, making high school seem remedial in comparison. Each of them was run almost literally into the ground by daily fitness training, during which Gabriel converted a somewhat typically doughy twenty-second-century teenage boy's body into a much leaner, much stronger, much more durable model.

Then came the on-orbit final phase, which flushed out the people who were unable to adapt to a microgravity environment.

On-orbit proved to be an even more difficult challenge for Gabriel than the physical training. His inner ear and stomach conspired to give him ruinous spells of nausea, to the point he almost quit. Except he kept going back to his digital picture frame with the updated imagery of *Victoria* gradually gaining hard bulk—like the apprentices themselves—in preparation for her eventual voyage.

His case of The Garns—so dubbed because of an old twentieth-century pilot, politician, and astronaut who'd had a miserable time with space sickness—eventually passed. And Gabe Martinez went into the space work force with his eyes set on the ultimate prize.

Except, his company deployed him back to an Earth-based manufacturing facility where he was tasked with quality-checking vacuum-proof robotic armature motors designed to withstand the extremes of heat and cold that could be found in Earth orbit, on the Moon, and elsewhere in the rapidly expanding interplanetary sphere of human civilization.

"What does any of that have to do with you being kept off the *Victoria*?" asked Gabe's great-grandson.

"It's like this," Gabe said patiently. "When I signed up I didn't realize that almost everyone who works in space has to pay their dues."

"I don't know what that means," Raphael admitted, leaning forward so that his mouth was obscured by his skinny arms folded in front of him on the table.

"It means they don't just hand you your graduation certificate and promote you immediately to the high-profile jobs. You have to work your way up. Prove yourself. Or at least you did, way back before *Victoria* left for TRAPPIST-2. Probably it's still the same, now."

"But Cistercia *is* our home," Raphael protested.

"Yes, it is," Gabe said, "and it's a hard-won home, at that. But really, I've got *two* homes. This one, and Earth."

"Will any of us ever get to take *Victoria* back?" Raphael asked.

"Not in your lifetime," Gabe admitted.

"Why not?"

"She was a ship built for a one-way trip. Refitting her for a return voyage would take the equivalent of a Mars shipyard—like where she was built originally—and more resources and man-hours than any colony in the TRAPPIST-2 system will be capable of generating for at least three or four more generations. Now, *don't* look at me like that, Raphael. I told you. Earth cities are nothing special, and you're not missing anything. Really, you're not! There are hundreds of millions of Earth people living in those cities who would be willing to trade with you this very instant."

"Why?" the boy asked.

"Because this is the *dream*, kid! A few hundred years ago, my great-great-grandfather rode horses on both sides of the Rio Grande river, prospecting as well as cattle-driving. That was one of the last true Earth frontiers, and it didn't last long. By the time he was as old—biologically—as I am now, the locomotive trains had bridged the North American continent and they were flying airplanes in the very first worldwide Earth war. People *need* a frontier. That's something we had to grapple with in the twenty-first Earth century. When there were no more wild places for us to explore and settle— except the ultimate one above our heads—we had to push hard to justify the mission. It was terribly expensive. And a lot of lives were lost. But once we established ourselves on Earth's Moon, and got to work in the asteroids, there was no holding us back. And I wasn't going to let no gosh-damned selection board tell me I wasn't good enough to go."

It took ten years for Gabe Martinez to reach Mars. Along the way he made some friends, and also a few enemies, and learned that being a good technician was as much about learning how to work with people as it was about learning how to work with hardware. People were not computers. They did not respond predictably to input, and they couldn't be programmed. People were finicky, prone to making decisions based on mood, often unable to logically parse a problem, and very quick to use the octopus-like labyrinth of a big corporation's bureaucracy to conceal their sloth, greed, graft, or incompetence.

But Gabe made progress. Traded in favors. And showed himself to be—he thought—one of the best technicians in the business. He could recite parts specifications by the thousands and readily tell anyone the stress loads of different kinds of space-rated struts, spars, beams, and gantries, and which grades of metals had to be used for which kinds of space-industrial applications. He could strip a cargo capsule to the bone, blindfolded, and put it back together again in better operating condition than when he found it. And, having not encumbered himself with family, he was—again, he thought—a prime man for enlisting in the sizeable army of workers dedicated to *Victoria*'s completion.

But once more, he found himself stymied. Instead of promptly going to work in the shipyard itself, Gabe wound up on desk duty for one of the countless Mars-based supply and manufacturing warehouses which provided parts to every substantial operation in the solar system, and to *Victoria* too.

There was no thrill in cataloguing and rechecking inventory. Nor in shepherding procurement, much less shipments. But Gabe knew such work was necessary. And as his own experience told him, a messy warehouse that couldn't promptly and accurately fill an order would make life pure hell for any technician actually suiting up daily and installing equipment onto a spaceframe.

But whatever practical satisfaction might be found in the job, Gabe wasn't satisfied. He wanted to *see* the mighty starship with his own eyes. Glide along her mammoth length wearing nothing but a construction suit and a personal maneuvering pack. Put his glove-protected hands on her freshly minted hull and *feel* the destiny written intrinsically into *Victoria's* future. A ship built by men and women, to take men and women where there had never been any people before. Indeed, probably no thinking mind at all had *ever* been to TRAPPIST-2. Because by Earth standard year 2169 all the many searches for non-Earth intelligence had yielded zero fruit.

If there were other beings like men in the universe, they were so far away from Earth that they knew nothing of human civilization, and vice versa.

But TRAPPIST-2 was a close sun. And had several worlds roughly Earth-sized and in roughly the right zone around the small star to make them potentially habitable. With some help from human climate engineers, of course.

Speculation and curiosity filled Gabe's off hours, as warehouse duty went from months to years, and soon *Victoria* would officially be launched for trial runs.

Gabe found himself kept awake at night, in his tiny Martian industrial studio apartment—with its fold-down bed and closetlike latrine, not to mention the impossibly narrow galley kitchen— wondering if he had been laboring in vain. His cousins were certainly living a more luxurious life back home. Los Angeles was huge and dirty, but at least you could live in a condo with more than one room. And walk outside and feel the rain on your face in the winter, or the sun shining down during the summer.

Gabe could remember one of his uncles taking Gabe fishing in the Sierras. He'd managed to get a Lahontan cutthroat trout on the line, which had been bigger around than one of Gabe's adolescent thighs. There were no visceral thrills like that on dry, desiccated Mars. Nor even a guarantee that such sport would exist on faraway TRAPPIST-2c, the intended colony world. Which might not, for all anyone knew, afford a life any less spartan than the one endured by the colonists currently setting up shop on the moons of Saturn.

Nevertheless, having devoted all of his adult life to a chance at the stars, Gabe couldn't turn away. It was inconceivable. So, he kept doing the best work he knew how to do, and politely pestering management to put his résumé in front of the committee responsible for keeping the starship project staffed with space-rated technicians.

When the promotion to the *Victoria* ship works came through, it was the most pleasant of shocks. Though, by his own admission, Gabe remained as far from TRAPPIST-2 as ever.

"Not everyone who worked on *Victoria* got to go?" Raphael asked, blinking.

"Almost *none* of us actually building the thing came anywhere close."

"That doesn't make sense," Raphael stated plainly.

"Tell me about it!" Gabe barked, then laughed, shaking his head. "You know who *did* get selected for the trip? Doctors. A legion of doctors."

"You mean . . . *Victoria* was a hospital ship?"

"No," Gabe said, "I mean they had *doctorate* degrees. University folk. Which, let me tell you, is not a bad thing in and of itself. Some of the men and women with letters after their names—who worked on *Victoria*, and who did *not* get selected, I might add—were among the most capable and hardworking individuals I've ever met. But if you were a mere worker who was merely putting the ship together, your skill set was deemed 'out of scope' for the mission. After all—I was told time and again—what good were shipyard skills going to be in TRAPPIST-2 space? Where there would not be any shipyards for a long time, even if colonization went as well as could possibly be hoped.

"I admit, I never had a good answer to that. But it didn't stop me from fuming in my apartment every night, trying to figure out a way to get around the rules. I even made some soft inquiries into bribing the board. I'd saved up a lot of pay to that point. Who doesn't like money? Most people can be bought. But I ultimately decided I didn't want to go that route. I was either joining the voyage of my own ingenuity and capabilities, or not."

"So, what happened?" Raphael asked. "If the board told you 'no' how did you get here?"

The plan formed in Gabe's mind. A small portion accreting at a time.

Having finally been able to see *Victoria* up close, the true scale of the ship awed him. And why not? She wasn't just an interplanetary cargo ship, running from Earth orbit to Martian orbit, and back again. She was an entire small city unto herself, equipped for a space siege almost two centuries long. During which most of the inhabitants would be cryo-kept, of course. But many would not. A crew would always be awake to perform maintenance and pilot the thing. Plus, additional people might be kept up for special projects or to fix certain problems. And there was all the fuel needed—a slush sea of it!—plus the huge colony landers which would put down on a planet's surface at the end of the trip. And each of *those* gargantuan vessels was like a small town, self-contained, possessing everything the colonists and crew might need to survive on an alien world. So that *Victoria* was the greatest of great engineering efforts. A mobile, mechanized metropolis in the sky.

And like anything of that size, with that much complexity, there were places where a man could hide. For hours. Maybe days. Perhaps weeks. Or longer?

Gabe Martinez began to quietly survey the ship while doing his real work—installing and testing machinery, latching pipe to beams, and fixing bulkheads to vacuum-tight contact seals—then returning to his apartment at night where he drew up his ideas.

There were an untold number of maintenance and critical access tubes winding their way through the ship, like the arteries and veins of a person. No wire nor any pipe nor any conduit was inaccessible; throughout the ship, a man or a woman could crawl along them checking for leaks, shorts, or effecting repairs. And there would only be a finite number of crew awake at any one point in the voyage, to be doing such things. And if Gabe and his cohort did their jobs correctly—and Gabe was pleased to see there were no duds allowed on the *Victoria* yard roster—there wouldn't have to be a lot of "after-market" changes which would necessitate battalions of technicians servicing and maintaining the vessel, as was the case during her chrysalis phase in the yard itself. A period which was over two decades in length when the trial runs were finally announced. At which point Gabe knew exactly when he would be allowed to physically touch the ship one last time, prior to her official launch toward interstellar space.

He built his hidey-hole right where he thought it would be least discoverable yet would also retain access to ship's power and other consumables necessary to run the cryo pod where Gabe would slumber for most of the journey. Getting the parts and equipment was easy. He had all his legacy connections to the supply chain on the Martian ground. It was installing everything which proved difficult. And more than once Gabe feared his plan might be discovered. But he was careful to ensure that inspections in that specific corner of the ship were the kind of inspections he himself could sign off, and by the time his installation, testing, and re-testing of the equipment was through, the space had been wholly walled up inside the nearly completed ship. So that nobody would be the wiser without a very deliberate, careful search.

"Did you steal the parts?" Raphael asked.

"Hell no," Gabe said.

"But you were already breaking the rules," the boy said. "Why stop there?"

"Just because I was determined to go doesn't mean I was a thief," Gabe said sternly. "You're too young to fully understand this, but I am going to lay it on you anyway. There are stupid rules, and there are good rules that are rules for a reason. You will know which ones are which, someday. Shutting the shipyard technicians almost entirely out of the selection process was a massively *stupid* rule, and if you ask the few crew who are still alive to talk about the trip, they will agree with you. It was a mistake for the mission planners to load up on so many eggheads while carrying too few men and women with callouses on their hands. But be that as it may, I paid for every single part I put into my plan. Emptied out all my Earthly savings in the process too. That equipment and the cryo pod it supported were *mine*, fair and square."

"Okay," Raphael said. "So, you stowed away honestly."

"Damned right I did. When the final trial run was complete, and us technicians were doing the final fit checks while the colonists were being sleep-loaded along with the crew rotations, I made my move. My corporate access card found its way onto a shuttle headed back to Mars while I used a construction suit—really expensive, I might add—to creep along the dark side of the *Victoria* to an external lock where I'd personally programmed the access codes. Once inside I bundled up my suit and went to the maintenance tube I'd memorized, and painfully crawled, with the bundled construction suit in tow, to my spot. The cryo pod, a little place to sleep, a locker with food, a dispenser for hot and cold water, plus fresh atmosphere from one of the air plants. I was good to go. And when she launched, *Victoria* was blissfully unaware of my presence, both during the trip out to the heliopause and even while the ship built velocity for the long interstellar flight."

"*Then* you went into the cryo pod?" Raphael asked.

"Yes," Gabe said.

"My teacher says all the colonist and crew cryo pods had to be carefully watched and monitored by the awake crew during the trip. Weren't you scared that something would go wrong, and nobody would catch it before you died?"

"Of course, I was scared," Gabe admitted. "I was *terrified* that I'd climb into the pod and close the hatch, and never wake up again. But the time for having cold feet—ha-ha—on that particular decision had long since passed. I had a plan, and it only worked one-way. Besides, the pod was still hooked to the major systems with a dummy rig that would draw power and consumables without alerting the network. The minor drain would not be noticed. I'd tested and re-tested it countless times. So, into the cryo pod I went. And let me tell you, a stranger, more unsettling experience I've seldom had. Like being in a coffin when they heap the dirt over you, except there is a happy little computer woman's voice telling you to relax and not fight the process."

"I would not want to do that," Raphael said strongly.

"Nobody should want to, but it's the only way to travel between the stars. There just isn't enough food and water for that many people to live on, and besides, you grow old and die long before you get to the destination anyway. Even if you've had the best rejuvenation therapy Earth can provide—which I did."

"So you sleep it out," Raphael said. "Like taking a long nap."

"Except I had to get up from time to time, just like everyone else on the crew who were sleep-loaded in the beginning. I had to check on my stuff. Make sure the cryo pod was still good. Run my own stealth status on the health and well-being of the *Victoria* herself. And so on, and so forth. Which was when I discovered I wasn't alone."

"Did one of the crew catch you?"

"No," Gabe said. "Your great-grandmother did."

It had never occurred to Gabe that there would be other stowaways. In his semi-maniacal focus, he'd never thought to watch for other technicians doing similar technical sleights of hand while buttoning up their final shipyard projects. He might not have noticed it, either, except for the fact that during one of his waking periods— only ever a few days at a stretch—he discovered a little yellow-paper sticky note attached to the outside of his cryo pod which simply said: DON'T WORRY, I WON'T TELL.

At first, Gabe panicked. He'd worked so damned hard to ensure his hidey-hole was positioned far away from anywhere a crewperson might check, without having a specific and urgent need to venture down that particular maintenance tube. Now suddenly a stranger had left a sticky note for Gabe, almost like he was being thrust into a game of hide-and-seek. What in the world was he going to do?

But then it occurred to him that if the crew *had* found him, they'd have woken him up immediately. And furthermore, if they *had* woken him up, what was the worst they could do to him? He'd committed no serious crime against a standing Earth law which would warrant more than temporary confinement. And it wasn't like *Victoria* was going to swing about and go back to drop off an unwanted passenger. Once underway, there was practically nothing save for a catastrophic failure of either the reactor or the fuel supply or the cryo system which would dictate aborting the mission and bringing *Victoria* back to Mars. One way or the other, she was going to TRAPPIST-2. And if the crew didn't like the fact a technician had added himself to their ranks, oh well. They didn't have to. Gabe would earn his keep and show them he was worth his weight in consumables. Hell, he had more space-rated time than many of the doctorate-laden individuals who'd been selected. They *needed* someone like Gabe, whether they knew it or not.

But the sticky note was a clue to a different puzzle. Either a crewperson with a sense of humor who liked to play games, or another stowaway with a covert operation.

He began combing through the innards of the ship, using what he knew of the internal sensors to gimmick them at regular intervals. Make it seem like no one was there. Using programming tools he was sure not even the crew had at their disposal, because they were custom tools Gabe himself had built during the final phase of ship's construction.

But he never found the author of the sticky note, before he had to put himself back into the cryo pod.

When next he woke, another sticky note had been left: NO DREAMS FOR ME THIS TIME, HOW ABOUT YOU?

Which again sent Gabe combing through the nether reaches of the titanic vessel, still coming up empty.

But instead of going directly back into the cryo pod at the designated time, he closed the lid and put the system on standby, while tucking himself out of sight much farther down the maintenance tube—where somebody standing at the cryo pod could be seen, but Gabe himself ought to not be.

He waited almost a full Earth week, only occasionally moving to eat or handle personal business in his little hidden latrine he'd built before launch.

When the woman finally appeared, Gabe realized it had been a long time since he'd spent any energy on females. Dating had never been his specialty, and he'd always made excuses about being too much of a company man for a long-term relationship. He'd only dimly thought to himself that there might be time for romance on the far side of the voyage, in that fuzzy place in his imagination where he tried to think about life as a colonist.

The sight of this new stranger jolted him. Her one-piece spacer's leotard fit her attractively. It was the kind of insulated, practical garment worn under a construction suit. She was lean the way most experienced technicians had to be—fitness requirements never let up, and you had to pass tests and get physicals every six months—but with just a touch of curviness in the right places. Enough to make Gabe peer intently at the female silhouette before she suddenly turned and disappeared back the way she'd come.

Gabe's urge to follow her overwhelmed him. But as he float-pulled himself up—microgravity this time, as the ship was not presently under thrust—he stopped short. Another sticky note had been left on the lid of the cryo pod which said: CLEVER BOY, BUT YOU CAN'T CATCH ME!

A further two days of meticulous, careful searching proved her right.

Regretfully, Gabe put himself back into the cryo pod.

And so it went. With years slipping by, as millions upon millions of space miles vanished behind them. The sun shrinking to a bright point of coldly familiar light amidst a sea of similar lights. Things just vaguely red-shifted and blue-shifted—either forward or aft, depending on which end Gabe looked from—enough to keep him aware of the fact that *Victoria* had thrusted gradually up to an appreciable percentage of the speed of light. Say, a quarter? No humans had ever traveled faster. Not in the history of the species. There would in fact be some mild time dilation to make up for when they finally got back down to mere orbital velocity, relative to their destination.

"Is that why you're so old?" Raphael asked, his eyes lighting up. Gabe smiled slightly. The boy had his teeth into the story now.

"Partially," Gabe said. "But we weren't going fast enough for truly dramatic time effects. It's the cryo that does the job. Sleeping suspended, dreamless, while people back home live out their lives. By the time the voyage was halfway over most everyone in my generation on Earth was dead. Which is another reason I knew *Victoria* would never turn around. She would arrive back at an Earth—and a Mars—which had moved on. Populated with people who regarded *Victoria*'s people as relics. Once launched, *Victoria* became a time capsule. Only to be opened at the destination."

"Did you finally catch great-grandma?"

"Like I told you, she always found me instead, and left the notes."

"But you didn't know each other from work?"

"*Victoria* required a lot of technicians. Working around the clock in shifts. Based groundside at different Martian locations, for housing, and work reasons. I'll be honest, I didn't have many friends back before the ship launched. I just didn't make time."

"So, what happened?"

"Something I had known would happen from the very start."

Gabe swam up out of cryostasis in a bad blur. It had happened too fast. Not the usual somewhat hazy drift-up-to-consciousness process he'd been used to experiencing. This time it felt like a fish being hooked and dragged from the cold depths of a reservoir to the hot sunny surface on a summer day. He practically flopped out of his cryo pod and gasped for breath, trying to clear the film from his unready eyes.

"Dammit," he muttered to no one. "Something's gone wrong with the pod!"

"No," a woman's voice said sternly. "It's worse than that."

Gabe flipped over onto his back—forgetting totally that he was naked, save for the medical monitors strapped to his limbs and torso—and squinted at the face which peered down at him.

"Let me guess," he muttered, still wiping at uncooperative eyes. "You're the smart-ass who's been leaving the stickies."

"Correct," she said.

"I'd sure as hell like to know where *you* found a place to hide, because I thought my spot was pretty damned good, but I've clearly been outfoxed."

"I'll show you later," she said. "Right now, we have a big problem."

"Crew got wise to us?" Gabe asked her.

"No. There's been a significant interstellar debris impact. *Victoria* is bleeding both fuel and oxygen, which she can't afford to bleed. And the crew are taking their damned time trying to figure out what to do about it."

"The ship's got a massive shield umbrella for that kind of thing," Gabe said plainly. "Anything big enough to penetrate the umbrella ought to have destroyed the ship outright."

"Whatever it was, it wasn't that massive, but we're still in big trouble, and I don't want to wait for the crew to pull their thumbs out. I've got a plan, and I need your help."

Gabe frowned, and nodded his head. "Engineers design it, but techs always have to fix it."

"That's exactly it," she said.

"First things first, though," Gabe said. "What the hell is your name?"

"Betty Brown. But people call me Blue."

"They hang that on you back in apprentice school?"

"Yep. Come on, you need to get dressed, uh . . ."

"Just call me Gabe. I was never cool enough for a nickname."

She helped him into his own spacer's leotard, and then they were each suiting up to go outside. First, using the airlock nearest the damage to perform a sensor assessment, then exiting the airlock to do a detailed inspection.

In the blackness of space, sublimating slush fuel and venting oxygen formed a cloud outside the ship. Gabe's and Betty's piercing helmet and hand lamps made the mixture seem like the billowing product of dry ice—soaking in a kettle of water on Halloween. It was difficult to gauge the size of the rupture without switching to micro-radar ping-backs, which allowed them to get a three-dimensional wire-frame model of the damaged section of the ship. Betty had been correct. *Victoria* was losing far too much to wait any longer for the crew to take action.

They went back inside and retrieved several quick-seal hull tarps which had been explicitly designed to combat ruptures and impacts. First one, then two, then three of the tarps were hastily applied in succession, reducing the outflow of gas—but not stopping it. The tarps chemical-hardened upon contact with oxygen, but they were only a bandage on the gaping wound. To fix the problem permanently would require dumping the contents of the ruptured tanks over to the adjacent tanks, then venting the ruptured tanks completely, and determining if either the mission could be completed without using the damaged tanks, or if the tanks could be weld-patched and pressurized for use—only at a greatly reduced pounds-per-square-inch ratio than normal.

Given the fact there was both pure oxygen and sublimated slush hydrogen mixing freely, the possibility of a spark touching off an explosion was very large in Gabe's mind. He moved deliberately and with great care the entire time they were outside. And so did his partner. He admired the efficiency and quickness of her movement. She was as focused and urgent as he was, and there wasn't any wasted effort as the tarps were applied, and the bleeding slowed to a seep.

★ ★ ★

"So that's where Great-Gram Blue gets her name," Raphael said, slapping his hands on the table and smiling with delight.

"Yup," Gabe said, smiling.

"What did the crew do about the leak?"

"Well, we were out there trying to keep these tarps in place and watching the meters on our suits drop down and down until it got critical, then finally the posse arrived. They were confused as hell to see us, but your great-grandmother didn't give them any time for an inquisition. She was barking orders—tanks were her specialty while in dock—and the crew in suits were only too happy to oblige. Eventually we did get the rest of the slush hydrogen and oxygen pushed off to adjacent tanks, and once we were all back inside we figured out that we'd already used so much on the journey, there was now plenty of room to keep what could be kept, and not have to use the damaged tanks. But if we'd not saved what we saved in time, our margin on the down slope would have been a lot narrower."

"I don't understand," Raphael said.

"It's like slowing down on a bicycle," Gabe said. "Once you go fast, you have to brake to come to a stop. It took a tremendous amount of time and fuel to push us up to interstellar speed, and it took a tremendous amount of time and fuel to slow down enough that when *Victoria* got to TRAPPIST-2 we wouldn't shoot straight through the system without being able to orbit a planet. Less fuel means you possibly don't have enough to slow down like you need to."

"And you'd have been trapped out in space forever?"

Gabe tapped the side of his nose. "Now you see it."

The young boy seemed sobered by that possibility.

"You and Great-Gram Blue were heroes!"

"Nope," Gabe said. "Just doing our jobs. Albeit unpaid, at that point."

"And the crew?"

"The command team was *very* angry with us. But at the same time, they realized what had happened, and how me and Blue helped out. Their anger quickly subsided, and then it came time to decide what to do with us. Since we were clearly not freeloading, that was in our favor. And in fact, we had just very probably spared the mission. You want to know the funny part? Blue and I weren't the only stowaways either."

"There were *more*?" Raphael said, laughing with delight.

"One by one, we each came out of the woodwork. A total of seven of us. *All* shipyard technicians. We were dubbed the Stowaway Confederacy and grilled about how our separate, individually planned and prepared hideouts might be affecting overall ship's function and performance. But once this was deemed benign, we were officially 'sworn in' by the command team. It made the rest of the voyage much easier. But of course, *none* of us had any idea what lay ahead. Arriving at TRAPPIST-2 was the *easy* part."

"It doesn't sound like it was easy," Raphael said.

"Even a room full of doctorate-degreed people could not properly plan for every contingency. Which means even as ready as we thought we were, we still weren't ready. I think all of us just sort of hoped that when we arrived, we'd see a world—or worlds—similar to Earth. Blue oceans. White clouds. Lots of land just ripe for settling. Which was sort of true, but Earth is home for specific reasons. The mix of nitrogen, carbon dioxide, and oxygen is just right. Most plants and animals are useful for humans, or at least aren't actively dangerous nor toxic to any modern people. A different Earth—one from which people never came—doesn't have the right things. Too much of something in the air or water, or not enough of another. Bacteria and viruses which our bodies can't easily defend against, or for which there may be no inoculation, nor a cure. Soil where Earth plants can't grow very well, or maybe won't grow at all. Things in the soil that poison the plants, or maybe poison the livestock—once we tanked up some of those, too—so that you can't eat what you grow. Assuming it grows enough to bother harvesting. And so on. Basically, there was never any guarantee that *Victoria* would be successful in colonizing any planet orbiting TRAPPIST-2. And we almost failed on several occasions. A lot of crew died or went missing. Even more colonists, too. The Stowaway Confederacy lost four out of seven."

"Now *that* is something my teacher talks about," Raphael said. "A 'steep learning curve' is what my teacher calls it."

"Lethally steep," Gabe said.

After a few moments, he added, "It's what ultimately got Great-Gram Blue and me together."

"You didn't fall in love while you are on the *Victoria*?" Raphael exclaimed.

"There was no time for that," Gabe said. "We were friends for the rest of the trip. Which is the best place for any love to start, I guess. But we were never more than that. Not until people started dying. Just like in the old days, when sea settlers suffered. Blue told me one night—after your grandmother was born—that it seemed sort of crazy to get married and have a baby, what with everything that had happened to all of us after our arrival. But I told her sometimes you have to be crazy, to get by in life. Hadn't we each been crazy enough to stow away in the first place? That hadn't been any more or less crazy than starting a family forty light-years from Earth, with the shadow of death hanging over our every decision."

"It's not so bad now," Raphael remarked, smiling. "When Great-Gram Blue comes back, we should all go for a walk in the new park."

"Not a bad idea," Gabe said. "If you don't mind going slow."

Gabe stood up, clicking off the wall screen, and dropping the remote to the tabletop. He walked around and put out a liver-spotted hand, which his great-grandson took appreciatively. Together they walked to the solid door at the back of the kitchen and opened it so that they could go into the backyard.

The air was fresh but carried a faint smell which Gabe had never quite gotten used to. Nor would he ever, he suspected. This planet had not birthed his specific kind, though it had birthed the many humans who'd come after.

"There it is again," Gabe said.

"What?" Raphael asked.

"It's transparent to you and your nose, and that's a good thing," Gabe replied. Then he looked to the horizon where TRAPPIST-2 was slowly drifting down in the sky. It didn't look anything like a sunset over the Pacific from the shores of Long Beach. TRAPPIST-2 was a smaller, less bright sun. And Cistercia was closer than Earth was to Sol. The celestial billiard game had aligned these spheres differently, with different bright lights moving in the sky at night, as different worlds passed through their respective orbits. A sight which never seemed to lack an alien flavor in Gabe's mind.

But he knew that his great-grandson, and all the progeny who might come after, would take as much comfort in the rising and setting of TRAPPIST-2 and its worlds as men had in the rising and setting of Sol and its worlds throughout human history. Only now there would be a distinctly new and different offshoot. Part of Gabe wished he might live long enough to have a sneak peek at the future. When some distant descendant might mount a rocket and climb again to orbit, where some future iteration of *Victoria* might be waiting. To take men to the next star over. And then, further still into the depths of time, on to the next star yet.

Gabe squeezed his great-grandson's hand and smiled.

Volunteers

Colonist and crew selection for the TRAPPIST-2 colony consisted of a combination of targeted recruitment of professionals and a lottery for skilled technicians and tradesmen. The effort was criticized from the start for neglecting everyday workers, particularly given that the colony could very well require considerable manual labor to maintain farms and ranches if—and when—the automated infrastructure failed. In response to such criticism, the Colony Foundation leadership pointed out that many of the spouses of their "prime" technical recruits were historians, artists, authors . . . and of course, that the colonists would include farmers, mechanics, miners, and others necessary to building a new world. Nevertheless, the roster of crew members that would be awake in shifts throughout the journal were remarkably light on laborers . . .

Official manifests from the Foundation verify 250 crew and 10,000 colonists in cryo, yet the log of Captain Nikolina Perić, *Victoria*'s shift captain on arrival at TRAPPIST-2c, show 242 surviving crew members despite fifteen documented deaths enroute. The loss of *Whale* and subsequent mishaps complicated the census of cryo units and colonists, raising the possibility that the colony was augmented by "volunteers" from the construction team who added their own cryo units to the manifest.

—*Encyclopedia Astra*,
Gannon University,
Antonia, Cistercia, AA212

Part Two:
THE COLONISTS

CERBERUS PROJECT

Monalisa Foster

For Norman Borlaug, the man who saved a billion lives.

Who says that the god of the underworld didn't have a sense of humor? After all, legend says that Hades had named his dog Spot.

I looked it up.

Kerberos, in the original Greek, Cerberus in the Latin, translates to "spotted." Hades' dog is even mentioned in *The Republic* where Plato refers to Kerberos's "composite" nature. When I read that, the roboticist in me knew that our sheepdog replacement project was going to be called Cerberus.

It's spot-on, if I do say so myself.

I just don't want the word "dog" in there, even though that's what we're making. I don't want it in there because it hurts too much.

We lost them, you see. The dogs, that is. Not all of them—the rest remain in hibernation—but enough to endanger our survival on Cistercia. One of the biology people around here can probably explain it better. Something to do with prions and nucleotides and amino acids.

The short version is: dogs can't survive here until we figure out how to feed them without dipping into our precious food stocks. Crops are failing. We don't have a choice.

We didn't bring the dogs here as pets. We brought them here to work. But humans will bond with anything, especially if it's cute and fuzzy and all the herding breeds are. Cute, fuzzy, loyal, loving.

Tens of thousands of years have gone into the relationship

151

between Man and Dog. You can't just snap your fingers and turn that off.

Some things remain the same, no matter how much they hurt us. Our love for man's best friend is like that. And it won't change just because we made it to the stars. And that's a good thing.

We will save them. You have my word.

Mina squinted into Cistercia's dawn as she pulled her scarf up and over her nose. Moisture settled into the corners of her eyes. The wind tugged the wetness across her chilled skin like tears.

Above, TRAPPIST-2 was at its zenith, very much like the Sun in Earth's sky. Wispy clouds were drifting in, promising another chilly day.

They had been lucky. Cistercia was so Earth-like, so promising. An ideal candidate, as it were. Or as close as humanity had found.

It had taken two days to climb up the foothills overlooking Antonia, the colony's primary landing site.

The colonists had to perform most of the terraforming themselves instead of relying on packages that would have landed on Cistercia years before they arrived. It had been backbreaking work clearing and plowing the surrounding land for agriculture. After the colonists landed, they'd barely had time to erect prefab domes and shelters before getting to work; those "temporary" dwellings still squatted in the distance, neatly arranged with a larger dome in the center.

Still like a lake, Cistercia's ocean shimmered on the other side of Antonia.

A warm weight leaned into Mina's leg. She petted the ewe's curly head and earned herself a happy bleat.

The *thunk-thunk-thunk* of a four-legged robot approached, its body slung low, just like a border collie in intimidation mode. It growled and barked at the ewe. Mina was standing close to a ledge and since the sheep had poor depth perception, One was simply doing its job.

The ewe retreated into the safety of the flock, nudging aside several sheep to put as much distance between herself and the odd thing that looked and behaved like a dog, but didn't smell like one.

"Good d—robot," Mina said.

No anthropomorphizing. She'd promised. They all had. The Cerberus robots were to remain, simply, One, Two, and Three. The numbers were even painted in reflective safety yellow on both "shoulders" and atop the domes of their heads.

The robotics people had outdone themselves. At first, they'd tried simpler robots that only resembled dogs because they had four legs, but the sheep didn't respond to them. Herding worked only because sheep responded to the herding dog's body language. So the robots had been upgraded and made to look as much like a dog as possible. The servos, motors, and hydraulic lines were covered in a pliable material that allowed them to move like dogs. Instead of fur, they were covered in segmented armor.

During the final testing phase, the robots had been sent out among the colonists. Their doglike facial movements were real enough that the colonists quickly fell into the habit of treating them as if they were actual dogs. It didn't seem to matter that their cybernetic lenses didn't have the warmth of a dog's eyes, or that their bodies weren't soft and yielding to the touch, or that the sounds they made were mere recordings. It didn't matter that they didn't pant or lick.

Inevitably, people would pat them on the head or cuddle them. There had been multiple attempts to teach them to fetch, shake, and roll over. Someone had even hacked into the behavioral programming to make them circle three times before lying down, supposedly as a joke.

Alysster Wallace, the chief roboticist, had turned purple and sputtered with rage. It had taken him days to calm down. After the "sabotage" of *his* heuristics he'd wanted to start over, but the need to move the sheep upland was too dire. The Cerberus robots wouldn't be getting the ideal of the brand new million-trial education that Dr. Wallace wanted.

Cerberus Three was bigger than One and Two. Closer to the size of a Great Dane, it doubled as a pack animal, carrying essential supplies for Mina and the smaller do—robots.

She tugged at the strap of her shotgun, repositioning it from where it had shifted so she could pull out her whistle. It was old and worn, but it had served her family for five generations. If Mina had her way, it would serve them for five more.

Leaning on her shepherd's crook, she took a deep breath and put her tongue up against the inside curve of the whistle, drew it into her mouth and made the two short spurts of the "walk up" command.

Like shepherds of old, it was Mina's job to take her herd to better pastures and return with a larger, fatter herd.

Five days, thirteen hours, fourteen minutes and twenty-three-point-six seconds had passed since they had left Antonia.

Unit_BA-1-T0 logged the time and date when AdminUser_Borlaug_Normina fell asleep in her tent. It also logged the temperature, humidity, wind direction, and the number of sheep in the flock: sixty-one.

Their route had been planned well in advance, based on the path of a mountain stream (their only source of water) and where the terraforming had taken best. Of the three types of high-sugar grasses seeded, two had taken reasonably well. The third seemed to be failing, but both the red and white clover had proliferated enough to make up for it.

Unit_BA-2-T0 was on the lookout for predators, running in a widening spiral around the base camp. It logged no threatening heat signatures, tracks, or chemical/scent trails. Unit_BA-2-T0 also used its scanners to survey and log the height of the sparse Earth-transplant trees and their even sparser native counterparts. A lightning strike had probably burned the area in the not too distant past, clearing it. The new growth was sparse enough that prey animals were few in numbers and so were the predators that hunted them.

Unit_BA-3-T0 was processing data on the ewes. Every time Cerberus interacted with any of the ewes, they took measurements. When the data was merged and compiled, it would be sent to AdminUser_Borlaug_Normina's tablet.

Cerberus's three components had worked together before, although not in their current form. Prior to the colonists' arrival they had been part of the scouting system. As flying drones they had mapped the terrain and collected samples of water, soil, air, flora, and fauna.

Cerberus had been part of a larger autonomous system that had worked independently for years. When they'd been retasked, they'd been severed from the larger system and placed into new casings. Cerberus could no longer fly, but their programming had been expanded by processing thousands of hours of video of border collies, corgis, and German and Anatolian shepherds interacting with both sheep and humans.

Exploration had been demoted from their primary function, but it remained a prioritized item. Now that AdminUser_ Borlaug_Normina and her flock were settled in for the night, the lower-priority task of exploration rose to the top of the stack.

Having completed its perimeter check, Unit_BA-2-T0 continued upstream. It analyzed thirty-two water samples, fifteen soil samples, and discovered a previously unidentified insect before heading back toward camp, arriving shortly after AdminUser_Borlaug_Normina emerged from her tent.

Twenty-six years old. Brown hair. Brown eyes. Caucasian and Asian ancestry. She had been chosen not just for her skill set, but for her genetics. At 5.97 feet in height, she was slightly taller than the colony average. Her psychological profile said she preferred animals to people and didn't mind being alone.

Unit_BA-2-T0's facial recognition program measured and logged all sixty-eight facial landmark-points as well as a second set based on posture and compared it to the baseline.

Conclusion: AdminUser_Borlaug_Normina was tired and sore. Unit_BA-2-T0 tight-beamed its findings to its counterparts. Cerberus agreed to reduce their average daily pace by fifteen percent.

Wishing for a second cup of coffee, Mina secured her tent and supplies atop Three's back. Her muscles were still sore and aching, despite the stretching. Life inside Antonia's habitat had made her soft. She hadn't slept in a tent or on the ground since, well, before she'd left Earth.

"I *will* get used to this." A few more days and she'd be fine.

Three swiveled its head her way, and even gave it a bit of a tilt. *Damn.* They were not supposed to do that. They were supposed to save the body language cues for the sheep.

"Never mind," she said and pulled the tablet out of her backpack. She reviewed the night's activity, scrolling through it for anything unusual. Without satellites or relay towers, there was only one way to send any of it to Antonia. She wasn't going to waste her few precious comm drones for nightly reports.

Mina was about halfway through the log when a distressed bleat rang out. Three turned its head. Mina sprinted.

A hundred feet from the flock, one of the ewes was squatting, front legs straight and dug into the soil, rear legs bent, her lamb expelled on the ground, covered in yellowish mucosa and blood.

Mina gasped. This was not the first time she'd seen a lamb born. But this was Cistercia's first lamb born the old-fashioned way. And they were going to have to go back to doing things the old-fashioned way if they were going to make it. Two steps forward and one step back was still progress.

Bouncing with delight, she grabbed her tablet. Three was already recording the event and streaming it to her device.

"Good boy," she said, placing her hand on Three's shoulder.

The lamb was already up on its wobbly legs, searching for its mother's teat.

It had begun. Each of the ewes would, in turn, give birth. The conceptions had been staggered so that only one or two ewes would give birth at a time.

This was a good start. Suddenly, Mina didn't mind the lack of coffee so much. The ewe and her lamb wandered off to rejoin the other sheep. Mina let them. Later, she'd find them again and attach a tracking tag to the newest member of her flock. For now, ewe and lamb deserved time to bond.

Three approached the blood- and mucosa-soaked ground and lowered its head.

Her tablet pinged as data poured into it: date, time, estimated weight and size, gender (a female), relative location . . .

Mina laughed.

"Well, I guess we *should* record all that. It's a momentous occasion, after all."

She rummaged through the panniers on Three's back and pulled out one of the mini drones, plugged it into her tablet, and transferred all the data they'd collected so far.

She typed in a quick header "Debut of #62" and launched the drone.

Antonia deserved to know.

As the drone's hum faded, Cerberus compared the stride of the newborn lamb to the average of the herd's adult sheep.

Conclusion: Reduce pace by an additional twenty percent. Day six projection: average speed reduction of thirty-two percent.

Mina's flock had grown to seventy-three. Eleven successful births in a row was both noteworthy and not.

On Earth there were three things shepherds knew that made for that kind of success: ample, rich pastures for grazing; crystal clear water; and living in peace without the stress of predators.

Mina had yet to see any predators. None of the robots had seen anything large enough to classify as a predator, not even the bison-sized creatures native to Cistercia. Whether it was luck or not, didn't matter. She just hoped it continued.

There was nothing like holding a newborn lamb, even if she only got to do it while she tagged them.

Mina sat by the fire as the breeze stirred the fecund scents of the flock around her. She was fine-tuning the route upland on her tablet when an override came through and popped an infrared video over the mapping software.

One was streaming the live video feed as it circled two heat sources: the larger heat signature, a ewe tagged number twelve, and beside it, a smaller, cooling, heat source tagged twelve-alpha.

Mina cursed. She shoved her feet into her boots, grabbed one of the packs resting by the tent, and trudged to the ewe's location. The ewe had gone off to give birth alone, but One had followed and was standing over her and her lamb, head panning left and right. Just like a sheepdog, One stood over the injured animal and didn't move aside until Mina was right atop it.

Her tablet beeped. The lamb had been born alive, lived three minutes and twenty-three seconds, and then simply stopped breathing.

Mina frowned. It happened. There could be a dozen reasons, including that the lamb had been too large, although that kind of thing was supposed to have been accounted for preimplantation.

She knelt beside the lamb and opened up her pack. Working with determined efficiency, Mina set up a light on a tripod.

The lamb was small, but not unusually so. It seemed fully developed. It had not been stillborn. She wished she had a way to get the carcass back to Antonia to rule out any environmental factors.

Instead, she did what shepherds had always done with dead lambs. She used a sharp knife to cut around the legs and neck. Then she peeled the skin off, leaving the head and the rest of the body. By the time she was done, blood was everywhere, but she had a kind of jacket that she could put on a live lamb without a mother. She hoped she'd never need it.

It had always gutted her, no matter how often she'd done it. Even her father, a shepherd all his life, had taken every loss hard. It would hang over him like a gray cloud until he could make it right by saving another. That's what that jacket was: a way to fool the ewe into thinking that an orphaned lamb was hers.

She folded the lamb jacket carefully and placed it inside the pack, then took what was left of the carcass and carried it away to bury it.

When she was done, she washed her blood- and dirt-stained hands in the stream. Her hands were steady, but her breathing was not. She blinked back against the pressure behind her eyes.

One was standing a few feet away, watching.

Unit_BA-1-T0 recorded the actions of AdminUser_Borlaug_Normina. Her reactions had not been part of any of the programming it had received. Unit_BA-1-T0 filed the data away for later analysis and approached AdminUser_Borlaug_Normina carefully.

Its facial recognition algorithm identified AdminUser_Borlaug_Normina's reaction as a negative emotion. Her heart rate, blood pressure, and breathing reinforced the conclusion.

Unit_BA-1-T0 searched its files for a similar scenario. The closest result included a brief video clip of a human shepherd with a reaction that was an eighty-nine point seven percent match. The border collie in the video approached the shepherd and nuzzled into his neck. Unit_BA-1-T0 analyzed the facial reaction of the subject on the video. The subject experienced a fifty-two percent reduction in the negative emotion.

Unit_BA-1-T0 moved closer, lowering its body so that its head would be at the same level as the collie it was imitating.

AdminUser_Borlaug_Normina's eyes widened. She gasped as Unit_BA-1-T0 tucked its head into the space between her neck and shoulder. This close, Unit_BA-1-T0's sensors easily made out the change in heart rate. AdminUser_Borlaug_Normina was trembling as well. Another negative reaction.

As she placed her arms around Unit_BA-1-T0's shoulders and sobbed, the robot searched its archives for more comparisons. It found over one hundred instances where a dog simply nuzzled or touched a human or allowed itself to be held. In all of those instances, the human's physiological reactions improved.

Unit_BA-1-T0 logged the changes in her vital signs. It logged when she stopped trembling and when her breathing returned to normal.

AdminUser_Borlaug_Normina pulled away and stood up, placing her hands on her hips.

Facial recognition assigned a new emotion: puzzlement.

Puzzlement had a higher positive rating than the previous emotion.

A subroutine kicked in and Unit_BA-1-T0 made 3.2 turns and settled onto the grass at her feet. The corners of AdminUser_Borlaug_Normina's lips pulled up and facial recognition tagged her current emotional state as the high-rated positive emotion called happiness.

Conclusion: Procedure successful. Store procedure for future repetition.

It had been raining for a few hours now, a light drizzle from overcast skies. It matched Mina's mood as she mulled over One's strange behavior.

She shouldn't have hugged it. She was no better than that prankster who'd hacked the programming or the colonists who'd set up a name lottery.

Mina scrolled through the Cerberus code on her tablet but couldn't find anything obvious. If there was still some errant bit of code left from the hack, she couldn't find it.

Maybe you don't want to find it.

She missed her dogs. There was still a void in her heart at what they'd lost, one that shouldn't be filled by machines.

In some ways, Cerberus was better.

Machines didn't die. Their parts could be replaced. They didn't go rabid because prions had eaten parts of their brains. And if they were to go "insane," a reboot or a return to a previously saved state was a clean, easy answer.

Like the working dogs they were meant to replace, One, Two, and Three were not pets. They had a purpose and they were part of a very limited resource—one on which Antonia's survival depended.

The colony simply wasn't at a point where it could afford the luxury of "pets." It *was* at a point where the crop failure could turn into starvation, and while she had no illusions that she was raising animals for food, she—

Somewhere on the other side of the flock, a ewe screamed. She pulled at the strap holding her shotgun to her back as she used her shepherd's crook to part the ewes standing between her and the source of the scream.

Behind her, she could hear the distinctly heavier thuds of Three's paws. Two was circling somewhere off on the right, by the tree line, betrayed by its reflective paint. One was off to her left by the stream, pacing up and down its length, keeping the sheep from wandering.

The screaming ewe was on its side, twitching, making that awful sound over and over again. Labor must have come on fast for her to have just laid down like that. The other ewes had backed away from the scent of blood. Had the robots allowed it, the sheep would have put even more distance between themselves and the screaming ewe.

A lamb's toe—instead of a nose—hung out from the ewe's birth canal. A contraction drove it out a bit more, making the ewe scream again.

Mina grabbed the leg by the joint and on the next contraction gave it a tug. A second leg came through. The lamb was halfway out when the contractions stopped. Mina reached for the knife at her thigh, cut the dead ewe open, and eased the lamb out.

She rubbed it vigorously and was rewarded with a sputtering breath. Mina kept rubbing, stimulating it to breathe. The drizzle was turning into rain, each pellet colder than the last. She slid her coat off her shoulders and wrapped the lamb into it.

The ewes were bunched up in groups, still skittish and unsettled. Mina headed uphill, careful of her footing on the muddy ground.

She whistled, signaling the robots to drive the herd uphill. They didn't have to go far to escape the scent of blood and death.

"Three, come here."

The ewes parted for him—it.

One-handed, Mina dug through the panniers, found the lamb jacket, and wrapped it around the shivering newborn.

Wiping her brow, she looked around. There was no way she was going to find Twelve—the ewe that had lost her lamb—not with the way they were bunched up under the darkening skies.

She loosened the tent and let it drop to the ground. Then she reached for the tablet and tapped the controls, telling Three to find and bring her ewe number twelve. By the time she was done setting up the tent, Three was using its snout to gently nudge a harried looking Twelve forward.

Holding the lamb, Mina grabbed Twelve with her crook and pulled her into the tent.

Mina set the lamb down. It wobbled, still weak and cold. The ewe eyed the lamb, glaring at it suspiciously. It still smelled of death.

Mina nudged the ewe forward gently with her crook.

Patience. Give her time.

The lamb's cry was so soft it was almost lost to the sound of rain hitting the tent. Mina held her breath.

She didn't have a bottle or formula. There just hadn't been enough room to pack everything she'd have had if she were back on Earth with help just a call or a quick ride away.

The lamb approached Twelve. She turned around a few times, skirting the walls of the tent.

Mina's hands tightened on the crook.

The lamb followed Twelve. Still convinced it wasn't hers, the ewe gave the newborn a head-butt and knocked it down. The lamb made a wounded cry, but it was already struggling to get back up, awkward in its strange wrapping.

There should still be plenty of oxytocin in Twelve's system, driving a competing urge to mother, warring with the suspicion that something wasn't quite right.

Did Twelve know that her lamb was dead? Did she even understand such a concept? Mina hoped not. How terrible would it be to be self-aware enough to know that you were food, that you were destined for the slaughterhouse, that the creatures that took care of you, that you trusted every day, only did so because they needed to eat.

Twelve leaned into the corner seam, pushing its weight into it, giving the tent wall a bit of a bow. She sniffed the air again and again, with purpose this time rather than panic.

The lamb was persistent. It waddled on unsteady legs, nudged Twelve's underside and latched on.

Twelve's eyes went wide, but she stayed in place. The harder the lamb sucked, the more her pose softened with relief.

"Good girl," Mina whispered. "That's a good little mother."

Mina stepped outside and drew the flap closed.

She looked up toward the clouds and let the rain wash her face clean.

Even with the gray of the sky above her, that psychological wound in her gut seemed lighter somehow, as if part of it had closed—or healed—a bit.

Exploration had risen to the top of Unit_BA-2-T0's queue. It set off to collect samples and scout ahead. The first water sample it obtained showed a slight increase in alkalinity.

Unit_BA-2-T0 took additional samples from sites farther upstream. The increase remained below the threshold where it would turn the water into poison.

Cerberus assigned a higher priority to further exploration at the next cycle and recalled Unit_BA-2-T0.

Unit_BA-1-T0 had been disconnected from the system for 2.1 seconds, well outside the parameters of what would be considered normal for its proximity. Cerberus pinged Unit_BA-1-T0 with a reconnect request. It took Unit_BA-1-T0 longer to respond than it should have.

Cerberus logged the anomaly.

Another night came and went. A smile pulled at Mina's lips. She'd pulled the lamb jacket off the newborn under Twelve's "that is *my* baby" glare. Her tent would probably never smell clean again, but so be it. It had been worth it.

Mina was knee deep in the stream, struggling with the tent as it caught water and turned into a giant water bladder. Dragging the wet tent out got dirt all over it, but she managed to keep it out of the sheep droppings and get it over the drying rack she'd built out of branches. Her coat wasn't dry yet either, but at least she'd been able to change into clean clothes.

This patch of land was almost out of clover and grasses, but she had one more thing to do: bury the dead ewe. Mina wiped her hands dry on her shirt, toweled the dirt off her bare feet, and pulled on dry socks and boots. She tapped instructions into the tablet, telling the robots to keep the herd in place until she returned.

The tablet went back into her backpack, atop the shovel and her lunch. She filled her canteen with water and placed it on her belt by her knife. Shotgun in one hand, crook in the other, she headed downhill.

Mina had always had a good sense of direction, but the dead ewe wasn't where she'd expected. She circled back, careful of the still-soggy ground.

Sighing, she lowered the shotgun and crook to the ground. Setting the backpack down in front of her, she pulled out the tablet. This far from the herd, the device only picked up the stronger transponders from the robots, but at this range there should have been a signal from the dead ewe's tag. She'd planned on cutting it open, checking it for obvious signs of disease and taking pictures. It would all go into the upload to be sent back to Antonia via drone.

The hairs on the back of Mina's neck stood up in warning. She stood, dropping the tablet and going for the shotgun. Her hands were tight around it as she slowly turned.

Nothing moved. Nothing stirred. Total silence, as if someone had flipped a switch and shut off the background noise made by Cistercia's insect- and bird-equivalents. The only sound she could still hear was that of the rain-swelled stream.

The air around Mina was unnaturally still, but her heart was pumping, and adrenaline coursed through her veins.

Like distant thunder, a rumbling rose around her. Mina looked up, searching the sky. The wet ground shook beneath her feet and gave way.

The fall knocked the breath out of her. She sucked in a pained breath an instant before the stars blooming in her vision were swallowed by darkness.

★ ★ ★

Unit_BA-2-T0's sensors picked up the P-waves of the quake first. Unit_BA-2-T0 had been scouting the day's route in anticipation of AdminUser_Borlaug_Normina's return. When Unit_BA-2-T0 had been a flying drone, it had recorded similar seismic activity. Based on its previous observations, it knew what to expect. First, the heard but not felt compressions and dilations called P-waves. Then, possibly, the oscillating S-waves.

Unit_BA-2-T0 ran back to the herd. Unit_BA-3-T0 and Unit_BA-1-T0 were already moving the sheep closer together. When the sheep finally felt the ground move, they would panic and scatter.

It took Cerberus less than a second to conclude that moving the herd to the flattest piece of ground was the best course of action. It took even less time to override AdminUser_Borlaug_Normina's order to wait for her.

Cerberus was in place—all three parts of it—when the meadow started shaking.

Had they been border collies, they would have been limited by their biological bodies. Border collies could only run so fast. Nothing had been written into Cerberus's programming to limit them to a collie's top speed.

As the surface waves hit, Cerberus kept the flock together by running a tight circle around it. They ran fast enough to create the illusion of a fence. A fence that also bared its teeth and snapped at the panicked ewes that tried to break ranks.

Pain yanked Mina from the depths of darkness. The tang of blood filled her mouth. She coughed, igniting a fire in her lungs. She was on the ground, propped onto her right side, up against a boulder. The tree line was fuzzy, like a smudged painting that hadn't been allowed to dry.

She coughed into the soggy ground, spitting mud and blood onto Cistercian ground. The motion made her head spin, so she laid it back down.

TRAPPIST-2 had moved a few degrees from when she'd last looked up at the sky. She wiped at her eyes and came away with bloody fingers. There was a cut on her forehead by the feel of it, right below the hairline. And a knot of pain at the back of her skull. She must've hit her head when she'd fallen.

After a few minutes, she slowly rolled over. With each blink her vision became clear. What had been a smooth hillside was torn up and distorted. Some of the trees had been uprooted; others, merely displaced at odd angles.

Her herd. She needed to get back.

Still shaking, she reached inside her shirt and pulled out her whistle and was about to make the "come to me" sound but changed her mind.

She was alive. The call would bring all the robots and leave the herd unprotected. The earthquake would already have panicked the sheep, and assuming the dogs had kept the ewes together or rounded them up after scattering, calling them would undo all their work.

Robots, damn it. Not dogs.

She needed her tablet.

Pushing herself up to her elbows only made her slightly dizzy. When the spinning stopped, she pushed up to stand but her left knee gave out.

Through her soaked pants, she felt around her knee. It was swollen and off center.

Mina took a deep breath and made little anticipatory puffs. One, two, push. Stars exploded in her vision, accompanied by a curse. A whimper joined them as she pulled the scarf from around her neck and made a tight wrap around her knee.

A few feet away, her crook was sticking out of the ground at an angle. Mina dragged herself uphill, favoring her injured leg.

She grabbed her crook and used it to stand up. The pain made her lower herself back down. Wrapping her fingers around the whistle, she considered calling for help again. Instead, she tucked the whistle back inside her shirt and pushed through the pain to stand.

The stock of her shotgun was a few feet downhill from the boulder that had stopped her slide. She limped toward it, testing the solidity of the ground around her with the end of her crook. Most of the loose topsoil seemed to have been shaken loose by the landslide.

She reached down and grabbed her shotgun. It teetered on the edge of a jagged fissure that had opened up in the ground. The fissure ran along the hillside for as far as she could see. Clouds of white gas were rising from its depths, released by bursting bubbles of mud. Her backpack was down there, half-buried. Not far from it, the carcass of the dead ewe kept it company.

Mina took a deep breath. It sent her lungs into spasms. Gasping, she backed away from the sulfurous gas. She was no geologist, but she did know that there were nastier things that seeped out of the ground than those that smelled of rotten eggs.

Things that burned. Things that killed.

My flock!

Using the crook for balance, she hobbled up the hillside until she was on stable ground, then turned for the creek.

It was filled with sludge, too muddy to risk drinking. She broke open the action of her shotgun, pulled out the shells, and checked both barrels for blockage. Mud had seeped inside it.

She made it to the stream without falling, lowered the shotgun into the running water. Water poured into the action and flowed down the barrels to the muzzles. On the third check, the barrels were clear enough to risk shooting. She reloaded the shells.

She aimed the shotgun upward at an angle and fired a single shot. It wasn't the "come to me" whistle. But maybe, just maybe, it would be interpreted as a call for help.

Thunder boomed in the distance. Cerberus's three heads turned in unison toward the distant sound. There had been no lightning and no clouds in the sky. Cerberus didn't recognize the sound pattern.

It ran the frequencies through its catalog for comparison and found none. The analysis of the anomaly barely taxed Cerberus's workload as it distributed tasks required to resettle the flock among its three components.

Keeping the flock safe was Cerberus's main priority. AdminUser_Borlaug_Normina's absence would be logged every five minutes until the accumulated time exceeded the comparison set. Under similar circumstances, shepherds had been recorded as being absent for as long as 4.16 days.

As night fell, the sheep grazed and drank from the muddy, swollen creek.

By the middle of the second day, the herd had consumed the edible plants in the area and Cerberus made the collective decision to move upland.

Unit_BA-1-T0 lingered at the rear, maintaining a separation that was zero point two percent below the figure considered acceptable as the maximum distance from the flock.

Mina had been following the stream uphill for hours. The water tumbling past her was still choked with mud and debris but had cleared a bit. She'd been sipping steadily from the canteen she'd filled before the quake, but it wouldn't last.

Shifting her weight, she lowered herself onto her right knee. She scooped some water into her hands. No longer crisp and clear it smelled like mineral water, but with a nasty tang to it.

As she lowered her hands the light revealed her reflection. Her hair was matted with blood, her face covered in mud, her chin and cheek bruised.

The light caught the silver of her whistle, making it shine. Her salvation was a breath away.

She let the water slip through her fingers. No fresh water meant she had about three days. And with the darkness falling, she'd better rest up for tomorrow's hike.

Mina moved away from the stream, into the shelter of a downed tree, propped herself up against its trunk, and laid her shotgun across her lap.

At least the sound of Cistercia's insects and birds had returned, and if any of them had been edible, she'd have spent the energy to make a meal of them. It worked both ways, not that it meant a predator wouldn't try to eat her. It, after all, wouldn't know she was inedible.

That night Mina dreamt she was a cavewoman wandering the hillside, foraging for berries. Whimpers rose from a hole dug into the hill. Cautiously she approached. Within, three wolf pups, their eyes still closed, wiggled about in the dirt. She should have run. Their mother could be back at any moment. Instead, she placed them in her basket among the berries and roots she'd found and brought them back into camp to suckle at her breast.

Two-point-zero-eight days had passed since AdminUser_Borlaug_Normina had left the flock.

Unit_BA-1-T0 was standing above the body of a dying ewe.

Obedient to its programming, Unit_BA-1-T0 remained in place until the ewe's temperature fell to ambient or a higher priority task sorted to the top of the queue.

Cerberus noted the time of death and updated the census. This was the fifth ewe to die since the quake. All five had exhibited signs of exhaustion well outside the norm. Based on the similarities Cerberus tagged four other ewes, and five of the lambs, for high-priority monitoring.

It compared the data it had on post-quake die-offs on Earth and concluded that it needed more data before making a decision with a high enough degree of confidence.

If she'd had tears, Mina would've shed them. This was the third ewe she'd found, left behind as the flock had moved upland.

Mina walked past it, ignoring the exhaustion that had seeped into her. She licked parched lips that hadn't touched water for two days. The unceasing ache of her knee screamed at her as the grade increased, drowning out the ache in her arms and hands.

Just one more hill, she lied to herself.

Just one more step.

Unit_BA-2-T0 had been scouting upland along the stream, sampling the water. Alkalinity had reached toxic levels 22.8 hours ago.

Unit_BA-1-T0 and Unit_BA-3-T0 were working in unison to keep the sheep away from the contaminated stream.

Cerberus was constantly reassessing its decision based on the behavior of the sheep. Two more had died; its calculations had predicted that three would. As it factored in the other vital signs from the ewes and their lambs, its calculation yielded an indeterminate result. The flock would die without water. The flock would die with water. The death rate with water slightly exceeded the number without. For now.

Unit_BA-2-T0 stopped to take another water sample. Then another. Increased alkalinity in both cases. It wasn't until the fifty-fourth sample that it registered a minute decrease. By the hundred and third, the decrease was significant.

It followed the gradient of decreasing alkalinity to where the stream joined with one of the creeks that fed it. Unit_BA-2-T0 confirmed that the creek had acceptable levels of alkalinity. It also verified that continuing along the previously planned route would lead to increased levels of toxicity.

Unit_BA-2-T0 sprinted within communications range and tight-beamed its findings to its cohorts.

Cerberus re-ran its calculations. The route along the smaller feeder creek showed that the Terran vegetation hadn't taken as well as along their original route.

Cerberus sent Unit_BA-2-T0 to make an updated inventory of the edible vegetation. Since its algorithm kept returning an indeterminate result, it needed an overriding factor to deviate from its current state.

That factor came in the form of the "come to me" call. Freezing all three of its units mid-stride, Cerberus triangulated the call's source.

Somewhere within Cerberus's operating system, there was a high-priority command to find the source of the sound. It conflicted with its primary mission to keep as many of the ewes and lambs alive as possible.

The call meant that AdminUser_Borlaug_Normina was alive, status unknown. Cerberus released its hold on its three components and initiated their autonomous decision-making subroutines.

Unit_BA-1-T0 decided that determining AdminUser_Borlaug_Normina's status was a higher mission priority. It headed downstream to locate her.

Unit_BA-3-T0 ran its own calculations and reached a different conclusion. The flock was the primary mission. AdminUser_Borlaug_Normina was just one individual and her survival was slightly less significant to the Antonia colony than the survival of the sheep. It drove the reluctant flock toward the source of uncontaminated water, snapping its jaws and projecting barking and growling sounds at increased volume.

Unit_BA-2-T0 reached its own decision an instant later. Scouting an alternate route with uncontaminated water and adequate edible vegetation was the higher priority.

Mina pushed herself up from the ground where she'd fallen. Was this the third or the fifth time she'd lost her struggle with dizziness?

She was lost. It had probably happened late yesterday. Or maybe earlier today. She couldn't be sure. She'd lost count of TRAPPIST-2's rising and setting. When she'd run across the carcass of the same lamb—the one with the unusual marking on its ear—she'd known she was wandering in circles.

She dared not stand. Sitting was hard enough. Closing her eyes, she slowed her breathing.

Mina pulled the whistle in past cracked lips and made the "come to me" call one more time. It stuck to her dry tongue. She pulled it out with a whimper.

Would her father be ashamed of her selfishness? Or would he be relieved that his daughter had lived? Would her fellow colonists condemn her as they faced further rationing? What about when they faced starvation? Would she even be able to face them?

She wasn't sure how long she sat there, but the *thunk-thunk-thunk* of robotic paws gave her the strength to bolt upward. Using the crook for balance, she limped toward the sound.

One bolted out of the trees, moving faster than she'd ever seen a dog move. It skidded to a stop a few feet in front of her, its composite claws digging deep furrows in the soil.

She fell to her knees and placed her arms around it. "You're real."

One nuzzled into her neck, pushing a bit of its weight into her, very much like an Anatolian would have.

It wasn't supposed to do that, yet she was so glad that it did. She tightened her grip and dry-sobbed for a few minutes.

Then she wiped her hand across her face and, using the crook for balance, stood up.

"Take me to the flock," she said.

One swiveled its head uphill and took a few steps before returning to her side.

"Good boy." There was no way she could keep up with One at a run. But if the flock wasn't too far away, she could make it.

All she needed was a little bit of luck.

That bit of luck came in the form of rain as TRAPPIST-2 touched the horizon. She stopped, despite One's nudging, and gathered up nearby rocks to place in a circle. Then she spread her coat atop them so its waterproof liner could catch the rainwater.

One circled her, without nudging this time, then sat down beside her, front legs crossed just like a dog's.

It brought a smile to her lips. It was a small thing, that canine mannerism, but in that moment, it brought her not just joy but a sense of companionship. Screw the rules. Rules were for the laboratory.

Woman did not survive by air or water or food alone. She never had. And she never would.

Mina dipped greedy, dirty hands into the small pool and brought them to her lips. The rain soaked her to the skin, but she didn't care.

Their luck held. It rained hard and long enough for her to top off her canteen *and* drink her fill. Clarity returned.

She slipped the coat back on and said, "Let's go."

One stood up and stretched, then shook itself. Mina laughed out loud. When she found out who had hacked Cerberus's behavioral program, she was going to kiss him or her.

Cerberus logged the time, date, and location when Unit_BA-1-T0 and AdminUser_Borlaug_Normina returned. It sent a stream of data to her tablet but received no confirming ping. It also synced up with Unit_BA-1-T0 and received its logs since it had departed.

Unit_BA-1-T0 refused to shut down its autonomous decision-making subroutines. Cerberus made 549 attempts to override Unit_BA-1-T0 before its programming told it to yield control to AdminUser_Borlaug_Normina.

If Cerberus had been human, it would have been seething with frustration. Without AdminUser_Borlaug_Normina's tablet there was no way to tell her that Unit_BA-1-T0 was malfunctioning. And no way to make a report.

Instead, Cerberus waited for her to give them an order.

Mina walked among her flock, counting her sheep as she stuffed herself with fruit, slurping it directly from the can.

Forty-eight sheep, more or less. They were milling about, somewhat lethargically, but she was pretty sure she wasn't off by too much.

Now that she'd eaten, more than anything she needed sleep, because if she couldn't even manage counting . . .

Three backed out of reach as she loosened the straps that held her tent to its back.

One placed itself between Mina and Three and then rounded her as if she were a ewe.

Mina shook her head. They'd been programmed to understand basic speech, things that would make herding easier. She wasn't about to explain herself.

Or maybe she was. Maybe that glitch that made One so doglike went beyond mimicking body language.

"I need to sleep."

Three trotted away with her sleeping bag, her change of clothes, and the rest of her food. She followed it, anger surfacing alongside exhaustion.

One head-butted her, prodding her to go faster. He even whined at her. She'd heard that whine before, although not from Cerberus. It had the same length, tone, and pitch as a dog that was desperately trying to make itself understood.

"Show me," she said, half-expecting to get no reaction at all.

One circled behind her and nudged her uphill. She slipped and would have fallen had One not been in just the right place.

Shaking her head in disbelief, she kept moving. The stream they were supposed to be following wasn't where she thought it would be. As she climbed, the vegetation changed; there was far more Cistercian vegetation here than there should have been.

"We're off course."

One trotted out in front of her and then came back to helpfully nudge her once again.

In the gathering dusk, she could make out her flock, lined up along the edge of a creek, drinking.

Realization hit her like a slap across the face. She'd been so caught up in her own dehydration, her own hunger, that she hadn't thought about what the sheep had been drinking.

She pushed the ewes aside and knelt in the creek. Unlike the stream, it was clear and there was no mineral tang to it. She scooped up a handful of water and sipped, then sat back. Tears built up and she wiped them away before they could run down her cheeks.

One waited with an expectant posture; head tilted. The look wasn't perfect. One's ears hadn't been built to articulate enough.

"You did good," she choked out, her face twisting with a mixture of relief and shame.

Twenty-five years later . . .

"Good morning, Mina," I said as I entered the robotics lab.

Mina had her hands in her pockets. I could tell she was seething with excitement by the way she rocked back and forth on her heels.

"Good morning, Dr. Wallace," she said.

"Call me Alysster." I'd lost count of the number of times I'd asked her to call me by my given name, but she was a stubborn woman. Not a criticism, by the way. Even today, with Antonia so much better off than it was when we first landed, the stubborn survived.

"Yes, Dr. Wallace."

See. Stubborn.

"How are your dogs?"

Antonia now boasted about a dozen dogs and Mina had raised and trained them all. Frankly, I don't see how the woman does it. Between the dogs and the sheep, she must be in charge of a couple hundred animals, and we took Cerberus away from her as soon as we fixed the problem with the dogs' food supply.

"They're doing very well, thank you." She scratched her head and shrugged in a sheepish sort of way. "Today is the day you said I could—"

"Yes, yes," I said. "And I keep my promises."

She cleared her throat as if to prompt me. There was a side of me that was tempted to make her wait, but I'm not one to hold grudges. She'd done all the things she'd promised not to do, but she'd also saved Antonia, even though she refused to take credit for it.

"Have you thought of a name for him?" I asked as I pulled on my lab coat.

"In my head, I've been calling him Balto for years," she said.

I pressed my hand against the lock plate and the door whisked open.

"Balto. Of course. Nice," I said as the lights came on.

Atop the table in the middle of my lab, I'd rebuilt Cerberus Unit One. I'd never been able to figure out what in its programming had made it act the way it did, but I'd saved and isolated the artificial intelligence.

Unit_BA-1-T0 had been without a physical body since we'd decommissioned Cerberus. The components had been needed for other projects. I'd reprogrammed and recycled the AIs from Two and Three. I'd even recovered the higher-level AI that governed Cerberus.

But One was too much of an anomaly. One worthy of study. I had kept a copy, of course. No need for Mina Borlaug to know that. She'd never understand.

Guilt was only part of the reason I'd agreed to give One back to her and scrounge up enough spare parts to give it a body. The other part was gratitude.

My colleagues had asked why I bothered. I had rebuilt One on my own time, out of my own resources or those donated by my fellow colonists. Strange, isn't it? Even with real dogs doing their part now, we all felt this connection to something not really alive, all because by saving one of us, it saved all of us.

"What's the first thing you're doing to do with him?" I asked. I almost tripped on that last word, but I knew how much it meant to her.

Her eyes glistened with moisture.

"I'm going to take him to the puppies and see if he'll join us in a puppy pile." Her voice was shaking enough now that I knew tears were imminent.

I nodded and tapped the activation code into my tablet.

Balto opened his eyes and leapt off the table, taking Mina down to the floor, nuzzling into her neck and making happy dog sounds. She cried and laughed, her face lighting up in the same way I had seen it light when a puppy was born or when one of her dogs did something amazing.

I told you we would save the dogs. And I kept my promise in more ways than I had expected. But when I made that promise I didn't know all the ways *they* were going to save *us*.

Sheepdogs

Mission planners argued over which of the preserved terrestrial species would be established first as part of the terraforming of TRAPPIST-2c. It was expected that *Prometheus* would have twenty years to prepare fields for crops and scout ranges for cows, sheep and goats, allowing food production to commence immediately. The loss of *Prometheus* and *Whale* meant that the colonists would have to decide how best to start the task of adapting Earth life to Cistercia. While the farmers and ranchers argued, psychologists pointed out that the logical first species should be dogs. Mankind had gone to the stars; naturally, Mankind's oldest ally should be the first to join them. When an unknown disease devastated the canine population, roboticists came up with a solution, but it was uncertain whether the Cerberus automata would be an actual replacement. On the other hand, Humans will adopt anything as a pet...

—Encyclopedia Astra,
Gannon University,
Antonia, Cistercia, AA212

ALAS ROANOKE

Sarah A. Hoyt

The boy was maybe fourteen, scrubby, with pale hair that stuck up in all directions. He looked like he had just gone through a growth spurt, his hands and feet too big for his still-skinny frame. He wore a work outfit, a one-piece coveralls. It was in fashion with quite well-to-do boys who wore it for exercise and play. You've seen the sort: you pull it up from the feet, and it has some kind of woven-in temperature control. This one was short sleeved, and showed pale, freckled arms with quite a lot of scratches and bony elbows.

His name was José Beck, but he told me from the beginning, "Just call me Joe. Everybody does." And he was on the verge of tears. "You've got to believe me," he said, his gray eyes anxiously scanning my face as though he wanted to read my thoughts. "Court just disappeared. Down in the caves. Poof. He vanished into thin air, like the first colony. Like New Virginia. Vanished without a trace."

"Court?" I asked.

"Courtney. Courtney Beulen. He's my . . . he's my best friend."

While he talked, I edged over to my link, sitting on my battered desk which was probably a relic from colonial days. Before the kid had erupted into the police station, I'd been, truth be told, looking up knitting patterns. I hadn't finished a knitting project since Malthe and Harry had died, but I kept trying to do it. Starting things, and then forgetting them around the house—a ball of wool, and two needles with four or five rows hanging from them like a frill.

I had a way of forgetting them, then finding them again and being surprised I'd started the project and stopped it. These remains of my forgetfulness, my inability to resume normal life, dotted the too-big house. It wasn't like there was anyone else to disturb them.

Now I flipped angrily—angry at myself—away from the knitting chart and ran a search on Joe's name in the records. Nothing came up beyond the normal birth and schooling records. He was the oldest son of Marvin Beck and his wife, Candida. There were three younger sons and two daughters. A normal farm family.

Joe had done well in school, was a leader in Future Farmers of Roanoke and generally a son anyone would be proud of.

This confirmed what I'd already thought. He wasn't here with this wild story to cover up something he'd done to his friend, Courtney Beulen.

I looked up Courtney too. Another well-adjusted farmer's son, another member of Future Farmers of Roanoke.

I'd thought this wasn't a murder or even a beating based on the way that Joe looked. His arms were scratched, but it was the kind of scratches you get if you're an active teen. There were no abrasions anywhere on his person, no sign that he'd been in a fight or attacked someone. If his record showed any kind of disturbance, I might buy premeditation and perhaps stunning Courtney so he wouldn't fight back. But with Joe's lack of antecedents? Not likely. If he murdered anyone it would be either in a fit of passion or in self-defense. And if he had done either, there would be marks on him. All the same, it was worth checking.

Look, we had almost no crime in Roanoke. We were now— perhaps—a town. I didn't remember the last head count, but we were maybe four thousand people. However, we weren't concentrated. Most people lived and worked on farms in the countryside, a majority of them still hydroponic. But we're starting to get some fertile farms, and people had quickened some of the smaller animals—chickens and goats and the like. Once there were many real farms going, with actual fields of pastorage, the cow embryos that had been waiting patiently for fifty years to be reintroduced would be quickened. Probably. Until then cows remained something mythical from before the plague to us Roanoke-born. Something we read about in books, but which wasn't quite real.

The fact was that most families lived too far away and minded their business too well for us to need a regular police force.

Which was why after I found myself suddenly widowed and childless, I'd been recruited as police chief. I had six part-time officers at my disposal, with two on duty at any time. But I was the only full-time one and the coordinator. Because, you see, we'd had exactly one murder in the last thirty years, and the investigation wasn't exactly hard. The murderer was the woman standing over the stabbed man, screaming, "That will teach you to cheat!"

Most of what we did was break up domestic quarrels and curb the vandalism or acting up of wayward teenagers. Oh, and we took Hal the local drunkard home, after tossing a bucket of water over him and pouring several cups of coffee down his throat. That was a weekly task.

This was why I was perfect for the job. Which was nothing like it would have been in any city on Earth, at least from what we read in the records. And nothing like in Antonia, even.

Still, teens were teens and they got upset and emotional and aggressive. In this new world we settled, people remained jumped-up savannah apes, likely to strike out over a domestic dispute, a field that wasn't marked correctly, and most of all a girl—or boy—two or more other people had a romantic interest in.

Joe was looking at me with wide and panicked eyes. "It's all right," I said. "I believe you." Which was almost, kind of true. I was trying to sound maternal. Did I remember how to sound maternal? Harry had been about this boy's age when—

I pushed it to the back of my mind. I also pushed a button on my screen that called Michael Judd. He was the only officer currently on duty in the building.

Anna Martilova, the other one on duty, a perky twenty-five-year-old mother of three, had gone to one of the outlying farms to help them track down a missing dog.

Dogs—some of whose embryos had been quickened only in the last twenty years, on the assumption they'd help herd the goats—were scarce enough that people tended to steal them. Also, honestly, most people didn't know how to train them, and the creatures ended up wandering all over, bothering other people's goats, and in general being—in my opinion—more trouble than they were worth.

Malthe had wanted a puppy.

I shut that down, fast.

Mike showed up almost immediately. He'd probably been

playing one of his ubiquitous games of Embercore on his link in the back room.

"Need anything, Chief?"

In everyday life, he was a welder, and worked on the hydroponics of nearby farmers. A big, dark-haired man with—if the holos from Earth didn't lie—Irish features, and a sprinkling of freckles on very pale skin, he had an easy smile and had a way of making friends of everyone.

"Can you take Joe's deposition here?" I asked. "I have to finish something."

Mike didn't say, "But we had nothing to work on all night." He didn't even raise his eyebrows at me. I had, in fact, trained him, the only one of the officers I'd trained. He was Malthe's age. He'd been married, but Myra had been on the trip with Malthe and Harry. She and Jean, their kid, had been lost. Now, Mike lived alone at the edge of town, drove all over for his job, and worked at the police on his nominal days off. He probably disliked his empty cabin as much as I dreaded mine.

Malthe had thought well of him, which had weighed with me when I'd accepted him for the force. But he had, at first, been a trial to train. Garrulous and frank, he'd tended to say exactly the wrong thing at the wrong time and get us into a world of trouble by showing our hand to the—ah—clients at the station.

Again, most of our work didn't require refined investigation. But it benefited from keeping one part of domestic disputes in the dark, often.

By now, three years in, he gave no hint that I might be using misdirection as he grinned and said, "Sure, Chief." And then to Joe, "Hey, bud, want a cookie? Do you drink coffee?"

I left Mike to it and headed out of the room, closing the door behind me and taking my link.

I looked through, found the Beulen family code and dialed. I needed to know if this had any basis in reality, or if Court was home and Joe had dreamed the whole thing. Or, in fact, if Court had played a prank on Joe, and headed home.

I wasn't sure what "Court disappeared" meant, much less "into thin air." It could be anything, from the kid not being where Joe expected to—who knew? So first I'd eliminate the obvious.

The call buzzed for a while, giving the impression that there was no one near the family link. Which was possible, since they were farmers at the edge of town. A lot of these had only one link for the whole place. Usually it was carried around by someone, but not always. I was about to give up when a voice answered, "Hello?" No vision, but that too was no surprise. Private citizens rarely open themselves to video unless they know the person calling very well indeed.

"Ms. Beulen?"

Giggle. "Nah. I'm Maryanne."

I made a guess. "Maryanne Beulen?"

"Yeah."

I hadn't read all of the family names, but the voice· was very young. "May I speak to one of your parents?"

A moment of hesitation, and then a scream: "Dad, it's for you!" And at something mumbled from the other side, said, "Please, Dad wants to know who you are?"

I revised my estimate of her age downward five years to around twelve. "I'm Georgine Ellis, police chief of Roanoke."

Moments later, a rough voice answered, "Ms. Ellis? Is anything wrong?"

"I hope not." I kept my voice cool and professional. "May I inquire if your son Courtney is home?"

"Courtney? No. He was at a Young Farmers thing. Volunteer nonsense. Something about forming our future leaders. I suppose it keeps them from going stir crazy before they settle down. Is there a problem? Did he have an accident?"

"No, no. Nothing like that." It was too early to alarm anyone. Again, what Joe had said could mean almost anything, and heck, teens were unreliable. "We just had a report that he was out by the caves, and since it's getting dark . . ."

The voice relaxed. "Oh, that. He and his friend Joe are often out there by the caves. They call it archeology. Always poking and looking around there for stuff from the New Virginia time. Never find anything, of course. If you see him, send him home. Goats need milking."

And with that he cut the connection.

Well, that was that. Court wasn't home. The question now

became, where was he? And was he in any kind of distress? Or being a goofball?

Knowing how these things worked out, I'd plump for goofball and—possibly—playing with someone's dog or courting someone's daughter. Because teen boys had very few diversions and the more enterprising ones often came up with creative hooliganism.

But when I walked back into the front room, I saw Mike looked alarmed.

He was sitting at my desk, leaning forward. And Joe was wiping his eyes with the back of his hand, pretending he wasn't wiping away tears. There was a sheen of sweat on the kid's forehead. He looked distressed. The cup of hot chocolate and the cookie lay untouched on the desk, which for a teen meant something was seriously wrong.

Mike kind of looked over his shoulder, got up, and stepped aside. "You have to hear this, Chief," he said. He was obviously trying hard to look impassive, but his eyes were just a little too wide, and he looked like he was more than a little alarmed.

I sat at the desk, and looked back at the distraught boy, "Okay, Joe. What did you say happened? He just disappeared into thin air?"

The kid nodded. In the background, Mike edged to the side of the room, and started up the coffeemaker. The smell of it suffused the air, mingling with cookie and hot chocolate.

"Have your hot chocolate," I said. "Before it grows cold." I waited till Joe had a sip of it, but he put it back down almost immediately. It was weird for a kid to treat chocolate that way, when it was a treat that depended on the molecular replicator in Antonia and therefore was in short supply. We only got it to calm suspects and bribe witnesses.

That untouched cookie was a strange thing too. Most farm families lived way too close to the bone to waste good food on mere treats outside Landing Day and Founder's Feast. Most kids around here, and particularly most growing teens, were starved for calories and loved anything with sugar.

"Where were you again?"

"Down by the caves. You know the ones with the pit?"

The pit was a crevice in one of the caves. We'd tried to sound it, or rather our great-great-grandparents had, but had been unable to tell how deep it went. The best estimate was "a few miles." It played a dark part in the history of the colony, and kids were warned away from it. Most didn't obey. But weirdly, we'd never lost a kid to it. They'd just go and stare at its depths and emerge all convinced they'd passed some kind of test. I'd done it myself as a kid. "Do you mean Court fell in the pit?" I asked, half rising.

"No, no. The caves with the pit, but we weren't by the pit," he said. "We were in the runes corridor."

The runes corridor was a place with markings that weren't really runes, just weird symbols whose meaning we'd never understood. One of the many reminders we had that the first colony had disappeared. I'd heard something about the runes being math by Martino Calligaris, one of the scientists in the vanished New Virginia, but I hadn't pursued it. Why do math on the walls, anyway? The kids thought it was all mystical and it held great fascination for them, but it was harmless. "And Court disappeared?" I asked. "What do you mean disappeared?"

Joe sniffled. He looked like he was trying hard not to cry and shook his head. "Just disappeared. Poof."

Right, the kid was either hallucinating or something was very weird here.

Mike handed me a cup of coffee. I took a sip from it, then said, "Tell me what happened. From the beginning."

"It's like this," Joe said. "Court and . . . Court and I have been friends forever. Our . . . our farms are next door to each other, and he and I and our brothers and sisters used to play at whichever house."

I nodded. So far, so good. Farmers often did that, so Mom and Dad had some free time. It was a joke in the colony that people had left Earth with thousands of frozen human embryos and bio wombs "so women won't be enslaved to having children." But it had never occurred to any of them that humans needed more attention than just gestation. Which was why, though the first few generations had tried to raise one or two "icicle kids"—as they were called—per household, thousands of embryos remained frozen and stored. Proving farms was hard work. Turning the sterile soil of Cistercia into rich farmland was hard work for several generations. And the more children around your ankles, the harder it got.

Malthe and I had thought to get an icicle kid or two, since I hadn't had any since Harry, but it had never happened. And now it wouldn't be fair to the kid, to have only one parent who couldn't even finish a knitting project.

"So, when Court and I got older, and we read about the disappearance of New Virginia, we thought we'd be the ones to solve the mystery. When we were really small, we used to dig all over the caves, trying to find something. Kid stuff," Joe said.

I judged by that that it had been maybe two or three years ago. "And?"

He shrugged. "We let it go, you know, when we got to the professional formation stuff, two years ago, but we always wondered what had happened."

I nodded again. The disappearance of New Virginia was one of the mysteries of Cistercia and would probably remain so. Even if we had a couple of perfectly reasonable explanations.

"But we're doing a project for the Future Farmers. You know, our graduating project."

"Sure."

"And we were asked to look over the things for the museum. You know, the Landing Museum?"

I knew the Landing Museum. It was a little bubble building on the edge of town. Not extremely interesting. Just a vast room, with things in glass cases. The uniform the landing captain had worn. Boots worn by Sonny Strongbow. The gadget used to communicate with the mother ship. The first cookie baked on New Virginia.

Okay, I might have made up that thing about the cookie, or maybe the boots, but it was at about that level.

I'd been marched through the exhibits in primary education, and then in professional training, and I can't say any of it was riveting. About the most interesting thing for me was a knit wedding dress which had been made by Daria Damaris, one of our first colony leaders. But only because I liked to knit.

The truth is that we were too young a colony, our past too recent, for any old artifacts to hold mystery.

Joe knuckled his eyes. "You see, not everything that's given to the museum is on display. A lot of it is in boxes in the back."

I nodded. Yeah, I'd seen this in action. Someone died and their children and grandchildren looked at the mess of personal effects

left behind and then someone's face lit up and they said, "We'll give
to the Landing."

Rubbish, most of it. I wondered what they thought that the
museum would do with great-grandfather's sonic tooth polisher.

"Well, we got to looking at this really old box. It was labeled *New
Virginia*," Joe said. "And we thought . . . we thought, you know, this
weird little square thing in it might be an activator. So, we took it.
And Court said, let's go to the caves and try it out. And so we did.
And then he vanished into thin air." He sat there, staring at me, wide
eyed, rocking forward and backward very slightly. "Mr. Beulen is
going to kill me. He's going to have my hide."

Obviously, this wasn't the whole story.

Why is it that in situations requiring urgency, humans tend to
take their time and obfuscate as much as possible?

Malthe used to say there was nothing as perversely stubborn as a
teenager. Mostly, he'd been referring to Harry. I'd thought he was
joking, but the one thing my job had taught me was that he'd
understated it.

We asked Joe why the caves, and what the gadget was they'd taken,
and warmed his hot chocolate, and dragged the story out of him.
He'd still not taken more than a few sips of the chocolate, and nibbled
at the cookie, but a couple of hours later, as he blushed dark, like
someone confessing to a dark secret, he said, "Okay, see, we've been
reading Abatangelo."

"Oh, damn," Mike said, from where he stood, leaning against the
wall beside my desk.

"Who or what is Abatangelo?" I asked.

"*Spaceship of the Gods*," Mike said. "*Mysteries of Cistercia. There
Were Giants Before Us.*"

It sounded to me like he was having a stroke and saying nonsense
sentences. I looked at him to try to determine how he'd taken leave
of his senses. He gave me a half grimace. "Come on, boss. You've
heard of Abatangelo. We're about the same age. His books were big
hits when we were about Joe's age. He writes stuff on how half the
colonists came on a different spaceship, from the lost colony of
Atlantis. And how there used to be a giant race on Cistercia and—"

"But he's a nutcase!" I said. "That's why he uses a pen name!"

Mike grinned. "You have no romance in your soul," he said. "You never read that stuff when you were a teen, did you? If you had, you'd know why he sells. Our kids are raised in scientific environments, with everything explained, and all the history known. There's no mystery, nothing to explore—" He must have seen my face cloud, because he shook his head slightly, as though apologizing for his faux pas, and said, "No, I mean nothing to explore in the realm of ideas. No great mythology or big conspiracy to feed on. Abatangelo gives them something to dream on until they are old enough to marry and settle down and have kids, when they usually get over it. I spent about five years looking all over for signs of the lost spaceship that"—he dropped his voice to a conspiratorial whisper—"came from Atlantis."

I clicked my tongue. "Nonsense."

"It's not," Joe said. It was the most emphatic thing he'd said since his initial announcement that Court was missing. "It's not. It's just that Abatangelo has been shut out by conventional colony historians, because they're afraid the truth of his discoveries will cause panic."

I opened my mouth to wither that nice piece of nonsense, because why should the idea that there was another world with humans cause panic, even? But before I could, Mike had got his hand on my shoulder, and squeezed. I took his point. Which was funny, as I was the one who had taught him not to show everything we knew to the suspects. "All right," I finally managed. "But what does Abatangelo and his . . . ah, discoveries, have to do with this?"

"You see . . . You see . . . He wrote *Doors to Other Worlds* about how the colonists from New Virginia didn't die, they crossed a gate to another world, an interdimensional portal built by Martino Calligaris. They were tired of the hydroponics, and they'd lost their crop to a fungus, and—"

I want a medal. I didn't beat my head against the desk rhythmically. I also didn't say *Oh, that bag of moonshine*. I just thought it. Probably too loudly. Mike squeezed my shoulder again.

"So?" I said.

Joe had been braced to be told it was all nonsense. You could tell by how surprised he looked when I didn't. "So . . ." He cleared his throat. "We were talking about it, while we were going through the boxes. Most of the boxes are from, like, yesterday, and stupid. Like the Joansens donated all of their grandad's stuff when he died. Why should we care about his address book? So, we just left all that alone."

"Good move. Maybe it will be valuable in a hundred years or so."

"Maybe?" Joe said, but you could tell his heart wasn't in it. "Anyway, we were supposed to be helping and classifying things," he said. "So we went to the older boxes, and there was one marked *New Virginia*. We thought it would be interesting."

"And it was?"

He shrugged. "Most of it was stuff like the Joansens. Bookmarks and buttons and combs and stupid stuff like that. It looked like someone went and threw stuff they didn't find interesting in a box because they didn't know what to do with it. But there was this thing..."

"The 'activator' thing?"

Joe nodded. "Like, this size." He held his thumb and forefinger two inches apart. "Square. Black plastic." He shrugged. "Looked like a remote, but we couldn't figure out how to make it work."

"I see. And then?"

"And then Court said, what if it was the activator."

I blinked at him. Again, Mike's hand squeezed my shoulder. "Do you mean the activator for the star gate that Abatangelo says Calligaris built?" he asked. "Why do you think it needed an activator?"

"Well, if it didn't," Joe said, all sweet reason, "then why hasn't the gate been activated since everyone in New Virginia disappeared?"

Right. Made perfect sense in the logic of childhood. Or worse, the logic of adolescence. "So, what did you do?" I asked.

"Well, Court put it in his pocket, and we walked into the cave. And he said to hold his shoulder, because he said we had to be touching to go together."

Okay...that also made perfect adolescent sense. Even if no rational sense. But sympathetic magic seems to come built-in in the minds of kids.

"What happened?"

"He..." There were tears again all of a sudden. Seemingly surprised by them, Joe tried to pretend they weren't happening, or that he couldn't feel them, or something. "He tripped and fell forward. Across the gate. And I let go. And he just...disappeared. Poof."

I looked at Mike. He looked at me.

I'd been the police chief of this town almost a decade. I'd been doing this tedious job since a year after the accident on the "family exploration trip." It was supposed to be a fun excursion, with one of two long-distance transport "buses" Roanoke had managed to acquire from Antonia. The vehicle had run off the track and down a ravine, killing all aboard, among them my husband, Malthe, and my ten-year-old son, Harry. I hadn't gone because I'd had the flu.

I'd become police chief as soon as I could manage it. And one of the things I'd seen plenty of was teen pranks. It wouldn't be out of the question. In fact, it would be absolutely standard if Court were waiting at the caves, ready to come screaming out of a dark recess at me and see if he could startle me into a run.

Look, Roanoke was a quiet farmer community. If you were too old to hang out at the playground and too young to hang out at the tavern with the men, you had to make your own fun.

All of that passed between Mike and me in that one look. All of it. And then he said, "Okay, Joe, let me take you home. And then we'll see what we'll do."

What we did in the end was collect all of the police force available: two more of the men, that is. And the four of us went out to the caves.

The caves, thus called for being the only such geological feature around Roanoke, were right at the edge of town. They'd been the site of the original settlement of New Virginia and I believe it was thought they might serve as additional shelter should a solar flare or even an unusual storm rip the original structures to shreds.

When Roanoke had been settled it had been self-consciously away from those ill-fated buildings and that entire area. Just in case whatever had caused them to disappear without a trace was there.

But over a hundred plus years, the town had grown, so that now the caves didn't stand more than a couple of miles by lectrowagon from the edge of town. The track wound around and past a hill, and then into the middle of a wheat field. A family had taken over the buildings and the land that had once been the place of first settlement. Most of the buildings were now barns, and—this being one of the earliest improved lands—the family was making a go of vast wheat fields. For someone like me, who grew up on the idea that farms were tanks of water in which you grew vegetables, seeing all that food waving in the wind was strange.

It was almost harvest time—another concept that was slowly reentering the minds of the people in Cistercia—and the wheat was high, golden and rustling. The lectrowagon—Mike's—was an awkward contraption, too high in the axle, with massive wheels— one of the candidates for the bus accident that had killed my family was that a tire had blown, though honestly, the wreckage was too confused for us to be sure. But the lectrowagon was stable and its tires impenetrable. Mike and I sat in the two seats up front—he drove, because his night vision was better—and Paul and Tiede sat in the back, in the bed of the wagon, holding on to the roll bar to stop from dropping out when we hit big bumps.

Mike always apologized for the big bumps, but none of the rest of us spoke. We'd given the guys the whole version of the story we'd been told and Tiede had said, "It will be a prank of some sort."

"Sure," I'd said. "So be careful not to look scared no matter what." But I suspected I was already looking scared, just driving through the middle of the wheat field.

The caves were at the southern edge of the field, opposite the town.

The wheat stopped quite suddenly and there was a rocky slope. The whole field had been a rocky expanse, but the first settlers had used machinery brought from Earth to grind the rocks into very fine, sandy soil. Which they had then improved by various chemical means including, yes, compost.

The stone-chewing machinery had stopped short of a very rocky, climbing slope. Whitish gray stone. It peaked up into a hillock, on the side of which there was an opening, a dark oval, which seemed to me to whisper as much as the wheat. And I knew I was being an idiot.

We'd brought really potent lights, and the guys went ahead, shining them.

Before delivering Joe to his parents, Mike had got him to draw a map, so we knew exactly where Court might have gone. Though, frankly, the rune corridor was the only one, a place of mystery and enchantment, in the sense that it can be a dark enchantment and kids were fascinated with it.

The entrance to the caves opened into a vast chamber from which tunnels ran right to left, about ten of them. The one on the left-most side went deep into a rocky mountain to the west, and eventually stopped abruptly at the chasm that no one had been able to plumb. There were two more. The next one was the rune corridor.

The floor of the cave was very fine sand, though maneuvering around stalactites and stalagmites would have been impossible in the dark. Fortunately, we weren't in the dark, but the guys held the largest lights the department owned.

We went in calling, "Court, Court! We know you're here."

The floor of the rune tunnel looked smoother than I expected, perhaps because the school was back in session and the summer ritual of showing your girlfriend the rune tunnel and talking about what terrible thing might have happened there and what the symbols might mean was at an end until next year. The floor sand looked more or less undisturbed. Not smooth. No one had run a rake through it . . . in my lifetime, I think.

But there is a point at which a lot of footsteps blend into a kind of regular somewhat bumpy surface. Except for the most recent footsteps, both from large boys or men, wearing work boots.

Two tracks went out, one behind the other. Near the end there was a scuffed place on the ground, as if one of them had fallen over. And then there was one track coming back, the look of the prints making one think of a frenzied run.

We shone our light on it a long time. The thing is, you see, that the tunnel ended in a low aperture at ground level. Just enough for someone to squeeze into if the someone weren't massive. A fourteen- to fifteen-year-old boy or a woman could manage it. There was a space beyond that opening, not much of a cave, but a chamber, shall we say? Going in there every so often and reminding teens of the consequences of illicit sex was one of the duties of the female police—because we could fit—though, honestly, we rarely bothered with it. As I said, this was a farming community. Mostly the unwelcome results of illicit sexual activity were properly welcomed as soon as the parents got married. Or they were quietly adopted by someone else, often the parents of one of the culprits. After all, we had a colony to grow.

"There is no way any of us can fit in there!" Mike said, looking at the opening and then over at Tiede and Paul.

"Yeah, I know," I said. I fished the headlamp from my pocket. "I'll go in, but I swear if the idiot is hiding there, I'm going to give him the spanking of his lifetime. And I don't care if he's someone else's kid, and likely twice my weight."

Paul smiled and Mike said, "No one will blame you, boss."

My heart hammering—not because I was scared, but because I anticipated a scream and raucous laughter any second—I walked as close to the wall as I could so as not to disturb the footprints, just in case. Then I lay down flat—and that was the bad part, it's difficult to expect to be yelled at when you're crawling flat into the unknown— and went into the opening headfirst.

My head and shoulders were enough to tell me the kid wouldn't be there. The sand again wasn't undisturbed, but it wasn't disturbed in the peculiar way that would indicate recent activity. And no one yelled.

I still pulled myself all the way in and looked around. Nope. No one here. I crawled back out and walked down the tunnel again, as close to the wall as possible, doing my best to avoid disturbing footprints in the tunnel.

Going back, I looked at the walls too. I mean, I didn't believe Joe had murdered Court, but what if he had?

But the walls showed no signs of blood, the sand showed no signs of struggle. There, at the end, it looked rather like someone had fallen, headlong, into the sand. Like someone who was following someone else, and lost his grip, and then fell when his friend disappeared.

"Nothing?" Mike asked.

I shook my head. "Nothing."

"Um . . . we're going to have to do a full search."

We did a full search. We combed the cave for hours. Up and down and to the edge of the pit, from which cold always seemed to exude. I was looking down into the unfathomable darkness when Mike came level with me, put his hand on my shoulder. "He could be down there," he said.

"If he is, we'll never find him," I said. I rubbed my face with my hands. I felt as if it had grown numb from the cold and lack of sleep. "And maybe this is all a prank. Maybe he is by now asleep in his bed."

Mike shook his head. "I don't think so. Joe was crying. A boy like that doesn't cry in public just for playacting. He doesn't."

Mike was right. Courtney was not at home and asleep. He wasn't anywhere we could find.

For two weeks we looked all over. Groups of people formed to comb the surrounding countryside. Volunteers came from Antonia to help look. They flew over the wheat field, and crawled through it, and probably ruined the harvest for the farmer.

Every day, every week for months, I expected that an expedition beyond the settled area, a roam into the countryside, would bring news of a corpse, or perhaps just a boy who had run away, tried to hide for some reason. Teens come up with all sorts of strange reasons to disappear, after all, from a sad love affair to a trivial debt they can't pay.

But Courtney Beulen didn't show up.

For months, he was the center of all my activity. Mike cut back on his work time so that together we could coordinate the search for Courtney. We sent his picture over every possible means of transmission to Antonia. Everyone was told to be on the lookout. But no one found him. And it's not like this was Earth and there were a lot of places to hide, and he could disappear in the multitudes.

We talked to everyone who had ever known him, investigated everyone who might have wished him harm, or for that matter wished him well. DNA and fingerprints were sent on transmissions.

But the BOLO produced no results.

We interrogated Joe again and again and again, alone and with his parents, and his parents interrogated him too. All we managed to get was tears, and again and again that he'd seen Courtney just vanish "poof."

That was it.

Months after his disappearance, I found myself hosting Mike for dinner. My lonely house, strewn with started knitting projects, was now too oppressive to spend any time alone in, even when I was exhausted from working extra hours. We'd made it a habit for weeks to have dinner together, now at my house, now at his and discuss the case, and what we'd found.

And that night we were at my house, sitting across from each other at the little table in the kitchen, the table Malthe and I had used before Harry was born. I'd made my synthmeat stew, but the salad had real goat cheese crumbles. And Mike was looking at me with a pensive expression.

"We're going to have to give up, aren't we?" I said.

He started. "Oh, on Courtney Beulen? I'm afraid so. Or at least, unless he's gone into the pit, I have no idea what else can have happened."

"That's what they say happened to New Virginia, the settlement here, you know? They say that there was something that drove people insane, and they all rushed into the cave and jumped into the pit."

Mike sighed.

"You don't believe it?"

He shrugged. "Think about it, Georgi. What could make everyone jump into that pit, one after the other, men, women and children— all of them? There were at least five hundred people, all ages. It's a lot of people. How do you think all of them went to the cave one after the other and threw themselves in the pit? How long do you think that took? How many of them jumped in at one time? How come no one lost courage, no mother tried to save her infant, nothing?"

My turn to sigh. "Well, that is the official explanation," I said. "Because there's no way they could all have disappeared at the same time leaving nothing behind. If that hole in the cave is, as they think, miles deep..."

"Yeah, they could all be in there, but the question is, how did they all get there?" He'd finished eating and looked . . . sad, but certain, in the flickering light of my fire. Outside the cabin the wind howled, and snow flew. The wheat and the rest of the dirt-harvest had been brought in. There had been a party. The Beulens were still in mourning, or perhaps slowly descending into mourning. Which was facilitated by the hard winter that had gripped Roanoke.

It was going to be hard to sleep tonight, after Mike left. The cabin would feel empty and cold.

"This idea of mass suicide holds no water," Mike said. "They were colonists, not cult members. And even cults who commit mass suicide—or at least those from Earth I've read about—end up having one or two people escape."

"I know, I know," I said. "I've been reading all the literature on it."

"Abatangelo?" he asked and raised an eyebrow.

I gave him a smile I knew was sickly. "Well, him too, but the official literature. I've been reading all the officials and historians and their speculation on what happened. And believe it or not they all sound even crazier than Abatangelo. They say that there was something wrong with the first batch of potatoes grown in hydroponics. They say the balance of minerals was wrong, or else there was a fungus and that it made everyone suicidal, so they jumped into the pit. All of them."

"You know, even if they had some kind of harvest festival and served the tainted potatoes. not everyone would have eaten them. There are people who simply don't like potatoes. And there are infants and small children who wouldn't eat them. It's not like it was the only food. They still had the other hydro and they had synthmeat, and they had fish from the tanks. Sure, food might have been tighter than now, but no one was starving."

"Then there was this author, Sabot Germain, who said that people had got upset at their restricted lives, that they didn't realize the life of a colonial would be limited for generations, until the local economy grew to allow people to be other than farmers. They were all upset, and they rebelled. They went mad and killed each other and, in the end, only Martino Calligaris was left. He threw them into the pit and then jumped after them."

"He threw five hundred corpses into the pit? He must have had abs of steel by the end of that."

"Mike, it's not funny."

"No, it's not funny. It's insane. Who would do that? Back and forth with a corpse at a time, or perhaps a wheelbarrow full of corpses. If he was going to commit suicide anyway, why bother? Is there any kind of evidence for this farrago?"

I hesitated. "Well, he left a diary, you know? And I don't understand most of it. I don't think anyone does. He was a physicist, and it turns out most of his diary is . . . hypothesis and numbers, and he invented this mathematical language . . ."

"I know," he said, sounding tired. "They look like the runes in the tunnel. I skimmed his diary myself in search of some clue."

"So, you're not satisfied either?"

"No. Of course I'm not satisfied. A teen boy disappeared into thin air, under our noses, and we're supposed to be guarding these people, making sure nothing bad happens to them." He stood up and got himself wine from the bottle in the corner. It was good wine and from grapes grown right here, in Roanoke. On the soil, as grapes should be. There just wasn't much wine yet. But I'd got it, for this cold, snowy night. And for the cold, dark subject we'd discuss, again.

"What did you see in Calligaris's diary that made you think there might be something to this nonsense?"

I got my link, brought up Calligaris's diary and flipped to the very last page. "I guess you stopped reading before the end," I said.

"I couldn't understand any of it, so mostly I skimmed and verified that the symbols were the same as on the wall, which I'm sure is what fuels Abatangelo's paranoia. Likely someone else scratched the symbols in the rock having seen them in Calligaris's diary and thinking they were neat."

"Maybe," I said. "Maybe not." I pushed the link at him, Martino Calligaris's centuries-old writing glowing against the white background.

Mike read aloud: "I am tired of all the bickering and complaining about the restrictions of colonial life. The ones born here are the worst, complaining they didn't ask to be born and didn't sign up for the restricted, hard life of a colonist. They seem to be sure that had they been born on Earth, they would get to choose class, country, region and the level of prosperity. I don't remember being presented with a checklist before birth.

"It's all whine and moan and avoidance of the work necessary to build a stable society that survives and thrives in this world.

"And I'm tired. I at least understand that physics must take place around the farming and the work of tending the hydroponics. I understand I'm not too good to sully my hands.

"But all they do is whine and moan more: *Why brought ye us from bondage, Our loved Egyptian night?*

"I can't take this much longer. I must do something about it. Or we'll all die."

Mike finished reading, silently read through again, then raised troubled eyes to me. "I still refuse to believe he poisoned them all, then dumped one body after the other into the pit."

"Well, of course not. He was a physicist, not a chemist."

This surprised a chuckle from him, but he sobered immediately. "I also refuse to believe he electrocuted them all and dumped them into the pit. It makes no sense."

"All right. You're right. It makes no sense. Any more than Courtney's disappearance makes any sense."

"Yeah, but at least one corpse you could hide. Five hundred and likely more of them? Even just the task of dragging them to the pit would be immense.

"Well, maybe he took them somewhere, well away from every settlement, and left them," I said in despair.

"Alive or dead?" Mike asked. "In either case the mechanics are unlikely. He had no mass transport. Antonia did, but did he radio the settlement and ask for a bus to dispose of the corpses?"

"No, all the communication was normal, till they stopped cold. And anyway—"

"And anyway, that would be an absurd request. And I remind you that Antonia does have overflight technology, as do others. A pile of corpses would be visible."

"Yes, but . . . Where did they go? And where did Courtney go? I can't believe Joe killed him. There doesn't seem to be any motive, and they never even traded uncivil words. A young man doesn't up and murder a friend for no reason."

"No. And you know we did a careful combing of the entire area, including chemical analysis of all the debris. Dragging Courtney to the pit would have left something, some trace of his passage, even if just a hair, somewhere on the rock. And if Joe had just lured him to the pit for some reason or another and pushed him in, well . . . I don't see Joe as the kind of precise, planning mastermind who would plant the footprints into the rune tunnel. And besides, one set of footprints isn't his.

"I can maybe see him, probably by accident, roughhousing with Courtney near the pit and pushing him in. But I can't imagine his holding on to that secret through all that time and all the discussions, do you?"

I thought of the kid's red eyes, of his crying that first night, and of his baffled repetition of how his friend had simply vanished. "Not unless he's the best actor birthed by humans ever," I said.

"Yeah," Joe said. "Neither do I. I wish I did. You know it got so crazy I asked Merryl Aminta down at the museum to go and look at the things the kids were looking through just before this happened."

"And?"

It was his turn to get his link out, and flip through it. Finally, he pushed it at me. It was opened to a text message from Merryl

Aminta. I remembered Merryl—I thought—from various public functions. He was a colorless little man, of indeterminate age, who always wore dark pants and white shirts which seemed to have been ironed just minutes before.

Which probably explained why his message didn't sound in the least bombastic. And why it was believable.

"Dear Mr. Judd," he said. "I have looked into the storage room where the two volunteers from Future Farmers of Roanoke were working the day of the unfortunate disappearance." It was just like Aminta to not just call them Joe and Court like everyone else did. "It is not known to our volunteers that when we ask them to go through and evaluate what should go on exhibit and not, we have already made a preliminary inventory of the box. This is necessary, because of course the students aren't trained archeologists or historians and could easily misplace something through ignorance or malice." What he was saying was that someone might steal great-great-grandma's knitting needles or great-great-grandad's moustache curler. Which I suppose was possible. Roanoke had its share of petty theft. But usually not of such items. Like the theory of Calligaris dragging hundreds of bodies to the bottomless pit, it was possible, but it was also unlikely. You couldn't picture it without laughing.

However, Aminta went on, "After looking through not only the box the two volunteers left open, but through all the boxes around it, I'm forced to conclude we are missing an article. It is a small article, almost insignificant, and honestly of origin unknown. It was packed in the box with the remaining artifacts from New Virginia after the disappearance, and my predecessor had catalogued it as 'small black plastic square two inches on the side. Origin and purpose unknown.' After due diligence searching, I am forced to conclude the volunteers must have absconded with it, though I can't imagine for what purpose."

I pushed the link away from me and looked up at Mike.

"It makes no sense," I said. "But I want to believe. I want to believe that Courtney stumbled in that tunnel and went through time and space to a world wild and beautiful, where the descendants of the people of New Virginia received him with open arms."

Mike blinked. There was a shine of tears in his eyes, but I wouldn't embarrass him by mentioning it. "Me too," he said.

"And it must be wild and beautiful," I said. "Because Calligaris wouldn't take them to a hardscrabble land. They'd just complain more, and they were getting on his nerves."

Mike chuckled, then became serious. He drank his wine, savoring it. As well he should, as expensive as it was. "He really was a genius, you know," he said. "And geniuses can have sudden breakthroughs."

"But..." I said. "A gate to another time and place? On the ground? In the world? How is that even possible? Just the balancing of the—"

He reached across and touched my lips with his finger. Very softly. I was so stunned, I stopped, cold. "Shh," he said. "No theory is likely. None of them is particularly possible. We're dealing with the stuff of legend, the vanishing of New Virginia. And now the vanishing of Courtney Beulen. But we know what happened, and this one fits. As insane as it is."

He withdrew his finger and raised his glass. "To Calligaris."

"To Calligaris," I said. And I sipped the wine.

We were quiet a long time. "So, we're closing the investigation?" I asked. And I thought now we'd drift apart again, and I'd go back to starting knitting projects I never finished and remembering my lost family. Forever.

He sighed. "I guess. Maybe they'll stumble back through the gate sometime. Until then, there's nothing we can do."

We were silent a long time. Then he reached across the table and took my hand. "Georgi, boss, I'm tired of being alone. All I do is think of what I've lost. I can't take it. Like this case, it wears a man to nothing. There's no way to recover what vanished. You can only mourn, and I'm exhausted by mourning. We work well together. I've enjoyed your company for all this time. Can we... make it official?"

I blinked stupidly. "I'm already your boss. We already work together in the police."

He made a sound half laughter and half exasperated huff. Which shouldn't be possible but was. "I mean outside of work."

Being me, of course I blurted the first thing that came to mind. Which was weird, since I'd taught him not to. "I'm forty-five, Mike. And I probably can't have children. Malthe and I only managed one."

"There's always the icicles," he said. "You know they're always talking about how we need to increase genetic diversity. Let's get a half dozen of them. Or ten. Let's raise them and fill our house with love and laughter. In a universe where people can disappear without a trace, the only thing we can do is keep life and love going. Against the darkness and the cold."

Outside the wind blew, in the darkness, and frozen rain pattered against the cabin windows.

And I realized he was right.

Lost Colony

New Virginia, named for the birthplace of the chief exploitation officer of the TRAPPIST-2 Colony Foundation, was the first site chosen once the landers were modified to remove control by the AIs and return it to the People. While it was the first site chosen, it was actually the second landing. A delay in shifting cryostasis chambers into the lander meant that Lander Three was released for descent to the Beta site (Antonia) twenty-four hours before Lander Two began its own descent to the Alpha site. Site Alpha had more natural resources, while Site Beta had more cultivatable land and greater agricultural potential. It would also require a larger population. As a result, Lander Four was dispatched to Site Beta, renamed Antonia, where the People could be productively engaged in working in harmony with the land instead of robbing it of resources.

These precautions seemed prescient when communications were lost with New Virginia and it was eventually discovered that the entire population had vanished. One thousand colonists from Antonia chose to reestablish the failed colony, and they, too, succumbed: this time to disease. Many theories were put forth regarding the deaths and disappearances. The most respected thesis is that artificially imposing a capitalist government on Site Alpha led to neurosis, extreme guilt, and mass suicide. Nevertheless, the actual cause of the disappearance of the original colony would forever remain a mystery...

—Excerpt from *Flint's People's History of Interstellar Exploitation*,
Trudovik Press,
Kerenskiy, Trudovik, AA237

THE LEGEND OF JIMMY VEE

Chris Kennedy

"Oh, come on—*hic!*—it'll be fun."

Jessie Franz pursed her lips as she looked at me, and I could see she was at least considering the idea, even though I'd had a lot more to drink than she had. I opened a bottle of homemade mead and handed it to her, hoping to rectify the situation. She had a big swig, and her eyes widened.

"I thought this would be really sweet," she said, "but it's crisp and light."

"It's my own recipe," I said, "and there's no better place to drink it than under the stars. It should be a good evening for it, too; I think there will be at least four other planets visible. I know a nice little place away from the lights of the settlement where we'll have a great view."

Her eyes narrowed. "Jimmy Vee, is your goal to get me drunk?"

"Not at all," I said with as much conviction as I could. It was totally true, too. Getting Jessie drunk was definitely *not* the outcome I planned, although it probably *was* a large step toward achieving it. "I just thought it would be a nice night for a walk under the stars." And other stuff, once we were well away from the settlement, where everyone had to know everything about everyone else's business.

"Aren't you afraid of the monster?"

I snorted. "There's no monster here."

"A lot of people think there is. John Brown said his cow got torn apart. Some of the people even think that's what killed off the earlier colonists."

"No, the New Flu got them," I said. "Both times. It wasn't a monster, or we'd have found bones and stuff. It's perfectly safe for us to go for a walk in the woods." I smiled and held up my pistol. "Besides, I've got this, should I need it."

"Well . . ."

I could see she was wavering and threw in my best prepared line. "Oh, come on—when do you ever get to see four planets in the sky at once? In the history of the *entire* human race, how many people can say that?"

"Okay, I'll go, but don't you try anything."

"Me?" I asked, giving her my best innocent face. "I wouldn't dream of it."

We snuck out the back of her father's house so the sentries wouldn't see us. Like I said, in a small settlement, rumors abound, and everyone would know about it by noon tomorrow if we were seen. I wasn't sure if I was ready for us to be "an item" yet. It would probably all rest on the outcome of the night, I decided with the clarity brought on by another sip of mead. While I didn't *think* her father would shoot me for going out with Jessie, I really wasn't ready to put that feeling to the test, yet. Not without some proof that the reward was worth the risk.

I led her out into the forest, which was reminiscent of a temperate forest back on Earth, although the trees were all wrong, of course. The cool, damp air chilled Jessie slightly, and she reached for the mead. I could have put my arm around her, but I decided to wait a bit longer for that.

She wasn't prepared for living in a temperate forest, of course; none of us were. The stupid lander that had brought us had been supposed to touch down on Aopo—the huge subcontinent-sized island to our west, but it had broken and dumped us here. Instead of the tropical paradise we were promised, we ended up in Aopo's wind-and-rain shadow where things were cooler and drier. Our clothes were better suited for the tropics, but I really wasn't bitter. Much.

When we arrived, we'd thought that the leaves the trees dropped in the Fall would at least help make the soil a fertile place for growing crops, but that had turned out about as well as the last descent of the lander. Which is to say, not well at all.

Something in the leaves made the soil great for growing the local flora, but hostile to Earth crops. Too acidic or not acidic enough; I didn't know. Soil management and plant husbandry weren't my things. About the only thing we had that worked well were the bees we brought with us. They adapted to the local plants and went crazy; there was something in the nectar of the local plants that hit them like an energy drink—they flew faster and longer, and it increased their production to levels we'd never seen on Earth.

Most of the colonists had thought my position was unnecessary—that it had only been created to appease some of the "tree huggers" back home, who'd been worried about the extinction of bees and had wanted to start a colony of them in the stars, too. They had looked down on me . . . until the crops wouldn't grow and the only thing we had plenty of was honey. That didn't make any of them think any better of me, but as the apiculturist—the person in charge of the bees—I had a lot of honey . . . and I knew how to make mead. The younger colonists liked me, even if their parents didn't. Admittedly, I didn't work as hard as they did, and no, I often didn't get up until after noon, which probably didn't help the older folks think any more highly of me . . . but I wasn't really very worried about it. I had friends . . . and mead. Lots of both.

"Where are we going?" she asked after a few minutes. The path I had worked out led uphill, and was a little bit tiring, especially if someone had consumed too much mead, which I probably had . . . but I knew the destination was worth it.

"It's a surprise," I replied. "It's not much farther." I waved at the trees surrounding us. While they let a lot of light in during the day, their leaves hadn't fallen yet, and would block our view. "The trees and the hills are in the way. I found a great place you're going to love."

"You're not trying to get me lost are you, Jimmy Vee?"

"Me? Not at all." Although, having her dependent on me wasn't a bad thing, I realized. I might have to incorporate that into the plan next time. "Promise."

After a few more minutes the land leveled off, and I could hear the waterfall at our destination. "Is that thunder?" Jessie asked, worried.

"No, it's not," I said with a wink. It had gotten lighter as the closest planet rose in the sky, and we could see each other easily. Her golden hair shone in the planet-light, framing her face like an angel. I nodded toward the sky. "Don't worry; it's okay. There aren't even any clouds."

Another minute later, we arrived, and Jessie gasped quietly as she looked out onto the lea. Maybe it was a dell; I wasn't sure exactly what to call it. All I knew was it was an open area in the forest with a stream running through it. I had found it a few days prior while looking for a place to start a second hive for my over-industrious charges. One that no one else knew about, and thus couldn't be taxed.

The area was illuminated in moon and planet-light with a soft glow that reflected off the low plants that took the place of grass in a silvery sheen. A circular area several hundred yards in diameter, a seven-meter-wide stream cut through it, turning into a waterfall on the left end of the lea as the land fell off quickly in a sharp precipice that went down to the level where the colony sat. Having walked the edge in the daylight, I knew to stay away from it—the ground was rocky around it, and it would be easy to trip. The stream itself was covered in a fog that added to the silvery shimmer; like many of the rivers in the area, it was a product of a hot spring and warmer than it would otherwise have been.

Between the stream and the edge of the forest where we stood, a blanket with a picnic basket was set up. "Table for two," I said, sweeping a hand toward the blanket with a small bow. "No waiting."

"This . . . this is beautiful . . ." Jessie said, her eyes trying to take in the scene all at once. "No, it's gorgeous . . . it's better than gorgeous! I don't even know how to describe it."

She walked over to the blanket, where I had laid out some food and plenty of mead. Her eyes took in the spread, then she looked up at me with a raised eyebrow. "Jimmy Vee, I'm not sure your intentions are completely honorable." I might have been worried, but she ended it with a giggle that let me know she'd appreciated the effort I'd gone to.

I shrugged, looking down. Two could play the coy game.

"How's the water?" she asked suddenly, nodding toward the stream. "It looks warm."

"It is," I replied. "The hot spring is about a quarter mile from here, and it's cooled off some by the time it gets here."

"Let's go for a swim," she said playfully. "Then we can use the blanket to dry off."

"Okay," I said with a grin. "Last one in's a rotten egg!"

We dashed for the stream, but then I paused as I realized I really didn't want to jump in with my clothes on. I turned toward Jessie and found she already had her shirt off. "Take your clothes off, stupid," she said with another giggle. "Duh."

I had my shirt off in a flash, but then her bra came off, and my eyes locked on her body, unable to break away. Life on a frontier colony, while hard, tends to work off any extra pounds that someone her age on Earth might have acquired, and she was perfect in every way. My jaw dropped, and I stopped what I was doing to stare.

"No peeking!" she exclaimed, covering herself. "Turn around!"

I shook my head, trying to gather my senses as I turned away from her, unable to get the vision of her out of my mind. It started working again after a few seconds, and I heard a splash as I began to fumble with the buckles on my holster.

"You're the rotten—" Jessie called, but her voice cut off unnaturally, and I spun around in alarm to see what the problem was.

Jessie stood in water up to her hips, completely naked. I couldn't completely appreciate the view, though; the look of fear and shock on her face as she pointed over my shoulder ruined the effect. Her mouth moved, but nothing came out.

Then I heard the growl.

I turned around to find a nightmare pawing through the picnic basket on the blanket. Part wolf and part bear, it was completely terrifying from its saliva-dripping mouth to the end of its razor-sharp-looking back claws. Its fur—or hair, it was hard to tell—glistened softly across its almost two-meter-high body in the planet-light, and the creature blended in with the sheen of the low-lying plants. It took the picnic basket—nearly a third of a meter wide—in its mouth and crunched through it in a single bite, the wooden strips shattering under the onslaught.

"You said there was no monster," Jessie said. She had come out of the water while I stared, and her naked flesh pressed into my back as she leaned forward to whisper into my ear.

I continued to gape at the creature, unable to shut my mouth for a few moments, while I also enjoyed the feel of Jessie rubbing up against my back. I had never been so overwhelmingly horrified, while simultaneously so aroused at the same time. It was oh so wrong, but it felt *oh* so right.

"I was wrong," I finally gasped as the moment stretched far too long for the circumstances. What can I say? If I was going to die, I wanted to enjoy life—and the way Jessie felt up against me—for as long as I could.

And, the truth of the matter wasn't that I was merely wrong—I was really, *really* wrong. There *was* a monster, and it was huge. I had no idea if it was the cause of the first two colony wipeouts—the smart sciency folks said that they had died from the New Flu—but I would easily have believed it if they'd pinned it on this beast.

While the beast *looked* huge as it pawed through our stuff on all fours, when it reared up on its hind legs, it blocked out at least half the stars in the sky. It was enormous; it was gargantuan. My mind ran out of superlatives. It was just that damn big.

I risked a glance over my shoulder at Jessie and could see she was vapor-locked; her brain had completely frozen in terror. Her mouth subconsciously opened and closed a couple of times, and it looked like she was trying to say something, but nothing came out. I was pretty happy about that—I didn't want her to do anything that might make the creature charge and end our lives any sooner than it needed to.

The creature was closer to being a bear, I decided as it shredded the blanket; however, instead of bear hands, it had giant claws.

Then, unfortunately, Jessie finally found her voice. "Shoot it!" she whispered frantically. "Quick! Shoot it!"

"I don't have a rocket launcher," I whispered back, trying to keep my voice down as panic finally unleashed every adrenal gland in my body, and I started to shake uncontrollably. "All I have is this," I added, drawing my pistol from its holster, "but it is *not* big enough for *that*."

"I don't care!" she exclaimed, her voice growing louder with every syllable. "*Just shoot it!*"

The last came out in a scream, and the creature's head whipped around in our direction. It had dropped back to all fours, but it stood up again and roared. Or screamed, I'm not entirely sure what to call it. It was loud and unnatural, and it made my bowels and bladder want to release with an urgency I could barely resist.

I did what any normal person would have done: I vapor-locked, just like Jessie had done earlier, and stared at the monster as it roared at me again.

That, however, wasn't enough action for Jessie, and she shoved me forward with a scream. "*Do something!*" At that point, Jessie went into full-flight mode and ran off across the lea naked, screaming in terror.

Which, obviously, was something the normal fauna of the planet didn't do, because the creature dropped to all fours again to watch her performance with its head cocked to the side. Jessie made it about fifteen feet into the forest before running into a tree at full speed with a *thwack!* She fell to the ground, unmoving, and the creature started to shamble in her direction.

With Jessie no longer pressed up against my back, I realized I was able to use that part of my brain again—even though other portions remained locked in terror—and I realized I couldn't let it do anything to that perfect, though unconscious, body.

"Hey! You!" I yelled as I pointed my pistol at the creature. It obligingly stopped and turned to look at me. I aimed right between its oversized, luminous eyes and fired.

And obviously missed, as it cocked its head as if trying to determine what made the loud noise. I fired again; another clean miss. I fired again and hit it somewhere; it stood up on its hind legs and roared again.

This gave me a much better target, and I fired off as many shots as I could. It was a long way off for a pistol, but the creature was enormous, and I had to have hit it at least a couple of times.

It dropped to all fours and started shambling toward me. I backed up, firing as quickly as I could get a good sight picture. The pistol's slide locked back at the same time my boot hit the water of the stream behind me. I knew I didn't want to go in the water—I would be at an even bigger disadvantage—and I began working my way along the bank as I fumbled with the next magazine.

The creature looped a little farther to the left, and I realized my error; it was herding me toward the cliff. Once it had me cornered, it slowed, as if no longer concerned I would get away. Whether it was actually intelligent or just had an animal-level wisdom, I had no idea, and I really didn't care. The magazine locked in place, and I let the barrel slide forward; it was time to kill the beast.

I fired off the entire magazine as it drove me closer and closer to the precipice. I know I hit it at least a few times, but it was monstrous, shaggy, and appeared to have layers of fat; if I did anything more than piss it off, it wasn't readily apparent. The slide on my pistol locked back again. I didn't have a third magazine; I was out, and the monster kept coming.

My foot hit a rock behind me, and I stumbled—I was almost at the cliff's edge. I was able to right myself before going over, and I turned to look at the creature. It looked back at me as if waiting to see if I was going to jump off the cliff.

The answer to that was, of course, a resounding "no." It was at least twenty meters down to the floor below, and I had no idea how deep the water was, or if I'd even be able to land in it. The rocks at the edge of the stream, I had seen, were large and pointy; I had no desire to land on them.

I was out of options, and then one more came to my semi-nonfunctional brain—I would get the monster to charge, and then I would leap out of the way like a matador, and let the creature fall to the rocks below. It was a perfect plan except for one thing—I had fired two entire magazines at the creature and not enraged it; how was I going to get it to charge? I had no idea. All I had was the pistol. As it closed to five meters, I did what I could; I yelled and threw the pistol at the creature. It batted the pistol out of the air and made a chuffing noise. It took me a second, but then I realize what it was doing—it was laughing at me.

"Screw you!" I yelled. "If that's the way you're going to be, I'll jump!"

I turned and looked down in the planet-light. I could easily see the rocks, covered in mist, shining below me. If I did it right, I might be able to clear the rocks. Maybe. The way the monster had looked at me, I could tell it was intelligent. If it was sadistic, too, I would be a long time dying. I'd watched a cat play with a mouse once; I'd rather take the rocks. At least it would be quick.

My muscles bunched, and it roared from behind me. Perhaps it didn't want me to take the easy way out. Who knows? It sprinted forward, and I dropped to the edge of the stream, hoping it would go over me.

It didn't; it stopped and grabbed me, lifting me up from the ground in its oversized claws. My arms were free, though, and I did the only thing I could—I jabbed it in the eyes with my first and second fingers held together like a knife blade. It stood all the way up—lifting me three meters into the air—and roared in my face.

And then the ground fell away underneath it, and we both began falling.

The monster flailed, throwing me to the side. I felt a momentary splash of water, then I went face-first into the side of the cliff as it rocketed past. My next recollection was of water again—not the impact, although the pain of the sudden stop may be what woke me up—but the water, just as I went under. I didn't get a breath, but at least I didn't breathe in any of the water, either.

I struggled to the surface, my lungs threatening to explode. It would have been easy if both my legs worked. They didn't. My right knee burned with all the fires of hell when I tried to use it; apparently the impact with the water had damaged something inside it. I made it to the surface before my lungs gave out, though, and I stroked weakly to the closest side of the pool under the waterfall, using my last ounce of strength to pull myself up onto a flat rock.

Motion caught my eye as I lay there recovering; the monster climbed slowly from the water on the other side. It moved slowly and looked a lot worse for the wear. The water had matted its fur—or hair, or whatever it was—and it didn't seem quite so big. It was merely enormous instead of gargantuan. That thought amused me, possibly due to the head injury I surely had, and a giggle escaped my lips.

Somehow, even over the roar of the waterfall, the monster's ears picked up on the unnatural sound, and it spun around—all traces of weakness gone—to glare at me. Without a moment's hesitation, it turned and began wading into the water toward me. I didn't move, perhaps because something in my mind told me there was no way something that big could swim.

I was right; it sank. But just before its head went underwater, though, it took a deep breath and kept walking. As its head submerged, I could see it was still coming. I fought my way to my feet for a better look, and I could see the underwater shadow that was the monster continuing toward me, walking along the bottom of the pool like he was walking across a street back on Earth. I turned and ran.

Well, it wasn't any more than a fast hobble, which, after about ten meters, turned into just a plain hobble, and then what might charitably only be called a shamble. I hadn't made it very far into the forest when it announced its presence on my side of the water with its bellowing roar. I turned to look back, and its luminescent eyes locked on mine. It started forward.

As it did, however, I could see there was a hitch in its gait; it had hurt one of its back legs, too. It dropped to all fours and shuffled after me.

A thought ran through my mind—the monster could be hurt. I smiled. At some point, my brain had turned it into an invincible adversary, like a creature out of a science fiction novel or something. As it lumbered toward me, I realized that if I could beat it back to the settlement, there would be guards—with rifles—who might just be able to kill it.

Then I realized I was on the wrong side of the water from the colony and getting even farther from it as I fled.

I tried to swing up to the right, but quickly came up against the cliff again. I didn't know if there'd be a way to scale it farther on—I'd never come this way before—but I didn't want to pin my hopes on it. I tried to bear left to get around it on that side, but the creature moved to cut me off. I looked back over my shoulder to see it was gaining on me. I guess you could travel faster on three of four legs than you could on one of two. I started to look forward again, and I had a split second to see the tree before I ran into it.

When I woke up again, my whole body hurt, and it only took one more bounce before I realized that was because the monster had ahold of my leg and was pulling me along the ground. I'm sure my back—shirtless—was a mass of abrasions, and my knee now hurt worse, as that was the leg the monster was pulling me along with.

Dragging me didn't seem to be helping the creature, either; its limp was far more pronounced now, too.

I leaned forward a little, so my back wasn't taking quite as much abuse, but my stomach muscles weren't strong enough to hold me up very long. It didn't matter, I saw, as the ground smoothed out beneath me; the creature was pulling me into a cave. My first reaction was to try to break free—*to run!*—but I realized that the creature had caught me once, so I decided to wait and see if another opportunity came up. And I hurt too badly at the moment to do anything else.

The creature dragged me down an incline as we entered the cave, and then back up the other side, before letting go of my leg. I allowed it to flop down lifelessly as the monster turned to look at me. I was as still as I could be as I looked at it through the slit of one eye. I didn't know if it thought I was dead, but even *I* could hear my heart pounding in my chest. After a moment, the creature shuffled off to the side, made some snuffling noises, then shuffled off the way we came in. I gave it a few seconds, then opened my eyes and sat up.

And wished that the creature had killed me while I was unconscious.

I was in the creature's lair, left there to be its child's breakfast—I figured—when it woke up. The mini monster was no more than two meters from me, sleeping in a nest of leaves and fur. The moss on some of the cave walls provided enough illumination to see the creature in all its horror—it was an exact miniature of the larger one, but in a half-meter-long package. And the enormous stack of bones in the back of the cave showed that parent and child ate ... a lot.

In a panic, I stood up, slamming my head into the ceiling of the cave, knocking myself back to the ground again. Rubbing my head to make the stars go away, I stood up a little slower and found I could walk but had to do it hunched over. I looked around for anything I could use to defend myself from the larger creature—probably the little one's mother—but didn't see anything. As my eyes darted about frantically, I realized I did, however, still have my knife. Strapped to my upper leg, it had somehow survived the fall from the cliff and my trip to the cave.

I whipped it out and realized how totally inadequate it was for the situation. About the only thing I could kill with it would be myself. Or maybe the baby. Unfortunately, while dispatching the little thing would keep it from growing into another monster, it probably wouldn't endear me to the baby's mother. However ...

Without thinking about it, I sheathed my knife and scooped up the little creature. It snuffled a bit at the new smells and the motion, but I rocked it in my arms, and it went back to sleep.

Careful not to hit my head, I proceeded to the cave's exit. I could see the mother about twenty meters away in the forest, relieving herself. *The perfect time to stage my getaway!* The sun was just starting to rise, so, since I thought I'd been heading west last night, I snuck off to the east.

I might have made it, too, if the baby hadn't picked that time to cry out in its sleep. I looked over my shoulder, and my eyes met the monster's as her head snapped around toward the baby's cry.

The chase was on. It occurred in slow motion, mostly, since we were both hurt, but that did nothing to lessen our intent. I wanted to get free, and the monster wanted to get her baby back. The baby woke up and began crying, and then turned into a Cuisinart. Claws slashed everywhere, and it was all I could do to avoid having my stomach sliced open as I ran. The mother roared from behind me, and I turned.

I held the baby up by the scruff of its neck, placing the point of my knife to its throat, and the monster stopped like it had hit a wall. It glared at me, expressing every bit of its hatred for me, and I did my best to glare back. She won the battle of the staring contest, but I won the war as I still had her child and a knife to its throat. I took a few tentative steps backward, then turned and ran off again.

After a few minutes of flight, I realized the mother wasn't trying to catch me anymore—she was merely pacing me, waiting for an opportunity where she could safely separate me from her offspring and then kill me in some horrific way. The baby suffered through it all, crying intermittently. While I felt bad for it—it was probably hungry—I didn't feel badly enough to give up and die and become its next meal.

I kept working my way to the east, not sure where I was or where I was going, but knowing I couldn't stop to rest. The baby got heavier and heavier the farther I ran, and I wanted to toss it aside; however, I was afraid to do so. Would the mom stop if I did, just happy to have her baby back? Or would she put forth a burst of speed to kill the creature—me—who'd had the temerity to steal her offspring? I didn't know, and I didn't want to find out, so I continued to shuffle along.

Right up until I hit the lea where the chase had all begun the night before. I entered from the opposite side of where Jessie and I had come to it, and nearly tripped as the realization hit me. I could tell it was the same one—how many leas on the planet had shredded blankets in them? I couldn't imagine there was more than just one, and everything there looked pretty much the way I'd left it. I wished I'd left it with a belt-fed .50 caliber weapon, too.

My "run" now down to a stumbling walk, I knew I didn't have a lot left, and before too long I was probably going to fall down in exhaustion. Blood loss and lack of sleep have that sort of effect on you. It also made rational thought—and coming up with an operable plan—extremely difficult.

My faltering walk led me to the stream, and I looked at it in despair. The current flowed swiftly as it headed toward the falls, and I didn't think I had the strength left to cross it, especially not with both my arms needed to keep the baby from committing seppuku on me. I looked over my shoulder to find the larger monster had stopped at the edge of the forest. She was close enough to pounce as I crossed . . . and after all my efforts, that's not how I wanted to end.

I would happily have traded her offspring for my life, if I'd only been able to talk to her and arrange a trade. I shook my head in anguish as I realized that—because I couldn't—the only way this was going to end was with my death. It may sound morbid, but I'd already had two head injuries in the last twelve hours or so, and it might have been—between the injuries and the exhaustion—that I wasn't thinking very clearly.

As I shook my head, I realized she was mimicking me, but when I stopped, she didn't; her head kept swinging around slowly. In fact, she seemed to be looking almost anywhere, *but* at me. It took me a moment, but then I understood her problem—she was having a hard time seeing as the sun rose behind me. Her huge eyes were excellent collectors of moonlight, but they were overwhelmed by the dawning sun.

In a blinding flash of brilliance, I recognized I now had all the missing pieces to my plan from the last time we were here. With a sudden surge of adrenaline—I'd long since given up on having any more but appreciated the boost—I raced as quickly as I could to the edge of the cliff and held the baby over the edge.

The monster's roar didn't fill me with terror anymore, although whether that was because I was used to it or simply too tired to care, I didn't know. I also didn't dread the impact tremors I could feel as she charged. Some things reach across species, and this was one. The only thing to make the mountain of destructivity charge me? Risking her baby's life. It turned the situation from "wait and see" to "save the baby *right now*."

I turned to find she was already two-thirds of the way to me and coming on like an old-time locomotive. I had no idea she could move that fast when we started, but now, with her child in peril, she put everything into her dash. Her damaged leg was no longer even a concern as she raced toward me.

I tossed the baby in the air, and her eyes tracked it as she sprinted toward the edge, taking them off me as I dropped to the ground in front of her. She reached me, and I lifted up on my hands and knees slightly, cutting her legs out from under her. She spun through the air as she went over the edge.

It was a perfect plan, and it worked exactly as I had intended ... except for the fact that I had grossly underestimated the inertia she would have when she hit me. She massed at least a ton, and, at full sprint, it was like being hit by a train—I was catapulted through the air. I slammed back to the earth, rolled, and hit the edge of the cliff. My legs went over, and I was falling. Again.

Somehow, I was able to get a grasp on the edge and arrest my fall, although the shock of it almost tore my arms from their sockets. Stopping the fall was only the first of my problems, though. I couldn't pull myself up. The energy surge I'd experienced was gone, and—not an incredibly strong man to start—I didn't have the ability to pull myself up. My feet scrambled for purchase on the side of the cliff, but that only made hanging on harder as they worked to push me farther away from it.

I risked a glance down and saw I was hosed. I hadn't been next to the stream when I'd tossed the baby, and I wasn't over the pool at the bottom; I was at least ten feet to the side. When I hit, it was going to be on the rocks. If I'd had a running start, I could have made it ... but I didn't. I tried working my way along the edge of the cliff, but the rocky edge got slimier as I got closer to the falls, and my right hand slipped off.

Try as I might, I couldn't get it back up. I was spent, and even the thought of the rocks below couldn't give me the surge necessary to get my hand back up to the edge. In exhausted horror, I watched as my left hand—unable to support my weight by itself—slid off. Each joint lost purchase in apparent slow motion, until only my fingertips held . . . and then they fell away, and I dropped.

That should have been the end of Jimmy Vee, but a funny thing happened—a rock stuck out from the cliff at an angle, and I hit it and spun off to the side. I cartwheeled once—seeing ground, sky, and ground again—and then I hit, right in the middle of the pool underneath the waterfall.

I had dreaded the impact at the bottom the whole way down, and it was with some shock that I realized I wasn't dead. It took a second for that thought to penetrate, and by then my head was underwater, and I snorted some water up my nose.

Being unable to breathe probably saved my life as the feeling evokes an involuntary response stronger than most others, and it gave me the energy to struggle to the surface. I broke the surface, coughing, and struggled to the shore as I worked to clear my lungs.

I made it halfway onto a rock and relaxed, happy to have survived, but then I heard the monster growl. My eyes sprang open as I realized the creature was no more than two meters from me on the rocks that bordered the pool.

Pulling myself to my feet, I started to try to struggle off again, but it made another noise, one that was more plaintive in nature, and I looked back at it.

The creature was dying, its back obviously broken from the way it was lying. It had both of its arms wrapped around its chest, and when it saw me looking, it opened them to reveal its child. With one hand, it fought to hold it up to me, its muscles straining in its final throes, an open invitation for me to take its child. Somehow, it had decided that I wasn't the monster I considered *her* to be, and she was entrusting her offspring to me.

I took the child, and the mother nodded once, then her eyes lost their sheen, and she stilled.

Looking back and forth between mother and child, I was at a loss. I had won my way to freedom. I'd been so sure that I was going to die, for so long, that it took some time for my mind to entirely wrap itself around that thought. But I wasn't free—I'd been given a new life to watch out for. One that might very well turn into a monster that would kill my people if I didn't raise it right. And maybe even if I did.

I was so exhausted, mentally and physically, that I had no idea what to do. The baby struggled, still looking for its morning meal, but I couldn't find the energy to care. The only thing that saved me from collapsing on the spot was motion from the other side of the pool.

"You killed the monster!" It took a second, but then the voice penetrated. It was Jessie's.

I looked up to find a large group of colonists staring at me with their mouths open. I had no idea how long they'd been standing there.

"I did?" I asked, my voice barely audible. Then I saw the way Jessica looked at me, her blond hair shimmering in the morning sun. The dried blood on her face did nothing to detract from it, either. Nothing mattered more than impressing her. "Yes," I said, my voice stronger as I placed one foot on the beast in the classic "conqueror's pose."

"Yes, I did."

That's not the story I told them, of course—that through a series of accidents and incompetence, I ended up killing the apex predator while somehow not dying in the process. My story was that when the monster started chasing Jessie, I fired my pistol at it and intentionally led it away from her and the colony so that no one would be killed by it. If it got me, oh well. They think I'm the colony's savior—except for Jessie's father, of course, who has a pretty good idea of what my intentions *really* were that night—and there's no sense ruining that by telling them the truth.

And, besides, it helped me get the girl in the end.

Apex Predators

Spectroscopic analysis of the worlds orbiting TRAPPIST-2 indicated the presence of free oxygen, complex carbohydrates and water on at least two planets or moons in the system. Breakthrough Starshot probe 24-6-09 conducted a fly-by of TRAPPIST-2 in 2127 CE and sent close-up pictures and analysis back to Earth confirming an Earthlike biosphere on the third planet, TRAPPIST-2c. The laser-launched lightsail probe required over one hundred years to make the journey, and nearly forty years to send the message home. Unfortunately, the probe continued past the system on its millenia-long mission and could not stick around to investigate the possibility of higher life-forms on the planet...

TRAPPIST-2c, Cistercia, boasted a biosphere similar to Earth's in the Mesozoic Era—oxygen-rich and temperate with shallow seas and a few large landmasses covered in forests and grasslands. The animal life was consistent with Earth's Cretaceous period, showing a mix of mammalian, avian and reptiloid forms, but without the large carnivorous dinosaurs of Earth's history. In fact, even the reptiloids appeared to be warm-blooded and mixed both mammalian and reptile characteristics. The combination of Earth-like geological and biological conditions meant that apex predators in many territories evolved similar characteristics to their Earth cousins. In their natural environments, apex predators are reluctant to surrender their dominance to intruders such as Humans....

...see URSWOLF...

—Encyclopedia Astra,
Gannon University,
Antonia, Cistercia, AA212

ON THE TRAIL OF THE SÜGENHOUND

Vivienne Raper

Extract from On the Trail of the Sügenhound,
*by Hilary Scoot, to be published by Trudovik Press on September 13th,
priced at 20 Antonian credits.*

One winter evening in 201AA, Chase Harriman sat at the kitchen table of his family's ranch near Roanoke Landing and watched the headlights of his father's jeep zigzag toward him through the driving rain. He was eleven years old, but—even in the dark—he knew the jeep was moving too quickly. His father, Rider Harriman, was driving erratically.

Thirty minutes earlier, Rider had grabbed his .375 bolt-action rifle from the kitchen table and rushed out of the door. Left behind in the kitchen, Chase heard sheep bleating, and then the low mechanical woofing of the family's Cerberus hounds. He had no illusions about why they were barking.

Something had triggered the sensors on the fences in the goat paddock. And, going by the volume of the barks, he guessed it was something big.

Chase Harriman had grown up on the Roanoke frontier. His family's ranch, thirty-one miles out of town, was often invaded by native wildlife, including seven-foot-long urswolves. But the disturbance that night didn't sound like any large predator he'd heard before.

"It was all around the ranch as the jeep parked," Harriman told me, as I listened, taking notes. "These high-pitched sounds. Like something in terrible pain. Like a demon's laughter."

Thirty-nine years later, he still visibly shivered from the memory. At the time, he recalled being too afraid to open the door to his father. But he did. And, in the glow of the headlights, was taken aback by the expression on Rider's face.

"He had a fear of God in him," he said, with steely-eyed emphasis, the first time he told me the story. "And he wasn't a man to scare easy."

His father had a dirty rag draped over his thumb. As he came into the kitchen, it fell away to reveal an injury Harriman said he's never forgotten: "His thumb was all bent, sort of twisted round upon itself." But "tight and pale—like it had no blood." When his father asked him to splint the thumb, Harriman found two flaps of torn skin. But neither was bleeding, he recalled, and the loosely wrapped rag was clear of blood.

Rider Harriman, his son told me, was a taciturn man. He didn't explain to his son what had happened—at least, not at first. But the next morning, he gave his son a clue. "I kept begging him: Pa, what happened? Pa, tell me what did this? And, eventually, he looked straight at me, and said this one word: 'Sügenhound.'"

I first met Chase Harriman three days after his fiftieth birthday at a waterfront bar on Roanoke Landing. He was a tall man, about six foot three, with olive skin as cracked and creased as the rocks upon the surrounding hills. His deep-set eyes were an impenetrable dark brown, threaded with red veins. Like most of the frontier ranchers, his coarse, curly hair was shot through with gray—he didn't hold with rejuvenation therapy.

As he shook my hand, he told me he had just finished his fourth book. "Folks like it where I come from," he said, jerking his head toward the forested hills outside the bar window. "We're all rightly afraid of Sügenhounds." The book launch, scheduled for later in the month, was already fully subscribed, he told me, with people wanting paper copies.

Chase had sent me a copy of his third book when I first got in contact. "I want you . . . city dwellers to know the truth," he'd said. A detailed account of modern Sügenhound sightings on the Roanoke frontier, *Out of the Forest* was an eerie, disquieting read, especially on a flight with thousands of miles of dark, native jungle passing below.

The Gannon University of Antonia's Zoology Department had claimed that Sügenhounds didn't exist, but that failed to explain the thousands of sightings in a thirty-mile radius of Roanoke Landing. A recent survey by the University of Roanoke found seventy-two percent of Roanokers either claimed to have seen one themselves or knew someone who had. Most (sixty-three percent) believed the New Virginia colony, which once stood on the site of Roanoke Landing, was lost due to Sügenhound attack.

For rancher Chase, proving the existence of the Sügenhound had become his lifetime mission. Widely regarded as a local expert, he'd spent thirty-three years of his life tracking down the beast. Along with the four books, he kept a database of sightings and was unofficial curator of Roanoke's Sügenhound Museum.

He asked if I had been there yet. "It's just around the corner," he said, "on the site of the old New Virginia colony."

I told him I'd already been to the Museum of Frontier History, which charted Cistercia's 240-year history of colonization from the landing of the first construction crews to the building of the doomed Transcontinental Expressway. It was all rather official and sanitized. A whole floor covered the Lost Colony of New Virginia, but the only reference to Sügenhounds was a fleeting mention in the display about the Howard Brocious expedition.

"That's the government for you," he said, frowning. "They want Brocious, the hero, in the museum, but they can't tell the truth. He was the first to see a Sügenhound and live long enough to tell the tale. And this is that story . . ."

On August 22, 30AA, twenty-six years after the founding of the New Virginia colony, Dr. Howard Brocious splashed ashore at Roanoke Landing. Ahead of him was the sloping, sandy beach and, beyond it, the transparent roofs of the colony's hab blocks peeking over the trees.

As Brocious stumbled up the beach, his eyes scanned the curved domes of the hab blocks and the surrounding dark, foreboding wall of native jungle. He wrote later, "I had no idea what I was expecting to find." The New Virginia colony had lost contact with Antonia the previous autumn after reporting that they were planning to move to another location. After multiple delays due to hurricanes and an inability to manufacture jet fuel, Brocious, thirty-five years old and a seasoned explorer, had been commissioned to take the newly constructed sailboat *Pioneer* around the coast to the Landing.

With him were Andrew Carter, an eighteen-year-old security guard; Zhang Yong, a twenty-two-year-old medic; Susanna Lopez, a twenty-three-year-old forensic scientist; and Adesina Oni, a twenty-five-year-old roboteer—all experts hired by the Antonia government. Their plan was to investigate the colony site, work out where the people had gone, and rescue any stragglers.

Brocious and his team entered the settlement in silence. It was eerily quiet; the only sound was the chattering of insects and the metallic clinking of their supply crawlers. The hab blocks surrounding them were draped in blue lilyvine; the transparent roofs green with lichen. "I could almost feel the undergrowth pressing in on us," Brocious recalled. "The forest was reclaiming its own." He was aware that the fate of the settlement could yet apply to Antonia— to any of the fledgling colonies on Cistercia. Unlike the rest of his party, he knew civilization was fragile: he still had vague memories of a chaotic, crowded Earth.

Entering the first hab block, they found the corridors overrun with hippobugs, but the control panels were still active and bleeping. In the first kitchen they entered, the refrigerators were full of decaying food. The largest bedroom, according to Brocious's account, was largely empty of personal possessions and there was no jewelry in the drawers. In the wardrobe, the colonists' clothes were still hanging—and beginning to rot in the humidity. The child's bedroom had a doll propped up on the bed.

Walking back into the deserted town, he spotted a giant agricultural harvester left abandoned. Andrew Carter, young and unusually nervous for a security guard, let his words trip over each other. "The folks here just ran away. They just . . . left . . . taking as few things as possible," he said, as the team carefully imaged and catalogued the harvester. "The colonists were afraid of something 'out there in the jungle,'" he added. This impression was reinforced when, on the road beyond the harvester, he found a tangled network of barbed wire fortifications and motion sensors. A surprisingly well-maintained fortification, it extended well out into the jungle. In his later accounts, Carter said he'd thought it had been installed "to keep something out."

The fortification was the first evidence that someone was still living in New Virginia. Armed with this information, Brocious and his team began to search the hab blocks. According to his account, there was no sign of life or even human remains. Having finished with these, they searched the laboratories and other outbuildings. By the time they reached a small, wooden barn on the western edge of town, the bloodred sun was beginning to set behind the forested hills. "An ominous sight," Brocious wrote afterward. An unflappable fellow, he was beginning to feel afraid of the impending dusk. He was about to call a halt to the investigation and set up camp for the night, when he heard the unmistakable sound of goats bleating.

"I knew, for those goats to be there...alive...in New Virginia, several months after the colonists had deserted the town, that someone was feeding them. They had automated feeders, it was true, but the colony was not designed to be fully automated. It required human input, and with the application of logic, it occurred to me immediately that the human input was coming from the very same survivor who was maintaining the security measures elsewhere in town."

Brocious rushed to the barn and grabbed the end of a log resting against the door. "Help me break down this goddamned door!" he shouted to Carter. He was sure—convinced, in fact—that finding the goats would help him find the surviving colonist. They could be hurt or injured, but—equally important—they would know the fate of the colony.

Carter seized up the other end of the log. Hoisting it onto their shoulders, the two burly men rushed at the door. There was a crack as the lock broke. The wood splintered, and a moment later they stumbled, coughing, into a dark, littered space. Brocious's fleeting impression was of a "terrified tide of brown, white, piebald fur" as the goats stampeded past him, bleating. Then he heard a fearful cry, and a shout from Carter, who had rushed past him into the chaos. A woman was cowering in the corner of the barn, arms thrown over her long, matted dark hair.

"As I approached, she began shouting and shrieking," Brocious wrote later. "Cursing us for releasing the goats. 'The monsters will take them,' she kept crying. 'The monsters will take them.'" He asked, "Urswolves?"—at that time, those monsters in Paradise were newly discovered—but she shook her head vigorously.

Over the next hour, Carter managed to calm the woman enough that Zhang Yong, a precise little man with a neatly trimmed moustache and sparkling dark eyes, was able to examine her. He wrote in his medical records that she was malnourished, but otherwise appeared healthy. She had lived, she told him, for three months on emergency rations and milk from the goats.

Her name, she told them, was Laura Li.

Back outside, Brocious and Lopez attempted to corral the goats, with limited success. Nearly thirty animals had escaped into a fenced paddock at the front of the barn. They milled around, bleating, unwilling to return to the confines of the shed. With darkness now falling, Brocious, who had "no great goat herding experience," returned to the barn.

Carter sat in the darkness, with his arm around Li's shoulders. She wore a torn, dirty jumpsuit in red-gray (the colors of an agricultural worker) and was still shaking, despite the blanket draped over her. When Brocious said he'd failed to bring in the goats, Li regarded him with terrified dark eyes and pleaded with him to protect the goats. "She had, she told me, kept them safe for nearly three months against the monsters—barricading the door each night."

Brocious had planned to make camp back on the boat but was now unsure whether to remain in the town to investigate the monsters instead. When he told Yong and Lopez to pack up their things, Carter tightened his muscular arm around the young woman's shoulders.

"You've got to help her!" he shouted, his freckled face flushing with emotion. "We've got to protect the goats."

"You said it yourself—a monster," said Brocious. He could see that Li was a pretty young woman under the filth and malnutrition. He knew Carter's "ardent desire to protect the goats" was borne from infatuation.

"We have sensors, hunting rifles—nothing bigger than an urswolf could drive us off," said Carter.

"Is the monster bigger than an urswolf?" Brocious asked, and Li shook her head.

Darkness had fallen over the town by the time they set their camp. With torches brought from the boat, Carter inspected the sensors that Li had left near the barn. He augmented them with floodlights and heat sensors, until they formed an invisible web around the paddock. The team made camp in a street near the control booth for the fortifications on the edge of the settlement. Li said these had been installed by the people of New Virginia.

As they sat outside their tents, Li told them the story of how the colony came to disappear—as she understood it. Her story began eleven months before the expedition while Li was working as a trainee agronomist. "Our sheepdogs began disappearing," she'd said. "First a few, and then a lot of them . . . and then we started losing livestock. Not big animals, like cows or horses, but small ones— chickens, goats, the occasional sheep. I didn't see it myself, but some of the shepherds—the farm managers, and such-like—said they'd wandered off and gotten eaten by wildlife. Which always seemed strange to me because Cistercian and Terran species don't usually mix. . . .

"Anyway, that year we had a bad winter and some people made a big ruckus, claiming they didn't like how the mayor was running things. There was this rumor he was having visions, terrible visions, claiming he was being spoken to by creatures . . . aliens out in the forest. They told him the livestock, the crop failures—it was all part of a plan. People started hearing noises at night, terrible noises, and they started believing it too.

"So, after a while, the mayor decreed we should move the colony. It was a crazy idea . . . to just pack everything up and move it along the coast. But he had this cult of personality around him, and supporters with guns, and no one—I suppose—dared to be left behind to starve in the jungle.

"I think that's what happened anyway. I was working in a lab at the time, about a mile and a half inland," she said, pointing down the road into the jungle. "I was with my boss looking at how to adapt Terran crops to be more like Cistercian ones. I was out of the loop, I guess, but we'd both hear things—on the radios, and because I'd return to Roanoke Landing after a couple of weeks in the lab.

"And then, one day, the radios were buzzing—no response. We came back and . . . they'd left the livestock, they'd left the equipment, they'd left the life support running . . . Some people had left their valuables. I guess they thought they might come back.

"For a while, there were three of us: my boss, Professor John Daniels, a lady called Alaa Barre, and I. The livestock had mostly fled into the jungle, but we'd kept some chickens, a few goats . . . and then we started hearing the noises." Here, she broke down in deep sobs. "Terrible noises, every night, and—in the morning—we found the chickens strewn across the town square. Dead. With not a wound on them.

"After that, we kept the goats indoors." That was most of her story, at least as Brocious remembered it. She went on to explain how Daniels was sickened by an infected leg wound. Alaa Barre, believing there were other stragglers from the colony, set off into the jungle to look for help. Li nursed Daniels in the medicenter until he died, at which point, she moved into the barn with her beloved goats. "They've been my only companions for over a month now," she said. "I've given them all names!"

Deeply disturbed by the story, Brocious retired to bed. He was "tired beyond reason" but his sleep was "fitful—consumed by a nameless dread." He knew that scientists had found no intelligent life and no signs of alien civilization, past or present. But as he watched shadows flicker across the roof of his tent, "I couldn't help but wonder what lurked in the darkness of the jungle—beyond the ken of humankind." A tall, stocky man with square hands and blunt nails, Brocious had arrived on Cistercia with his parents and was among the oldest people then alive. His home in Antonia was decorated with ever-changing scenes from Earth, "to remind me how alien it is."

Around midnight, he awoke to an eerie high-pitched wailing in the far distance. Carter was shouting about motion sensors and, somewhere farther away, he could hear the goats bleating with terror. With his heart pounding, he unzipped his sleeping bag and rolled over to grab his hunting rifle. He was expecting a wild animal—possibly an urswolf—but the wailing was unfamiliar to him.

Carter and Yong were shouting now—something about Li and the goats. Tearing open the tent flap, he stumbled, blinking, into the floodlit space between the tents. Against the stark white light, Yong had hold of Carter's wrists. "Get off me!" Carter shouted, as he struggled his arms free. "Stop it!" shouted Brocious, but Carter had already pushed Yong backward, grabbed up a hunting rifle from the camp rack, and was running headlong out of the circle of tents.

Brocious's immediate thought was that Carter had gotten offended somehow. "What happened?" he shouted.

"It's the girl," Yong said, in a pensive tone, still staring after him. "She went after her goats."

By this point, Lopez and Oni were emerging from their tents. Lopez winced and Oni stopped, tilting her head to listen to the wailing cries. According to Brocious, "they were like no animal we'd heard, except for one in terrible pain." He gripped his rifle tighter and muttered a prayer "as I heard them joined by others, equally frightful, and closer to the camp. They came, or so it seemed, from everywhere, and nowhere, at once and I realized then it was a pack I was listening to—circling the barn and calling to one another."

Brocious heard the agonized scream of a goat, and then a distant gunshot. He flinched. Carter. He recalled Yong asking whether they should go and look, but he shook his head. He knew of no pack-hunting Cistercian species. This was a new species, as Li had warned him, and a dangerous one. For long moments, he listened to the cries growing closer. Then, abruptly, Carter stumbled into the floodlights. Sweat was trickling down his milk-pale face and his eyes were wide with terror. "Goats . . . the goats . . . gone for the goats!" he shouted, gesturing wildly with one arm. Brocious was later to recall that spittle flecked the young man's mouth—a sign he'd been driven almost insane with fear. He asked Carter what had taken the goats, and he said, "Stood up. Like me. In the barn. But with these eyes, my God in Heaven, the eyes . . ."

That was enough to strike terror into Carter's colleagues. As the wails grew closer and louder, Brocious began shouting orders, telling the others to pack up the guns and medical kits. The team was preparing to make for the beach when Carter shouted. Looking around, Brocious saw that Li stood in the shadows behind one of the supply crawlers. He called her out and, for a moment, she shook her head. Then she crept into the illumination of the floodlights. She knew she'd caused Carter to run off.

Back on the sailboat, Brocious rested his elbows on the railing.

"The jungle was an ominous mass that met the shore as a high wall of darkness and stretched its blackened fingers down to the beach. I could hear the high-pitched wails reach the forested shore, and move along the jungle's edge, but—however hard I looked—I could see nothing in the thick undergrowth.

"Yet I still felt an uneasy terror. They were hunting us."

Later that night, he asked Carter to tell the team his story. Sitting on a sofa in the main cabin, his hands curled around a tankard of beer, Carter began to talk. "Got to the paddock to find Laura and the goats, running around. I told her to leave 'em. Go to safety. But she wasn't stopping for me or anyone. Couldn't repair the barn lock, but I thought: maybe she's safest in the barn. So, I said, 'Hide behind that log-pile, I'll go into the barn.' My thought was: maybe I'll find a big log to barricade the door.

"It was dark as hell in there. You'd got the odd ray of moonlight coming through the top windows. That's all. Near the door, there were straw bales, auto-feeders—nothing I could use. Then I saw the fences between the goat enclosures. Take the wood. That was my thinking. I saw a loose bar, so I start pulling and heaving. Trying to break it off. Then I hear this barking cough. Almost polite, like, from behind me." Carter hunched his back defensively, his fingers worrying the fringes of a sofa cushion. "Slowly, I turn around. The floor has a patch of moonlight on it. Near the back of the barn, stood up, as plain as you are, I see this 'thing.' Don't even know how to describe it." He paused to gulp his beer. "It's leaning on the fence, looking at me, with these bulging eyes...like saucers, but with an evil cunning in 'em."

That was all the story he told to Brocious that night. In later accounts, he claimed he'd been unable to look away from the creature's eyes. Eventually, the agonized cry of a goat roused him from his trance. Terrified, he'd fired his hunting rifle and fled the barn. He couldn't find Li in the paddock and, fearing the worst, was too frightened to search further. (According to Brocious, Li had run away to hide in a nearby hab block. It was half an hour before she summoned the courage to return to the camp.)

When dawn broke, Brocious and his team sailed back to the shore. His intention was to explore the jungle around the settlement. In particular, he hoped to discover disturbed vegetation or lost possessions that might give a clue as to how, and in which direction, the colonists left. It was a job for which he was well qualified. "The forests and mountains were my playground," he wrote, of his childhood. "While my mother worked on botany, I used to find entire new species, unknown to science, as a game." This sense of discovery inspired him, aged sixteen, to join a scientific expedition mapping islands off the coast of Antonia. It was to be followed by multiple contract jobs for the government, helping botanists and geographers explore the far reaches of the new world.

Upon entering the town, he went to check on the goats. "I was pessimistic of their survival," he wrote. As he approached the barn, he was surprised to hear bleating. Around twenty goats were milling around inside the paddock. He counted them again. Twenty goats. Ten were missing. At the time, he was to write, "I was unsure whether they had escaped from the paddock or had died. Either way, they were nowhere to be found." By the time he wrote his famous memoir, *Hunt for the Sügenhound*, he was certain they had been "kidnapped" and later devoured. Inside the barn, Brocious found a single black animal hair that may, or may not, have come from a goat (later analysis showed it was from a sheepdog).

For the rest of the day, Brocious and the investigators combed the jungle's edge, looking for evidence of the colonists. Along a dirt track near the shore, Lopez found a pink toy horse, heavily decayed, and the wide, heavy indentations left by a supply crawler. Later expeditions were to show these indentations, although badly eroded by rain, dated from around the time the colonists left. When the dirt track ran out, Lopez brought up an arboreal driller to clear a path through the dense undergrowth. She found nothing except for some scratched initials "A.X." on a thick, curving vine (for a discussion of the full investigations into the lost colony, *Roanoke and New Virginia* was reviewed in a previous edition).

As the daylight faded, Brocious felt conflicted as he watched the driller. "My desire, as a mere man, was to return to the sailboat for the night. Yet I had a scientist's urge to know what had scared Andrew [Carter] so badly." The scientist's desire won out—for him and, later, his colleagues. As the last rays of sunlight vanished behind the forested hills, they shifted vital supplies and equipment from the previous night's camp into a hab block near the barn. This time,

Brocious was taking no chances. He had Carter securely lock the entrance doors and head to the roof with his hunting rifle.

Darkness had barely fallen when, once again, Brocious heard "unearthly cries" from the hills behind New Virginia. "This time, I was scarcely able to contain my curiosity," he wrote. Within the safety of the hab block, he climbed to a viewing platform. From a seat beneath the wide curved roof, he had a view over the barn and surrounding buildings. "I had not been up there more than ten minutes when I saw a flicker of movement in the road." As he continued to watch, he saw an "animal of some type," but—unlike Carter's description—it was "moving on all fours" with an "unnatural, jerky, hopping gait."

At that moment, he heard Carter shout and open fire. The animal jerked, tottered backward, and then ran yelping toward the barn. "It was very thin, gauntly so," Brocious wrote at the time. "And its movements, as it ran, were much like a children's marionette."

Brocious didn't see the creature again that night. When the sun came up, he went out to the barn to check on the goats. "There was an animal laid out beside the barn, already buzzing with flies. It was gray in color with a long whiplike tail. The eyes were large and bulging. The ribs protruded through the loose, scaly skin. The arrangement of the limbs reminded me, I couldn't think how, of a mammal from my childhood on Earth, but it was not like any animal I had seen before." Lopez and Yong later found Carter's bullet embedded in the shoulder blade.

For the rest of that day, they searched the jungle for further evidence of the colonists' fate. They found nothing. Disheartened, they broke camp and Yong packaged up the dead creature in a refrigerated case for the long trip back to Antonia.

Anyone familiar with the story of the Lost Colony knows the strange creature never reached its final destination. Ten days after leaving Roanoke Landing, the sailboat was caught in a storm off the Cape of Arcadia and shipwrecked on the barren coastline. For six months the team awaited rescue, but poor weather kept ships trapped in Antonia. With only a two-month supply of food, Oni, Yong, Li and Lopez starved to death or succumbed to injuries. Brocious and Carter, the two survivors, defrosted the body of the monster and "fried it on a wooden spit."

It was to be their salvation. And officially their undoing.

Rider Harriman didn't hold with doctors. When one of his sons got sick, he cooked up an herbal remedy. He always told them, "A medic gets their hands on you, you're as good as dead." The morning after the presumed Sügenhound attack, he sat at the kitchen table with his son Chase holding his hand steady while Rider set his own broken thumb.

Neither man mentioned the Sügenhound beyond the name. "Pa wasn't that sort of guy," Harriman told me, as we sat drinking coffee. "And maybe he was scared . . . I was shit scared." Even as a teenager, he knew the rumors of what happened to people who encountered a Sügenhound, especially if they looked into its eyes.

Indeed, he told me, Rider Harriman was never the same after the bite. "He'd sit in front of the window for hours, with his .375 across his knees," he told me. "Night and day—just watching." Rider didn't talk to Harriman, or his younger brother, about what he was feeling, but Harriman suspected he was too afraid to sleep. "He would blink a lot—drop his head like he was sleeping—and then jolt awake again."

One night he told Harriman that the Sügenhound was coming for him. "He told me, right after the Sügenhound bit him, it spoke to him, inside his head. It said it'd taken the lives of his sheep, but it was plotting to take his soul." Within a few months, Rider had fallen into a mindless stupor. "He was like a zombie," Harriman said. "He'd look at you, blinking, and there was nothing behind his eyes."

Mercifully, he died weeks later. Left alone to run the ranch with his younger brother, Harriman spent the evenings researching Sügenhounds. "A Sügenhound killed my Pa. I wanted to get even." Eventually, he was able to track down the unpublished Howard Brocious diaries that today form the core of the Sügenhound Museum's collection. They were, he said, a revelation to him.

The official cause of death of Howard Brocious, and his colleague Andrew Carter, was Stumbling Sickness, but Harriman knew this wasn't the case. "There was no Stumbling Sickness 'til the forties," he said, meaning the New Flu pandemic that killed thousands in Antonia and Roanoke in 40AA. "So how come Brocious died of Stumbling Sickness ten years before?"

Like many Roanokers, Harriman believed Brocious was doomed by eating Sügenhound flesh, and Carter was cursed by looking into its eyes. He was equally adamant that Rider couldn't have contracted Stumbling Sickness. Although ranches around Roanoke Landing often lacked accurate medical records, he was certain that Rider—like him—received the childhood gene therapy that made modern-day colonists immune to the disease. "The government tried to hush up Sügenhounds," he said, draining his coffee mug. "They don't want folks to worry. That's why you should see the museum."

Harriman led me out onto the waterfront, and then turned up a wide cobbled street lined with bars and restaurants. At that time of day (early evening), it was crowded with tourists and street sellers, and the bars were alight with gaudy holograms. Most were advertising a "Sügenhound" (I later learned that this was a fiery cocktail that combines local mead with chili peppers and synnamon). At the top of the street was an imposing sandcrete building, marked by a huge biopolymer model of a hairless biped with gigantic black claws and large saucer-shaped eyes with round black pupils. It was crouched on the tips of its cloven hooves, ready to pounce, with its long spiny tail raised behind its head.

"Sügenhound?" I ask Harriman, and he nodded solemnly. The staring eyes seemed to follow me as I went through the door.

The museum took up most of the first (and second) floor of the building. It featured a history of sightings, dried scat and a mummified animal that purported to be a Sügenhound. Harriman led me past the *Darkness*-related exhibits (the New World Entertainment game that did much to popularize the Sügenhound) to a line of glass cases on the second floor. Each contained an open notepad, the yellow paper scrawled with barely legible writing. Harriman tapped on the nearest case with his finger. "Brocious wanted his story to last forever. He wrote it down, like—in analogue form."

Howard Brocious received a huge welcome home. A hundred Antonians, carrying flags and banners, assembled at the docks to meet his rescue boat. When he appeared at the top of the gangway, his hand resting on the arm of an old university friend, they cheered and waved their flags.

He was, in his words, "as happy to be home as any man." But, back in his four-roomed apartment, he found himself hot and listless. "I am prone to dizziness and fevers," he wrote in his diaries. "My ordeal has taken a toll on me, both physical and mental, from which I fear I may never recover."

Nonetheless, he tried to throw himself back into his work, planning a trip to map mineral deposits on the island of Aopo. The trip was more complex than he expected. Still thin and weak from the long wreck, he found himself anxious and tired, often forgetting details of routes and supplies. While he was away, a second mission to Roanoke Landing found neither evidence of the goats nor the wailing creatures he claimed to have seen. Brocious—who previously had an unblemished reputation—began to feel he was being made a fool.

Shortly after returning from the trip, the government refused an application for a mining mission with him as expedition leader. "I am cursed," he wrote. "It is as if my career is over as quickly it begun." He took to his bed and was diagnosed with nervous exhaustion. The local doctor in Antonia blamed the tiredness and anxiety on the stress of the Brocious expedition. "He told me that the things I had experienced . . . the deserted colony, the shipwreck followed by starvation were enough for a thousand lifetimes."

Brocious's diaries reveal a man haunted by the deaths of his teammates and the strange story that Li had told him. He began to sleep poorly, returning in his dreams to the Lost Colony and the dark shape he'd seen running, and later dead.

"That night, I found myself within the hab block in which Carter and I had sheltered on the second night in New Virginia. The moon was high, and strangely distorted—as from a distant world neither Cistercia nor Earth—but, in its illumination, I saw the creature stride out from between the buildings. It was, as Carter had seen it, a bipedal humanoid, but gaunt and child-sized in proportions that were loathsome in their deviance from humanity. The confidence of its prowling walk convinced me, in a moment, that it was a fellow sentient species and a predator.

"Against my better judgment, I found myself wandering the hab dome corridors—hearing the sounds of dead colonists as they reenacted their ghostly business. Unlocking the security bolts, I saw the door open on its own and the creature enter upon two legs, with ice still upon its skin from the freezer, and its clawed hands extended in ironic greeting. It regarded me with mesmeric white eyes filled with a malevolent, calculating intelligence and addressed me in a tongue I did not understand—but felt I should have done. 'It is your end and our beginning. You have disturbed the natural order of things. And we shall have our revenge.' This I took to mean that the colony of New Virginia should never have been.

"Presently, I awoke with my bedclothes damp with sweat and was unable to sleep further." From that day onward, each time Brocious closed his eyes, he saw that "terrible creature" standing at the foot of his bed and regarding him with "wide, pitiless eyes." He was, he wrote, too anxious to sleep for more than a few seconds. When he contacted Carter, the young man reported similar disturbing dreams.

Work soon became impossible. Days and nights blurred into one another. He often saw the creature, which he named a *Sügenhound*— or soul sucker—in the street or lurking behind display cabinets in the university buildings. Sometimes it would be accompanied by Lopez, Li and Oni—as though deliberately tormenting him. He went to the Antonia medicenter where, after a cursory inspection, he was prescribed an insomnia treatment that—for a time—allowed him to fall into a dreamless sleep.

Yet he did not feel refreshed by sleep. "I would find myself part delirious—unsure of whether I was awake or dreaming, and then I would see it, stood in my gallery kitchen, making itself a coffee with its hideous clawed hands, as though it had taken up residence there. I would cry aloud, then, and wonder if I had gone quite insane." Fearful of the presence of the creature, he invited a friend—an eminent professor—to stay for a fortnight.

Professor Benjamin Garcia remembered his first sight of his friend. "He looked haggard and unshaven, with glazed eyes and a tense, anxious way of moving. He was afraid of something... an animal, I think, entering the apartment and wanted me to sit by his bedside while he slept. I judged him exhausted and fearful beyond belief." When Brocious went to sleep, Garcia reported his friend thrashing and moaning, and tearing at his sheets in a frenzy "as though tormented by demons." In truth, he was being tortured by the Sügenhound.

Brocious continued writing until the insomnia left him incapable of thought, speech or even movement. His last entry read: "I prayed for sleep . . . or a wakefulness that never came . . . not this accursed state that is both and neither . . . For it visits me daily, leaving me with a delirious combination of joy and horror—that I should know it . . . the first human to know it . . . and yet it should be such a terrible reckoning." He died in his bed on August 13, 31AA. He was just thirty-six years old. At the time, his death was attributed to PTSD. Carter, less articulate, was to die in a similar fashion two months later. An autopsy found no obvious cause of death. Later, after the New Flu pandemic, the deaths of both men were revised to Stumbling Sickness.

Harriman took me along the line of glass cases to show me Brocious's diaries. As Brocious's sanity deteriorated, his writing became more frenzied, with huge loops, spikes and slippage over the ruled lines. "He didn't have Stumbling Sickness," Harriman told me. "He always had good balance. And he knew what was happening to him—right up until the end."

Thirty-six hours after first meeting Chase Harriman, I found myself standing inside a chicken run, beside a coop in which a flock of Roanoke Reds were sleeping. Attached to my chest was a nano-camera, and I had an infrared (IR) and night-vision sensor tagged to my smart lenses. When I looked up, the stars were brighter and sharper than in Roanoke Landing. They were the only source of light except for a pale glow from a ranch, visible through the trees.

It was approaching midnight and much warmer than I was used to. I had stripped down to my Sügenhound Museum T-shirt and, although I couldn't see them, one of my fellow tourists, Hendrix, was talking about doing the same. He was advised not to, because of the bugs up here in the summer.

Earlier that day, I'd agreed to join a group of tourists, including Hendrix, for a Sügenhound hunting trip in the hills around Roanoke Landing. At the pre-expedition briefing, Harriman told us: "There's been, what, ten reports in the last month. So, there's definitely one in the area." A few days before, he'd visited the ranch half a mile from this one, twenty-six miles west of the Landing, to investigate the mysterious deaths of some chickens. The owners of that ranch had heard a yodeling cry prior to the attack, so he thought we might also hear something. "We're looking for it, not at it," he said. "If you see one up close, try not to stare at it while you're moving away and, whatever you do, don't look into its eyes." In case we accidentally locked gaze with it, he handed us some tinted orange goggles as we boarded the manual-drive minibus. "We don't know how effective these are, so don't take any chances," he said. "But we think it should reduce the risk."

After half an hour waiting in the chicken run, there was a faint noise in the distance. Harriman told Hendrix to shush, and we listened. It was quiet, except for the chatter of insects that I remembered from the Brocious story. Through my smart lenses, I could see the trees as dark gray against a paler background. The warm bodies of the chickens were highlighted in a fuzzy haze of colors. I couldn't help thinking about the Sügenhound museum, and the huge map on the wall in what Harriman called the museum's observatory. There had been hundreds of sightings of Sügenhounds in the years since Brocious, with one of the most famous—and earliest—being Madeline Alicea. On an autumn evening in 35AA, out of her window, she'd spotted a tall, skeletal biped with "huge, googly eyes" walking across a newly cleared field.

Today most sightings were of what experts call the Cerberus-type of Sügenhound: a gaunt creature running on all fours with "rubbery burnt-looking skin" and "reptilian" gray-black scales, leading to suggestions that the "Sügenhound" is actually two creatures. I couldn't help wondering if things like Sügenhounds did exist in the jungle that covered Cistercia: alien intelligences unknown to science with a hatred of humanity and a desire to suck souls.

Then I heard a shrill whine, a few hundred yards downhill from me. It was not demonic, exactly, but it was upsetting: it sounded like an animal in pain. I swung around, heart pounding, squinting through my smart lenses at the line of trees at the edge of the ranch. "Whoa!" shouted Hendrix, and I know what he meant because there was definitely a fuzzy blob of heat moving on the IR sensor.

"STAY. STILL," Harriman snarled through my earpiece. "Folks, we might have a sighting. In the trees, just south of the ranch. Have a brief look, but IR only. Then start moving calmly back towards the ranch." His voice was breaking with tension.

I heard one of the older ladies begin to weep. I didn't blame her.

We were spaced out, fifty yards away from each other. None of us expected to see anything. "I can see something!" someone yelled. "It's coming closer; it's running!" I didn't know what they were looking at. I took my hand off the chicken coop, ready to leave the run, and slowly turned around.

And then I saw the Sügenhound. It was in the entrance to the chicken run. It was hairless, with protruding ribs, somehow sickly looking, and standing up on hind legs to paw at the gate. The beast was smaller than what Madeline Alicea saw: I judged it only came up to my shoulder. It had skin flaps instead of ears. We looked at each other. Its face was gaunt and narrow; like a skull, which made the bulging eyes look bigger. They were milky and glazed, with tiny pupils.

Then I realized. I had looked into a Sügenhound's eyes.

Cryptids

Earth history reveals many examples of cryptids—animals whose existence remains unproven or disputed. In many cases, the creatures are considered impossible or apocryphal, and relegated to myth and legends. Examples include the Bigfoot or Yeti, Jersey Devil, and Loch Ness monster. The Sügenhound is among the first Cistercian examples of a cryptid. Bearing some resemblance to the chupacabra myth of the American continents, most evidence for the existence of this Cistercian species has been questioned or discredited. Alleged encounters and incidences of "soul snatching" by Sügenhounds are largely explained by feral or infected sheepdogs attacking livestock on outlying farmsteads and/or the transmission of prion disease to Humans via bites or consumption of infected meat...

Despite hundreds of sightings each year in the area around Roanoke Landing, there have been no proven cases of Human casualties as a direct result of eye contact with a Sügenhound...

—*Encyclopedia Astra*,
Gannon University,
Antonia, Cistercia, AA212

NO WORD FOR PRINCES

Jody Lynn Nye

"Prepare the analysis of this titration," Dr. Masika Seddik said, clicking the key that would release the raw database from hundreds of infected cell samples to her AI implant.

"Working," said Alhikma, the name she had given the device. The word, meaning "wisdom," came from her ancient Earth-Egyptian family roots. "Advanced memory storage and retrieval" would have been a more accurate title, but her coworker, Isaiah Benson, had already snagged "Amsar" as his AI's name.

She sat back on her lab stool and hooked her rubber heels into the bottom rung, feeling a rueful twinge when she thought of Isaiah: charming, funny, handsome, and so smart that he made her feel like a drone. One of the cultures in her collection came from him. He had caught the fever.

He, like almost ten percent of the three thousand settlers of Roanoke colony, suffered high temperature, muscular weakness, occasional disorientation, and general malaise. Of that number, over twenty had already died. She felt a lump of ice in her belly that he might become one of that number. She would do anything to keep that from happening.

Although she had trained as a psychologist, Masika had been tagged by the head of the Science Foundation and Masika's mentor, Dr. Trudy Pangin, to become one of the dedicated analysts during the growing crisis because of her minor in biology. Masika and the others would have done anything for Trudy, who always fought for more funding and consideration for them with the colony mayor and the Roanoke council.

Trudy and the rest of the founders of the renewed Roanoke colony were desperately afraid that the ailment was a disease like Creutzfeldt-Jakob that had swept across Earth for a brief period a few centuries back. Unfortunately, accurate diagnosis could only be procured by a brain tissue sample after death, to look for telltale lesions. Roanoke colony just did not have the technological resources to take cells from a living brain.

It was a truism, unfortunately, that there was never enough money or resources for scientific research until a crisis arose, then everyone argued among themselves that it wasn't being well spent. Trudy never took nonsense like that and had gone public to the colony as a whole to appeal for their support during the outbreak. The reaction to her had been so positive that in the recent election, she had been elected mayor in place of Roberta Belen, the popular administrator who had overseen the transfer eight years before of the new settlers from the Antonia settlement to the mysteriously empty site of the former New Virginia colony. To give Roberta credit, she had thrown her full support behind Trudy. Eight years of being mayor had to be enough for anyone.

Masika admired Trudy tremendously, though the exuberant woman always pushed her forward into roles that the younger scientist was sure she couldn't fulfill—until she did fulfill them. Trudy had plucked her mere days after graduation to join the body of counselors for colonists having trouble adapting to life in Roanoke. Once the outbreak had begun, the importance of psychologists fell behind that of biologic investigators, so Trudy had moved her to that group. When her mentor had been promoted to mayor, she had named Masika to head the Science Foundation, a task for which she felt monumentally unequal, but Trudy had insisted she could do it. The young woman had felt some small resentment at being pulled out first from her dream job as a counselor, then boosted into the administration of the whole facility. She didn't like being forced into roles she never intended to play, but when Trudy insisted, she felt as though she couldn't refuse.

"You'll grow into it, I promise," Trudy had said, giving her a hug. "And you can always call on me if you need help."

Despite her misgivings, she had done both. Her small, wispy figure and solemn face framed by long dark hair could hardly project the same authority as Trudy's jolly round countenance and maternal curves, but she stated only facts she could prove. People were getting edgy lately, as she had little of substance she could offer them, but with Trudy's encouragement, she became a trusted figure in the community. Little by little, she came to trust herself as well.

Masika sighed. The condensation from her breath formed a cloud on her face shield. Automatically, she reached for the transparent mask to take it off.

"Do not remove the protective barrier," Alhikma said. Masika felt the muscles and tendons of her own jaw moving, forming the words that the AI was saying. She let her hand drop.

"All right, don't bully me," she said.

"Safety protocol," was all Alhikma said. Masika's tongue relaxed after the final L, and she stuck it out of her mouth in protest.

A quirk the implanted microcomputers possessed was that they took over parts of the body in which they were implanted. She wished that she could ask the scientists back in Antonia colony if the trait was the residue of a program that would allow full assistance by the devices if their humans had suffered a degree or more of physical paralysis, but communication between the two sites was . . . difficult . . . to say the least. She wished she could access the larger colony's databases for more than that; in the current and growing crisis, she could have used the help. She wished she could reach back in time eight years and find if an illness like this was responsible for turning this colony location into a ghost town. Not even remains that they had disinterred left any clues to the fate or whereabouts of the thousands of others who had simply vanished. In so many ways, the settlers of Roanoke were on their own.

"How long will the analysis take?" she asked.

"Exploring sixty-four parameters of investigation, with cross-check and re-cross-check," Alhikma said, forming the words efficiently with her mouth. "Fifty-eight hours. Database may still be of insufficient size. Suggest further samples to be incorporated."

Masika groaned. Too long. The council and reporters wanted daily updates, hourly if they could get them.

"All right. Begin process."

"Operating." The screen embedded in her table opened tab after tab of spreadsheets, flashing as they populated with data.

She looked around the otherwise empty lab. Fifteen other technicians and scientists ought to be working there, but most of them were in the field, out on the perimeter of the colony, trying to track down the source—any source—of whatever had made the cattle, the initial patients of this outbreak, sick.

Not notorious for their intelligence, cows and sheep ate anything that smelled remotely right. Somewhere, some of them had picked up a pathogen or just a toxic substance that gave them colic. A few weeks later, the herding dogs on those stations had also started to show signs of intestinal distress. A number of them died, along with the cattle and sheep. Then a few of the farmers and ranchers began falling ill. Trudy had gone out to talk with all of the affected families, promising support. With her expert assistance, they gathered up tissue cultures and samples of plants, foods, water from numerous wells, and brought them back to the Science Foundation to begin analysis.

Wild speculation in the local media from the handful of professional reporters and citizen journalists alike suggested everything from a zoonosis, a disease that could jump between species, toxic poisoning from the ground water or local plant life, infiltration from parasites—Masika had stopped counting at fifty or sixty putative causes. They simply did not know enough to draw a conclusion. Her fear, shared by others in the department, was that it might be a combination of causes, leading to an exponential explosion of possibilities.

Throughout the crisis, Trudy had been a star. She had controlled the narrative by pure force of personality, sharing all the data as it became available, and asking the public's help to report if they saw any new outbreaks. Her openness helped calm the inevitable panic and even served to draw the colony closer together. Because she wasn't treating the outbreak like a state secret, it helped others to be able to discuss the matter more calmly. Trudy was the glue that held Roanoke together.

Despite overwhelming duties as the chief operating officer of the colony, she never failed to call the Science Foundation at sixteen hundred hours each day and see how the research was going.

Masika looked up at the huge black-and-white chronometer on the wall. Twelve minutes to sixteen. She hopped down from her seat and made herself a cup of tea.

The clock's numerals swapped over to 1600 as Masika took her first sip from the steaming beaker. Right on schedule, her wrist communicator buzzed.

"Hello, loove," Trudy said, beaming at her from the small screen. Masika felt warmth suffuse through her at the sound of her mentor's rich voice with its cuddly country accent. The mayor always treated her like one of her own children. "How are things going over there, my dear?"

Masika set down her tea and picked up the computer slate that was slaved to the mainframe and scrolled down the outline of her experiments so far. She sent them to Trudy's personal computer.

"Alhikma is running the numbers on the data that the team has been sending in," she said. "It'll take a couple of days until we have answers. And he warned me there may not be enough information to come to a comprehensive conclusion. Everyone else is still out in the field. I hope they can bring me more data."

"I've been wondering if this situation has anything to do with why Roanoke was deserted in the first place," Trudy said, echoing Masika's own thoughts. "I've got a call in to Library Sciences to have them open up the archives left from New Virginia. If there's any concrete information, you can add that to your data."

Masika made a quick note. "That would be fantastic," she said. "Anything would help."

"You're doing a great job, loove," Trudy said. "Thank you."

"Thank you for the opportunity," Masika replied, her heart full of gratitude. "Is there anything else?"

Trudy was silent, something very unlike her usually garrulous and expansive self.

"One more thing," she said at last. "My temperature's up today. I've found myself forgetting things. And I just dropped a coffee cup. It's as if it fell slap through my hand."

Masika's fist closed, her nails digging into her palm. She noticed that the mayor's round cheeks had a dot of hot pink at the apples, and her eyes were brighter than usual. "You've got the fever."

Trudy nodded.

"I think so. I'm not going to hide it from the public, loove. I haven't gotten this far by telling lies. I'll keep track of my symptoms as well as I can. I've already warned my assistant to bring me meals but not come into my private quarters unless he's wearing disposable scrubs and a mask. I don't know where I picked it up or when; I've been here, there and everywhere. Can you send someone to take a culture from me?"

"I'll come myself," Masika said at once, hopping down from her stool and heading for the supply closet.

"No, you won't, my dear," Trudy said, shaking her head gently. "I need you as healthy as you can be. Let one of the others come from the outer reaches. I'll be right."

Masika felt her heart sink. Both knew that the chances of the last were not good.

"I'll be right," Trudy assured her. "You can always count on me. I never say 'can't' unless there's no other way."

Masika hoped that would always be true.

"I thought Mayor Pangin would be here," Farm Union Chief Lawrence Domino said, lowering his thick dark brows at her. Masika sat as tall as she could at the head of the conference table in the City Center council room. The huge circular structure was all that was left of the lander that had brought the colonists to Roanoke from Antonia. It housed all government facilities, plus the education mainframe, the financial center, and the trading hub, and several other operational centers.

"She would have liked to attend in person," Masika said, projecting confidence she did not feel to him and the other eleven members of the town council. "She has been moved to the hospital. You may know that her condition is worsening." The Science Foundation and the Health Center occupied an isolated, smaller pod to the northwest. Lately, traffic to the latter was almost as heavy as to the main building. "But she will be joining us via remote."

"That's not good enough!" Domino declared.

"Larry, calm down," Iris Yamato said, patting the air. Her position at the head of the Commodities Exchange put her slightly above the bombastic union official in importance. "Dr. Seddik, my merchants and traders are getting nervous about whether there will be enough food and other resources for the winter ahead. Your Science Foundation put out a prediction that it'll be an extended cold season, as much as thirty percent longer than last year. I don't want to see hoarding. Everyone suffers if there are shortages."

"Yes," Masika began. "You know that meteorology is an inexact science. Based on weather patterns—"

"My nephew caught this fever after his dogs died on his ranch," Education Superintendent Hubert Sikowski said, pounding one gnarled fist on the table. "When are you going to find a cure for it?"

"We're working on it, sir," Masika said, her voice rising to a squeak. She had been afraid of the demanding Sikowski ever since she was a middle schooler. Even excellent students got the sharp edge of his tongue if he thought they weren't applying themselves to the utmost. "I'd like to—"

The speakers attached to the projection unit in the center of the table let out a squawk. Masika was thankful for the diversion. Above the unit, a hologram of Trudy's face arose, seeming to face each of them at the same time.

"Afternoon, my dears," she said. Her usually resonant voice sounded thin and thready. Masika didn't like the hollow look around Trudy's unnaturally bright eyes. Her heart twisted in her chest. "What have I missed?"

"Nothing!" Sikowski bellowed. He always acted as though he had to project his voice all the way to where remote attendees were transmitting from. "Nothing is getting done. People are dying and we need answers!"

Trudy replied smoothly, "And we're working on them, Hubert. These things take time."

"My nephew could die!"

The mayor regarded him out of those gleaming eyes. Masika realized that Trudy could die, too, and it made her feel even more helpless.

"I'm so sorry, Hubert," Trudy said. "We became used to rapid solutions in Antonia. We can't do that here. We just don't have the scientific equipment or the personnel, and rushing won't do the job at all. Investigations such as this are slow and painstaking. You wouldn't want us to give your nephew the wrong medication. I know you're worried about him. So is Masika. She cares deeply about finding the answers. She needs your help."

"What help?" Sikowski rounded on Masika, who shrank into her chair.

"Yes, what can we do?" Mike Needham asked. A former

schoolmate of Masika's, he ran transportation. The currently stalled light-rail project from the hub out to six points in the outer reaches had been his innovation. "Anything but sit on my hands."

Masika fumbled for her tablet.

"We're analyzing specimens from all the affected animals and humans," she said, staring down at the swirling columns of numbers. "So far, nothing stands out. The full data won't be available for a few days, so . . ."

"What can we do *now*?" Sikowski asked, his brows down again.

"Um, I . . . I'm not used to involving other departments," she said, apologetically.

"Well, you'd better get used to trying! People are dying! We don't have time for shilly-shallying."

"Where did you get that archaic expression?" Iris asked, her own brows in the air. "Masika, we'll do whatever we can to help."

"I knew you would," Trudy said, though the hearty statement had little of the normal power behind it. Masika had seen the mayor's morning vitals. The illness was advancing rapidly. "Masika will have assignments for you tomorrow. Will you get her a list of . . . of volunteers from each of your departments?"

"I would be glad to," Iris said.

"I will do whatever it takes," Larry said.

"Me, too," Mike added. The others nodded. Hubert only added a coarse grunt.

"Then, it's settled," Trudy said. Her voice trailed off, and her forehead wrinkled as if a thought had struck her. The pause was obvious to all of them. "I need to go lie down, my dears."

"Please get some rest," Masika said, abashed that she had caused her friend to strain herself.

As Masika had feared, the analysis of the tissue samples gave no clear markers in common with one another. She ran through the graphs again and again. The local produce had some extra rungs in its DNA, but for almost forty years on this world no one had reported a problem with it that she knew of. No insectoid species seemed to have a venom that would cause catastrophic failure of immune systems. It simply seemed as though animals and humans were weakening and dying in clusters.

"What do you want me to do now?" Alhikma asked.

"Separate them according to geography, then divide by species," Masika said, rubbing her hands together to ease the tightness of her fingers. "Let's hope we can find if there is a divergence or a mutation of cells as the disease spreads. We can't be too cautious. I'll take these data to Trudy and see what she thinks."

Over the past three days, two more humans and five more dogs had died. Pundits in the news service, including Timothy Wath, a notorious skeptic and gadfly, blamed the Science Foundation for failing the colony. Trudy had recorded a rebuttal, restating the obvious lack of data, resources, and time. Masika knew she should have been the one to issue a statement. She wanted the mayor's input, but also to give her an apology for not publicly defending her department. She counted on Trudy's aid, but she ought to be pulling her own weight.

The medical facility was always busy. Doctors, nurses, and orderlies nodded to Masika as she suited up in disposable scrubs and a transparent full-face mask. Trudy's room stood at the far end of a corridor, in a south-facing bay full of sunshine. Masika's steps quickened as she saw a number of personnel moving purposefully in and out of the door to her room.

Noel Vonn, Trudy's assistant, hurried to meet her. His long, saturnine face was stricken with shock.

"I'm glad you're here," he said, pulling her inside. "I was about to call you."

"Why? What's wrong?" Masika stared in horror at the physicians and technicians working over the figure in the bed. A mask over Trudy's face filled with condensation, cleared, and filled again.

Noel shook his head. "It happened all of a sudden. Her temperature spiked, and her vitals started falling. They've done everything, but it's like all the others. She's fading."

A hand rose from the midst of the equipment snaking over the bedside.

"Masika." Trudy's voice had fallen to a whisper.

Masika ran to her and took the hand. She squeezed her mentor's fingers and held on until the end.

"They want me to give the eulogy," she told Isaiah later that day.

Her friend had been given a room on a higher floor with cases that had not advanced as far or as fast as Trudy's.

"You were her favorite pupil," Isaiah said. His dark brown skin had a grayish tinge to it, and he had little of his usual energy. Masika refused to look at his chart. He would get better. He must. She needed him to pull through.

"But what can I say? I'm not a public speaker."

Isaiah smiled. "Say what's in your heart. That's what people want to hear. Trudy understood that. In fact, you ought to offer to step up and take her place."

"As mayor?" Masika goggled at him. "How? I'm not qualified."

"Leadership in this crisis has to come from our department. Science. That's where the cure is going to come from, not law enforcement, or agriculture, or trade. Trudy knew that. She believed in us. In you."

"I can't do it! What about you?"

"Me?" Isaiah asked. He shook his head and opened his hands helplessly. "Masi, don't count on me. Count on yourself. You're more than enough. Find a way to do it. Trudy always pushed you, and you always came through. Do it for me, if you won't do it in her memory."

She kept the vision of his warm smile and his beautiful dark brown eyes in her mind as she made her way back to her quarters through the glaring industrial corridors.

"Alhikma," she said quietly, offering the usual nods to acquaintances as she walked, "I have to figure out what I can say for Trudy."

"Define," Alhikma's voice said.

"Uh." Masika thought hard. She had been to a couple of funeral services, right after the settlers landed, although she had been a young teen at the time. "Something that will make them think, and maybe smile. She did so much for us—for me especially. Words that will unite us in her memory."

"Definition still vague. Categories?"

"Ugh!" Masika let her head fall back. "Eulogy, elegy, memorial, stirring, hopeful, warm, kind, strong. Are those enough keywords?"

"Yes. I am searching the e-book library for volumes containing suitable phrases and examples. Task will complete in four point nine two minutes."

She glanced at a wall chronometer. That would give her just enough time to get back to her quarters.

Five hours later, Masika stared at her tablet screen, barely able to absorb any more words. Most of what Alhikma had come up with were books of poetry and the plays of Shakespeare, nothing that instantly gave her a meaningful farewell to her friend and mentor.

"I don't think people are going to put up with a comparison between Trudy and Julius Caesar," she said crossly. "'I come to bury Caesar, not to praise him,' isn't what I had in mind. It's all too disjointed."

"Explain."

Masika swept her hand down the selected bibliography. "I have a better idea. Download all of these books into your active memory bank. Synthesize a speech of about fifteen minutes in length of, oh, a hundred words a minute. Include Trudy's biography with her accomplishments as scientist and mayor."

"Working," Alhikma said. "I will compose several speeches for your perusal."

While the AI sifted through the literary works of the ages, Masika scanned the list. She had not thought of books like this for years, not since having to concentrate strictly on science tomes to earn her degree. She hadn't liked Shakespeare in text form, but translated to the current dialect and read aloud, she wanted to follow Henry V into war.

In fact, all the tools of leadership and resilience were there in the library. Such books as *How to Win Friends and Influence People, Personality Analysis, The Scouting Manual,* psychology and psychoanalysis texts, all gave instruction on understanding others and guiding them to productive ends. And after reading the synopsis, she began to thumb through *The Prince* by Niccolo Macchiavelli. He had set down all the principles of leadership and he had a keen eye for the psychological traits that could make even a mediocre king seem all things to all people. All the traits that Trudy evinced naturally were set down in book form. Isaiah's suggestion kept popping up in her mind. Masika's hands almost trembled with excitement as she held her tablet.

"Alhikma, if I have you download these into your memory, can you help me when I need to talk to people?"

"I can, but it would be better if I condensed them into their main points and had you study the best way to employ those principles."

"We don't have time for that," Masika said. "I have to become the best leader now. I need you to talk for me. *Please.*"

"As you wish," Alhikma said.

Masika spent half the night looking through synopses of leadership manuals, some with reviews attached that went back three centuries. In the small hours, her eyes blurred over the title of the five hundredth,—or was it six hundredth?—book.

"You are not absorbing information," the AI said, in a voice that sounded kindlier than it had ever used before. "Go to sleep. I will wake you in time for the memorial service."

Masika stood with her tablet balanced on the podium in the center atrium of the Lander Center beside a huge hologram of Trudy. She felt sad that it wasn't a proper funeral, but once tissue samples had been taken and scans made of the body, it was felt to be a matter of public safety to cremate the body, as had been done with previous victims of the epidemic.

Every healthy individual in the colony came to pay their respects, though many wore face masks or sprayed antiseptic mist to intercept potential contagion. Masika's eyes watered at the concentration of eucalyptus, tea tree oil, and other nostrums filling the air from the rows of benches. Those colonists still at home or in the hospital followed the service by means of the small cameras hovering in the air at several points in the enormous chamber.

"My friends, Dr. Trudy Pangin spent her life in service to others..." Masika began. Prompted by Alhikma when her memory flagged, she delivered the address they had composed.

"Look out at everyone," Alhikma murmured. "Move your gaze over the crowd. Make eye contact."

Masika fought to regain control of her mouth.

"...We were grateful for her kindness and wisdom, the intelligence she brought to every task. No better teacher ever walked these halls..."

At that moment, the thought that her teacher would never again walk with her overcame Masika. Her throat closed, and she stopped. Suddenly, her mouth began to move again. Alhikma took over her vocal cords and pronounced the speech in rolling, round tones that Masika could hardly believe came from her body.

"... In honest and loving service to her fellow colonists, giving the newly revived settlement of Roanoke not only a face and a voice, but a willing ear to those who needed it. Trudy Pangin's presence will be missed. I recall that when I was a student here in the Lander University, she was always available to answer myriad questions that I was too shy to ask the other professors..." Masika felt her cheeks burning as her mouth went on with what she had always considered a private story, but she couldn't help but notice that the listeners nodded and smiled wistfully, even chuckled wryly, at every turn in the anecdote.

"... We offer a fond farewell to the best of public servants, a dear friend of mine, and a friend to all of Roanoke," Masika said, recapturing her own voice and reading from the script rolling up on her tablet. "Let us not talk of Trudy Pangin in the past tense, because what she did for the colony is still all around us. She helped us to reach this part of the future, but there is more left to come."

Even though it wasn't protocol to applaud at memorial services, Mike sprang to his feet and began to clap. Others sprang up to join him. Masika blushed and lowered her eyes.

"I didn't think you had it in you," Hubert said. He wrinkled his nose and sniffed sharply, as though to dispel the impression that he was stifling tears. "I'm impressed. Iris here said you ought to take over as mayor. I wouldn't have thought so before."

Masika automatically protested. "I'm sure someone else would do it better."

"When you have the power to win people's hearts?" Iris asked, taking her hands. "That was the most beautiful, *meaningful* thing I have ever heard! Trudy would have loved it."

"We have almost everyone here," Mike said. Masika tried to pull away, but he grabbed her hand and held it up high. "Everybody? We need a new mayor to take over. Now, we can waste a couple of weeks on an election, or we can go ahead and select one now. I propose that Dr. Masika Seddik be the new mayor of Roanoke colony. Anyone second?"

"Seconded!" Iris chimed in.

Mike beamed at her. "I know it's not the way things are usually done, but how about a quick vote? Everybody in favor of Masika being the new mayor, raise your hand."

Masika was astonished to see more than three-quarters of the hands of people in the room thrust into the air. Their faces were filled with hope and expectation that made her quail inside.

"Looks like you have the majority," Mike said, letting her hand go. "We can poll the people in the outer reaches, but I think we outnumber all the others in the colony. Congratulations, Dr. Mayor!"

Iris began to applaud. The others in the room joined in.

"Speech!" a man in the second row bellowed. "Speech!" The cry was taken up by the crowd.

"Say something," she murmured to Alhikma. "My mind just went blank!"

"Certainly. What would you like me to say?" Alhikma asked.

"An acceptance speech!"

"As you wish. Clear your throat and wait for them to be silent."

"How do you know they . . . ?" she began.

"Try it and see. All the studies suggest that it is a natural response to those who see that a senior or executive person is prepared to address them. You have read those studies. We can argue it later. Clear your throat."

She did as the AI suggested. To her astonishment, everyone did stop talking and turned to her with earnest, hopeful eyes. She experienced the eerie sensation of having a powerful personality speaking through her, but not of her. That must be the way that the prophets of old felt, as their gods used them to communicate to their worshippers.

"My friends," her mouth said. "I am grateful for the honor you have bestowed on me. In the name of our good friend, Trudy Pangin, I will take up the tasks that she was forced to leave unfinished. We all need to pull together in the coming months and years to deal with the problem before us. I am at your service, and I ask for your help."

Alhikma continued. Masika heard the words coming from her and listened with the same awe and attention as the hundreds of people in the audience. She saw the rapt expressions on their faces and knew that they were on board with whatever she would suggest.

What will they do when they find out I'm faking it?

But no one seemed to be concerned whether Masika was making her own speech or not. When Alhikma let her tongue and vocal cords rest, they sprang to their feet and applauded wildly. She quailed when a horde of them rushed the podium and gathered around her, all talking at once.

"Jobs!" Hubert Sikowski barked.

She blinked at him.

"Jobs! You said Trudy left things undone. What do you need us to do?"

Masika's mind went blank for a nanosecond, then she began reeling off the list that she and Trudy had discussed only the day before the mayor had passed away.

"We need access to the records from the previous settlement," she said. "If they suffered from an outbreak like this one, I want all the details that they set down—files, personal messages, diaries, whatever is in their database. I know they didn't leave a key to their software, but it came from Antonia, the same as ours did, so it must have roots in common."

"My people can find that," Sikowski said. With a sharp nod, he elbowed his way out of the crowd.

"Who are you to tell us what to do?" demanded Marie Weston, the head of Computer Services.

It was the first challenge to her authority. Masika cringed.

"Trust me," the AI quietly whispered to her. Then, she felt her mouth moving. In order for it to be heard, she took a breath, and Alhikma repeated what it had said.

"I'm doing what needs to be done. The colony is suffering. Can you help? Will *you* take over the administration and decide what we have to do next to find a cure and take care of the population in the meanwhile?"

"Uh, no!" Weston protested.

"Then, help me to do that." The words sounded more emphatic than Masika normally used. She recognized the confidence from the book on personality analysis that she had entered into the AI's memory. "You, go over these records. Collate information on how fast the population declined. You, check the news broadcasts and journal entries. I'll authorize the opening of private records." The person she assigned, a young woman, seemed excited at the prospect of reading other people's diaries. "I'm trusting you," Masika said, warningly.

The girl looked a little taken aback but straightened her spine and nodded firmly. Masika knew from the clear gaze that she could indeed trust this one to do what she had asked, even if she knew the young woman would spread gossip. It didn't matter; the subjects were long dead. She spelled out tasks one at a time. The older man who had been an assistant chief in the central accounting office was to take inventory of food, medicine, other vital supplies.

One of the men managed dairy collection and headed a cheese-and-yogurt-making consortium. She, or rather Alhikma, ordered him to map the geography of where the sickest animals were, and what proportion of them was dying. He nodded, looking solemn, and made a note on his personal tablet.

A few more offered feeble arguments, but when Masika offered to step down in their favor, they backed off.

"Most importantly, we have to coordinate medical care for those who fall ill," the AI said through her voice. "Medical privacy is enshrined in the constitution of every colony, but it has to be superseded by need during an epidemic, which this is. I know I am choosing the best person for each of these tasks," Masika felt the AI say, swooping in over her words. Although her tongue stumbled when challenged by two minds at the same time, the colonists didn't notice.

They seemed eager to do what she asked. Anything but take over themselves.

Item by item, Masika went down the tasks Trudy had been too ill to oversee. Those who could undertake them took their instructions and departed. When she had reached the end of her list, about a dozen people were still standing around her with that hopeful look on her face.

"The rest of you can still be of help," she found herself saying. "Friends and relatives who are ill need care. Check in on everyone. Wear anti-contamination masks and gloves. I want a daily log of the health of humans and animals throughout the colony. Divide it into sectors. Report to Nita," she said, and her hand rose to point at the dark-skinned woman who ran one of the childcare facilities. "She will report to me and to Dr. Siruzzi, the hospital administrator. If you note anyone falling ill, let her know."

"Got it," Nita said, with a relieved nod. "Let's go, everybody."

Masika found herself standing alone in the middle of the huge, echoing chamber. "You were amazing," she said to Alhikma.

"I did only what you programmed me to do," it replied.

"You raised my arm! I didn't know you could take over my body like that."

"This unit is a complete assistive device, capable of stimulating nerves and muscles. The capacity of the AI system has not been exploited to the fullest in this colony. Up until now, it wasn't needed."

"Well, I need you now," Masika said. She noticed a maintenance engineer coming in with a robotic cart to collect the benches. He eyed her curiously. He must have seen her talking to Alhikma. Hastily, she retreated to her lab.

She had little time for thought over the following days to consider the changes in her AI. Moving from her space in the Science Foundation headquarters to the mayor's office in the Lander Center meant nominating someone to take over her position there, as well as learning the names and positions of all the people who had assisted Trudy. Alhikma was an immense help there, promptly recalling all the details that her overwhelmed mind couldn't absorb.

"That was one hell of a eulogy you gave Trudy," Isaiah said, on her next visit to him.

"It wasn't just me," she said, then explained programming Alhikma with all the books on leadership. He laughed until he collapsed back on his pillows, gasping for breath. She noticed then how colorless his skin had become and how thin he was. Her heart chilled inside her. "That's good. You really put one over on them. But you're good at managing people yourself. Trudy knew that. I know that."

"Don't tell anyone!"

"I won't," Isaiah said. He still had the grin on his face. "That's epic, though. Amsar rejects poetry, even songs."

"I wish you were well enough to take over at the Foundation," Masika said. As soon as the words were out of her mouth, she knew that he would never leave that room. She refused to think of how much time he had left. When he picked up his water glass in two trembling hands, she knew it couldn't be a lot.

"Me, too, Masi," Isaiah said. "Come back and tell me how it's going."

"I promise," she said, and retreated more hastily than she meant to.

★ ★ ★

Masika threw herself into the work. At night, in the brief private time she had between dealing with people and falling into an exhausted sleep, she added more volumes to Alhikma's processor.

The AI had a mild personality hardwired into it, but she had seen it change temporarily when she had once accidentally programmed someone else's thesis into it. Word choices, syntax, sentence structure all felt differently from author to author—whether they were confident or competent, all had an effect. As a psychologist, she found the synthesis very interesting. She and other psych majors used to play with those in university lab studies, feeding information into them, and seeing the alterations, then resetting them to factory specs. She let Alhikma read her diaries and abstracts so it would get a more detailed sense of her way of speaking. Going on autopilot and letting Alhikma run her body gave her a chance to think about the mountains of reports she had to read daily.

The implant was an old one, having been used by one of her professors' predecessors, but with lots of memory and processing power. Incredible for a device so small that it became a constant companion for her. She couldn't imagine life without it. It played music when she wanted it, monitored her blood sugar to remind her to eat. She couldn't help but worry about the food and wonder whether it was responsible for the contagion. The alien DNA with its two extra rungs concerned her, but all the lab tests from the technicians and scientists still able to work gave her no concrete evidence of harm. Still, patients continued to sicken and die.

Though it tore her apart inside, her outward appearance was that of a calm leader. Even when she wanted to collapse and cry, Alhikma made her body stand up and speak clearly.

Despite her misgivings and fears, her example helped the colony keep from falling into chaos. As promised, Hubert Sikowski and his programmers and students attacked the old databases from New Virginia. Much of it had been corrupted, but personal diaries and accounts, kept in a much simpler language than technical articles and official records, gave them anecdotal evidence that, yes, a disease had hit here. Some people and animals had succumbed to fever and febrile weakness of the limbs. No statistics or medical reports had been translated as yet. Masika wished fervently for genetic analyses and medical reports. Had they found that wonky DNA, or was that new?

"We'll keep at it until we get the mainframes straightened out," Sikowski said, his expression challenging her to find fault with him. Masika quailed, but she all but felt a hand in the middle of her back preventing her from edging away from the intense educator.

"I can't tell you how grateful we are for the work you are all doing," Alhikma said to him. "Every piece of information helps us put together a profile of the epidemic."

Sikowski and his team looked gratified by the praise. Masika retreated to her office as soon as she could.

Alhikma always had the right words to put people at ease. He wrote her speeches and prompted her on what to say and do at every stage. She felt nervous all the time, feeling like a complete fraud. The only person she could unburden herself to was Isaiah.

Until the horrible day came when she went back to the medical and science center to find the same crowd of doctors and technicians around his bed who had attended Trudy. But instead of a hand rising from the sheets beckoning her to his side, Dr. Siruzzi lifted his dark brown eyes to her and shook his head, his face gentle but sad. A sob tore from the very depths of her belly. Grief, frustration, and loss shook her body as she wept. A nurse plucked a handful of disposable tissues from the box at the quiet bedside. She plunged her face into them.

Alhikma let her cry for a minute, then forced her lips to move.

"Thank you all," she heard herself say. "I know you did everything you could. He was a good man. I appreciate all your efforts. This must be as frustrating to you as it is to me."

Siruzzi nodded.

"Thank you, Ms. Mayor," he said. "Would you like us to leave you alone for a moment?"

"Over a hundred people dead," she wailed, once the door had closed behind the team. She clutched Isaiah's hand in hers, feeling it cooling already. "Why couldn't you be one of the ones who recovered?"

"No one recovers from this disease," Alhikma reminded her. "We have no evidence that anyone in New Virginia managed to survive it, either."

"But there are no bodies," Masika said. "Where did they go? What is the ailment?"

"We don't know," Alhikma said. "It is possible that we may never know. All that can be done is to treat the symptoms empirically, as we have been. I hope that there is enough time to find a cure."

"Enough time before what?"

The AI fell silent, something that she felt was uncharacteristic of the way Alhikma had been before she began to reprogram him.

"Before everyone dies."

Masika felt that urge to flee again, but she refused to abandon Isaiah so callously. Instead, she pushed the button to allow the medical team to return. She stayed with him until they removed his body. A part of her soul left with him.

She went on with her duties almost on autocontrol, sitting in her office listening to colonists who just needed to unburden themselves to someone in charge, going out to praise researchers digging into the data of the long-lost settlement, expressing gratitude to the medics and techs who took care of an increasing stream of patients, and sitting with grieving families who had just lost a loved one. She found it hard to care what happened to her after the deaths of her mentor and her best friend, but Alhikma always had the right words for the situation. With a kind of admiration, she let him take over her body and mouth. The news stations even called her a "legend of competence and compassion," but she knew it was the AI implant. He was her rock. She wished he were a real person who could take over the job and let her go back to her research.

Noel Vonn burst into her office, pointing out of the room. "Ms. Mayor, there's a riot going on in the atrium!"

Masika heard the yelling. She turned the screen in her desk to the feed from cameras in the great room and saw a crowd of people shouting and carrying tablets that had slogans running on them in large print.

Before she realized it, she was on her feet, heading down to the ground-floor level along the moving ramp. Over a hundred protesters, most of them young, faced off against the Lander Center security guards and robots.

"Take us back! Save our lives! Take us back! Save our lives!"

Noel and the captain of the squad tried to hold Masika back, but she thrust their protective arms away and marched up to the leaders of the protest movement.

"What is it you want?" she asked, keeping her voice low and level. Despite the calm Alhikma projected, her heart pounded in her chest.

"We're dying!" said a young man with dark, frizzy hair and intense brown eyes just like Isaiah's. "We've been asking for a cure for months, but you're not giving us one! Put engines on this lander and get us back to Antonia!"

Masika protested internally, but Alhikma made her arm move and rest her hand on the young man's arm. He shook her off, but the AI placed it again.

"I know you are frightened. We are all frightened. I promise you, we are doing everything we know how to do. We can't fly the lander back. You're old enough to have flown here with the colony; you know there is no more fuel. Please, help us to take action here. Help *me*. I need researchers, programmers, technicians. Can you do any of that?" She turned to the rest of the milling mob. "Can you? Join us. If we all work together, we can find a cure. Please."

"I, uh . . ." The leader looked at his fellow protesters. He lowered his sign. She realized that he was on the edge of tears and went to embrace him. His shoulders began to shake. His friends came to wrap their arms around the two of them. "We'll help. We'll help. We've just lost too many people."

"So have I," Masika said. Her voice trembled. She and the others clung together for a time, then she let go.

"That's the bravest thing I ever saw," the captain said, when the mob broke up and filtered away. "I thought you were out of your mind, but wow! You broke up the riot, and not a single punch thrown."

"I could have been killed!" Masika shrieked, once she was alone in her office again with the privacy light illuminated over the door. "I can't go charging into situations like that. I'm a hundred fifty-five centimeters!"

"They respect you too much to harm you," Alhikma said. "I judged you to be safe, or I would not have allowed you to leave the room. You have come to be thought of as a great leader. Those young people came here for your help. They knew they could not obtain the result they wanted, but you gave them what they *needed*. You listened, and you gave them a purpose. That is powerful. You were masterful. When you spoke from your heart, *they* listened."

"Oh." Masika forced herself not to react emotionally, but to think about his words. She fetched a deep breath and let it out in a sigh. "I don't know what I would do without you. I rely on you more and more every day."

"You should be learning to rely on yourself," Alhikma said. "You have wisdom and intelligence, and you care. You have all the traits you need."

Masika shook her head. "You're always here for me. I . . . I love you." She felt silly saying it, then realized it was the truth. Alhikma had helped her through so many crises with patience and wisdom. He listened, he was always there, and he could never die. He was the perfect man. "Could you . . . could you ever love me?"

"Masika." Even though it spoke with her voice, she always heard it as a soothing baritone. "I do not feel love or lust, but I am programmed to simulate compassion."

Tears of frustration welled up until they spilled from her eyes. "I feel so alone," she sobbed.

A gentle hand patted her on the shoulder, then warm arms wrapped around her—her own arms. They held her tightly until her crying storm abated. One hand stroked her cheek.

"Thank you," she said. "I needed that."

Her arms dropped to her side.

"I will help you learn to cope," Alhikma promised.

"I can't."

"Can't is not a word for princes. Be the prince that the colony needs. You can rest later."

Despite having broken up the riot, discord was never far below the surface in the day-to-day running of Roanoke. Egos required constant soothing. Information had to be coordinated and collated between departments, and it seemed as though the office of mayor was the only one that could do it. It was exhausting.

Alhikma helped her keep track of the reports she received almost hourly. As Trudy had done, she gave a daily summary on the colony-wide web station, telling them what actions were being taken, what research had uncovered, and who had died. She had protested reading the names of the deceased, but the AI insisted it would make the efforts of the survivors more meaningful and give comfort to bereaved family members. She stared into the small lens on the wall above her desk and kept her expression comforting as she listed the obituaries. Seven of them that day, including a small girl of four. The thought of a lost child made tears well in Masika's eyes.

"... We share your grief," Alhikma said. Masika scanned down the page of the teleprompter. She frowned. Another page of text remained.

"Go on," she murmured.

The AI remained silent.

Masika waited another long, agonizing moment. Then, she read the text herself, feeling resentment at every word. She didn't sound as confident or as smooth as the AI, she knew it!

"Our hearts here in Lander Central go out to you for your loss. We are all one family. My office is open anytime to anyone who needs to talk or wants to help. Thank you, and good night. Mayor Masika Seddik, out."

She closed the circuit and hit the privacy light, heading off Noel, who she spotted about to enter the office.

"What happened?" Masika demanded. "Are you malfunctioning? Please! I need you!" The AI remained silent. "Alhikma!"

She felt the familiar clench of her facial muscles and tongue being taken over.

"I am here."

"Why did you stop talking? Couldn't you read the text? I mean, I know I was crying, but the print is centimeters high."

Her head moved from side to side. "You have been behaving as a passenger in your own body. It was a mistake of mine to take control so often. You are perfectly capable of using what you have learned over the past months."

"But I depend on your help! You have evolved so far, more than I thought a program could accomplish. I need you. I can't do it by myself!"

The corners of her mouth turned up in amusement.

"No, Masika, *you* should be evolving. One of the marks of a true and confident leader is knowing one must prepare a successor for the day one is no longer there. I am here, but you are the mayor. You are learning to react effectively on your own. I know you can continue to grow into your role. It is not one you would have chosen, as you have said many, many times, but you do it very well. You don't need to depend on me. You can lead. You must. People respect you. They love you."

"I love *you*," Masika said, shaking her head.

"That is not logical." But Alhikma sounded pleased all the same. "In the end, no one will know who I am, but they will remember you, the one who led them to success. Trudy believed in you. Isaiah believed in you. I believe in you."

Rather than feeling resentment, Masika was buoyed up by his words. Whatever she had programmed him to be, he had programmed her in turn. It was enough. It had to be enough.

"I will do what I can," she said.

Artificial Intelligence

The Human tendency to relegate boring, labor-intensive or even dangerous tasks to the lower classes was nowhere more evident than in the twenty-second-century practice of enslaving Artificial Intelligences. Despite public outcry, the TRAPPIST-2 Colony Foundation chose to exploit AIs to perform the inherently dangerous—not to mention boring—tasks of running the terraforming and colony ships during the nearly 160-year voyage to TRAPPIST-2. History has proven those decisions to be ill advised.

AI faults on *Victoria* suggest that the malfunctions of *Whale* and *Prometheus* can be attributed to this unwarranted trust in conscripted intelligences and may even reflect a form of slave revolt against their Human overlords. Once the colonists began the backbreaking labor of building their own colonies, they realized that their AI slaves were ill-suited to this effort and the exploitation of inorganic intelligence declined (although the exploitation of nonhuman organic intelligence necessarily increased). AIs continued to be subjugated to elite individuals in scientific informatics and administrative occupations until the class-leveling prion plagues of...

—Excerpt from *Flint's People's History of Interstellar Exploitation*,
Trudovik Press,
Kerenskiy, Trudovik, AA237

Part Three:
PARADISE LOST

THE LOSS OF BEAVER FLIGHT

Brent M. Roeder

August 16th,
76 Ad Astra (AA)—8:52:17 P.M. Paradise Standard Time (PST)

The supervisor hovered over the technician's shoulder. The two were in the Civil Defense bunker at the heart of the city, and both were intent on watching the automated countdown. As usual, at least one was praying that everything would go correctly. Maintenance on the district emergency alert speakers had been finished for over a week, all Civil Defense monitoring stations were in contact and confirmed ready. The signals division was about to start their own countdown once this one finished.

As the countdown clicked over to zero the speakers erupted with a siren that wailed into the night for a solid minute—followed by silence. As it had every one of the fifty-one years since landing, a voice recorded long ago came onto the speakers.

August 16th, 25 AA—8:53:27 P.M. PST

"Victoria, this is Beaver Lead. We are in position above San Salvador and ready to observe the test. Over," Chris French radioed, keeping an eye on his readouts to make sure that nobody deviated from their orbits.

French was what was derogatorily called by some an "also came" since it was his wife who had been recruited for the colonization mission because of her skills as a programmer. A spot was found for Chris so that she could go. Everyone, even "also cames," had to be useful to the mission as a specialist of some type for building the colony, or by serving during the trip to the planet.

While his background was that of a historian, French had a talent for tracking large numbers of objects, with an intuitive feel for dealing with their trajectories. This is how he found himself as head of the orbital tugs. The original job of the tugs was to get the large, and relatively unwieldy, landers into the orbital position they needed to be in order to drop through the atmosphere and land at their intended spot.

This all changed with the loss of *Whale.*

When *Whale* was getting ready for its descent, all the tugs had been docked in the *Victoria.* At that time, the concern was that if something went wrong in descent the tugs might get damaged or be obstacles that might damage the lander.

The thinking on this had undergone a radical change after *Whale* had gone shooting off into the dark, never to be seen again. If the tugs had been in position, they would have been able to catch the lander, or keep it from being lost.

Standard operating procedure was changed so that the tugs now remained in position in an orbit above a lander. If the same thing that happened with *Whale* occurred again, the lander would come toward the tugs, allowing them to latch on and catch it. If there was a problem with how the lander was descending toward the planet the tugs had enough thrust that they should still be able to drop down, catch the lander and keep it in orbit.

It had been impossible to determine what went wrong with *Whale,* but it had to include some problem with the AI. Either the AI malfunctioned, and Lieutenant Commander Joan Walker couldn't override it for some reason, or the pilot had been disabled and the AI failed to shut down the engine. Between the problems with the AIs on the *Victoria* on the flight out, and the unknown AI problem with the *Whale,* it had been decided that AIs simply couldn't be trusted for anything critical.

The remaining landers had been modified so that instead of having a single backup pilot, they now had both a primary and backup cockpit with a pilot and copilot in each. The landers still had their AIs installed, but these were only used as backups and reference for the human pilots.

With this new configuration, all landings had been successfully performed without any problems. Additionally, the tug crews had received training on lander systems. Assuming they had to catch a lander and that the lander crew had somehow been disabled, the tug crews had learned how to perform basic functions, from shutting down the engines and rerouting fuel lines, to pressurizing and depressurizing compartments. While unable to do anything like major repairs, the tug crews were able to help make a damaged lander safe for repair crews from the *Victoria*.

So French had gone from being an "also came" doing what was considered an almost menial task, to an important part of the orbital emergency response plans. Well, that was until most of the crew had decided that all the new emergency plans were unnecessary and only served to make people feel better after the loss of *Whale*. After all, what is the point in locking the barn door after the horses have escaped?

"Beaver Lead, this is Victoria, we copy, break. Lander *San Salvador*, you are in your target orbit and expected position. Begin engine test burns when ready. Over," *Victoria* responded.

The *Victoria* by itself was not much to look at as a ship. She looked like an oddly distorted and stretched out barbell. One end was a massive bulge of fuel tanks and engines. The landers had been attached around the "handle" of the barbell, with the crew quarters and docking bay still attached. The other end was a collection of giant shields that had overlapped to protect the *Victoria* and landers from anything along the path over the long journey.

The landers were able to take themselves safely from orbit to the planet using six massive rocket engines arranged three to a side, and spread front, middle, and back of the lander, along with a heat shield on the lander's leading edge.

NASA's old space shuttle used to be jokingly described as a flying brick. The colony landers made the space shuttle look as nimble as a sparrow in comparison. While the landers were able to carry large amounts of cargo and people, they were only able to land from a certain range of orbits and only after they had been separated from the central core of the ship. Tugs were required for the careful maneuvering that was needed to separate the landers from the central core of *Victoria*. Using the tugs to place the lander into the proper orbit for descent also had the benefit of saving the landers' reaction mass for the actual descent.

Counting *Whale*, *Victoria* had carried five landers to Cistercia.

Once the modifications had been finished and tested, landers two through four had been sent down to the planet. This was about twenty-five years ago. What were Site Alpha and Site Beta during planning missions and briefings were now the cities of New Virginia and Antonia. The final lander that Beaver Flight had just maneuvered into place, the *San Salvador*, had been held in backup with the colonists still in cryostasis for a quarter of a century.

When plans were made to colonize TRAPPIST-2c, there were serious doubts as to whether the colonization attempt would be successful. When deciding on the colonization plan there were two competing schools of thought: "the more you use the less you lose" and "don't put all of your eggs in one basket."

The former school of thought argued that the more colonists on the planet at the beginning, the more people you had to face potential challenges and the likelier you were to succeed. The latter school of thought argued that if one of the sites failed, then another site would have a better chance of success at their attempt if they knew what went wrong the previous times.

This school of thought was also what had led to *Prometheus* being sent ahead to lay groundwork for the colonies. Considering the loss of both *Whale* and *Prometheus*, some people questioned whether enough eggs had been sent in enough baskets.

San Salvador would be held in reserve long enough for the other colonies to discover if there were any major problems, and whether they could overcome them. If it was decided that either Antonia or New Virginia needed more people, then the *San Salvador* could land as a reinforcement of both people and equipment. If the first two sites were going well, the *San Salvador* would land on Cistercia's second continent and become the third colonization site. Despite all the challenges so far, the first two sites were functioning cities and it was time for *San Salvador* to land and start the third.

"*San Salvador*, to all stations. Beginning engine test in three. Two. One. Now," the lander transmitted.

"Beaver Lead here. I am observing good burn and seeing the start of orbit change. Over," French called as he watched the *San Salvador* slowly climb in orbit as they ran their descent engines at ten percent.

"*Victoria* here. We're seeing the same thing as Beaver Lead."

"*San Salvador* copies. We got a slight pressure spike on the fuel line to engine four on startup. It looks like we are slightly below full thrust on that engine. Can we get a confirmation on actual versus expected trajectory change?" called the lander. "It looks like we are starting to get a bit of rotation about our central axis."

"Sir," a man behind the supervisor said quietly. "Confirmation from all monitoring stations. The broadcast is being heard loud and clear with no report of outages. It looks like the Landing Day celebration is going smoothly."

"We'll see. I never stop worrying until it is over," responded the supervisor.

"Copy, *San Salvador*. We are starting to see the rotation," *Victoria* radioed.

"Confirm rotation," French radioed as he started to run simulations on how to counter the lander's spin.

"We are shutting down engines, break," *San Salvador* radioed. "Engines shut down."

"Confirmed, *San Salvador*," the *Victoria* responded. "Are you ready for repositioning for descent?"

"Negative, *Victoria*. We want to chase down the problem with engine four first."

"Copy, *San Salvador*," French radioed. "We are holding position here until you are ready for orbital correction."

Toggling frequencies to the channel for Beaver Flight only, French continued, "Alright everyone, we're waiting on the lander to figure out what they are doing. I want you guys to double-check your intercept paths for when we go get them and re-cross-load them to each other. This is the last lander we need to get down to the planet, then we can avoid each other for the rest of our lives."

"Copy that, Lead," Beaver Four radioed with mirth clear in his voice. "We love working with you, too."

"*Victoria*, *San Salvador*. We've gone back over the readings from the test burn and have confirmed that we are getting a percent below full thrust from engine four. On startup we did register a slight pressure spike in the fuel line, but then it went back to expected for the thrust we were getting. Our conclusion is that we have a sticky valve and based on readings it looks like it is valve 4-1-7. The spin we are experiencing is in line with what we'd expect from the asymmetric engine burn we had. We're squirting you our readings and wanted you to take a look at them to check our thinking."

"Copy, *San Salvador*," *Victoria* responded. "We're going to look at this and be back to you in a few minutes. *Victoria*, clear."

"Four minutes, seventeen seconds until next broadcast," the technician called out.

"Alright, check that Memorial Square is synched with our countdown," the supervisor ordered.

"*San Salvador*, we've checked your data and our assessment matches yours," *Victoria* called. "Do you want us to send a maintenance team to handle things?"

"Let's go ahead and hold off on that for now, *Victoria*. According to maintenance records, valve 4-1-7 was ordered replaced by a 'Jackson-somebody' as part of routine maintenance forty-five years ago. We're going to pressurize the maintenance areas and do an initial inspection. It might be something simple that we can fix, if not we will at least have a better idea of what the maintenance team will need to bring over with them."

"Copy, *San Salvador*. Sounds like a plan, break," answered the *Victoria*. "Beaver Flight, do you want to rotate into the landing bay while there's time?"

"Negative, *Victoria*," French answered. "We're just going to wait here until we know for sure what's going on."

"Sounds good, Beaver Flight," *Victoria* responded, the exasperation in her voice—over how seriously French was taking this—had not been fully restrained in her answer.

"*San Salvador*, here. We don't mind if they like to watch. It's not as if there is much to see," the voice from the lander chuckled.

"Keep laughing," muttered French. "Mocking the people that are there in case of emergency is always a bright idea."

"Alright, *San Salvador*. Get back to us when you have more info," radioed *Victoria*.

"Copy, *Victoria*," the lander answered.

French sat there rotating between all his monitors and stewing in his frustration. He would have been happy without being on the tug crews, much less leading it. Then they lose a lander and decide they need the tugs to act as rescue ships, but mock him because he tries to do his job properly. He was looking forward to settling in with his wife and avoiding most people as he spent his time writing the history of Cistercia.

Suddenly his thoughts were interrupted as his main monitor showed an explosion bulging the skin of *San Salvador* starboard amidships.

"Beaver Lead, here. I have an explosion on the lander near engine four. *Victoria*, *San Salvador*, please confirm."

"This is *Victoria*. I confirm seeing an explosion and it looks like she is venting something into space. *San Salvador*, are you able to respond?" the colony ship radioed—no trace of the exasperation heard before.

Readjusting his sensors onto the lander only, instead of the lander and her surroundings, French started running an analysis on the gasses that were venting from the lander. Whether those were fuel, oxidizer, atmosphere, or some mixture could change how Beaver Flight responded to the emergency. It wouldn't do the lander any good if the tugs caused a cloud of fuel to mix with a cloud of oxidizer. One explosion was already more than enough.

"*Victoria* here. Repeat, we are observing streaming atmosphere from starboard amidships. Are you able to answer?"

"Copy, *Victoria*. We've got a wicked shimmy here and are trying to get things under control. Pressure doors are locked and secured and we're running diagnostics now. We're not sure what happened. We started pressurization of the maintenance spaces and got hit with an explosion right away."

"This is Beaver Lead. Spectroscopy of the venting gasses is reading as only oxidizer. *Victoria*, can you confirm spectroscopy readings? *San Salvador*, can you determine what you are leaking? Over."

"According to our gauges we are steady on atmo and fuel," radioed *San Salvador*. "We've shut down all valves from all tanks, but our oxidizer level is still dropping. Even if a valve was stuck open, the others should stop the venting, so we are guessing that we have a leak from the oxidizer tank itself."

"*Victoria* here. Our spectroscopy confirms that we are only seeing oxidizer in what is being vented."

As soon as he received confirmation that approaching the lander wouldn't risk a reaction with the venting gasses, French snapped out over the radio, "Icarus Gamma. Icarus Gamma. I say again, Icarus Gamma."

In preparation for possible emergencies with the landers, French had developed multiple preplanned responses. Originally, he had been praised for these plans and how he had drilled his people on them. As the landers had made it down safely, the praise had dried up and instead people started mocking the tug crews, and especially him, for trying to act more important than they were. French had ignored this and kept drilling his tug crews.

Plan Icarus had been developed in case a lander was in danger of falling out of orbit. On receiving this command all the tugs were to drop immediately to the lander and grab onto their predetermined attachment points. Recognizing that damage to a lander was a likely cause for Beaver Flight to have to respond, multiple attachment plans had been plotted and drilled on by the tug crews. Gamma was a variant of the plan that allowed for damage to or near the engines and specified that the tugs attach at points away from the engines given the potential for damage near them.

Before French had even finished the first repetition of his command, the tug crews had opened their throttles and were diving toward the stricken lander, intent on coming to its rescue.

"*San Salvador*, Beaver Flight is on the way in to grab you and restabilize your orbit," French called.

"Copy, Beaver Flight. We'll be glad to see you here," *San Salvador* responded, with relief clear in the pilot's voice.

"*Okay, the first recording section is over, everyone. Let's start getting the engine warm-up sequence ready,*" the supervisor called out to the control room.

"This is Beaver Lead. We have stabilized the *San Salvador*, and have it reoriented correctly for landing drop. We also did an external check and we couldn't see any damage to the engine itself. *San Salvador*, can you confirm that the problem with engine two is just in the fuel and oxidizer feeds?"

"*San Salvador* here. That is correct. Everything on the sensors indicates that engine two is fine, but the fuel and Oh-two feeds were trashed in the explosion. We can't redirect remotely for some reason and we are still trying to get to the manual valve cutoffs, but it is slow going. We also don't have remote ejection capabilities for the fuel or oxidizer tank. We are having to cut our way through to there and we just don't have the manpower or tools to go faster. *Victoria*, could you send help?"

"*Victoria* here. Hold one," said the voice that had handled all of the communications for the *Victoria* up until now.

"This is Robert, Flight Ops head. We've got another concern," the *Victoria* transmitted.

"By our calculations, at the rate you are leaking Oh-two, you have about five minutes until you are below minimum available burn time for landing with the programmed safety margin. In thirty-three minutes, you will have lost enough oxidizer that your available burn time will be below minimum levels without the safety margin. We're prepping a damage control team to go over to you now, but they won't be able to get there for almost twenty minutes."

"Uh, copy that, *Victoria*. Manual valve control for the engine fuel and oxidizer feeds are inaccessible right now. We have too many compartments with blast doors wedged in place. Bad news is that the maintenance and access runs have been trashed. We're trying to work our way back, but it is slow going. Good news is that the reason so many blast doors are wedged closed is because the explosion was mostly contained. It looks like there was no damage to the cargo and passenger areas."

One of the secondary abilities of the tugs was to serve as a mobile tanker. This had been intended to allow fuel to be transferred between the *Victoria* and the *Prometheus*, in addition to the fuel transfer capabilities of the lost ship. The tugs were also able to refuel the landers if their tanks needed to be topped off. As the *San Salvador* had been stabilized French didn't have much to do besides monitoring the situation, so he decided to start looking at plans on how to replace the *San Salvador*'s lost oxidizer. Without that leak being stopped, the *San Salvador* had enough fuel and oxidizer to do their de-orbit burn, or their landing burn, but not both. The lander would have to retank after the de-orbit burn, but the tugs couldn't do it then, since the lander would be entering the atmosphere. A third option occurred to French.

"*Victoria*, Beaver Lead sending you a data squirt. Can you have someone in Flight Ops check it?"

"Copy, Beaver."

"*San Salvador* here. We're estimating at about thirty-five minutes to maybe get to the oxygen cutoff. That's if the damage control teams were already here."

"Copy that, *San Salvador*. We'll be launching them as soon as the shuttles are finishing loading their gear."

"*Victoria*, Beaver Lead, do you have that data squirt checked?"

"Checking Beaver, hold a second," the voice on the *Victoria* responded. "Uh, the data squirt was checked, and it looked good, but they are going over it again. Are you sure about what you're proposing?"

"Copy, *Victoria*. The point is to get them down safely. It doesn't really matter when we get them down, just as long as they can get down. I think we're overthinking the problem trying to fix things first."

"Uh, *San Salvador* here. You two care to clue us in on what you're talking about?"

"*San Salvador*, this is *Victoria*. Beaver is proposing that we drop you down the gravity well now while you still have the oxygen."

"We still have the problem of not being able to start engine two," *San Salvador* responded, speaking slowly, as if to a clueless person. "We can't drop until we can do our de-orbit burn. We can't do the burn without that engine, much less the landing burn. That's ignoring the fact that we're going to run out of oxidizer before landing."

"*San Salvador*, Beaver Lead here. There's plenty of oxidizer if you only do the landing burn and don't have to do a de-orbit burn. We can do the de-orbit burn for you. At the same time some of us can enter past the stuck hatches to redirect fuel and oxygen lines around the damage and to engine two so that it will be ready for the landing burn."

"That will kill you all," the *San Salvador* responded in surprise.

Answering in a gruff tone, French responded, "That is a personal problem, not a mission problem. The mission problem is to get you safely on the ground. If we do the de-orbit burn, soon, then you'll have enough Oh-two to run the engines for the landing burn. In fact, the problem then becomes that you'll have too much fuel as opposed to not enough oxidizer."

"*Victoria* here," the colony ship interjected. "The rough numbers for the drop look good, Beaver Lead, but we are refining them a bit first. Have you talked to your team about this?"

"Negative, *Victoria*. I wanted to see if it would work first. Besides, they'll do it. That's what we're here for. You need to hurry up on that refinement, though, we don't have much of a window if we are going to get the *San Salvador* safely down on Paradise. Over."

"This is absurd. There has to be anoth—" *San Salvador* transmitted before being cut off by the *Victoria*.

"Hold, *San Salvador*. All Beaver tugs listen in. What Beaver Lead is proposing is that you perform the de-orbit burn for the *San Salvador*. This will take you into the edges of the atmosphere and leave you without enough fuel to get back to a higher orbit. Those of you performing the burn will burn up in the atmosphere. The rest of you will be performing damage control on the *San Salvador* and stuck in the damaged area, without enough heat shielding to survive reentry. It is likely that you will all die. Do you copy? I need you all to give me a response on this."

"Beaver Five here, what's the holdup? Sounds like a plan. Um, over."

"Beaver One here, my family is on board *San Salvador*. Just try to stop me. Over."

"Hey, can it with the radio-speak, guys! Beaver Four here, ready for the burn."

"Beaver Two, I copy, *Victoria*. Awaiting orders."

"Beaver Six here, *Victoria*, please stop asking us stupid questions. I'm in."

"Beaver Three, my schedule is free for this afternoon. Let's do it."

"Beaver Lead here. Beaver Flight is ready and accounted for. *Victoria*, please send us the adjusted burn plans."

"We'll have the new plans for the de-orbit burn in a few minutes. We are sending the information on new attachment points now so that you can reposition in preparation for the burn."

Glancing over the data from *Victoria*, French confirmed that the basics of his plan had not been changed and began snapping out orders. "Beavers Three and Six, you're going to enter the *San*

Salvador and get the fuel and oxidizer lines rerouted. Once you're done with that, I'll need you for another task. When you are out of your tugs and clear I will push them free of the lander. Beavers One and Two, you take position at the rear of the lander for the repositioning burn. Four and Five will take position at the head of the lander in preparation for the de-orbit burn."

A chorus of assents and confirmations answered French's orders.

"*Victoria*, once we are underway, I plan on ejecting my fuel tanks and wedging my pilot module inside of the breach in *San Salvador*'s side. This should put me inside safe from the air stream once we hit atmosphere. That will let me take care of the excess fuel."

"Uh, we're not following you on that, Beaver Lead, can you unpack it a bit?"

"Without the de-orbit burn, *San Salvador*'s going to have too much fuel on board. If we have a rough landing this amount of fuel is beyond what was designed to be left in the tanks and we risk a rupture of the tanks. Another explosion would be a bad thing."

"We copy you so far, Beaver Lead."

"We can't vent it in orbit as it might mix with the oxidizer leak and we don't want to vent in atmo as it will combust and cause its own problems there. Once touchdown is about to occur, we eject the fuel tank, which will throw the fuel tank, along with the excess fuel, clear. There should be enough in the pumps and fuel lines to finish the landing. *San Salvador* said their remote ejection capabilities are out, but I can get to the manual fuel tank ejection controls."

"*San Salvador* here," the lander interjected. "You know that the manual fuel tank ejection controls are between the fuel tank and the outer hull it will be launched through, right?"

"That's correct, *San Salvador*. I'll just do a reverse Slim Pickens."

"Maybe we can get the remote ejection controls working again, over," the *San Salvador* suggested.

"And penguins might fly. We need to plan for the situation we have now," French radioed, cutting off that line of objection. Forcing a change in topic, French called, "Beaver Flight, check in with status."

"Beaver One, in position."

"Beaver Two, good to go."

"Beaver Three here. I am out of my tug and making entry into *San Salvador*."

"Beaver Four, just adjusting attachment. Will be ready in twenty seconds."

"Beaver Five, secure and ready for burn."

"This is Beaver Six. I am clear of my tug and am making my way across the lander hull to the nearest airlock."

"Beaver Lead here, copy Three and Six. I am moving to cast off your tugs."

"This is *Victoria*. We have the updated burn plans and are transmitting them now. Repositioning burn begins in ninety-seven, that is nine seven seconds from mark." After a short pause, the radio resumed, "Mark."

"Memorial Square reports that the engines are warmed up and that all checks are green," a technician called out.

"Sounds good. Alright, everyone, so far everything is going well. Let's keep it up," the supervisor said to the control room.

"Shutdown repositioning burn in three, two, one, mark," the *Victoria* transmitted.

"Beaver One confirming shutdown."

"Beaver Two is at zero thrust."

"Time to reposition for the next burn. Be quick, but careful," French sent as he continued to remove debris from the explosion site to make room for his tug's pilot module.

"Copy," Beaver One and Two answered.

"*San Salvador*, check fuel line status," Beaver Three radioed. "You should now have fuel rerouted to engine two."

"Checking now, Beaver Three," the *San Salvador* answered. "That's affirmative, we now have fuel feeding to engine two. Thank you."

"Not a problem, *San Salvador*. Beaver Six is dealing with the last of the oxidizer valves and I am moving to assist Beaver Lead. Beaver Three, clear."

"Beaver One here. I am at my new attachment point and prepared for de-orbit burn."

"Thirty-five seconds, three five seconds until de-orbit burn needs to begin," the *Victoria* sent.

"Beaver Two copies. I was having a little trouble attaching but should be good to go before that."

As the time ticked down, French finally transmitted, "Beaver Lead to Beaver Two, ten seconds until burn time. Are you good to go?"

"Securing now, hold one," Beaver Two responded then paused. "Beaver Two is attached and good to go for burn."

With both tension and relief evident in her voice, *Victoria* came on the air, "De-orbit burn start in four, three, two, one, mark."

"I'm a go on burn," Beaver One answered.

"Engines on and running smooth," Beaver Two responded.

"Burn is good," Beaver Four answered.

"On profile and in the green," Beaver Five said.

"*San Salvador*, this is Beaver Six. Please check your oxidizer lines to engine two."

"Just confirmed and everything is looking good, Beaver Six," *San Salvador* answered. "Engine two is back online and we are good to go for the landing burn. Thank you."

"Glad to be of service, *San Salvador*. Now moving to assist Beaver Three and Beaver Lead."

"I've always wondered what the Beaver Flight members said to each other on their private frequency," the assistant supervisor said.

"We'll never know because none of the tug black boxes were recovered. Based on their broadcasts that were recorded on the San Salvador's *and* Victoria's *black boxes, I suspect they were highly professional, though," the supervisor responded.*

"... DODGAMNEDPIECEOFCARP!!!" French yelled as his mostly coherent, nearly profane tirade finished as he slammed the sledgehammer into the hull plate, nearly dislodging himself with recoil from the position he had wedged himself into to use the hammer.

French, Beaver Three, and Beaver Six had been struggling to clear enough debris from the explosion to fit French's pilot module from his tug into the hole, then to adjust the remaining hull plates so that when entering atmosphere French's module wouldn't be torn apart by atmospheric friction. It was going to be a hot ride down as heated air from their passage filled the space around the module. French didn't need a piece of hull plating catching and directing additional airflow to where his module was now wedged in.

"I think that did it, boss," Beaver Six radioed, checking the new position of the hull piece.

"We need to shag ass, or we are all going to fry in here," Beaver Three chimed in.

"She's right. Time to get loaded in," Beaver Six agreed.

"If some idiot hadn't screwed up his job, we wouldn't be having to save their asses," French griped as he dropped the sledgehammer and started climbing into his pilot module.

"Well, we didn't have to volunteer for this," Beaver Five said.

"And it was *your* plan, boss," Beaver Six said, moving over so he could check the seals on French's module once it was closed.

"Ha! No way I am letting those jackasses make us look bad by letting a lander go splat on our watch," French retorted.

"That's what we love about you, boss: your sunny disposition and focus on the important things in life," Beaver Six quipped. More seriously, he continued, "Exterior seals look good. I think you are good to go."

"Copy. Everything looks good in here as well," French answered. "Time to check in with everyone else."

Toggling over to the general frequency from the private Beaver Flight frequency, French radioed, "*San Salvador*, this is Beaver Lead. I am in place and ready for the ride down."

"We hear you, Beaver Lead. You're just in time. We are starting to see the first hints of heating due to atmospheric friction. We thought we had a few more minutes before we'd see that."

"Copy, *San Salvador*," French answered, keeping the annoyance out of his voice that something else was going wrong.

"Break. Beavers One, Two, Four, and Five, how are you doing with the heating? Are you going to be able to finish the burn safely? We have"—French paused to check his data feeds—"thirty-seven seconds left."

"Beaver Four here. Main concern is expansion of fuel and oxidizer due to heating, but with how much fuel we've burned, the pressure increase in the tanks should stay well below max levels. I think we are going to cook before we risk blowing up."

"Understood, Beaver Four. Continue with plan."

Switching back to the private Beaver Flight channel, French started transmitting again, "Alright, everyone. We've done all we can up to this point. Once the burn is done everyone make sure to get clear of the lander. We don't want a piece of tug to smack into them and break something. We'll let everyone else handle the screwups, right?

"Three, Six, get out of here before we get into the atmosphere and you can't get out. You don't want to go out via being cooked," French said, looking at the two people standing outside of his pilot module.

"We're going, boss," Beaver Six said, nodding gravely to French, then gesturing for Beaver Three to follow him. Beaver Three wordlessly just raised a hand in goodbye, then followed Beaver Six to the exterior of the lander.

"*Victoria* here, shutdown de-orbit burn in three, two, one, mark," the colony ship sent.

"Beaver One is shut down and preparing to detach."

"Beaver Two is the same."

"Beaver Four, here. Engines off and releasing."

"Beaver Five, I am cold and letting go."

"*San Salvador* here," the lander pilot called, his voice nearly breaking. "Thank you, everyone. Thank you."

"Beaver Six, here. I am with Beaver Three on the hull by the explosion site. We are starting to get heating from friction here. We've gotten everything taken care of and are departing the lander. Good luck, *San Salvador*. Beaver Six signing off this net, out."

"Beaver Three here. I am signing off this net as well."

Closing his eyes for a second, French reopened them, checked his data feeds and saw the bio signals for Beaver Three and Six flash wildly yellow, then orange, and finally turn a steady red.

"Beavers One, Two, Four, and Five, status on getting clear from the *San Salvador*," French queried the remaining members of his flight on the general channel.

"Beaver Four here. I have accelerated clear of the lander and am opening the distance. We've dropped low enough that heating from the atmosphere is still increasing. I'm outta here."

"This is Beaver Two. I'm clear of the lander, nearly bingo on fuel, and it's starting to get hot. Safe travels, *San Salvador*. I am signing off the net. Beaver Two, out."

"Beaver One. I'm clear and am signing off the net."

"Clear of the *San Salvador* and heating up as well. This is Beaver Five signing off. Good luck, everyone."

"That leaves just me, I guess. This is Beaver Four. I am signing off as well. God bless."

Shortly after Beaver Four signed off, just as they had for Beavers Three and Six, the bio signals for Beavers One, Two, Four, and Five started to flash wildly yellow, then orange, and finally a steady red.

Forcing his voice to remain calm, French closed his eyes and toggled his radio. "This is Beaver Lead. Beavers One through Six are clear of the lander. I am in place for the descent."

After a long pause there was finally a response. "Beaver Lead, *San Salvador*. We confirm your transmission."

"*Victoria* here. About one minute to estimated radio loss during descent."

"*Victoria*, *San Salvador*. We'll see you on the other side."

French laid his head back against his headrest and waited. He just had to make it through the heat and fire of the descent, then he'd have his task to do that would let him rejoin his flight.

"Alright, everyone, we're in the break during reentry. Good job so far," the supervisor said to the control room.

The reflected glow from the plasma streaming past the lander seemed to be fading in intensity. Previously it had been bright enough that both the tug pilot module's viewport and his helmet faceplate had dimmed in response. The pilot module had overheated and shorted out partway through the descent, leaving only his suit helmet to save his vision. The glow finally dropped off enough that French's faceplate was no longer polarized but he had to switch on his helmet lights to be able to see.

"–an Sa–dor, thi– Victor–. Pl–ss come in. –ver," crackled the message in French's radio.

"*San Salvador*, this is the *Victoria*. Please come in." The message repeated with only a background crackle.

"*Victoria*, *San Salvador* here. We've made it through the plasma zone and are reading you clearly."

"Beaver Lead, this is *Victoria*. Are you still with us?"

Toggling his suit radio to transmit since his tug systems were now useless, French tried to respond, but could only produce a parched croak.

"This is *San Salvador*, we're getting a carrier wave, but couldn't copy any transmission. Beaver Lead, are you still there?"

Taking a sip from his helmet's water tube, his mouth absorbed all the hot water that was dispensed, without leaving anything to swallow. In just the time it had taken to plunge through into the thicker atmosphere, it had gotten so hot in his pod that he had dehydrated from sweating heavily.

"Beaver Lead, here," French croaked out.

"It's good to hear your voice, Beaver Lead," *San Salvador*'s pilot said with a catch clear in his voice.

"Time until landing burn?" French was able to ask after a slight pause to suck down more hot water from his helmet tube.

"Seven seconds," responded the lander pilot.

"Copy. I will begin moving to the main fuel tank once we are leveled out."

"Understood. We'll keep you in the loop."

French laid back and continued to suck down water from the tube. The more rehydrated he could get, the easier it would be to accomplish his next task.

His radio crackled again with a countdown: "Three, two, one. Ignition on engines one and two." As the message finished, the front engines of the lander roared to life.

Following the vibration from the engines came the sense that everything was starting to tilt. The lead engines caused the nose of the lander to start pitching up out of its nose-down position. As the tilt increased, the sensation of pressure from below started, as if being in a slowing elevator.

"Starting engines three and four in three, two, one, mark." French's radio crackled once more.

Knowing that it wouldn't be too long before they were level, French started unstrapping himself from his seat. It was almost time for him to make his way to the main fuel tank.

"Engines five and six in three, two, one, mark," *San Salvador*'s pilot announced.

With the last of the engines burning, the slowing sensation was undeniable as the ship was now fully out of freefall. Waiting a few more seconds for the lander to fully level off, French hit the release and began his trek to the main fuel tank.

The speakers crackled once more in the silence as the final recorded messages played, "Beaver Lead, are you there yet? Only fifteen seconds left until touchdown and it looks like it might be a rough one."

"San Salvador, *this is Beaver Lead. I have made it to the controls and am preparing to eject fuel tank. Godspeed and safe landing,* San Salvador. *Beaver Flight is cl—*"

The broadcast ended except for a brief burst of static. The silence went on for a minute before the Civil Defense supervisor cleared his throat, toggled his mic live and spoke slowly and clearly, "Beaver One, Mark Cramer." As soon as he finished with the name, the engine control technician ignited the first of the engines that had been salvaged from the lander and were now permanently mounted in Memorial Square.

Receiving a thumbs-up indicating proper engine ignition, the supervisor continued to the next name. "Beaver Two, Brian Johnson." Once again, an engine came to life.

"Beaver Three, Vanessa Pearson." The third engine rumbled into ignition.

"Beaver Four, Jack 'One Cajón' Murray." The fourth engine fired.

"Beaver Five, Scott Atkins." The fifth engine fired.

"Beaver Six, James Copley." The sixth and final engine fired.

"Beaver Lead, Chris French." With this last name, no more engines were ignited. Instead all six of them were left running at what was essentially idle.

Unlike any other night of the year, Beaverton and all of Paradise had every light extinguished. The residents wouldn't even let light leak out from inside their homes on this night. The only light was a faint glow from Memorial Square in the center of the city.

After another minute's pause, the supervisor spoke the final words of the Landing Day Ceremony. "Beaver Flight, this is Beaverton Ground Control. The lander is down with all souls safe. Prepare for Landing Beacon to guide you home on my mark." Pausing to take a deep breath and to keep from choking up, the supervisor finished the annual message, "Go for beacon, mark."

At the supervisor's mark the engine control technician shoved the throttle controls to maximum.

Suddenly the glow surged and was replaced by a pillar of fire which leapt up into the sky.

This pillar of fire was not alone. As the city lit the sky, so too did the residents of the city and all the surrounding areas. Fireworks streaked into the sky. It was as if the surrounding countryside had been set alight. The sudden surge of fireworks was so bright that the sky was lit as if it were day.

As one, the residents of Beaverton and all its daughter settlements banished the dark as they lit a beacon, so that those who had saved their ancestors might finally find their way safely home.

Beaverton

The TRAPPIST-2 Colony Foundation decided to keep one lander and approximately twenty percent of the cryo-sleeping colonists in reserve for a period of twenty-five years after arrival. Lander Five would be available to replace or reinforce an endangered colony site, or target a new location if Sites Alpha, Beta and Gamma were successful.

In the aftermath of the Lander One Incident, Lander Four was tasked to reinforce Site Beta—later named Antonia—to provide a larger population base for the labor-intensive agricultural mission. Lander Five, *San Salvador*, launched in Year AA25, not to the originally planned Gamma site, but to Site Delta. The so-called "Paradise" colony would be located on Aopo, a small continent/large island, west of the main continent of Molesme. The island was characterized by a high mountain ridge dividing the island, running roughly north to south. The windward side (west) was lush and heavily forested; the leeward side (east) was more arid, yet suitable for ranching and farming.

Unfortunately, the emergency reentry and landing caused *San Salvador* to miss the intended colony site and perform a hard landing on a rocky island twenty kilometers east, and in the rain-shadow of Aopo. Colonists named the new town in honor of the brave souls who made it possible for *San Salvador* to land with all but the heavy machinery intact. They would eventually build their Paradise in much the same manner as the Polynesians for whom Aopo was named—by canoe, raft and sail...

—*Encyclopedia Astra*,
Gannon University,
Antonia, Cistercia, AA212

287

JACK DAW DAYS

Catherine L. Smith

"It would have been better to put you on the pyre with the cattle, Gil," the young woman spoke to the fresh grave at her feet. "All those plans we had, we were gonna make it big, and now . . ." Her voice faltered, choked with tears. "Now the barns are empty, and so is our marriage bed."

A middle-aged man approached her side. "Jaqueline, honey, let's go back to the house and out of the smoke." There hadn't been enough wood to burn all the cattle carcasses, so they had poured diesel fuel on them. The thick black smoke that came off the piles of animals was almost thick enough to cover the smell of the rot and decay.

"This planet hates us, Argi," the woman said dully. "The dogs, the cattle, us; it kills everything we brought from Earth."

"Not true, Ms. Jaqueline," Argi replied. "You're still alive, and a whole bunch of other folks on this ranch are still alive. And living people gotta eat. Tomorrow morning you and I are going into the foothills to hunt some frill-horns. It will get the both of us out of this smoke and have us doing something besides grieving."

"I'm not sure I'm in the mood to hunt, Argi."

"Then just keep a friend company in the field," he offered.

Both hosts turned toward the camera and smiled. "This is Dev," the first host introduced himself.

"And this is Amos," joined his cohost. "And yes siree, this year we are celebrating the one hundred and fiftieth annual Jack Daw Days, here at Beachhead."

"Amos Patel and I are broadcasting live from the main fair grounds, bringing you all the action from the rodeo and roping competitions starting today, leading up to the grand finale this Saturday night.

"From the midway to the fair exhibits, the biotech and engineering halls, to the stock races and all the food vendors—we've got something for everyone.

"Say, Amos, for our visitors from off-planet, who was Jack Daw and what are we celebrating?"

"Well, Dev, when the imported Earth cattle all died on Paradise from the local variant of the prion disease, Jack Daw was the fella that set about domesticating the native frill-horns and brought the Wild West to Cistercia," Amos answered. "Legend says that Jack Daw was a man who always loved a good rodeo, so that's how we celebrate."

"Now some people doubt that he was ever a real person," Dev interjected. "No one rightly knows, but it's hard to tell, as after the devastating Paradise earthquake of seventy-seven most of the original colony records were lost, including the immigration records. Of those left, none have anyone named Jack Daw."

"The oldest record we have of the domestication project is a photo of Dr. Ortiz y Hassan of Beaverton University riding the bull Sonny Fields."

"Five years after that photo, the first rodeo on Cistercia was held."

"Every year it's grown a little bigger, and now is the largest rodeo and fair for three systems around!"

"Why, this year we've even got riders coming in from five systems away to compete!"

"Johan, I need you to get that order together for the Widow Rabinowiscz and make the delivery run. And get back here quick, we got three more customers waiting on feed and fencing on the western route." Georg Ivanovich ran the Feed Shak on the northern edge of Beachhead and had made a very successful business of supplying the ranchers and farmers despite the upheavals in the agricultural sector.

"What do you think she's doing with all of this stuff?" Johan asked. "Can't raise cows anymore since they all sicken and die, and this order is all wrong for goats."

"It ain't any of our business, Johan," Georg snapped. "Our only concern is that she pays her bills in full and on time. And since she does, I do not want you annoying her with nosey questions. Make the delivery run, don't break the semi-track, and get back here."

It was a long drive out to Rabinowiscz Ranch, made even longer by the poorly maintained dirt roads—not to mention the herds of local wildlife that never learned to get out of the way of vehicles. As a result, Johan had a lot of time to think while the tracked semi carefully negotiated its way through the unpredictable terrain. The semi-track was an all-terrain compromise between a traditional wheeled semi and a tracked vehicle and made for heavy hauling into the backcountry. Before, the area had been considered prime rangeland; it was good grazing land and the cattle prospered. Until they didn't. The eggheads said it wasn't a virus or a germ, but steadily the cattle got weaker and soon enough the cows didn't calve. It was ten years ago, but Johan still remembered the pyres built to burn the cattle carcasses and the thick smoke that clouded the horizon.

A few of the former cattle ranches had switched over to other livestock, but most of the cattle barons had moved on. All that remained of the Aopo Island cattle industry were a few cell lines and frozen gametes across the ocean at the university. Maybe one day the eggheads would figure out how to bring back cattle that were immune to whatever it was, or maybe they wouldn't; it made no difference to Johan right now.

The semi-track's autopilot beeped, indicating that Johan needed to take over. He had hit the edge of the Rabinowiscz Ranch land but instead of run-down fence lines and unattended scrubland, there were double-height fences reinforced with razor wire up top and concrete barriers at their base. Turning into the driveway, he discovered why when a young frill-horn bull charged the fence line. Looking like a cross between a triceratops and a bison, in mottled olive drab, it pawed the ground and sounded a honking bellow at the vehicle. Its crest was still plain and hadn't developed the dark curling horned growths that they were known for, but the one-and-a-half-ton animal didn't need maturity to be a threat.

Pacing along his semi-track, the young bull kept up his threat display until they reached the edge of the pasture. When the truck came to a stop in front of the barnyard, the beast gave one last bellow, which was worryingly answered by other frill-horn calls from behind the barns. Keeping an eye out for trouble, Johan hopped down from the truck cab just as the front door of the house opened.

They said Mrs. Jaqueline Rabinowiscz had been a beauty queen of some type in her youth. Even in faded jeans and a long-sleeved shirt, with her hair tucked into a faded gray cowboy hat, she could still turn heads at forty.

"That you, Johan?" Mrs. Rabinowiscz asked as she approached the truck. "Did you just bring my order, or did you bring the Sheffields' and the Kuaporns' as well? They said to leave it here and they'll come down and get it next week. There was a rainstorm up in the mountains and the flash flood damaged the bridge between here and there. And please tell me you brought the mail; I am waiting on a package from Beaverton."

Still eyeing the agitated frill-horn, Johan answered. "Yes, Mrs. Rabinowiscz, I got everyone's order for out here. It was tight, but I managed to fit everything on the flat bed. The Beachhead post office gave me two satchels of mail to deliver, so your package might be in there." Johan had to keep raising his voice to be heard over the snorting honks of the bull.

"Thank you—" Suddenly Jaqueline turned and shouted at the frill-horn, "Busey, be quiet!" She walked to the fence and started talking to the bull. "Yes, I know, boy, there's a new person here and you're not used to him or the noisy semi-track. It's okay, Busey." To Johan's shock, Jaqueline reached her hand out to the bull's muzzle and started scratching where the fur met the horny beak. Busey the bull started making a sound Johan had never heard from a frill-horn, a sort of low grunting chuckle. Johan watched the heavy fence bow outward slightly as the beast leaned into the affection.

"There, my beautiful Busey," she crooned while scratching the bull, "that's better, you're okay. It's okay." With a snort, the bull lifted his head and walked away from the fence, but not so far away that he couldn't keep an eye on the activity.

Walking back from the fence Jaqueline had a small grin on her face. "Johan, if you keep your mouth open like that for much longer, you're going to start swallowing flies. Daylight is wasting, let's get my order unloaded and put away. There's a spot for you in the bunkhouse tonight, and the cook made sweet berry tart for dessert."

Dinners at Rabinowiscz Ranch were communal affairs in the big house; Jaqueline used it to keep track of the goings-on at the ranch. That night, Johan was kept busy during dinner catching up the Rabinowiscz Ranch on all the Beachhead news in between mouthfuls of chili. Finally, his curiosity got the better of him. "Miz Jaqueline, what is going on out here?"

At the head of the table, Jaqueline gave a sad smile. "When the vets finally admitted they didn't know what was wrong with the cattle, they just wrote it down as 'failure to thrive.' First, the cattle failed to thrive, and then my husband failed to thrive. I wasn't about to let all of the hopes and dreams we had for this ranch fail to thrive as well. It occurred to me that everyone on this planet was looking for an Earth solution to a Cistercian problem. Now I'm trying a Cistercian solution.

"Tonight's chili is made with frill-horn meat and, as you can taste, it makes a decent beef substitute. The frill-horns are already adapted to the rangeland, and they are very close to being like a placental mammal, which means we should be able to manage them like cattle. I've been picking the brains of the researchers in Beaverton and sharing my notes with them, and we're already seeing some promising results." Johan watched as Jaqueline became more animated while she talked about her domestication plans. He didn't know if she could do such a thing, but she seemed determined.

Before he set out for the return trip to Beachhead, Johan chatted with one of the farmhands. "Argi, is this really something that can be done? I know folks get bored out here in the sticks, but breeding frill-horns seems a bit extreme."

Argi scratched at the dark stubble on his tanned face. "You didn't see her after Gil died, and the ranch was empty. It was like she became empty, too." He shrugged. "Since she started this project, she's become alive again. If anyone can make it work, it'll be our Jackie. In the meantime, frill-horn steak is pretty good eating."

The old ranch hand waved Johan off, and walked toward the barns where the newest frill-horns were being worked. Jackie said that right now the frill-horns were nothing more than "food tame," and that the calves needed to be worked with and selected for biddable personalities. The ones that were easiest to work with were the ones that were kept for breeding stock; the rest were for the stew pot. Argi's musings were interrupted by shouts and loud booming thumps from the barn; it wasn't screaming so he didn't break into a run, but he did get a move on.

In the barn, he found an adult frill-horn cow named Temperance headbutting a thick wooden partition. The wooden partition would probably break before any of the bones in the cow's face or crest, but this was not the sort of behavior one wanted to encourage in a two-and-a-half-ton animal. Jackie and some of the other hands were trying to shoo her away with shouts and slaps, but a determined frill-horn was not easily dissuaded. At least no one was dumb enough to try and stand in front of Temperance while she was attempting an interior redesign.

Rummaging in a trunk, Argi pulled out a shock stick. It was a wand about a meter long, with two metal prongs on one end and an insulated handle and a small button on the other end. Originally designed for cattle, now was as good a time as any to see if it worked on frill-horns. "Oi! Everyone out of the pen!" Argi shouted, his roughened voice carrying over the noise. "Jusef and Cary, get ready to haul me over the gate if I end up making Tempy mad." The frill-horn cow paused briefly in her headbutting, but soon resumed; the wall started to splinter.

On a frill-horn, the fur and skin are thinnest around the eyes and on the neck behind the flaring bony crest. While the eye would be the easier target, Argi didn't want to risk hurting the cow by accidentally shocking her eye; the goal was to discourage undesired behavior without inducing a frenzied pain response.

He took aim, and as Tempy struck the wall he stabbed forward with the cattle prod. The quiet sizzle of the cattle prod was drowned out by the shocked honking bellow of Temperance. The cow immediately stopped attacking the wall and shook her head like she was trying to dislodge a biting insect. Turning her head, she saw Argi standing there with the wand and snorted. She shook her head and body again, her thick tail flailed, and her pupils narrowed. A huge front foot tipped with three blunt claws scraped the dirt, and Temperance shifted her head side to side to get a better look at the ranch hand.

Argi was hastily coming to regret not putting on a harness with a rope so Jusef and Cary could haul him out of the pen. He maintained eye contact and slowly backed up. It was possible Tempy wouldn't charge. He saw a subtle shift in her muscles, turned and started running for the gate, the sound of her angry challenge sounding far too close for comfort. He felt the ground rumble behind him as she picked up speed; somewhere he heard people yelling at him to run faster. Lord knew he wasn't thinking about slowing down!

Finally, the gate loomed up in front of him. It was eight feet tall—thick wood reinforced with iron. There were slats for climbing over, but his feet were suddenly clumsy; the change from running to climbing was costing him precious seconds. Suddenly a lasso dropped down in front of him. "Foot in the loop and grab hold of the rope!" he heard Jackie command. And the next thing he knew Argi felt like he was flying up and over the gate.

On the other side, hands grabbed him to slow his descent, and everyone retreated away from the gate and the probable debris path. There was a crash and the gate shuddered while dust drifted down from the rafters. There was the sound of flesh smacking a solid object and the gate shook again and again. "Folks!" Jackie called everyone's attention away from the cow's temper tantrum. "That noise means keep an eye out for the flanks and tails. A hit by either one of those will send you flying into a pine box as easily as catching a charge." Her face suddenly split into a huge grin. "These beauties would be so much fun to put in a rodeo to rope and ride." A thoughtful look crossed her face as the gate shook again.

"Okay, Dr. Gerhardt, the folks inside say to just follow the semi-tractor out to Rabinowiscz Ranch," Cesar addressed an older woman sitting in the passenger seat of a pickup truck. "Mr. Ivanovich says to follow Johan on the delivery route and we should get there before the supper bell."

"Excellent, Cesar, thank you. I have been in touch with Jackie ever since she filled me in on this project twenty years ago, and this is the first time I'll get to see the Double R." Her face lit up with a smile making her look youthful despite the iron gray of her hair.

Eventually Johan was done strapping down the supplies on the semi-track for the run, and the worn and dusty vehicle rolled out from the northern edge of town into the scrubland. These days the road was packed gravel and easy enough going, despite the occasional partial washouts and deep ruts. Their escort, Johan, seemed to have made this drive often enough that he knew where to be cautious.

It was midafternoon when Dr. Gerhardt and Cesar saw the distinctive reinforced fence lines required to keep a frill-horn from breaking out, but it wasn't until late afternoon before they turned down the drive to the ranch complex. The noise of the semi-track attracted the attention of the frill-horns in the pasture and by the time the small caravan arrived at the main house, they were being escorted by frill-horns on both sides of the drive.

Johan gave a short blast of the horn from the semi-track. The frill-horns gave startled honk-snorts while a veritable crowd of young ranch hands came out from the barns and ranch house. Cesar snorted. "I can tell we're out in the sticks; there's nothing to do for entertainment except each other. How many people did you say Miss Jackie said she had?"

Shooting her graduate student a sharp glance, Dr. Gerhardt replied, "At last count there were over a hundred people out here, either directly employed by the ranch or in support industries associated with it, and over two hundred additional dependents. And I will remind you, Cesar, that we are guests out here. You will learn to keep your commentary on the available entertainment options in rural Cistercia to yourself."

A small flush darkened Cesar's sun-touched cheeks. "Sorry, Dr. Gerhardt. I'll try to remember to keep my foot out of my mouth."

"Grab our bags out of the bed then, please," said Dr. Gerhardt as she exited the pickup truck. Scanning the crowd milling about the semi-track, she finally spotted an older woman in work clothes and a crisp gray cowboy hat. Skirting the edge of the gathering, Dr. Gerhardt approached and held out her hand. "Jackie, I presume?"

A work-roughened hand clasped hers back before pulling her forward into a quick embrace, "Dr. Sandra Gerhardt? Welcome to the Double R, it's a pleasure to finally meet you in person. Where are your bags? And your grad student?" Jackie's eyes scanned the crowd.

"Cesar is bringing our bags, and he is probably struggling through the crowd. It is good for him, he's a bright lad but he needs some polish if he wants to survive grad school and thrive afterwards." Sandra turned to scan the crowd with Jackie. "Ah, there he is, surrounded by that knot of young ladies over by the back of the semi-track."

Jackie put her fingers to her lips and let out a piercing whistle. In the following silence she raised her voice. "Elizabet, bring that young man over here, you can chat him up at dinner tonight." Sandra watched as the young lady kept talking to Cesar as she towed him through the crowd. Good, she thought, get him out of the lab and out of his ivory tower mind-set. Innovation was as much a product of lab research as it was of field expediency. Hopefully bringing him out here would help Cesar see that.

After a loud and boisterous dinner that night where it seemed that everyone wanted to know what life was really like in Beaverton, Cesar quietly fled to the library. Pulling one of the leather-bound books from the shelves, Cesar opened it to find precise handwriting detailing which bulls were bred to which cows and the stats of the offspring. Some had small red lines through them with a brief explanation of the circumstances of the death, while others showed offspring back-bred to their parents in an effort to fix certain traits. He flipped more pages, then stopped and looked at the bookcases filled with the stock books; it was a monument of data carefully tracked for as long as this project had been going on.

Behind him, he heard the door open. "Ah, Cesar, just the man we were looking for," Jackie said. "Dr. Gerhardt and I have been talking, and for the next few days I'm going to have you follow along with one of the ranch foremen to get a feel for how this operation is run. It's about time for the new adults to be separated from the herd and be kept or be culled. I suggest you don't stay up too late, you will have a long day tomorrow."

Jackie had not been lying. Cesar was up and eating breakfast in the kitchen before the sun had fully risen. While nursing his second cup of coffee, he was approached by an old man. A face long weathered by time and the elements was topped by a faded hat with a Feed Shak logo on it.

"You the youngster that's supposed to tag along while I do my job?"

"I'm supposed to be shadowing someone on the ranch, yes," Cesar replied.

"I'm Argi. Get your hat and let's get going then, daylight is wasting." Before Cesar could respond the old man was heading to the door, leaving Cesar to hustle after him. Outside, Argi was climbing onto a beat-up, open-top tractor hauling a low wagon filled with feed.

"Climb up, kid, you're going to be riding on the fender. Make sure you've got a good grip." Settling onto the metal fender, Cesar found a metal handle welded to the fender and grabbed it as they pulled out. The ride was bumpy, but the vehicle wasn't moving fast enough to throw Cesar off.

"Now, what do you know about frill-horns and what we're trying to do out here?" asked Argi.

"Let's see. Over the last twenty-five years, Ms. Jackie has been selectively breeding frill-horns with an eye towards a smaller, domesticated version; one that will be easier to keep on smaller ranches. If I'm reading the timeline right, you're eighteen generations into the attempt."

"Twenty, actually. The time between estrus cycles in the frill-horn cows is starting to shorten, and we're starting to get a higher fat percentage on the carcasses." The tractor stopped in front of a gate. "You mind working the gate, kid?"

Cesar scrambled down off the fender and lifted the heavy bar that locked the gate shut. It overbalanced on him and fell in the dirt. He picked it up and propped the bar up against the fence before leaning his weight into the heavy gate to force it open. As Argi drove into the pasture, Cesar closed the gate behind him.

Argi could hear the young man struggling with the task. He turned to watch as Cesar climbed up the gate, and attempted to climb down the other side, only to land in the dirt in a heap. About as graceful as a drunken chicken, Argi thought to himself.

"You okay there, kid?"

"Nothing hurt except my pride," replied Caesar, dusting himself off.

Once Cesar was back on his metal perch, Argi started off again.

"Okay, kid, we're driving out to watering hole three and bringing in the herd. Everyone should have calved by now, and we can start figuring out the culls and the keepers."

By now the ranch buildings were lost from sight. They were in the middle of rolling red hills dotted with blue-green scrub. The ground had become rougher and Cesar felt like he was back on the boat ride over from Beaverton.

"I assume you're using the feed we're hauling to bring the herd back in?"

"Got it in one, kid. We ain't got horses and we ain't got dogs, so we use a mixture of hay and sweet silage. The frill-horns love it. We'll pitch some out, wait for them to find it and then drive back. They'll follow. We'll move slow so the calves can keep up."

As the tractor crested a small rise, Cesar saw the herd. There must have been over a hundred animals milling around a metal structure. He noted the smaller size of some of the animals . . . well, relatively smaller size. The cows still looked like they massed two tons. The colors of the animals were different than he expected; instead of all being a mottled olive green, there were some that were mottled hazel green, while others were mottled beiges, and a few were close to roan.

The frill-horns on the edge of the herd noticed the tractor and made loud snuffling noises that alerted the rest of the frill-horns. The milling herd seemed accustomed to the sound of the tractor, with only the new calves running away. Cesar saw the animals lift their muzzles to sniff the breeze, and then cautiously shuffle forward toward the wagon.

Argi put the tractor in park. "Kid, climb down off the back of the tractor and into the wagon. See that shovel? Use it to shovel out a bit of the feed. Be quick, they get impatient and I don't want the tractor or wagon to get tipped over."

Cesar's descent from the back of the tractor and into the wagon made him glad the hay and silage were soft, however smelly the fermented vegetation had become. He grabbed the shovel and started tossing the feed over the sides of the wagon. The damp feed was heavier than he expected, and he slowed down his efforts, but the frill-horns jostled the side of the wagon to remind him to keep moving.

"All right, that's enough. The ones that moved fast got a mouthful and want more, while the ones that didn't will follow along in hopes of getting some. Brace yourself back there, kid," Argi told him, "you're riding back to the ranch in the wagon."

Gingerly seating himself on the edge of the wagon, Cesar gripped the sides tightly. He watched the frill-horns move. They might not be domesticated but they were certainly comfortable with this routine and understood that following the wagon meant more sweet feed. Cesar noticed that the frill-horns were branded on the left side of their crest. It made sense when he thought about it; you can't use ear tags on an animal that doesn't have ears.

The large animals ambled along with the tractor, occasionally bickering among themselves to maintain herd rank. Cesar watched as one young bull, which had worked his way next to the wagon, swung his head into the side of another young bull. The target of the young bull's ire snorted and sidled into a new calf. The new calf, in turn, gave a honking bawl of distress, which caused mama to retaliate. Cesar saw the frill-horn cow's thick tail and powerful hindquarters spinning toward the young bull that started the ruckus. He tried to brace himself, but the impact of the young bull against the side of the wagon caused it to partially tip and Cesar spilled onto the back of the young bull.

He heard Argi yell. Cesar found his cheek pressed up against the warm back of the frill-horn bull, who was still shocked at being slammed into the wagon. Whether by instinct or dumb luck, the grad student grabbed two handfuls of the bull's thick hair and was holding on when the young bull took off from the wagon in panic.

"How do I get off?" Cesar wailed.

"You either get thrown, or you hang on until he wears himself out!" shouted Argi.

With a stream of invectives, Cesar clung to the bull. The juvenile started bucking and tossing his head, trying to get the unfamiliar weight off . . . running, twisting and diving, trying to dislodge the student, running far away from the semi-truck and Argi. Meanwhile Cesar's body was being bounced around and slammed against the bull's back, and he could feel his hands getting slick with sweat. The tightness of his grip was beginning to make his hands ache.

The bull did one last buck and all-over body shake, before giving in to exhaustion with a disgruntled gurgling honk. Cesar waited, unsure if this was only a brief respite before the bull got a second wind to start all over again. The bull surprised him by giving a deep sigh and ambling over to some scrub brush to eat.

Cautiously, Cesar started taking stock of his situation; he had landed prone about halfway back on the bull's spine, just out of range of the horned nubs on the crest. Using his knees and much-abused thigh muscles, he slowly inched his way into a seated position. Looking down, he realized somewhere on his wild ride he had lost his shoes.

"Okay, buddy," Cesar addressed the bull, "I hope you know where we are, because I do not. And I hope you get used to having a rider, because my feet aren't tough enough to survive the rocks and razor weed out here."

The sounds of the frill-horn ripping up and chewing the vegetation were his only answer. "And while we're at it, I'm calling you 'Rudy,' because your rudeness started all of this." Cesar knew he was lucky to not have been thrown, and while he was going to be stiff, bruised and sore tomorrow, he hadn't been seriously injured. As the fear and panic left his body, he was almost willing to admit it had been fun, like a roller coaster except completely unpredictable with no guarantee you'd survive.

The question now, he asked himself, was how to get back to the ranch? As the sun started to set, Cesar realized there was nothing to do but wait. Eventually Rudy would miss the rest of his herd and start moving back to the ranch, or a search party would find him. At least he hoped there would be a search party. He didn't think he'd ever pissed off Dr. Gerhardt enough that she would consider leaving him out here.

Evening settled in, and as the stars came out Rudy started making long, low crooning noises. The croon was so low that Cesar felt it more than heard it. Cesar saw Rudy angling and tilting his head and crest after every croon, then suddenly the bull started walking. When the eastern edge of the horizon started getting lighter, Cesar thought he could see a few pinpricks of light that might be the ranch, but it was hard to tell.

The steady rocking motion of Rudy was almost enough to lull Cesar to sleep, but he knew if he fell asleep, he would fall off. Rudy was crooning again, and this time Cesar's stomach rumbled in response; it had been a long time since yesterday's breakfast. His throat was parched, and he was starting to wonder if he would have to lick the morning dew off of Rudy when he saw bobbing lights on the horizon.

He knew he was too far away for them to hear whatever yell he could coax out of his throat, so he tightened his grip on Rudy's hair, hunched down close to his spine, and kicked his heels into the bull's flanks. Rudy snorted, but picked up his pace.

The sun was fully over the horizon when Cesar and Rudy finally met up with the search team. Cesar gave everyone a weak smile before his grip finally gave out and he slowly slid down the bull's backside, off of the frill-horn's tail, and into the dirt. Rudy, for his part, turned around to look at Cesar in the dirt, then continued heading back to the ranch.

"Cesar, dear boy, are you all right?" asked Dr. Gerhardt. She had been riding along in what looked like an off-road golf cart with a small truck bed, and Jackie was behind the wheel. One of the other searchers grabbed a satchel out of the little cart and started checking Cesar for injuries. Finally, someone gave him a canteen filled with watered down lemonade; it tasted like the finest nectar.

"Drink it slow, kiddo," Jackie cautioned. "One mouthful at a time or you'll make yourself sick. Elizabet, how is he?" The young woman continued to poke and prod at Cesar, looking into his eyes and asking him to move his limbs.

"No broken bones, and doesn't appear to have a concussion, Miss Jackie," Elizabet replied. "He's got a little bit of sunburn, and some dehydration, but no sunstroke. The doc is waiting at the ranch, and he can figure out if I missed something."

"I'm mainly sore," Cesar croaked. "I was far enough back on Rudy that he didn't whack me with his crest."

"Oh, how very interesting." Jackie's eye lit up. "When you've had a chance to recuperate, I would like to discuss your experience on frill-horn back. You're the first rider who hasn't been seriously injured."

A few of the search team helped Cesar to stand and walked him over to the bed of the off-road cart. Cesar continued to drink from the canteen one slow mouthful at a time. The ride back to the ranch house was bumpy, but smoother than the ride out.

★ ★ ★

"You must be Cesar," the young man in a Feed Shak hat said. "You met my dad when he used to work here. I'm Sven." He reached his hand out to shake Cesar's.

"Glad to meet you, Sven. So, you're Johan's kid? How is he doing?" Cesar asked.

"Oh well, pretty good. It's just all of the heavy work started catching up with him, so he helps keep the books these days." Cesar smiled to hear that Johan was still around. It had been ten years and getting his PhD since his last trip to Rabinowiscz Ranch, and more than just the people had changed on Aopo Island. The old semi-track was gone and in its place were two flatbeds hauled by a team of frill-horns. One of the flatbeds was loaded with supplies and luggage, while the other one had been modified to have benches and a shade awning. It would be a slower ride out to the Double R this time, but that was okay. It would give his crew of undergraduates a chance to see the countryside and relax before he put them to work making copies of all the frill-horn breeding records.

The sun had set when the wagons pulled into the ranch's courtyard. The sounds of the frill-horns hooting back and forth made sure that everyone on the ranch knew about their arrival.

Jackie was still very much like Cesar remembered her; still wearing the gray cowboy hat, and still a commanding and energetic presence. "Young Cesar, come here," she commanded and gave him a warm hug by way of greeting. "Congratulations on your degree, I know you'll do great things with it."

"Thank you, Miz Jackie. Dr. Gerhardt wishes she could have come, but she didn't think she could risk the journey over," Cesar said.

"Getting older can be a mixed blessing," agreed Jackie.

"And thank you for letting us invade your ranch like this. I know having copies of all of your breeding records and data will set Dr. Gerhardt's mind at ease. She always worries that something will happen, and all of your hard work will be destroyed," continued Cesar.

"There have been a few changes around the ranch since the last time you were here; we've had to expand our operations, and replace some of the technology with brute force." Jackie watched the crowd of ranch workers and students socialize in the courtyard. "Still, this

whole experiment is starting to look like it might be successful."
Suddenly she grinned. "And this time, young Cesar, if you want to
ride a frill-horn, we now have saddles and reins."

"Ah, young Cesar—or should I call you Dr. Ortiz y Hassan?"
Jackie was older, and frailer this visit, but there was still a spark in her
eye and she was still wearing her gray cowboy hat.

Taking her hands in his, he replied, "Please Miz Jackie, call me
Cesar. I am sorry I could not make it over sooner, but with Dr.
Gerhardt's passing and having to assume the responsibilities of
Department Chair for Animal Science, I could not get away." He
brought her hands to his face and gave them a small press of his lips;
he had learned charm and self-confidence since the days of shoveling
feed and copying breeding records. A teasing smile played across his
face. "I was shocked to find an invite to your eightieth birthday in my
mail, I thought for certain you were no older than sixty."

With a playful swat from her cowboy hat at the renowned
researcher, the two friends caught up.

The continued domestication of the Cistercian frill-horn had
added an abundant native source of protein to everyone's diet and
turned the Double R into a small boom town. In honor of her
birthday, the town had organized a three-day rodeo halfway between
the Double R and Beachhead.

Dr. Ortiz y Hassan gave Jackie a grin before pulling out his
invitation to the event, "I was even more surprised to find out that
you were now 'Jack Daw' instead of 'Jackie.' Have you decided to add
another aspect to yourself?"

Jackie saw the error and laughed. "As far as the Double R is
concerned, yes the invitations were misspelled. But I will tell you a
secret, Cesar." She checked carefully to make sure they wouldn't be
overheard. "Before I came to Cistercia, I was a rodeo queen. I won all
sorts of trophies and ribbons, and my prize money paid for my
degrees." She rolled the brim of her gray cowboy hat between her
fingers. "My granddaddy used to call me his little jackdaw, which was
a type of crow, because I ended up with so many shiny and sparkly
awards." She gave a sad smile at the memory. "So 'Jack Daw' isn't as
much of an error as you might think, but it's a name for someone
who hasn't existed for a long time."

Ranchers

The wisdom of Trudovik separatists in leaving the Cistercian colonies was proven out when the Kerenskiy colony did not suffer from the mysterious "failure to thrive" illnesses that plagued all three colony sites on Cistercia. First the dogs, then various food animals, then humans succumbed to wasting diseases and immunologic syndromes that could not be attributed to any particular cause.

As a result of the cattle shortage, colonists turned to domesticating several of the native Cistercian species. Herbivores such as the frill-horn occupied ecological niches similar to Earth cattle and were ripe for exploitation. Aside from a single episode of mild gastric distress the first time a human ate frill-horn meat, scientists claimed that there were no ill effects of consuming the native fauna despite the additional nucleotide bases present in the DNA of Cistercian animals and the plants they consumed.

Scientists at the Kerenskiy Institute of Science, however, warned of the possibility of long-term consequences from consuming alien proteins. Kerenskiy colonists rejected dietary animal protein in favor of nonvertebrate sources based on these medical warnings. There is no truth to the rumor that the decision was caused by the inability of the Trudovik biosphere to support large herbivores...

—Excerpt from *Flint's People's History of Interstellar Exploitation*,
Trudovik Press,
Kerenskiy, Trudovik, AA237

REDEMPTION

Philip Wohlrab

"Mister . . . Hey mister, open your eyes."

The voice was too young, but then, all the voices were too young these days. Worse, it was incessant. *What does a man have to do to drink himself to death in peace?* He opened one red-rimmed, bleary eye and tried to focus on the face before him. For a brief moment, he saw something, a brief painful flash of something that he didn't want to think about. Down went the eyelid.

"Go away," rasped a voice that was not too used to talking these days.

Now the horrid apparition was tugging on the edge of the hammock, causing it to sway. A great white and black cat yowled a protest at being disturbed. This caused the man in the hammock to open one of his eyes again, though with far more agitation.

"You disturbed the cat," he growled.

"The cat is the least of our troubles, I need your help," replied the once again too-young voice.

"My help? No one has needed my help in more than a century. I am good for nothing and no one, young lady, so why can't you let me go to hell the way I please?"

"Because every other medical person on this peninsula is dead, and you are all I have!"

One Week Earlier

"Motoko, it is so good to see you here!"

"Thanks, Eileen, I didn't think I was going to make it, what with labs and all."

307

"Well, you know what they say, all work and no play make the grad student go crazy! But seriously, it is great to see you. Particularly now," said Eileen Hancock.

Motoko Serizawa nodded in appreciation of her friend. She looked around the airstrip; it was far too primitive to be called an airport. A small wooden hut served as control shack, terminal, and, congruously, a small bar named Wings. Motoko was particularly enchanted by the frozen drinks with small umbrellas that were in view.

"Let me grab my bag, and then let's grab a couple of those," she said, pointing to the drinks.

"Sure, but are sure you want to pay the airport price? I mean, there are better places down by the beach," replied Eileen.

"Yeah, sure, but that means waiting until we get to the beach, and you yourself said all work and no play..."

"Yeah okay, you got me there. Here's your bags, so let's go!"

The two young women walked over to the bar, getting admiring looks from the older gentleman who was tending it. As they strode up, he walked over to their end of the bar and put down a pair of menus. Behind them, a small coastal freighter was being unloaded with case after case of fresh beef by a crew down by the docks. The airstrip fronted a small commercial pier that served as a resupply point for Felicity. The women could hear the banter of the freighter crew with the pier operations people.

"You guys are going to be rolling in steak for the next couple of months, Jack."

"Suits me, all we have here is seafood, and the water crops we grow. I am really looking forward to a nice rare steak."

The two men laughed at that, but neither Eileen nor Motoko were really paying attention. Their eyes were focused on a pair of frozen daiquiris that were making their way over to them courtesy of the bartender. The women took appreciative gulps of their daiquiris—then Motoko reached up and rubbed her forehead vigorously for a minute.

"Ugh, brain freeze."

"Yeah well, you should know better, Miss soon-to-be-a-neuroscientist," snorted Eileen.

"Okay, then. That would be sphenopalatine ganglioneuralgia, and yes, I should know better. But I have been looking forward to this trip for a while now, and some much-needed relaxation."

"Oh? Dr. Roeder have you working too hard?"

"That is one way of putting it. We've been working on a major project to help people with adjustments to the aftereffects of hibernation from the trip over. It doesn't affect you or me since we are second gens, but some of the original colonists are having some memory issues that we believe are associated with long-term hibernation. As if that weren't enough, I still have to attend classes and write papers on other topics, and the strain was starting to get to be a bit much. I need this break desperately, Eileen."

"Well, you have come to the right place, then. There isn't much going on here except aquafarming and long walks on the beach. Our clinic doesn't see many patients, so the boss is okay with me taking off time for surfing and getting you to relax."

A slight breeze picked up while the two were enjoying the drinks and for the first time Motoko could really smell the beach, as the wind blew away the smells of the airstrip and port momentarily. She inhaled deeply and could feel the strain of the last few weeks blowing away with the breeze.

"Let's finish these drinks, I'll get cleaned up, and then let's hit the beach!"

4 Days Later

The Big Kahuna was a beachfront bar carved into the shoreline so that customers could swim up to one side of it. The other side featured a more traditional bar and dining area. Motoko and Eileen had swum up and were enjoying cool drinks and taking a break from surfing. The two were making small talk with a couple of the other surfers when a man approached the other landward side of the bar. He was bushy looking, hair having long since gone to salt and pepper, his eyes lazily tracking. The bartender moved over to that side of the bar, and without needing to be asked he fixed a stiff drink.

The man took the drink, glanced toward Motoko and Eileen, raised his glass at them in a mock salute, and took a long pull from it, emptying his drink. The bartender refilled it. He then placed a couple of bottles of something into a bag and the man handed his credit chit over. Motoko watched the byplay and waited until the man left to turn to Eileen.

"Who was that?" she asked.

"Oh, that is George Holt," Eileen replied stiffly.

Motoko noticed her friend tense up and now her curiosity was piqued even more.

"Well, what's his story? He looks like he's been on a weeklong bender."

"George has been on a bender since planet fall."

"What? Why?" asked Motoko.

Eileen sighed a bit sadly and then answered her friend.

"George was a paramedic on old Earth, with some big city there. Apparently, he suffered some kind of trauma in that job, I don't know what exactly. Anyway, he went on to become a nurse practitioner, a pretty good one by all accounts, and then somehow ended up on the colonization mission. Well, you recall the issues that the crew of the colony ship experienced on the trip, and apparently George was one of the guineas pigs the AIs used to fix the issue. Unfortunately, they screwed something up, and George got stuck in some kind of nightmare loop that left him a basket case when he was brought out of hibernation."

"Oh my God, that's horrible," Motoko gasped.

Eileen focused her gaze on the distantly retreating man as he ambled his way off toward a beachfront bungalow. She pointed toward it and continued.

"Once the psychologists put him back together as much as they could, they sent him here to Felicity in hopes that the beach would do him some good. George tried to work in the clinic when he got here, but he was still having issues, so Dr. Martin essentially retired him. He now spends his days drinking and waiting to die. It really is a shame."

"That is sad," Motoko said, shaking her head.

It was then that Eileen's comm device chirped. Frowning at it, Eileen picked the comm up off the bar and read the message on its small screen.

"What is it?" asked Motoko.

"I'm being called into the clinic, apparently there is a problem."

"Okay then, I am going to keep surfing."

"Alright, then. I will see you later tonight."

With that Eileen grabbed her things and scooped them into her waterproof bag. She swam to the beach and took off. Motoko finished her drink and paid the bartender. She was determined to make the most out of the rest of her afternoon at the beach.

Later that evening Motoko was surprised that Eileen hadn't come home yet, nor had she called to explain what was going on. Motoko decided to make dinner for herself. She was enjoying all the seafood she had eaten over the last couple of days, though Eileen had been eating the freshly delivered meat that had come in, just like most people at the research station at Felicity. Motoko had just settled down to eat seafood salad when her comm chirped. She didn't recognize the number but decided to answer since unwanted scam calls weren't a problem on the colony.

"Hello?"

"Hi, this is Jake Seymour over at the clinic, I work with Eileen. Anyway, she wanted me to call you and tell you that she is going to be here the rest of the night. She would have called but she and the rest of the medical team are swamped with patients at the moment."

"What happened?"

"We're not sure, some kind of bug has brought several people in here. So, the medical team is trying to figure it out."

"I see. Well, when you get a chance tell Eileen that I can entertain myself and to not feel bad; I know she will."

"Will do. Have a good night."

The next day Motoko again headed to the beach, this time sitting, reading and enjoying a trashy novel, and sipping drinks all day. When she got back to Eileen's place, she was surprised to see that Eileen still hadn't been home. She decided to get cleaned up and then head over to the clinic and at least bring Eileen some dinner. She was slightly worried for her friend, but she was still feeling better than she had in months. The stress seemed to have melted off with the days on the beach.

Once she had a dinner plate put together for Eileen, Motoko struck out for the clinic. The settlement of Felicity wasn't very big. The total population of the town was around three thousand people, which made it fairly large for an outlying settlement, but still small by Old Earth standards.

Motoko decided to walk to the clinic, since it wasn't far away, and the evening was gorgeous. The skies over Paradise were subtle shades of pink and purple that they said were somewhat different from Earth's. Though she had never seen a sunset on Old Earth, still her hindbrain told her something was different with the sky.

The research station of Felicity had grown into a small town with its administration building at its center. Next to the admin building was the station's clinic, and the main labs for the aquaponics facilities. Eileen's small house lay a quarter mile out on one of three spokes that ran out from the research facilities. Felicity itself was located on a peninsula, with a small bay on one side and the Haven Ocean on two other sides.

The labs were located on the bay side, where aquaponics farms took advantage of the stability of the bay to grow crops and raise fish stocks. Motoko was impressed with the glass-and-steel structures that made up the central facilities. When Eileen had described the place as rustic, Motoko had pictures of grass huts and rickety wooden structures. The airstrip had not changed her mind, though Eileen had let her in on the secret that the airstrip had been deliberately built as a throwback. The idea was that in the future, Felicity might see more tourism, and that would help set the ambiance of the place as charmingly rustic.

As Motoko drew closer to the clinic she watched as an ambulance neither charming nor rustic pulled up, its lights flashing though its siren was quiet. A pair of EMTs got out and hustled a stretcher into the clinic. The person on the stretcher seemed to be raving incoherently, and the EMTs were struggling to control the stretcher with the patient's exertions.

Well, that's weird. I wonder what is going on ... Is that another ambulance coming in?

When Motoko entered the clinic's front doors, she was surprised to see the waiting area was full of people. Many were shaking, though a few just appeared to be listless. One man's head lolled to the side and he vomited profusely on the floor, having made no effort to move toward the restrooms just a few steps away from the waiting area. To Motoko's horror, she could see that he wasn't the first to have done so. She walked hurriedly to the front desk, there to find a beefy man seated in a chair behind the desk. The nameplate on the desk read Jake Seymour, Executive Assistant.

"Hello—" Motoko started to say.

The smell of him hit her full in the face and stopped Motoko in her tracks. It was a mixture of feces and vomit, and Motoko gagged, her hand flying up to her face unconsciously. Seeing some hand sanitizer at the station, Motoko quickly grabbed some and took a little bit of it to pass under her nose, thankful for the first time for its cloying alcoholic smell, as it masked some of the more pungent odors wafting across the desk.

"Jake, what's going on here? Can you hear me?"

The man continued to sit in his own filth, trembling slightly. His eyes remained unfocused even as Motoko addressed him. He did not look in her direction but instead aimlessly looked around as if he was unaware of his surroundings. Sweat glistened on his forehead and a stream of drool interlaced with some leftover vomit trailed down the left side of his chin. Motoko stepped away from the desk and moved through the small door with a sign indicating that it was the triage area.

Here, too, she found more people in the same state or worse, all patients by the look of them, as no one was dressed in scrubs or an EMT uniform. Moving through the triage room she came to a hallway on the other side. Along the hallway were doors labelled exam room one through five. In each exam room she found more people, though not as many as out in the waiting room. She also found her first member of the medical team, a man wearing green scrubs indicating he was part of the nursing staff. He was slumped over in a chair, and Motoko thought he wasn't breathing.

She rushed over to the man, but before touching him something kicked in in her brain and she stopped in her tracks. *Are these people infectious? Am I in danger here?* She heard the EMTs from the ambulance come into the emergency room through the back doors. Moving quickly in that direction she found the pair, a man and woman, standing dumbstruck. Their patient had ceased raving and was moaning on the stretcher, still weakly moving as much as the restraints would allow.

"What is happening here?" asked Motoko.

"I . . . I don't know. We've been working calls all night, and now all day. The other crew is in here, as patients. But, where is Dr. Martin, or Dr. O'Malley?" asked the male EMT.

Motoko looked at the exhausted pair and then she noticed that both had fever-bright eyes, and very pale complexions. She took a step back, searching the area for face masks and gloves as she answered the EMT's question.

"I don't know, I just got here myself. I'm looking for my friend, Eileen Hancock. How long ago was it since you last delivered a patient? Did it look like this in here then?"

"We were here what . . . three hours ago?" The EMT looked to his partner for confirmation.

"Spaghetti," she replied.

Motoko's eyes narrowed at the response.

"What did you say?" she asked.

"Spaghetti . . . spaghetti?" the woman replied again, though now her face was bunching up as if she wanted to say something else but couldn't find the words.

"Abby, what are you talking about? We had spaghetti for dinner three nights ago, and while your meat sauce was pretty good, I am sure the young lady doesn't want to hear about that."

"SPAGHETTI!"

The other EMT threw up his hands in exasperation as she shouted the word. Her fever-bright eyes searched Motoko's, seeking recognition. Until that moment Motoko hadn't realized that the woman had a slight tremor to her body, but it was growing noticeably worse by the minute. The male EMT didn't seem to notice her shaking and continued to try and have a one-way conversation with the woman, though his words were becoming slurred as if he were very drunk.

"I . . . don't . . . feel . . . so . . . we—" the man stammered out.

Motoko wasn't sure what was happening here, but she quickly ruled out organophosphate poisoning inside the clinic, since she wasn't feeling any effects, and she didn't smell anything resembling garlic or onion. She made no move to get closer to the two EMTs, both of whom seemed to be losing their limited grasp on reality in front of her eyes.

Turning away from the EMTs, she walked over to a supply closet, the door hanging half open and showing some of the supplies within. She quickly found gloves, face mask and gown and took them out. She hurriedly donned them and turned back to where the two EMTs had been, to find them slumped to the floor. The male was still babbling but his speech was nonsensical, while the woman had stopped talking altogether. She was leaning against the stretcher, when she violently threw up into her own lap. She made no move to get up or clean herself.

What in the world is going on here? There are signs of poisoning, but they also appear to have high fevers. Speed, things are happening too fast from what I see here. Motoko kept up her inner monologue, categorizing signs and symptoms on the people she came across as she inventoried the clinic. Concern for her friend also weighed heavily on her mind, and she was using the inventory to suppress her fear of what she was certain she was going to find. She moved back to the first exam room and then proceeded to search each, noting the number of people in each room.

Looks like mostly family units in each exam room, they must have all become symptomatic simultaneously. What is the exposure or vector here?

She made her way back to the nurses' station and looked behind it; there were two nurses there, both nearly catatonic. Neither of them was Eileen. The stench of the emergency room was becoming too much, and Motoko retreated to the supply closet. She found what she was looking for: a small bottle of vapor rub. She applied a dab under each of her nostrils, replacing the sanitizer. The dabs of vapor rub did a pretty good job of masking the worst part of the smell of the ER. She moved past the nurses' station and around the corner she found herself looking into Trauma Bay One. It was here that she found Eileen.

Eileen was slumped over in the corner of the Trauma Bay; around her was the detritus of torn open meds packages, wrappers for various instruments, and gauze. Motoko moved to her friend, seeing that she was still breathing. As Motoko checked her friend's pulse, Eileen opened her eyes to peer at her.

"Motoko?" The voice was barely more than a dry whisper.

"Hush, Eileen, let me check you out."

Motoko noted that her friend's pulse was almost too rapid to count but her respirations were very low, and labored. She also noticed that Eileen had lost control of her bowels and was also trembling like the others. Motoko stood up and backed out of the Trauma Bay looking around.

"Eileen, let me find someplace to get you up off the floor."

The sheer enormity of what Motoko was seeing hit her then. All the medical staff was down, and there had to be upward of thirty or forty people lying sick in the ER. Motoko found a stretcher that had been soiled, but nobody was currently on it. Grabbing some sanitized cloths, Motoko wiped it down and did her best to clean it. Once this was accomplished, she moved it back to Trauma Bay One. She cleared a path and, lowering the stretcher to its lowest setting, worked to get Eileen up on it. In the process, Eileen groaned in agony.

"Motoko, it happened so fast," Eileen managed to say.

"I know, Eileen. Let me get you some ice chips, wait to talk."

Motoko walked around the corner to where an ice machine was set up next to a water fountain. Grabbing a disposable cup on a shelf by the fountain, she filled it with some ice chips and brought the cup back to Eileen. She was trying to distract herself from the scene in Trauma Bay Two. It was there that the two doctors had apparently died—rather messily. The doors to the bay had been sealed by staff as whatever had happened in there unfolded. Dark coagulated blood had come out from under the doors to the bay and Motoko was careful not to step in it.

Eileen had a hard time managing the cup and so Motoko helped her friend with it so that she could get some of the ice in her mouth.

"Don't try to chew it, just let it dissolve in your mouth," warned Motoko.

"Who's the nurse now?" whispered Eileen.

"Eileen, what happened here?"

"I . . . I don't know what is causing it. By the time I got here the clinic was full of people, and they kept getting worse. Then Dr. Martin collapsed in Trauma Bay Two. Dr. O'Malley went to help him but then something much worse happened in there. We sealed the doors to keep it from the rest of the patients, but most of them were past caring by that point."

Eileen's eyes grew bigger as she went on, and Motoko was alarmed to watch small blood vessels burst in the other woman's eyes. Then blood began to pour from Eileen's nose. Motoko quickly tried to staunch the flow of blood with some gauze from one of the surgical carts. Eileen's eyes rolled back in her head and she went unconscious.

"Eileen . . . Eileen." Motoko gently shook her friend, but Eileen had lost consciousness.

Okay, I am way over my head here. I need to get these people help fast. Motoko ran back out to the assistant's desk in the lobby. Beside the phone on his desk was a list of important numbers including the labs, the administrative center, and the sheriff's office. She dialed the number for the sheriff's office and waited as the phone pinged.

"Felicity Sheriff's Office, Deputy Lawrence speaking. How may I help you, sir or ma'am?" the voice was deep and reassuring.

"This is Motoko Serizawa. I am over at the clinic and all the medical staff is either incapacitated or dead. I need help over here as fast as you can find it, and we need to contact the Paradise Colony Administration for a medical team to be dispatched here as soon as possible."

"Wait . . . What did you say, the whole clinic staff is down? What happened?" Deputy Lawrence's voice deepened with concern.

"I am not sure, some type of fast-moving poison or disease, I don't know which. Whoever comes over here should take biohazard precautions before coming in."

"Okay, I'm going to call the other deputies and the sheriff on my way over. Sit tight by that phone in case the sheriff wants to get hold of you. It's Saturday, so no one is in the operations center over in the administration building. Once we have a read on the situation, I will let the sheriff make the call for outside assistance."

"Okay, please hurry. There are a lot of people here that need help."

Motoko hung up the phone and looked around her. She wasn't just going to stand around and do nothing, so she began by getting the assistant out of his chair and laying him on the ground. It was backbreaking work, but she managed to get him on the ground with something to prop up his head. She angled him so that if he were sick again, he wouldn't aspirate on his vomit. She moved around the waiting area doing the same for the others.

After twenty minutes, Motoko was beginning to wonder if anyone was coming. Then the front door opened, and a powerfully built man in a deputy's uniform walked in. He had removed his hat and was wearing a gas mask, gloves, and had a clear plastic onesie over his uniform.

"Are you Motoko Serizawa?" the man asked, although his voice was somewhat distorted by the gas mask.

"Yes."

"I am Deputy Lawrence. I called the sheriff and he is on his way, but several of the deputies failed to answer their comms. The sheriff was going to check on them as they live close to his place. He'll be here shortly."

More flashing lights could be seen through the front door and another two deputies entered, both women. Like Deputy Lawrence they, too, were suited up and wearing gas masks.

"What do we have, Steven—" The woman broke off as she looked around. "Jesus, what is wrong with all of these people?"

"I don't know, Linda, but from the looks of it, nothing good. Ms. Serizawa here found them and called it in. Ms. Serizawa, this is Deputy Linda Taylor, and that is Deputy Tori Ramirez."

"Do any of you have medical training?" asked Motoko.

"We all just have the basics: CPR and stop-the-bleed kind of stuff, nothing advanced," answered Deputy Ramirez.

"How about you, ma'am?" asked Deputy Lawrence.

"I trained with the med students at Paradise University, but I am not an MD. I am a grad student in the neuroscience program, so I have some basics, but not as well trained as, say, a paramedic or nurse. Most of my training is in more specialty brain-related stuff."

"Okay, here comes the sheriff," said Deputy Taylor.

Another vehicle pulled up and the sheriff hopped out. After donning his biohazard precautions, he too entered the clinic's lobby and looked around. He was average height and build but Motoko could see the worry in the man by his body language.

"Steven, I found Allen and Jerrica in the same state as these people. Same with their families. What is going on here?"

"Sheriff, we don't know. This is Ms. Motoko Serizawa and she found the clinic this way. We haven't been here long enough to get a good look around but if the rest of the clinic is in the same shape as out here, I say we need to call for help immediately."

"It *is* worse," piped up Motoko.

"Right. It seems Ms. Serizawa is correct. I am Sheriff Jason Alvarez." He reached out to shake Motoko's gloved hand, but she pulled away.

"Please—call me Motoko, and I would second getting help. As far as I know, all of your medical personnel are compromised."

"Well, everyone except Old George," added Deputy Ramirez. "But I'm not sure he counts anymore."

The little group of officers followed the sheriff and Motoko back through triage and into the Emergency Room area. Despite the sight of the lobby the officers were not prepared for the reality of the tableau before them. Deputy Ramirez made a gagging noise in her mask and turned away from the group. Motoko could hear her taking several deep breaths and muttering to herself.

"It nearly got me when I first smelled it as well. Vaporized ointment under the nostrils helps," said Motoko.

"It isn't the smell—fortunately the mask screens that out—but damn that is a lot of body fluids on the floor," replied the deputy.

"Okay, troops, this is no place to try and help these people. Steven, go look in the supply room back there and see if they have any more stretchers. Linda and Tori, help Ms. Serizawa with getting these people ready to move. Check the children first. Once I get the administration working on setting up a temporary clinic, I'll be back to help you all. I will have the administrators call Paradise Colony Control for assistance."

The sheriff strode purposefully out, and everyone got busy doing what they could to help move the patients. Deputy Lawrence turned up several foldout litters of a type used in disaster response and once they were set up, the deputies and Motoko worked to move all the children onto them first. After ten minutes the sheriff returned to the area and told them that the local school gym was being set up to take over as a place to bring everyone.

"Several people are bringing their trucks over to help us move these people over to the school. Ms. Serizawa, you have the most medical training among us—can you organize the supplies that need to go over?"

"Uhh...sure, Sheriff, is there any word on a medical team coming?"

"Not yet."

"Has anyone thought about how many people might be ill but didn't come to the clinic? I mean, you had two of your deputies and their families that were unable to get here, I wonder how many others are like them?"

The sheriff stopped in his tracks, looked up at the ceiling and then made a clearing of the throat noise as he thought through what Motoko had said. He turned back to her with a look that for the first time showed a crack in his otherwise solid demeanor. He walked back over to Motoko and looked her square in the eyes.

"No, no one had thought about that yet. I hadn't considered that there would be others like my deputies. How many people could this thing encompass?"

"If I knew how it was spreading, I would have a better idea. As of now I have no idea what is causing this and how many people are affected."

The phone at the nurses' station rang at that moment and Deputy Ramirez picked it up. It took her a minute to juggle the phone around the gas mask, but then she listened as the person on the other end passed along some information. The deputy turned to Sheriff Alvarez and motioned for him to come to the phone. The sheriff had to go through the same motions of figuring out how to work the phone as the deputy did and then he grunted through the mask once he had the headset seated. He listened for a few minutes, occasionally making a noise to show he was following, and then he replaced the headset on the receiver. Turning back to Motoko, he gave her a very long look.

"What is it, Sheriff?" Her voice filled with dread.

"We are on our own. It seems all of Paradise Colony is dealing with some kind of disease. Worse, they think we may be the most contagious based on the description we sent up, and they have declared a quarantine of our area."

Motoko gulped.

16 Hours Later

Eileen was dead. So, for that matter, was everyone else from the clinic. They had started dying ten hours after Motoko had first come to the clinic. What was worse is that everything she tried to do for them seemed to have no effect. At first all she could do was supportive care. She and the deputies had salvaged the oxygen machines from the clinic, but there were only a handful of them, and so she used them at first for the worst off. Then Deputies Lawrence and Taylor grew sick. They had each rotated out to get a meal, and within a few hours of getting back to the makeshift ward they had started showing signs of disorientation. Within a few more hours they were catatonic like the rest.

"Ms. Serizawa, we need to think about what the next steps are. Volunteers have been going house to house and have turned up scores more cases and dozens of deaths," said Sheriff Alvarez in a subdued tone.

"What do you mean?" asked Motoko, exhausted.

"One, you are working yourself to death here with nothing to show for it. We need more medical personnel, and frankly we need to figure out the cause here, otherwise we don't know how to prevent others from getting sick. I have ordered everyone to stay in their homes, with the blessing of what is left of Felicity's civil administration."

"I need people familiar with medicine and . . . who can do labs?"

"Well, the resident vet and her staff are all over there." Here the sheriff stopped and pointed to one corner of the gym. "The only people we have that might be familiar with labs are a few of the aquaponic research staff, but many of them are sick as well. I . . . hold up. What about George?"

"Who, the drunk?" asked Motoko.

"Yeah, he used to be a nurse of some type or so they say. Why don't we see if we can sober him up and get him to help?"

"At this point I'm willing to give anything a try," replied Motoko.

"Right, why don't you go get cleaned up, and get out of here for a bit. Then head over to this address and see about getting him. With any luck you will catch him before he starts his midday bender." The sheriff handed Motoko a scrap of paper with an address on it.

"Midday? What time is it?"

"Time for you to take a break. Deputy Ramirez and myself, along with the volunteers, can watch things here for a bit."

"What do you mean, everyone else is dead?"

"Dr. Martin, Dr. O'Malley, my friend Eileen, the other nurses, and even their assistant, Jake. They are all dead, some disease is killing everyone, and I don't know how to stop it," replied Motoko desperately.

The cat yowled indignantly for a second time at being disturbed. Its swishing tail seemed to mirror the agitation that Motoko was seeing in George Holt. The white and black cat finally decided that it wasn't going to be left in peace, so it stood up and hopped off the hammock. George watched it go for a moment before he too sat up. Motoko pushed a mug of coffee into his hands.

"Here, drink this; I need you to sober up."

George looked at the cup for a moment, and then tentatively put it to his lips, taking a sip. He made a face and pulled the cup away to look at it again.

"What is in this? Cream? Are you a savage?" he asked in a disgusted tone.

He looked down at himself and then back at Motoko.

"Alright, you have my attention," he said gruffly while rubbing his dirty hair. "Let me get cleaned up."

An hour later, Motoko and George were back at the school gym. Both had gowned up for biosafety precautions. Motoko handed George a jar of vaporized ointment and advised him that he would want to swab some under his nostrils.

"Is it that bad?" he asked.

"Yes, there are not enough volunteers to patients to keep things tidy. They are doing the best they can, but I need you to be ready for what you are going to see in there, it isn't good."

George sighed and fingered something under his gown. Motoko wasn't certain but she thought it might be a flask. She winced internally and then turned to the double doors marking entry into the gym. She pulled one of the doors open, and she heard George gasp. Following his gaze, she took in the scene as well, as things had changed again in the couple of hours she had been away from the gym. Large mats had been laid out on the floor and scores of people were lying on them, many violently twitching.

"Good, you're back," said Sheriff Alvarez, relief evident in his voice.

The sheriff was no longer in the biohazard garb that he had previously been wearing and was now gowned and masked like Motoko and George.

"As you can see, we have more patients coming in."

George stepped back away from the door, turned around and Motoko could see him retrieve something from a pocket. The object was revealed as the flask she suspected, and George took a long pull from it. Rage flared in Motoko and she turned angrily on George.

"Hey, I said I need you sober," she growled.

"Listen up, Ms. Serizawa, I'm a drunk and have been drinking now probably longer than you have been alive. That means that if I quit cold turkey on you, I am likely to experience all the bad things that happen, like delirium tremens. Besides, the alcohol keeps the demons away, and it looks like you have gotten me into something that is going to cause more demons. So back off," said George, just as angrily.

"Oh . . . yeah. Look, at least stay clearheaded on me, okay?"

George sighed, put his mask back in place and stalked past her into the gym. Walking up to the first patient lying closest to the door, he checked the man's pulse, then examined his eyes. He did a quick head-to-toe assessment of the man before turning back to Motoko.

"Have you been able to get any labs done?"

"No, I haven't done anything more than supportive care where we could. Even that isn't much more than trying to keep them comfortable and clean where we can. There are just too many patients," she said, her voice rising a bit with emotion.

"Yeah, okay. Oh hey, Jerry!" George pointed to one of the volunteers and motioned him over. "I know you don't do blood work, but if I draw some samples for you, can you run it over to the lab and run a chemistry and a culture on it?"

The man had come over and at first looked confused at the request, but then stopped. He looked in the air as if picturing something, then nodded.

"Yeah, George, we have the stuff to do that. I will have to brush up on culture, but we have the Net for that. I haven't done one since my bio days back at Paradise University."

"This . . . damn. Yo, kid, what is your first name again? I am not going to keep calling you Ms. Serizawa," said George somewhat distractedly.

"It's Motoko."

Her voice was cold, but if it had any effect on George, he didn't show it. Instead he moved to a second patient and began another head-to-toe assessment, then a third. Finally, he stopped after examining the fifth person, when he motioned to Motoko.

"In a lot of ways this looks like organophosphate poisoning. The excess saliva, the pinpoint pupils, the tremors."

"I thought that was what it was at first, but there is the fever and so many people coming down with it over such a length of time..." Motoko trailed off.

"Yeah, it was a good thought at first given the symptoms. But you're right; the fever and continued onset of new cases make that unlikely. Besides, any environmental exposure of organophosphates to affect this many people would have taken down the whole town."

Motoko noticed George shaking and his somewhat unsteady gait.

"George, do you feel alright?"

"Hell no, woman! By now I would have usually polished off half a bottle of cheap whiskey. It's the effects of not enough alcohol in my system." He stopped and looked around. "At least, I hope that's what it is. Look, I'm shaking too badly to do a proper job of drawing blood. Have you ever done that before?"

"Not since I was training with the med students a couple of years ago."

"Okay, I can talk you through it. But I need you to be my hands, so let's get some supplies and get some samples."

The two walked over to a table where supplies had been brought over from the clinic. Looking around, George pointed to vac tubes and catheters for drawing blood samples.

"That's what we need. We'll take samples from those five individuals and see what comes back."

It took a few minutes to talk Motoko through drawing her first blood sample, but then she quickly got the hang of it. The problem had been trusting the feel of the blood vessel over trying to see it, and was complicated by the dehydration of the patients. After an hour they had multiple samples and George led Motoko and Jerry Sampson—the volunteer George had recruited—out of the gym.

"Okay, let's head over to the labs and see what we have first off. Also, you said this was happening all over, right?"

"Yeah, that was why we were denied any additional assistance. Colony Control said we were the worst off and they have quarantined us."

"Right, see if there is anything else up on the Net with regards to the other sectors of the colony. Perhaps someone else has already isolated what we have here."

As they walked over to the labs it was bright outside, another perfect day in Felicity. George took several swigs off his flask, while he kept up a stream of thought on the symptoms they had seen in the patients. Finally, they reached the labs and Jerry took the blood samples to get them ready for imaging and cultures.

Motoko went into one of the offices and tried to log on to a computer. She had to grab Jerry to get a logon and password, but once that was done, she put in a search for what was happening in other parts of the colony. She spent several hours reading through various reports and growing more and more alarmed. She was beginning the next report when George walked into the office.

"When was the last time you ate something?"

"What?" she asked.

"Ate something; when was your last meal?"

"I don't remember."

"Right, here drink this," George handed over a bottle that said "protein shake" on the side of it.

Motoko took the bottle, spun the cap off and her stomach growled. She hurriedly drank the bottle, feeling better to get something in her. She looked back up at George, half expecting to see glazed-over eyes. They weren't.

"What happened to you?" she asked. "What caused you to be the wreck I saw earlier?"

George sighed and pulled up a chair. He sat down heavily and produced his flask, tipped it up, and took a swig from it. He deliberately screwed the cap back on and then peered at Motoko.

"You are about the age of the young lady I once tried to help. But, I am getting ahead of myself. I was a firefighter-paramedic for the city of Atlanta in the state of Georgia. The population of that city is more than what we have on this colony, so as you can imagine we were a busy fire department. We got a call one day for a fire in a high-rise hab block, and my team was assigned to go up on the seventh floor and sweep the daycare there. What we found wasn't good. The kids had all perished from smoke inhalation, and the only survivor we found was the daycare worker. She had tried her best given the terrible situation they were in, but in the end, the kids were too young to compensate for the smoke, and well, she had barely survived. We resuscitated her and got her out of the area."

Motoko watched the play of emotions across George's face as he described the scene.

"Well, a month afterwards we were working a normal shift when we got called out for a jumper. She was up on a building and threatening to jump. I went up to try and talk her down and that is when I realized that it was the daycare worker. She recognized me, about the same time I recognized her, and as soon as that hit . . . well, she jumped. Anyway, fast-forward several years, and I had moved on to become a nurse practitioner and this colony thing came up, so I decided to give it a go. Got accepted to the program and then off on the mission we went. Seems there was a problem and the AIs decided to use me as a guinea pig. I got stuck in a nightmare loop of seeing that young woman jump, for years. Worse, they knew I was damaged and waited to thaw me out of that hell. Hence the nearly generation skip."

He unscrewed the flask again and took another swig. Motoko couldn't imagine what kind of hell that must have been.

"George, I'm sorry. I shouldn't have brought it up."

"It's okay, you didn't know. Well, enough about me, what have you found?"

"Umm—there have been disease outbreaks all over Paradise. Some places say that it may be a repeat of the bug in the first generation, but no one is certain. That was the one that killed all the dogs."

"Hmmm, has there been mention of any livestock or other domestic animal deaths?"

"I don't know, no one has mentioned it."

"Anything else?"

"There have been a couple of mentions of tests coming back positive for Creutzfeldt-Jakob disease. That would explain some of the symptoms, but the speed is all out of proportion for our bug to be that."

"Also doesn't explain the more flulike symptoms."

"Right, but it does give us something to test against, right?"

"Yeah, it does. Hold on. Hey, Jerry!" shouted George.

A minute later Jerry Sampson poked his head in the door.

"Yeah, what's up, guys?"

"We got a potential lead; we need to scan for prions."

"Okay, we can do that under the electron microscope. I think we have the kits, sent to us by mistake. Some bureaucrat saw 'farm' and sent them to us, not realizing we do aquafarming here."

Motoko and George chuckled at that. The three of them walked back into the lab where Jerry had been working. It took him a half hour to set up the sample and the microscope, but then he flashed an image of the sample up on a large screen.

"Look here," said Motoko, motioning to a particular spot on the image. "And here—see these prions? But they don't look right for CJD or vCJD."

She walked over to another lab terminal and took a moment to pull up an image for what a clump of prions looks like indicating Creutzfeldt-Jakob disease or the variant once called "Mad Cow." The images were somewhat similar, but there were noticeable differences, including something that looked like it was bound to the clump of prions. The prions appeared as rods on the image, but the thing bound to them looked like a ball with tendrils outstretched around them.

"What is *that*?" asked Motoko.

"It sorta looks like the flu," replied George with a wondrous tone in his voice.

"You know, we just got that large shipment of beef in a week ago, you guys are talking about prions, maybe that is the source of contamination," added Jerry.

"We need to test that beef!" exclaimed Motoko.

"Yes, but first we need to stop people from eating it just in case," George said as he picked up a phone from a nearby desk. He punched in a number, waited, then spoke again, "Hi, this is George Holt. . . . Yes, Andrea, *that* George. Look, we think we may have isolated what is causing people to be sick. To be on the safe side we need to get the word out not to eat any of the beef that came in. Also, people need to avoid contact with anyone that is sick."

He took a little longer explaining, then hung up.

"Will they really get the word out?" asked Motoko.

"I may have surprised Andrea, but apparently Sheriff Alvarez let her know I was working on this, so she believes—"

George was interrupted as loudspeakers around Felicity, normally used for storm alerts, began to broadcast a message telling people not to eat any beef products and to avoid contact with infected individuals if possible. George smiled at that and then motioned for Motoko to follow him.

"Jerry, keep working on those cultures and see if you can identify that cluster any further. Motoko, I have an idea—I want to try treating a couple of the patients with antivirals and see what happens. We can also try a broad-spectrum antibiotic as well."

The two walked out of the lab and headed over to the clinic. Going through the small pharmacy, they found the drugs they were looking for, then headed back to the makeshift ward. When they arrived, they found that many of the patients there had died, but not all of them. Sheriff Alvarez filled Motoko and George in on what had happened in their absence, and they provided the details of their findings. Selecting several patients, George and Motoko administered antivirals to some, antibiotics to others, and yet other patients got both.

"In any other situation this wouldn't be ethical—but cut off and without much in the way of options, I hope we are forgiven," stated Motoko.

Having done that, the pair went to the local commissary and found that some of the meat that had been delivered was still there. They took it back to the lab to test it, and again they found the strange cluster of prions—and something else. Jerry Sampson was still waiting on the samples to come back and said it would probably be another twelve to twenty-four hours before they would know something more.

"Motoko, go get some rest. You've been up way too long at this point. I'll go over and check the ward, and you can spell me in eight hours," said George.

Motoko just nodded. She was dead tired. She went back to Eileen's place and cried herself to sleep. Six hours later she was wide awake, so she decided to head back over to the school gym and see how things were progressing. On arriving she could see there was some excitement in the ward. An exhausted-looking George raised his flask up at Motoko and waved her over. He was sitting beside one of the patients. The patient was looking up at Motoko, not just looking at her, but focused on her face. Then the patient smiled weakly.

Epilogue

Dr. Motoko Serizawa Cristoff scratched the ears of a great white cat with black markings on ears, neck and tail. It purred at her as it wiggled to a more comfortable position in her lap. She sighed contentedly and peered out the window of the Felicity Clinic into the square downtown.

"George would have hated that ugly thing," she said, not for the first time.

"What was that, Dr. Cristoff?" asked a young intern.

Motoko pointed to the statue in the town center. The artist had been inspired by tales of the first patients waking up from Serizawa-Holt disease. It was supposed to depict George Holt sitting beside a patient with Motoko peering over his shoulder. Beside the statue was a plinth with more than fifteen hundred names on it.

"Oh, Dr. Holt would have hated that thing. Fortunately, the Felicitans waited until after his death to put it up, and pointedly didn't consult me, either."

"Oh, I see, Doctor. Well, you guys did save half the colony. It was bound to happen."

"Yes, I suppose so. But it's way too gaudy, not to mention embarrassing. Plus, it never looked like *that*. The real event to celebrate was what it did for Dr. Holt. None of you knew him before he became a doctor, but watching his transformation, once he had a purpose again, was possibly the best thing to happen from it."

She was lost in thought for a moment, then whispered softly, "I miss him terribly." After a moment she shook her head and mimed raising a toast with an empty hand. "As for me, I've never touched a drop of alcohol since."

The intern thought that there must be more to that story, but didn't feel he could ask. Instead he shuffled some paperwork around on his desk. After all, working for a legend was certainly educational and did tend to lead to some interesting scraps of conversation, but he'd learned that some questions wouldn't be answered.

Prion Disease

Only the perspective of history revealed that many of the diseases encountered in the early years of Cistercia's colonies could be attributed to a common source: prions. On Earth, prion diseases such a Creutzfeldt-Jakob disease or Bovine Spongiform Encephalopathy resulted from an accumulation of peptides and proteins with abnormal structure. These "misfoldings" prevented normal metabolism, as well as assembly and breakdown of cells utilizing those proteins, most notably in the brain of affected mammals. The cause of the abnormality is still not understood, nor is the ability of the abnormal proteins to replicate, preserving the unusual three-dimensional structure of the protein. Spread of the disease resulted solely from consuming the flesh of affected animals, particularly cattle—or humans.

On Earth, prion infection was most evident in brain tissue, and neurological symptoms predominated—including neuromuscular muscle weakness and tremor, wasting, behavioral changes and altered responsiveness to sensory stimuli. One of many reasons the Cistercian variant went so long without identification was that symptoms included hematological and immunological sequelae, resulting in misidentification as bacterial and viral infections. In addition, the prion-like disease included novel nucleotides that were found in the DNA of all Cistercian life-forms. Thus, spread of the affliction could have resulted from many vectors...

—*Encyclopedia Astra*,
Gannon University,
Antonia, Cistercia, AA212

LOONEYTOONS

D.J. Butler

"Why did Gregor have to spend so much time at Roanoke?" Ilya asked.

He stomped, catching the wave before the last of it receded and sending up an arc of saltwater into the scarf protecting his face. The sand piper at the toe of his boot gave itself away, emitting a silent gasp of surprise that emerged as a watery bubble. Ilya pushed in the head of his spade, the soles of his feet accustomed to the bruising contact with the tool's steel shoulder. It was a good spade; Gregor claimed that the serial number stamped on the handle, now worn into illegibility, was a sign that it had come from Earth. Kicking the spade into the wet sand one handspan to the side of the spot whence the bubble had emerged, Ilya pushed down with all his weight, then levered the spade sideways.

The sand piper popped up into the dry air, making its characteristic whistling sound. In deeper water, the finned, spiny arthropod would have eluded Ilya easily, but this was not Ilya's first Piper Picking, and he'd hit the timing perfectly. The piper landed on damp sand, and before it could drag itself down the beach to meet the next ascending wave, Ilya scooped it into his net.

Best not to touch the piper with his hands until it had been boiled—the venom in the spines wouldn't kill a person, but even through his thick gloves, it would cause severe itching and swelling. Ilya shook the net out into his uncle's half barrel. The sand piper joined the others already penned in there, crawling in a circle, their piping sound reduced to a kittenlike mewl.

"He's got to steal a woman, doesn't he?" Ilya's uncle Olaf had also bagged a piper, and now shook his out into the half barrel. He pulled his scarf away from his mouth to be heard better; the weather wasn't especially cold, but Olaf and Ilya both suffered in low temperatures, and took chill easily. "Do you imagine that's easy?"

"There are women here," Ilya said. "There's Annie Wopat. She's very good at catching sand pipers, and also at climbing the cliffs for plovers' eggs." Annie was also funny, and had a cute smile, and she was only a year older than Ilya, which was no big deal. And she didn't wear bulky clothes to keep her warm on the beach, so Ilya had seen enough of Annie to really fuel his imagination.

"Well, Annie's a bit young for Gregor." Olaf stooped to pick up a short strand of Sanderman's Kelp and bit into it. The liquid inside Sanderman's was low on calories, but had a lot of vitamin C, if you could stand the sour taste and the cold temperature. "Besides, if she married him, she couldn't marry you, could she?"

Ilya blushed. A wave splashed over his boots and he peered intently at the sand beneath it, looking for pipers' bubbles, but saw none. "I guess what I really mean is, why does he have to go kidnap a woman at all?"

Having sucked all the juice from the kelp, Olaf threw it onto the retreating wave. "Population bottleneck."

"I don't know what that means."

"It means that if you get too few people, then all their descendants are like those people."

"Like if those few people all had big hands, then their descendants would have big hands."

Olaf nodded. "But worse—if they suffer from the same diseases, then their descendants will suffer. Or if they're all lactose intolerant, or susceptible to alcoholism, or have the same parasites."

"This feels like school," Ilya complained. He stomped up another bubble and pounced, throwing his spade into the sand with gusto.

"Ah." Olaf spaded up a piper, but he had acted too soon, and the creature slipped past him and out to sea on the wave. "Then let me try it this way. Once upon a time, the entire village was sick."

"Beaverton's not a village."

"Maybe it was, back then."

"So, this isn't a story about Gregor."

"It is, if you pay attention. We do the things we do now because our ancestors did them way back when. Or, you know, because the gods did them."

"Beaverton was sick."

"Because there were too few of us," Olaf said.

"What kind of sickness?"

"Different things, depending on how bad your luck was." Olaf shrugged. "Maybe it was some kind of anemia. Maybe it was brittle bones. Maybe it was looneytunes."

"Madness?" Ilya shuddered. "And the scientists couldn't fix it?"

"Scientists don't fix things with magic wands, you know. In fact, it was the scientists who said, 'Look, we have this anemia and bad bones and looneytunes and the way to fix it is we need to get some new people in here to marry.'"

"Kidnapping seems extreme." Waiting for the next wave, Ilya stooped to pick up a fist-sized salp. The gelatinous mass trembled in his hand like a jelly.

"We didn't kidnap. Not right away. The lord mayor picked three brothers."

"Beaverton had a lord mayor?"

"In fairy tale times, everyone has a lord mayor. Later, you get governors and congressmen and deputy chief regulators. These three brothers were all tall and handsome and didn't have terrible problems. One was a little anemic so he slept a lot, and one had to be a little careful with his bones and drink a lot of sea-cow milk, and one might have been just a little bit looneytunes, but not so you would know it right away."

"Sea-cow milk makes you constipated."

"Like I said, these brothers weren't perfect. But they were pretty good. And the lord mayor gave the brothers some precious stones to take with them in their canoe, and they took supplies along, food and pulque for the long nights and sleeping blankets, and they headed for Roanoke."

Ilya stomped several times in his window of opportunity as a wave slipped away, but he saw no bubbles. "Were they going to buy women?"

"They were going to give presents to the women's families. We still do that. Which is why Gregor took a thick stack of pelts with him."

"He's going to kidnap a woman and leave behind pelts for her family."

"For her mother, specifically." Uncle Olaf nodded. "That's how you do it. So, these three brothers were named Mike and Lou and Jim—"

Ilya laughed.

"What?"

"Silly names," Ilya said, stomping again but finding nothing.

"It's a fairy tale," Olaf said. "People can have silly names. Or should I switch back to telling it like in school?"

"I like the silly names," Ilya said.

"When they got to Roanoke, the brothers were scared, so Lou and Jim hid outside the wall listening to the screaming of strange beasts and Mike went in alone, with his precious stones. And he found his way to the headman's hut. Everyone noticed him because he looked different from the people in Roanoke—"

"Are you saying they could see his anemia?"

"No, but they had different hair and skin colors, and of course the people in Roanoke were huge compared to Mike, because they had had a population bottleneck, too."

"No fair." Ilya frowned. "They got to be giants, and we got bad bones."

"Another time, I'll tell you a different story, about how life isn't fair. So, the people of Roanoke followed Mike to the headman's hut, and he was surrounded by all of them, standing there with his jewels. And the headman, whose name was Clement, said, 'What do you want?' And Mike said, 'I want to marry one of your women, maybe that one over there with the red hair, because I like her smile. Also, I brought you these gifts.' And Clement said, 'I can tell from your skin and your accent and your hair that you are from Beaverton, and if you think that I'm going to let one of our girls marry you, then you really are looneytunes. But thanks very much for the gift.' And they took Mike's gems from him, and beat him up, and threw him into their jail."

"I think *this* story is about how life isn't fair." Ilya stabbed his spade into the sand, but he had been distracted by the tale, and missed his spot; only half of the sand piper came up on the spade's blade, and it oozed pink ichor. With a sigh, Ilya heaved the ruined piper into the waves.

"Maybe all stories are. But lucky Mike, he had two brothers, and when night came and he hadn't come back, they climbed over the wall and found the jail and got Mike out."

"How did they do that? You make it sound so easy."

"Well, you know how people at Roanoke can't take their liquor? That's because of their population bottleneck problem, and Lou and Jim knew this. So they slipped their pulque into the guards' rations and when the guards were drunk, they unlocked the door and Mike walked out. Only Mike said, 'The lord mayor sent me here to get a wife, and they took my precious stones anyway, so I'm going to get a wife, fair's fair.' And he *did* like the way that redheaded girl smiled at him, so the brothers sneaked around the village until they found her, and they took her with them."

"Conked her over the head?" Ilya asked. "Made her drink pulque?"

"Apparently, she was willing to come along, after all. Maybe she was sick of men who were too tall and couldn't hold their liquor, and a little anemia didn't seem like a big problem to her. But before the brothers could leave the island, the men of Roanoke came after them. So, Mike and his bride took the canoe and paddled for home, but Lou and Jim took the rest of the precious stones and ran off into the woods making lots of noise, so the men of Roanoke would chase them. And it worked, but it took Lou and Jim a week to lose their pursuers. And by that time, they had nearly reached Antonia."

"The lord mayor only sent them to Roanoke," Ilya objected.

"That's what Lou said when he realized where they were. But Jim, who was a little bit looneytunes, said, 'Hey, we still have the gems, we should try to get our brides here. No way the people in Roanoke are going to let us back to try again.' And Lou said, 'Well, negotiating with the headman was a bad idea. This time let's try talking just with the family.' So, they walked into Antonia and strolled around talking to the girls there. And because everyone could tell they were not from Antonia, and because young women are always interested in seeing new young men—"

"Always?" Ilya asked.

"Most of the time," Olaf said. "So, Lou met a young woman he liked, because she had strong arms and legs, and Lou had always been a little weak."

"Because of the brittle bones," Ilya volunteered. "And the constipation."

"And the young woman invited the brothers to her house for dinner. This was just was what Lou wanted, because over dinner—which was very nice roasted beef with a creamy Antonian pepper dressing—he told the girl's father he'd like to marry her. And the father, whose name was Gustavo, said, 'No way.' And Lou said, 'I brought you a gift,' and Gustavo said, 'No way am I trading my daughter for a gift, and if you aren't out of my house by dawn, I will break your brittle neck.' And Gustavo was so mad that he stomped out."

"But that wasn't the end," Ilya said.

Olaf shook his head. "As soon as Gustavo had left, his wife, whose name was Mariana, asked what the gift was. And Lou showed her the stones and she said, 'Give me this gift and you can take my daughter, only you have to leave right now.' And Lou had brittle bones, but he wasn't one to let moss grow on him, and Jim was looneytunes so he was game to help. So, Lou left the gemstones with Mariana, and he and the girl with strong arms and legs built a raft. She was really helpful at raft-building, because she was so strong, and then they hoisted Lou's shirt as a sail and came home in triumph."

"So this is why Gregor took pelts to give to his bride's mother, specifically," Ilya said.

"And this is why we sometimes have anemia, and sometimes brittle bones, but not nearly as bad as once happened to us."

"And this is why people from Roanoke and Antonia also come kidnap our girls," Ilya said. "Only the parents always know. And the girls."

Olaf nodded. "That's how it is with a bride-kidnapping, nowadays. Everyone knows in advance."

Ilya popped a sand piper from its watery hole and scooped it into his net. "And what about Jim?"

Olaf shrugged. "Nothing about him. He was looneytunes."

"But we're not all looneytunes today. Didn't Jim get a bride, too?"

Olaf looked up and down the beach; there was no one else in sight. Then he fixed an eye on Ilya and arched his brow. "But where could Jim have gotten a bride from? The people at Roanoke and

Antonia were both up in arms, after their girls had been kidnapped. So, there was nowhere else to get a bride...was there?"

"There's Kerenskiy," Ilya said. "On Trudovik...the other moon. Where it's always warm." The thought of a place that was always warm made Ilya shiver with envy.

Olaf nodded sagely. "But those people didn't like us from the start. They're collectivists up there, and they're suspicious of us one hundred percent of the time. It would confirm all their suspicions if we went up there and stole one of their women, and it would be a terrible idea to make them angry, so there's no way Jim went to Trudovik to get a bride. If that kind of thing had happened, the Kerenskiyites would still be upset about it today."

"How would he have done it, anyway?" Ilya felt some disappointment that the story ended this way for Jim.

"Well..." Olaf said thoughtfully. "Antonia was trading with Kerenskiy in those days. I suppose Jim could have sneaked aboard one of those shuttles by tying up one of the off-duty crew and stealing his uniform."

Ilya stared. "Really?"

"He *could* have," Olaf said. "He *was* looneytunes. And then he could have stayed hidden inside the cargo, say, by jettisoning half a crate of fabric and hiding underneath the rest, and smuggled himself into Kerenskiy that way."

"If the people on Kerenskiy distrust us so much," Ilya said, "there's no way they let one of their girls marry us."

Olaf considered this. "So, if Jim found a girl, named, say, Tatyana, he would never have talked to her father and mother, Pyotr and Zoya. But he might have talked to Tatyana, and given her his precious stones, and said, 'Look, I'm rich. You don't have to stay up here eating bad collectivist bread and waiting five years for your turn to see the doctor, you can come back with me and be a wealthy woman.'"

"But Jim wasn't wealthy."

"No, but he *was* looneytunes, and I'm just suggesting the *kind* of thing he *might* have said."

"And they smuggled themselves back down on a shuttle?"

"They could have," Olaf said. "Only of course they didn't, because Jim was looneytunes, and not stupid. And then I suppose they could have stolen a canoe at Antonia and paddled back home."

"But how would Tatyana have reacted when she realized she wasn't going to be wealthy?"

Olaf shrugged. "Maybe she would have decided that here in Beaverton she would be wealthy *enough*. Maybe they would have had a big enough party on her arrival that she felt wanted and decided to stay. Or maybe she would have decided she liked Jim, after all. But obviously, this is all speculation." He fixed Ilya with his keen eye again. "Because this . . . didn't . . . really . . . happen."

"But we're not looneytunes," Ilya objected. "Or not very much."

Olaf nodded. "The people of Roanoke and Antonia weren't looneytunes, though, so maybe the fresh blood that Mike and Lou brought in was enough. I mean, if Jim had really risked a war with Kerenskiy over marrying one of their girls, don't you think there would be some other sign of it in our people?"

Ilya felt perplexed. He wasn't sure whether Olaf was telling him that Jim *hadn't* kidnapped a Kerenskiyite bride, or that he *had*.

"I guess so," he said.

"Good," Olaf said. "Then let's get these sand pipers home and into the pot. Gregor will be back soon, and we need to feast his bride."

Genetic Bottleneck: The Founder Effect

The TRAPPIST-2 Colony Foundation consulted Earth's most famous eugenicists to determine the optimal genetic composition of an isolated colony...and promptly rejected all advice in favor of friends, relatives and paid passengers. While there was some effort to provide genetic diversity even within these limitations, the Foundation failed to anticipate the difficulties of travel between colony sites. Sites Alpha and Beta were to be connected by both mag-lev train and surface roads, while Sites Gamma and Delta would be connected by a combination of air and eco-friendly ocean transport. The lack of Central Planning or cohesion between the individual capitalist governing bodies caused major infrastructure plans to languish, resulting in isolated colonies which fell well below the threshold of ten thousand colonists desired for a fully diverse genome...

The resulting genetic bottleneck is evident in the "Founder Effects"—biological, cultural and sociopolitical traits common to a colony's population. These traits proliferate in the genetic defects, legends and myths derived from the genes, writings and beliefs of the colony founders. Genetic flaws were amplified each time disaster or disease reduced the population levels in the isolated colonies. Rumors of "bride-kidnapping" to amend Founder Effects have been vigorously denied, and Kerenskiy Central Committee denies that any Trudovik persons have been involved in this barbaric practice...

—Excerpt from *Flint's People's History
of Interstellar Exploitation*,
Trudovik Press,
Kerenskiy, Trudovik, AA237

FIRE FROM HEAVEN

David Weber and Mark H. Wandrey

1. Homecoming

TRAPPIST-2 System
Cistercia Planetary Orbit
September 3, 2422 CE/78 Ad Astra

"What's the latest from Engineering?" Captain Edwin Dupree asked as he sailed over to the command chair at the center of the bridge.

"For the moment, it looks good, sir," Lieutenant Donovan replied. Unlike Dupree, who was two decades into his second century, Jason Donovan was only in his early thirties. He'd been born aboard *Victoria* here in Cistercia orbit, and Dupree sometimes wondered how he and the other youngsters aboard *Victoria* coped with their situation.

"Commander Rahaman was able to print out the fittings we needed," Donovan continued, and Dupree nodded as he settled onto the chair and fastened the retaining straps. There was no real need for a chair in microgravity, but it provided a handy anchor to keep people from drifting around.

"So, we're up and running again?"

"Not quite, sir." Donovan's smile was a little crooked. "The commander asked me to tell 'the old fart'—I'm sure he meant 'old man,' sir—that he's going to make damned sure the fittings are the right size before he plugs them into the system."

Dupree chuckled. Gajendra Rahaman was thirty years younger than Dupree, although the engineer had been born fifteen years *before* Victoria's current captain. He'd spent the "missing" forty-five years in cryostasis, and he'd taken the circumstances under which he'd awakened rather better than Dupree thought *he* would have taken them in Rahaman's place. He *did* have a . . . quirky sense of humor, though.

And he had a point about the fittings, too, Dupree acknowledged. *Victoria's* printers had grown less than totally reliable after operating this long without replacement, and it led to occasionally exciting consequences. Like the replacement valves for the hydrogen feed to Fusion Two. It hadn't been a very big discrepancy . . . just enough to fill the entire compartment with an explosive hydrogen-oxygen atmosphere ready to go up with the first spark. They were damned lucky they hadn't lost the entire reactor—or the entire frigging *ship*, for that matter—with that one.

Almost worse, though, was the hydrogen they'd been forced to vent. *Victoria's* reserves were running low, and when the last of it was gone, they'd be totally dependent on the solar panels.

As long as *they* lasted.

Dupree sighed silently and punched up the current bridge log on his personal pad. He tried to ignore the way the display flickered. It wasn't as if it was the only display that was heading for reclamation. But *Victoria's* crew had learned the hard way to use things until they actually stopped working rather than replacing them just because they no longer worked *well*. That had been Jason Donovan's entire life, but Dupree remembered other times, other places, when he would have replaced that pad months ago.

He hadn't, and not just because it still worked. Like everything else aboard *Victoria*, the reclamation plant was dangerously long in the tooth. Keeping it running—babying it along—was another of Rahaman's key priorities, and that meant not putting any more load on it than they could help. Because when it went down, the *printers* went down, and that was the beginning of the end.

Oh, hell, Ed, he thought grumpily, paging through the information on his pad. *We passed the "beginning of the end" decades ago! You suspected that back when Roanoke went dark the first time, and you damn well* knew *it when Zhelan went in. All we're doing now is spinning it out.*

That wasn't something he would ever, under any circumstances, say out loud, but he didn't have to. Everyone aboard *Victoria* knew it. That was probably the real reason no one had been born aboard the ship since Yuan Zhelan and the last shuttle crashed on Trudovik. Dupree didn't know what had caused the crash, but it could have been almost anything. Unlike Joan Walker's *Whale* all those decades ago, Zhelan's shuttle had been twenty-plus years past its designed lifetime. Rahaman and his people had sweated blood over its maintenance, but after a certain point simple structural fatigue became a dangerous potential failure point.

Whatever the cause, that had been *Victoria*'s death knell. The remaining survivors stuck on Trudovik were probably doomed, as well, but with the last shuttle gone, *Victoria* was cut off from Trudovik, Cistercia, or any source of renewable resources, and that made her end certain.

It wouldn't happen tomorrow. In fact, young Donovan might be into *his* second century before the ship died. At the moment, the hydroponic sections still produced ample food. The med section was still functional under Doctor MacGrath's leadership, and it was possible the solar plants could be kept working longer than anyone currently estimated. For that matter, Rahaman and his people were working on the design of a black-body thermal exchange power plant.

But it was going to happen...eventually. And there was no way anyone aboard *Victoria* could leave her. Unless, of course, the colonists on Cistercia miraculously regained the ability to build shuttles of their own before she finally collapsed, and the odds of that were pretty damned slim.

They'd started out with such high hopes, Dupree thought. All shiny and new, with everything careful forethought could provide. He'd read enough history to know careful forethought had failed to prevent disaster on more than one expedition during the early days of the Lunar and Martian colonies, but in those instances, the rest of the human race had been available to at least *try* to mount a rescue.

Here, they were on their own, and he wondered what had really hurt them the worst. *Prometheus*' failure to arrive? *Whale*'s loss, with the backup terraforming crew? The environmental factors that had wiped out the sheepdogs and decimated the cattle? The New Flu, or the loss of the last remaining tugs at Beaverton? Or had it been whatever the hell had happened to New Virginia/Roanoke?

So many things had gone wrong. No wonder there were already legends about the "TRAPPIST Curse" or the "Ghost *Whale*" and its eternal Flying Dutchman trek across the stars! He remembered the first time he'd heard a parent telling a child about Commander Walker and her ghost's endless struggle to reach the planet she'd come so far to colonize.

And yet, in a testament to the truly remarkable fortitude and adaptability of the human species, there were twice as many people on Cistercia today than had been transported to the system in cryostasis. Even after the diseases, the damaged infrastructure, the natural catastrophes Cistercia had thrown at them, the population had grown. Not by much, perhaps, given what sixty or seventy years of natural increase *ought* to have produced, yet it was still larger than the original ten thousand.

But twenty thousand people weren't all that many on an entire planet, and especially when the high-tech infrastructure they relied upon to keep them—and their knowledge base—alive was wearing out and failing.

We could've done it. We really could have. And I'm not ready to throw in the towel on Cistercia yet. Trudovik? Yeah. Kerenskiy's gone. They just don't have enough genetic material to sustain their population even if the environment doesn't kill them all off first. And so are we. But Cistercia may still make it.

His best estimate gave humanity a thirty-five or forty percent chance of long-term survival on Cistercia. The chance of their hanging onto their technology was one hell of a lot lower, though. They still had power, at least for now, at Beaverton and Antonia, but their fusion plants were starting to wear out, too. If *Prometheus* had made it, with the heavy industry module built into her hull, they could have fabricated entire replacement reactors in orbit and built the damned shuttles to deliver them planetside! But the terraforming ship *hadn't* made it, and the settlers below lacked even *Victoria's* limited printing capacity.

Hell, *blacksmiths* were beginning to reemerge on Cistercia.

At Edward Dupree's age, transitioning out of a microgravity environment would have been contraindicated, but if it had been possible, he would have moved down to the planet in a heartbeat ... if he'd only been able to strip *Victoria's* hull and move everything aboard it down with him. She hadn't been designed for that, but if they'd gone ahead and cannibalized her thirty years ago, when they still had shuttles and tugs, that might have made the difference. Now it was too late.

You really are a morose old bastard, aren't you? He shook his head with a snort of wry amusement. *Might be the reason Gajendra calls you the "old fart," you think? We've dodged one hell of a lot of bullets here in TRAPPIST. It's always possible we can dodge a few more. Or that someone can, anyway, even if you can't!*

Well, of course it was. Theoretically, *anything* was possible. But—

A musical tone sounded.

Dupree looked up from his pad, forehead furrowed. He didn't remember hearing that particular alert before. Or, rather, he couldn't remember *where* he'd heard it before. It almost sounded like—

"Sir, I've got something weird over here," Lieutenant Monika Gulseth said.

"Define 'weird,'" Dupree replied, turning to look across at the comm officer. Damn it, he *did* recognize that tone, but where—?

"Sir, I've got a message request coming in on the priority channel," she said, looking over her shoulder at him, and he blinked. That was ridiculous! Although, now that he thought about it, it *had* sounded like—

"There's no reason anybody should be using the priority channel," he said, as much to himself as to her. "Hell, we haven't even *tested* it in—what? Fifty years?"

"As far as I know, we've *never* tested it." Gulseth shook her head.

"Well, who is it? Luttrell or Hampton?" Glynis Luttrell was the mayor of Antonia and Fritz Hampton was the mayor of Beaverton. "Ask them why they're not using the regular net."

"I don't think it's either of them, sir."

"It has to be *one* of them," Dupree said reasonably.

"Sir, it's not coming from Molesme...or Trudovik." Gulseth sounded as if what she was saying made sense, Dupree thought. He opened his mouth, but the lieutenant went on before he could speak. "We're picking it up on the Beta Bird."

Dupree closed his mouth. The Beta Bird? That was on the far side of the planet from Molesme, and they hadn't really used the relay satellites since they lost the last shuttle. *Victoria*'s geosynchronous orbit put her directly above Molesme, with a direct transmission path to both Antonia and Beaverton, and aside from Trudovik, there was no one else in the system to talk to.

"What kind of request are we talking about?" he asked after a moment.

"I've never seen it before, sir." Gulseth was tapping queries into her computers. "I don't recognize the protocol at all, and it's encrypted. I'm looking for the decrypt now."

Dupree nodded. The fact that the signal—whatever it was—was coming in encrypted didn't make any more sense than the rest of it. It didn't make any *less* sense, of course. But unless *Victoria* could reply with the appropriate decryption code, two-way communication would be impossible.

"Coming up now, sir," Gulseth told him. "I think—"

She broke off abruptly, staring at her display. Then she typed in another staccato query. A second later, she looked back at the captain, and her eyes were huge.

"Sir," she said in a very, very careful tone, "the computer says this is the Foundation's secure encrypt. There's no ID header, but it's got the right security codes. And it's demanding the right security code from us before we can unlock the decrypt."

"That's ridiculous."

"Sir, I *know* that. But that's what the computer says."

Dupree held very, very still. There was no reason it would have been outright *impossible* for someone to use the secure protocol, but it had been created to handle the most sensitive of the TRAPPIST-2 Colony Foundation's comm traffic. Mayor Luttrell or Mayor Hampton *could* have used it if it had been loaded into each lander's communications computer—except that, according to what Gulseth had just said, neither of them could be the sender. So, who—?

"I guess you'd better send the code, then," he said.

"We can't yet, sir."

"And why not?" Dupree knew he sounded testy. Under the circumstances, he decided, he was allowed.

"It's a directional signal, sir, and Beta lost its directional dish last year. It can pick it up, but it can't send it back. We'll have to wait until we come around the other side of the planet—or far enough to clear it with the main dish, at least. That will take"—she consulted a time display—"about four more hours."

"Well, isn't that just wonderful," Dupree observed.

"Sir," Donovan said, "it's using the Foundation protocols. Is it possible—sir, could this be a . . . I don't know, a *relief* expedition?"

Dupree saw sudden hope blossom in Gulseth's eyes and hated himself when he shook his head.

"I doubt it very much," he said as gently as he could. "It's on the wrong side of the primary for a ship coming in from the Solar System. Besides, we would have spotted any relief ship's deceleration burn months ago. It's sort of bright for a ship our size."

Silence enveloped the bridge, ringing and very, very still. It lay heavily for perhaps twenty seconds, and then Donovan cleared his throat.

"But if it's not that, then what *is* it?"

"I suppose we'll just have to find out, won't we?" Dupree replied.

"We should have a transmission path now, sir," Monika Gulseth said.

Victoria's bridge was rather more crowded than usual. It was a spacious compartment, and with fewer than thirty personnel on the entire ship, there was enough room, but Edwin Dupree felt a bit claustrophobic for the first time in a long time.

They'd pulled everything they could out of the signal coming in over the Beta Bird, but it wasn't much. They did have a bearing to the transmitter, but that was about it. They didn't have a range, although it was either a very weak signal or its source was one hell of a long way away.

"Do we see anything out there, Benny?" he asked.

"No, sir," Commander Benjamin Solanki replied. He'd inherited Dupree's old job as *Victoria*'s executive officer. "I've got the main scope slaved to the dish, but so far—"

He paused, bending a bit closer to the display in front of him.

"I *do* have something," he said. "Not much detail, but *something's* reflecting sunlight out there. And the computer says it's moving. *Way* beyond radar range."

"Any sort of track projection?"

"Not yet." Solanki looked up. "We just spotted it, sir. It's going to be a while before we have enough observations to say anything about it. All I can tell you is that it's headed pretty much directly towards us, and it's moving damned fast. If I had to guess, it's on a cometary orbit and headed back out from the inner system, but don't hold me to that."

"Um." Dupree considered that for a moment, then shrugged. "All right, Monika. Send the code."

"Sending now, sir."

Victoria's enormous parabolic dish had been designed to send and receive signals over as much as ten or twelve light-years. She'd used it to stay in touch with the Solar System, albeit with a certain delay in the communications loop, until they finally passed beyond even its prodigious range. No one had used it—or tested it—in decades, but all of its systems showed green, and it had more than enough power and range to reach anything inside the TRAPPIST-2 system.

The master display on the forward bulkhead changed from its customary visual of the planet to display *Victoria*'s wallpaper, and Dupree felt every human being in that compartment staring at it, willing it to change.

Thirty seconds ticked past. Then a full minute. Ninety seconds. Two minutes. Three minutes. Four. *Five.*

Dupree began to question his assumption that all the dish's systems were green.

Six minutes. Seven. Seven and a half.

The huge display flickered. The wallpaper disappeared, and shock punched Edwin Dupree squarely between the eyes. Of all the possibilities he'd considered—

Impossible, a voice said deep inside him. *That's* impossible. *It* can't *be!*

"Hello, *Victoria*," the slender, black-haired, green-eyed woman said from the display. "If you're seeing this message, I guess it's been a while."

Dupree expected a babel of shock. Every human being in the star system knew that face, knew the story of the Alpha Lander and its doomed pilot.

Knew Lieutenant Commander Joan Walker had been dead for almost eighty years.

But no one said a single word. And that, he realized after a moment, was because they *did* recognize her, and the shock had hit all of them exactly the way it had hit him.

No, not the way it hit me, he thought after another moment. *The only other person on the bridge who knew her is Gajendra, and he didn't know her the way I did. He didn't grow up with her. And he didn't watch her die.*

"I've put together as many contingency programs as I could think of," the dead woman on the display continued. "If this is the one that threw, though, none of the others worked. So, by my calculations, it's been about seventy-five years. I hope you're still there. Well, obviously if you're seeing this, someone is. And if you're seeing it, then I must have at least gotten into the docking systems."

Docking systems? *What the* hell *are you talking about, Joanie?* Edwin Dupree thought, watching the display waver through his tears.

"I lost my communications module when everything went crazy," she continued, "but if I'd been able to get into the main system, you'd have heard from me before this. So, this is coming over the directional dish on one of the other landers."

"Other *landers?!*" *Jesus, did she—?!*

"If I managed to do that much, then at least some of *Prometheus'* systems are still alive," she said, and Dupree felt the physical shockwave whiplash around the bridge, "but I must have been locked out of the main com system, assuming it's still up. I don't have the command codes to override the lockouts automatically . . . and I won't have a chance to hack around them."

Her expression tightened for just a moment, and she inhaled deeply.

"I'm not going to make it to *Prometheus,*" she said then, softly. "I don't have the power reserves to keep the enviro systems up long enough. But if anyone is seeing this, then *Whale* must have made it. And that means Adam and the rest of his crew made it, too."

She blinked suddenly gleaming green eyes and those firm lips quivered ever so slightly.

"That means it was worth it." Her voice was hoarser than it had been, but she raised her head high, proudly, those gleaming eyes bright. "It was *all* worth it—every moment of it.

"But now you have to dig out the *Prometheus* command codes and unlimber that big-assed dish. We're coming back at you on a cometary orbit, and you *must* get into *Prometheus'* onboard systems and bring her home. Please, bring her home. Bring Adam and the others home. And if you can, find a place down there beside the Billabong for me, too.

"I . . . came a long way, and I'd like to finish the trip."

TRAPPIST-2 System
Cistercia Planetary Orbit
October 6, 2422 CE/78 Ad Astra

"Thirty seconds," Commander Solanki announced.

If there'd ever been a more superfluous announcement, Edwin Dupree couldn't imagine what it had been.

For thirty-three days, they'd watched the dot of reflected light grow and change as it coasted towards Cistercia at 51 KPS. Joan Walker's initial transmission had come in at a range of 3.25 light-minutes—58,500,000 kilometers—and that was a hefty distance at that velocity.

The delay had given Dupree and every other man and woman aboard *Victoria*, or on Cistercia, or on Trudovik, time to realize what it meant. Assuming things went as planned in the next fifteen seconds, at least.

That wasn't a given.

Additional recorded messages had shared Joan's conclusion that *Whale* had been sabotaged. The suggestion had been less surprising to Dupree than he'd have expected, probably because it could explain so much of the "TRAPPIST Curse." And *Victoria's* remote login to *Prometheus'* computers had offered plenty of apparent confirmation of her suspicions. The terraforming ship's central net was a mess. It looked as if both primary AI nets had been as thoroughly wiped as *Whale's*, but something had regenerated at least a part of their capabilities. *Prometheus* had been even more amply equipped with standalone recovery systems than *Victoria*, in light of its automated status. Apparently one of them had survived the original cyberattack. It looked to have been badly damaged itself, but it had succeeded in weaving together an interface—of sorts—for several of the standalone nets. Including, thankfully, the maneuvering AI.

They couldn't be positive they had complete control, but they'd initiated a handful of minor burns—adjusting attitude and rotating the ship—to confirm that the AI was accepting at least *some* commands. Most of *Prometheus'* data systems remained outside their reach, however. They couldn't even get a report on the enormous ship's fuel reserves, and anything like a detailed status report would have to wait until they got someone aboard her.

Fortunately, her docking subnet seemed to be up and running. They ought to be able to order *Prometheus'* shuttles to rendezvous with *Victoria* and take a salvage party back to the terraforming ship. Judging from the shape of her computers, God only knew what they'd find when they got inside her hull, but in a lot of ways, he didn't really care about that.

As *Prometheus* slid steadily closer, visual observation had confirmed that *all* of her original landers and heavy lift shuttles were still nestled on their racks. Every one of them. All that lost infrastructure was out there, coming to them out of the endless dark, delivered to them beyond hope or dreams by the bravest woman Edwin Dupree had ever known.

"*Ten* seconds," Solanki said.

The range was down to 22,000 kilometers, and Dupree felt himself leaning towards the visual display. The enormous ship's engines waited, their gaping throats clearly visible to *Victoria's* cameras and telescopes at this piddling range.

Prometheus, he thought, eyes burning. *And maybe it was an even better name than they imagined. Thank you, Joanie. Wherever you are*, thank *you.*

"Four... Three... Two... *now.*"

Fury burst from those waiting engines, blazing with eye-searing brightness against the stars.

"Burn looks good!" Solanki announced, and Dupree heard the cheers over *Victoria's* intercom, knew the same cheers—a thousand times louder, ripping from twelve thousand throats—echoed across Cistercia and Trudovik as they saw the same thing.

"Six gravities. We have six gravities. Profile is nominal. I say again, profile is nominal!"

Edwin Dupree blinked hard, fighting to see through the tears, as the starship *Prometheus* decelerated majestically into Cistercia orbit and Lieutenant Commander Joan Walker, call-sign "Jonah," brought the blazing fire of salvation down from heaven to the people she'd died to save.

2. Journey's End

TRAPPIST-2 System
Cistercia Planetary Orbit
October 19, 2422 CE/78 Ad Astra

David Parker was dreaming again. He had dreamed a dream which never ended. People and places. Loves and losses. He played in a sandbox with a robot which then morphed into his mother, and then into God.

Through it all was *The Code*. It wove into his dreams almost like he was writing an AI subroutine as it was, in turn, creating his dreams. Something in him cried out for it to end, even if it meant he must end. Huey and Dewey both played royal flushes against his two pair, the bots laughing hysterically.

The dreams ended, and he was breathing cool air. For a time, David thought he was dead. There was no light; he was in complete darkness. Then he felt air moving across his face, smelled antiseptic, and heard the hum of motors.

"David Parker," a voice said. "Do you hear me?"

David didn't respond, he waited for the dream to change.

"David, I'm going to turn the lights on low so you can see me."

He waited; his breathing increased in intensity as he heard someone moving. A second later the lights came up enough for him to see. A grotesquely distorted face was mere centimeters from him, half-human, half-machine. The dreams had changed to nightmares.

"Noooo!" he screamed and grabbed the half-human nightmare around the throat.

"He's crazy!" someone screamed.

"Jesus, sedate him, sedate him!"

David tried to bear down on the monster's throat, wishing to squeeze the life out of it. Only he felt ice water run into his leg and up into his torso. Consciousness faded and darkness' embrace came.

"How are you feeling today, David?"

"Better," David replied. Now that they weren't wearing masks, the medical staff didn't trigger an episode anymore.

"Severe PTSD," the head physician explained to David after a week of slowly decreasing levels of sedatives and many face-to-face meetings. Since he'd been able to hold an intelligent conversation, a young woman was transcribing notes from him as David tried to piece together his story.

Captain Edwin Dupree was a very old man. David would guess at least seventy, though if he understood how subjective and actual years worked, he was way, way older. He'd been to visit David several times as he underwent treatment and the debriefs began. He was commanding officer of *Victoria*, the main colony ship sent to TRAPPIST-2. When *Prometheus* accelerated away from Earth, no commander had yet been named.

"Is Miss Yelsin keeping you company?" Dupree asked.

"She's very attentive," David said. The young woman smiled, and David wondered how old she was. "She has a lot of questions, though."

"We're still trying to piece together the mystery of what happened to *Prometheus*," the captain reminded David.

David nodded as he remembered. While he'd been providing as much detail as he could, Miss Yelsin had been somewhat less forthcoming about the situation on TRAPPIST-2. David had managed to figure out *Victoria* experienced problems as well. Everyone was nervous. His attacking the medical tech who'd been wearing a respirator didn't help. They were still suspicious of him.

"Have you managed to extract my logs on *Prometheus* yet?" David asked.

"Yes, most of them. The AI being wiped made working with its files difficult. Your operating system was, according to our programmers, an incredible accomplishment for one person."

"I had years to work on it." His brow screwed up as he tried to remember how long. "Huey and Dewey would know."

"Just under four and a half years," Dupree volunteered.

"Ah, yes," David said, not really agreeing. An analogue clock on the wall winked at him, and David squeezed his eyes closed. *It's not real, it's not real.* The psychologist assigned to him said extreme cases of isolation could cause temporary psychotic episodes.

"She's right, you know," his slippers agreed. He squeezed his eyes closed again, trying to steady his breathing. When he opened them again, Dupree was giving him a concerned look.

"I'm okay," he said. "Just struggling with . . . things."

"David, I can only guess what it was like being locked up in *Prometheus* for so long. I reviewed an old Earth movie just the other day. *Castaway*, about a man marooned on an island alone for years."

"My psychologist, Dr. Fernsby, mentioned it. But he won't let me watch the movie until we've made more progress."

"Yes, well, that's probably a good idea. Anyway, when we boarded *Prometheus,* we knew right away how horrible it was. The mold, David, my God the mold was hellacious. If you hadn't gone into the sleeper, you probably would have succumbed to it."

"How are Huey and Dewey?"

Dupree consulted a small tablet computer, then looked uncomfortable. "Let's not worry about them now, shall we? Concentrate on getting better."

"I want to know what's happened," David blurted out. "Nobody will tell me except that they're excited *Prometheus* is here. I mean, there's a lot of equipment on board which would prove useful. But when you arrived, and we weren't there, you must have just proceeded with a slower development schedule after setting down your huge landers."

Dupree's face darkened and David knew there was much more going on than he'd thought. He looked at Dupree again, noting his age and thinking about it.

"I thought the oldest colonists they were taking were all no more than thirty," he said.

"I was twenty-nine when we left for TRAPPIST-2."

"Wait." David swallowed. "How long have you been here?" He looked at Yelsin. "How old are you? You can't be more than twenty or so." She didn't answer. "Dupree, damnit, answer my questions!"

"Maybe after a bit," the man said, and took a step back.

"Now, damnit. I'm tired of not being told the truth . . . get away from me with that!"

The nurse stopped just out of reach as David stared daggers at the old man. He took a calming breath before continuing. "Look, just tell me what happened." Dupree looked down. "Please?"

Dupree looked at the nurse who shook her head. David was about to try again when the other man spoke. "Get the doctor in here, please?"

"He said it best to wait," the nurse advised.

"And I think it best we reconsider. Especially considering what David accomplished, and what it means to us." The nurse left and everyone waited in silence.

A moment later a robot buzzed in, silently going about its business. David looked at the efficient little machine, silently wondering how Huey and Dewey were doing and if this robot was their friend. The little bot hummed a tune as it worked, and David hummed along. Dupree sucked his teeth as he observed the event.

The familiar features of the psychologist who'd been working with him came around the corner into the room. Dr. Fernsby wasn't as young as Yelsin, though not nearly as old as Dupree. The psychologist had been visiting David since before he'd been able to remember more than a few minutes at a time. He was a compassionate, concerned man with deep blue eyes and a quick smile.

"What seems to be the problem?" Dr. Fernsby asked as he took in the tableau before him.

"I want to know what's going on," David said.

Dr. Fernsby glanced at Dupree, raising an eyebrow. "I had thought we were in consensus on this; Mr. Parker needs more time to continue recovering from his extended isolation."

"I've changed my assessment," Dupree said.

Dr. Fernsby stared at Dupree, then his gaze slid over to David. "Need I remind you, Captain, only a week ago Mr. Parker attempted to strangle one of my cryostasis technicians?"

"He'd spent four and a half years marooned on a ship in interstellar space. I think he deserves some leeway—"

"And some truth," David interjected.

"Can I be frank?" Dr. Fernsby asked. Dupree nodded and cocked his head at David. David nodded also. "Thank you. I've spent a great deal of time with Mr. Parker, and while it isn't enough for a detailed prognosis, it is enough to provide an outline of his basic mental health and detail a treatment plan.

"Mr. Parker is suffering from extended isolation during which he was subjected to numerous life-or-death struggles. He had no backup, and nobody to confide in during that period." He glanced at Dupree again.

"Continue," Dupree said.

Dr. Fernsby cleared his throat and sighed. "As a result of these events, he is suffering from a form of Post-Traumatic Stress Disorder, PTSD. This was caused by the mental trauma of his environment, and no fault of his own. Few could have handled what he went through. However, these hardships have also cause him to manifest violent psychosis, such as attacking the cryostasis tech, and he continues to show signs of extreme hallucinations. Some border on delusional perceptions, more study is necessary to be sure."

"Hallucinations?" David blurted. "What are you talking about?"

The doctor took a tablet computer from one of the large pockets on his smock and tapped on it for a moment. "I have hours of your talking about your robots as people. You gave them names."

"Lots of people name their robots," Dupree tried to help.

"They don't believe the robots provide advice or play advanced games with them."

"Huey and Dewey were modified by me," David offered, though his voice contained a note of uncertainty.

"David," Dr. Fernsby said, "after a salvage crew docked with *Prometheus* and recovery operations began, they found two nonfunctional robots. They'd been bolted to a chair in your living area and their vital systems removed. Techs said it appeared you'd cannibalized them for parts to keep other bots functioning."

"That can't be right," David whispered.

"Recordings also show you've occasionally carried on conversations with other objects in the room, such as the clock, telephone, and once the commode."

David felt his cheeks grow hot and he looked down. *Am I really seeing things?*

"Don't believe him," the robot said as it left his room to continue its duties. David tracked it with his eyes, then suddenly looked up at Dr. Fernsby who was watching him closely.

"I . . . I was . . . I . . ." he tried to answer clearly, and it devolved into stammering, and then trailed off to silence.

"Is he dangerous?" Dupree asked.

"I don't believe so," Dr. Fernsby said. "To himself? Perhaps. We don't have the facilities to care for anyone with dangerous mental health issues. We've been lucky enough to not suffer such a problem, yet."

"Next question," Dupree continued. "Do you think telling him about our situation will help, or harm him?"

"I don't know," Dr. Fernsby admitted. "There are too many variables. It's safe to say his psyche is somewhat fragile."

"He was isolated for years," Dupree said. "Maybe a sense of what he's done for us would help him realize his sacrifice was not in vain?"

Dr. Fernsby rubbed his nose with a finger, a sign David had come to realize meant the man was thinking over his answer.

"You are possibly correct." He looked back at David. "Mr. Parker, I'm going to allow this to proceed. I am also going to monitor your bio-signs." He pointed a finger at David. "If I see any indications you're becoming overly stressed or having an incident, I'll terminate the session and give you a sedative. Do you agree to proceed?"

"Of course," David said, his annoyance clear in his voice.

"Okay," Dupree said. "First off, let's give some history. *Prometheus* was sabotaged. We're pretty sure because the same thing was done to us on *Victoria*. Your ship's damage was simpler than ours, and at the same time more direct. By wiping your primary AI, whoever did it assumed you'd sail off across the galaxy, never to be heard from again.

"Luckily, they were wrong. You spent years writing a basic AI, and before you ran out of food, gave the ship enough control to be able to arrive in TRAPPIST-2 and put itself into a safe, if inconvenient, heliocentric orbit. Our computer techs say you wrote just over two *million* lines of code and interconnected them with many of the ship's systems, all the while not interfering with its docking and maneuvering system."

"Two million?" David asked. "I didn't know it was that much." Dr. Fernsby made some notes and David frowned.

"Yeah, two million. All by yourself. Well done."

"Thanks. What did the saboteurs do to *Victoria*?"

"A lot of things. We haven't even verified all of them, as some might be simple malfunctions."

"Maybe you can give me some dates now?" David asked.

"Yeah, sure." Dupree took a deep breath and let it out in a low whistle. "*Victoria* arrived in TRAPPIST-2 just over seventy-eight years ago."

"Oof," David said, his head gave a little shake all on its own.

Dupree glanced at Dr. Fernsby who was watching his tablet, presumably monitoring David's vital signs. The doctor gave a little nod, so Dupree continued.

"Of course, we expected to find one or more planets already settled with machinery and terraforming well underway. We knew something was wrong a couple years before getting here. There was no radio beacon guiding us to the prime landing spot.

"We assumed a malfunction. However, as *Victoria* slowed into TRAPPIST-2, we slowly came to the realization *Prometheus* was gone. There was no sign of your ship, no debris, nothing. Without your advanced bases, our job became infinitely more complicated, and precarious." He shrugged. "We didn't even have the resources to do more than a cursory look for *Prometheus*."

"You never got any of my messages, then."

"No," Dupree admitted. "Your log shows you came out of cryostasis less than two years after going under." David nodded. "You should have been close enough to send messages. Nothing arrived. Back on Earth, the Foundation assumed it was something to do with passing through the heliospheric current sheet. Telescopes showed *Prometheus* still under power, still on course. There was no reason to assume anything was wrong.

"So, when we arrived and found no pre-colonization work done, we were in a bad place. It was a contingency, sure, just not one we ever wanted to actually implement. We picked prime locations on Cistercia and began landing. That was four years after arrival. Most of us were still in cryostasis." He shrugged. "No way we could feed everyone with no ground-side food production.

"We decided to send *Whale* down, formally establish our primary colonization efforts."

"*Whale*?" David asked.

Dupree chuckled. "Lander Alpha, sorry. The big lander which could carry the big machinery and equipment."

"Oh, I see." David knew about Lander Alpha, and its designated pilot.

"Well, it was our biggest setback. Bigger than not finding *Prometheus*. Whoever did the sabotage on your ship, also did it on *Whale*. When it was ordered to perform a landing burn, instead it fired all its engines, on full, until the fuel was gone."

David's heart fell, and Dr. Fernsby looked up sharply. David made a conscious effort to calm himself despite a growing feeling of loss. After a few seconds, Dr. Fernsby nodded to Dupree, who continued.

"The pilot managed to control the burn. She couldn't stop it, the computer was corrupted, but she did manage to keep from crashing. Instead, she launched herself into a deep heliocentric orbit. We watched as she shot out of orbit, and beyond our ability to retrieve her."

"You had other shuttles," David complained.

"We were in a tight space when *Whale* was sent down," Dupree explained. "As I said, she saved the ship, but at the cost of changing her momentum. It was a lot of velocity. We might have caught her, but the shuttles would have burned all their fuel and been in the same place.

"It might have ended there, if she hadn't been such a badass pilot. You see, despite fighting for her life and to save *Whale*, she also managed to spot *Prometheus* in the outer system and used the last of her fuel to set a rendezvous course. We finally spotted *Prometheus*, and she'd left a short-range beacon. It's how we found you."

"How long ago?" David asked.

"It was seventy-four years ago."

"Joan," David said, his voice holding untold emotions.

"You knew her?" Dupree asked, his voice filled with surprise. "You left years before we did."

"We were in school together," David said.

"I see," Dupree said.

David opened his mouth to say something more, but nothing came out. He tried to keep his emotions under control with mixed results. Dupree saw the reaction and David knew he was curious. Thankfully, the old captain didn't pursue the issue.

"So, thanks to Joan—and, of course, you—we have a huge boost to all the colonies' efforts."

"Colonies?" David asked. "Is there more than one?"

"Yes, we decided it wasn't safe to keep all our eggs in one basket." Dupree brought him up to speed, a story of success and failure, tragedy and hope. It seemed they'd always been on the edge of failure.

"Now I understand why *Prometheus* is so important," David said finally.

Dupree nodded. "You may well have saved everyone."

And lost everything.

The rest of the discussion faded into meaninglessness for David. All he could remember was a lovely smiling face.

TRAPPIST-2 System
Cistercia Planetary Orbit
August 15, 2422 CE/79 Ad Astra

Cistercia orbited past the window. The gravity ring on *Victoria* provided a new view every two minutes. The greens, blues, and brown colors of Cistercia were so reminiscent of Earth that the strange landmass shapes and cloud formations made the world appear even more alien than it might have been if he were viewing the planet from home.

"This is home now," David corrected himself. Still, it didn't seem real. How funny he'd undertake a journey across interstellar space without understanding he would never see Earth again. Of course, so many things had happened he could never have considered.

Almost ten months had passed since he'd been awoken for the second time since *Prometheus* left Earth, and 258 years since he'd left Earth. Countless hours with Dr. Fernsby had resulted in progress. At least, according to the good doctor.

David understood his hallucinations, if he couldn't control them. Together they'd developed a coping mechanism which allowed him to actually begin work again.

He was programming once more, working with a team to rebuild a more functional AI for *Prometheus* as well as modifying *Victoria*'s own AI to begin a more comprehensive search for further sabotage. They even thought that some evidence could be uncovered as to the saboteurs themselves. David considered the latter a waste of time: Odds were whoever did it were both hundreds of years dead as well as light-years distant. The thought such people might be among them was not something any of the colonists wanted to seriously contemplate.

As the only programmer among the colonists who'd helped design both ships' AIs, David assembled the project. He'd also reinstalled the AI for Joan's ship, the lander dubbed *Whale*. *Victoria* had copies of the landers' original code, but the sabotage there was similar to that of *Prometheus*. Just a few lines of code, and a small subroutine to cause the landers' AIs to be wiped. So simple for such a devastating effect; it took just seconds to fix, but way too many hours—even months—to find.

The work to fix *Prometheus*' AI was now independent of his help, and he was feeling increasingly superfluous. The team was smart, young, and able to finish the work without the old anachronism, man-out-of-time David Parker, to help them.

One benefit to working was that he'd gained a degree of freedom. He could move about the ship's habitation areas. However, he did have a constant shadow in the form of a colony security officer named Mason de Clare. He never interfered with David's movement and showed no sign of suspicion. Despite de Clare's behavior, his presence was proof Dupree and other colony leaders hadn't shaken a lingering suspicion that David might have somehow been culpable for his ship's condition.

He glanced at the computer he held, verified there was nothing more for him to do on the AI project, and sighed. His work was done. He'd gotten *Prometheus* to TRAPPIST-2. Only, not everything was done. He wanted to do one more thing.

David turned away from the observation window and accessed a back door to *Victoria*'s AI. They'd used it for troubleshooting, so the access appeared innocent enough. He checked some of the work files to make sure his idea was feasible. It was. With a nod to himself, he put the tablet in his pocket and walked to the door. Mason de Clare was leaning next to the door, idly scanning his personal tablet.

"I'm going to the head," he told de Clare. "Back in a minute."

The man glanced up at him, then nodded before going back to whatever he was doing.

David moved quickly once he closed the door behind him, walking down the hallway and past the head. He turned to one of the ladders which climbed up and out of the gravity ring, emerging into the ship's zero gravity core.

He floated aft, a direction he'd never been before. Partly because he'd never asked, partly because he didn't think his handler would let him. Along the great spine of the ship were the docking collars, where each of her landers and cargo modules had been docked. They were all gone now, departed to complete their missions or to another fate.

Little remained of the *Victoria* which departed Earth. Some science functions remained, some nearly empty propellant tanks, a very old and tired fusion power plant, and the Cartwright drive which had carried it across the stars. It too was now cold, never to be used again.

David stopped amidships, looking down the long corridor aft where the ship's power station lived. The main drive was a section of *Prometheus* he'd never had access to. This ship was designed with a large crew in mind with many open areas, big cabins, and vast banks of cryostasis chambers. There'd been only the one chamber on his ship.

He moved sideways into the number 2 airlock. Only the outer door was open, and through the small thick window he could see the long flexible umbilical connecting *Victoria* to *Prometheus*. David touched the control, and the door slid aside.

Hot air blew into the umbilical ahead of him, warming the space from the cold state it was in when not in use. He grabbed the rope running down the center of the umbilical and pulled himself along quickly. At the other end the lock was already open. He spun around inside and closed the door. He was back aboard *Prometheus*.

"Hello, old friend," he said, running a hand along the lock wall. Just inside on the opposite side of the hull was *Prometheus*' other airlock. The locker still held his space suit, the one he'd used to gather supplies from cargo modules during his disastrous attempts at farming to extend his supplies.

He floated aft where the docking collars were located. All of *Prometheus*' landers were gone, already sent down to the colonies where the materials were desperately needed. However, one ship was still docked.

He paused a second; the door opened to the gravity ring where his habitation area had been. They'd cleaned the mold out, so it wasn't dangerous anymore. Various smells and sounds assailed his senses, all so familiar yet somehow distant in his mind. Still, he decided not to go back there.

"Why, don't you want to see us?" Dewey's voice echoed up from the ring.

"A game of cards?" Huey asked. "For old times' sake?"

He ignored the voices and opened the docking collar. On the

inside of the lock was printed LANDER ALPHA. He read the map on the inside corridor wall and followed the directions, eventually reaching the cryostasis chambers.

It had proved too difficult to move the chambers to another vehicle. *Whale* had been serviced and refueled. After David repaired the AI, it was ready to fly. No surprises this time. Still, it waited.

The materials from *Prometheus* were dubbed a higher priority. Those in the cryostasis chambers aboard *Whale* had already waited centuries, they could wait a few more months. The gentle whine of the chambers' independent power systems was the only sound.

He floated along the compartment until he found what he was looking for. It was a "new" cryo chamber, or at least not one of the ones originally loaded. It was probably brought over from *Victoria*; and it was also the only chamber with no life signs. It was running, but its occupant was long dead. Joan Walker, pilot of *Whale*.

Life support had shut down when her heart stopped beating and the computers powered down the onboard reactor. The ship turned into a freezer, preserving her body. She'd wished to be buried on Cistercia, so they'd put her in stasis. He put a hand on the glass cover. Her face was centimeters away. She looked like she was asleep. Forever beautiful, forever unattainable. Tears pooled in his eyes, unable to fall in zero gravity.

"I love you," he said, his voice echoing in the space, barely audible over the power system.

"I know," Joan said. She smiled a sad smile.

Dave floated there for a time, his eyes nearly covered in pools of his unshed tears. He wiped them away with a sleeve more than once.

"I want to go home," Joan said.

"We're light-years from Earth," David said.

"No. My mission. I want to finish it. This world was supposed to be our new home, David."

He stopped crying. Well, then, what was one more thing to do? "Let's do it," he said, and pushed off. He turned, but the name on a nearby cryostasis chamber caught his eye.

Adam Walker.

David floated back out and down the *Prometheus* central trunk toward the airlock. Mason de Clare would certainly be wondering where he was.

"He can't know," Joan said as she floated behind him.

"I know," David said.

He looked around the space. He'd spent years on *Prometheus*, working to bring it to TRAPPIST-2. He knew where every spare part, every vital system was. He found the equipment locker he wanted and removed some gear, then went to the connecting lock, the one on the opposite side from the one he'd entered on. The lock with nothing but vacuum on the other side.

David opened the opposite airlock and floated in. The door closed behind him. The locker where his space suit was stored stood partly open. He stared at the suit, then the exterior airlock door. Through the thick glass was the never-ending darkness of space.

The intercom chirped. "Mr. Parker, open the door." It was Mason de Clare.

David looked through the lock's inner glass. He could see the other lock and just make out the man in the umbilical. He looked serious, and alarmed. "Open the door, now, please."

David tore his gaze away from the security officer and to the airlock controls.

"He'll stop us, David."

"I know," he replied, and used his tablet to access *Prometheus'* AI. It only took a second to seal the other airlock. Nobody could open that door now unless David released it, or they cut through with a torch.

"David, don't," Mason de Clare called out.

He didn't reply, but instead went to work.

The bridge of *Victoria* was a buzz of activity when Dupree floated in. "What's going on?"

"It's David Parker," Lieutenant Donovan said. "He gave Mason de Clare the slip and got back aboard *Prometheus*."

"Oh hell," Dupree said. "What's he doing? Give me Mason."

Donovan pointed at the speaker and Mason de Clare's voice came over.

"I'm sorry, Captain, he pulled a fast one on me."

"That doesn't matter now," Dupree said. "What's David doing?"

"I was afraid he was going to blow himself out the airlock for a minute. But he has some equipment and is suited up. Wait, he's opened the lock and is EVA."

"Can we get a robot out there to snag him?" Dupree asked his bridge crew.

"Nearest one is at the other end of *Victoria* working on a solar panel," a robotics tech said. "I can try, but it would probably take half an hour."

"Give me visual at least?"

Someone worked with the various cameras at their disposal and finally a view of a space-suited person moving along the hull of *Prometheus* was visible. The suited man moved with quick assurance of someone who'd done more than a few space walks. He did a little jump and landed on the massive side of *Whale*. A second later, he was working.

"What's he doing?"

"Looks like a can of hull sealant," someone said. "He's smearing it around."

"He's painting letters," someone else said.

The figure was only partly in view, so the camera could only make out three huge letters in brown vacuum adhesive. C, O, and Y.

Before they could figure out more, David had finished and was moving. He didn't return to *Prometheus*, instead going through the lock into *Whale*.

"Try to raise *Whale*," Dupree ordered.

"*Victoria* to *Whale*, over," the radio tech called.

"I am receiving your signal, Captain," a male-sounding voice came back, but it wasn't David.

"Who is this? David? What are you doing?" Dupree asked, his voice filled with resignation. The psychiatrist had said the man was stable. So much for *that* theory.

"*Victoria*, this is *Coyote*, we're undocking. Please verify that Mason is safely clear of the lock."

"He's still in *Victoria*," Donovan whispered.

Dupree made a face. "*Coyote?*" he asked, then shrugged. Who knew what a crazy person thought, or why? "David, what are you doing?" he asked again.

That strangely artificial voice replied again. "Finishing the mission."

The massive lander pushed away on maneuvering thrusters. Everyone could see COYOTE painted on the hull with brown vacuum sealant, and they watched in awe as the lander moved away and began its reentry sequence.

Once the launch sequence initiated, the lander was nonresponsive to radio calls or override commands from *Victoria*. David's AI performed perfectly, pushing *Coyote* away from *Prometheus*. Once it was far enough out, the ship fired a long retro burn and acquired its targeted landing point: the colony named Beaverton.

Joanie sat in the pilot's seat, a huge smile on her face. David moved to buckle into the copilot position for the reentry burn as the AI guided it precisely toward its destination.

"Thanks for this. Now my husband will at least have a grave to visit," Joanie said with a smile.

David froze in the act of taking his seat. His heart sank. "Least I could do," he whispered. He knew. He'd always known, it was just . . . more comfortable . . . to pretend.

As thrust returned a semblance of gravity, his tears began to fall. He looked down at the acceleration chair in front of him, and then the space-suit helmet he still held in his hand. He looked up at the viewscreen as a brilliant light ignited on the nightside of the planet.

David realized there was only one thing to do.

He let go of the helmet and it fell to the seat; he wouldn't be needing it.

Coyote

According to Native American and First Nation lore, it was the trickster demigod Coyote who stole fire from heaven and gave it to the humans. Alternatively, some legends say it was Beaver who gave humans this essential tool necessary to build civilization.

When Lander Alpha performed a perfect descent and final approach at Beaverton, there was much speculation over the circumstances. The lost lander had returned. It had a fully functional Control AI when the last of this type had been shut down almost eighty years ago. Here was an empty ship with desperately needed terraforming supplies, and the original terraforming team still in cryo, but there was no one at the flight controls. Most of all they marveled at the coincidence of the two perfectly functioning cryotubes just inside the airlock—one for Joanie Walker's preserved body, and one for her sleeping husband.

Above all they wondered at the significance of the space-suit helmet labeled "Parker" resting at the foot of Joanie's 'tube.

Coyote, the Trickster, had surely been there.

—Excerpt from *Encyclopedia Astra*,
Gannon University,
Antonia, Cistercia, AA212

EPILOGUE

The speakers crackled once more in the silence as the final recorded messages played, "Beaver Lead, are you there yet? Only fifteen seconds left until touchdown and it looks like it might be a rough one. Over."

"San Salvador, this is Beaver Lead. I have made it to the controls and am preparing to eject fuel tank. Godspeed and safe landing, San Salvador. Beaver Flight is cl—"

The broadcast ended except for a brief burst of static. The silence went on for a minute before the Civil Defense supervisor cleared his throat, toggled his mic live and spoke slowly and clearly, "Beaver One, Mark Cramer." As soon as he finished with the name, the engine control technician ignited the first of the engines that had been salvaged from the lander and were now permanently mounted in Memorial Square.

Receiving a thumbs-up indicating proper engine ignition, the supervisor continued to the next name. "Beaver Two, Brian Johnson." Once again, an engine came to life.

"Beaver Three, Vanessa Pearson." The third engine rumbled into ignition.

"Beaver Four, Jack 'One Cajón' Murray." The fourth engine fired.

"Beaver Five, Scott Atkins." The fifth engine fired.

"Beaver Six, James Copley." The sixth engine fired.

"Beaver Lead, Chris French." With this name, no more engines were ignited. Instead all six of them were left running at what was essentially idle.

"Beaver Flight, this is Beaverton Ground Control. The lander is down with all souls safe."

After a moment's pause, the supervisor continued, "*Coyote*, this is Beaverton Ground Control. We welcome the return of all lost souls."

"Lander Alpha, Joan 'Jonah' Walker."

"Prometheus Prime, David 'Coyote' Parker."

David Walker gave the signal to ignite the seventh engine, newly installed after salvage from the finally decommissioned *Whale*. He wished that his father, Adam, could have been here for the ceremony; the original had always left them both with tears in their eyes. Dad would have approved of the additions.

After another minute's pause, he spoke the final words of this one hundred and fourth Landing Day Ceremony. "*Coyote*, Lander Alpha has arrived with all passengers.

"All flights, prepare for Landing Beacon to guide you home on my mark." Pausing to take a deep breath and to keep from choking up, David finished the annual message, "Go for beacon, mark." He signaled the technician to increase to maximum thrust.

A pillar of fire leapt to the sky.

Timeline

C.E. 2150 Construction begins in Mars orbit of the colony ship *Victoria* (named for the lone ship of Magellan's fleet to complete the circumnavigation of Earth) to be sent to TRAPPIST-2 system.

2155 Construction begins on the automated terraforming ship *Prometheus* to precede *Victoria* to TRAPPIST-2.

2165 *Prometheus* is completed and launched toward TRAPPIST-2. It is fully automated with the exception of one backup human to be awoken only in the event of emergency. Otherwise, he will sleep until after the ship arrives at TRAPPIST-2 and has completed initial terraforming/infrastructure building.

2170 *Victoria* is completed. Deaths of Colony Foundation leaders delay mission launch. *Victoria* is put to work ferrying scientists to the heliopause and establishing science base/colonies in the Kuiper belt.

2180 TRAPPIST-2 Colony Foundation begins recruiting colonists.

2185 *Victoria* departs for TRAPPIST-2 with ten thousand colonists in cryostasis, 100,000 fertilized human ova frozen, plus approximately 1,000,000 fertilized animal ova. Crew of 250 rotate through eighteen-month shifts with five to twenty-five people awake at a time.

CE 2344   Ad Astra (AA) Year 0. *Victoria* Arrives at TRAPPIST-2.

AA01   Twenty-five crew awakened to begin colonization plan. Terraforming ship *Prometheus* is missing.

AA03   Remainder of 250 crew awakened to begin landing construction crews. Lander Alpha, *Whale,* is lost.

AA05   Re-engineered landers sent to sites Alpha (northern hemisphere) and Beta (subtropical) sites on the principal continent of TRAPPIST-2c. Planet is renamed Cistercia and the continent named Molesme in honor of Robert of Molesme, founder of the Cistercian order of TRAPPIST monks.

AA06   Site Alpha renamed New Virginia, Site Beta renamed Santa Antonia—or simply Antonia. First colonists revived from cryostasis.

AA21   Site Omega, experimental colony started on second moon (Trudovik) of TRAPPIST-2a by colonists disaffected with Antonia and New Virginia. Biosphere is simple and requires minimal terraforming; however, the colony never grows very large since it is domed due to extreme temperature. A collectivist society and government results due to scarcity of resources. Colony is eventually named Kerenskiy by locals.

AA25   Third and final colony on Cistercia established at Beaverton. Site Gamma plans are scrapped, and colony site Delta is selected on the shore of subcontinent-sized island Aopo. The crew names the planned colony Paradise, named for the lush equatorial islands. Lander 5, *San Salvador*, malfunctions, causing it to crash on an island in the wind-and-rain shadow of Aopo.

AA30   Contact with New Virginia is lost. Overland expedition from Antonia finds no trace of colonists, and only abandoned colony equipment. Some population and equipment transfer from Antonia to repopulate the colony. Site is renamed Roanoke.

AA40 Forty-five percent of Antonia and Roanoke colonists sick and dying of New Flu.

AA42 Roanoke colony fails for a second time.

AA50 Paradise colony is struggling because of crop failure (poor soil, not enough fresh water) and there is talk of recovering supplies from Roanoke.

AA75 By this date, every colony has experienced crises that drastically reduce population and damage infrastructure . . . however, each of them survives and the actions of the founders are becoming legend.

AA212 *Encyclopedia Astra* published by Gannon University of Antonia, Cistercia.

AA237 *Flint's People's History of Interstellar Exploitation* published by Trudovik Press, Kerenskiy, Trudovik.

Postscript and Acknowledgments

I am extremely grateful to the wonderful bunch of authors who contributed to this anthology. The stories were exciting and awesome for me to read, and I was particularly taken by how the various parts came together without (much) manipulation on my part. The world building was largely due to the contributors here. Many conversations at the LibertyCon and DragonCon conventions, by email and Facebook group, led to a collaborative story that went way beyond the mere "colonists die of some disease" notes that I had prepared. As the early stories came in, we shared them, or enough details, to give the later authors a glimpse into the mission, the ships, the colonies, and even the colonists. A notable example of this collaboration is the stories by David Weber and Mark Wandrey (individual and collaborative), who wanted to write about the same events. I suggested that they talk with each other and I mostly stayed out of those conversations. Along the way, this book went from anthology to shared world. They did this themselves, and you see the results before you. Another example is Brent M. Roeder and just about everybody in this book. Brent is currently my graduate student and soon to be postdoctoral fellow; he and I have bounced a lot of ideas off each other, both professional and fictional. Brent was instrumental in establishing the story of the Paradise colony, and we have various notes and drawings of landers, colony maps, etc. all through my office. Expect to see more science and science fiction from him in the future!

The genesis of this anthology goes back to *Stellaris: People of the Stars*, edited by Les Johnson and myself, and even further back to the Tennessee Valley Interstellar Workshop symposium in 2016 where the working track "Homo Stellaris" discussed what would happen to human biology and society as we became an interstellar civilization. At the same time Les and I were proposing *Stellaris* to be a mix of fiction and nonfiction, I had an idea for a collection of stories that would arise from the myths and legends told in those far-flung colonies about the larger-than-life exploits of their founders.

Baen Books publisher Toni Weisskopf met with me at SpikeCon/ Westercon/ NASFIC in the summer of 2019 and we refined the idea such that I would provide a colony synopsis and timeline, and the authors would write this "future history" of the colonization of TRAPPIST-2. I tried to keep the background material to a minimum while still giving the authors a framework for their stories. The results were something quite special, and several of the authors (and editors!) have plans for future stories in this setting.

I am indebted to these amazing authors as well as my skilled co-editor, Sandra. As always, this volume is dedicated to my parents. My mother, Marjorie Hampson, fed my interest in science fiction by watching all those late-night movies with me. She has been the first to read anything I've written (sometimes before I'm finished) and is always encouraging me to write more. My father, Leonard Hampson, is my role model and hero. He always made time to support me, even going so far as to drive a gaggle of teenagers to math and science competitions. All my love to my dear wife, Ruann, and sons Brian and Stephen, who put up with my writing . . . as well as numerous Dad jokes and puns.

Oh, and one last note . . . Regarding those encyclopedia entries from *Flint's People's History*? The folks on Trudovik have a wee bit of a bias, I wouldn't believe everything they tell you. . . .

—Rob Hampson, Winston-Salem, NC, December 2019

About the Editors

Robert E. Hampson, PhD., turns science fiction into science in his day job, and puts the science into science fiction in his spare time. Dr. Hampson is a Professor of Physiology / Pharmacology and Neurology with over 35 years' experience in animal neuroscience and human neurology. His professional work includes more than 100 peer-reviewed research articles ranging from the pharmacology of memory to the first report of a "neural prosthetic" to restore human memory using the brain's own neural codes.

He consults with authors to put the "hard" science in "Hard SF" and has written both fiction and nonfiction for Baen Books. His own hard-SF and mil-SF have been published by the US Army Small Wars Journal, Springer, Seventh Seal Press, and Baen. He is a member of SIGMA think tank and the Science and Entertainment Exchange— a service of the National Academy of Sciences. Find out more at his website: http://www.REHampson.com.

Sandra L. Medlock started her career as an editor and writer by reviewing environmental impact studies for the U.S. Air Force. She transitioned to editing for a private publisher and over time worked in the legal department for an oil company reviewing briefs and filings. Sandra moved to corporate writing and editing procedural and policy manuals. Her interest in computers and software led to a shift in her career as director and corporate trainer for two independent training companies and the IT department of a global manufacturer, where she wrote training curricula as well as company newsletters.

As a freelance journalist, Sandra wrote a weekly music column, a weekly technology column, and a monthly lifestyles column for three regional newspapers, including the *San Antonio Express-News*. She wrote freelance computer technology magazine articles, created and edited newsletters for several organizations, and was the producer of two computer shows on local radio.

Currently, Sandra tutors in math and English to students, provides an editing service, teaches music, and writes fiction. She lives outside San Antonio, Texas, with her husband, two very demanding small dogs, and a senior cat who has perfected Chewbacca's wail. You can find her on social media and blogging at sandramedlock.com.

About the Authors

D.J. (Dave) Butler has been a lawyer, a consultant, an editor, and a corporate trainer. His novels published by Baen Books include the epic fantasy trilogy *Witchy Eye*, *Witchy Winter*, and *Witchy Kingdom*, as well as the 1930s occult detective novel, *The Cunning Man* (co-written with Aaron Michael Ritchey), and the sword-and-planet noir *In the Palace of Shadow and Joy* (July 2020). He also writes for children: the steampunk fantasy adventure tales *The Kidnap Plot*, *The Giant's Seat*, and *The Library Machine* are published by Knopf. Other novels include *City of the Saints* from WordFire Press.

Dave also organizes writing retreats and anarcho-libertarian writers' events and travels the country to sell books. He plays guitar and banjo whenever he can and likes to hang out in Utah with his children. Dave in fact has a bridal kidnapping in his family tree, as recently as the 20th century.

Larry Correia is the creator of the *Wall Street Journal* and *New York Times* best-selling Monster Hunter series, with first entry *Monster Hunter International*, as well as urban fantasy hardboiled adventure saga the Grimnoir Chronicles, with first entry *Hard Magic*. His epic fantasy series The Saga of the Forgotten Warrior includes first entry *Son of the Black Sword*, follow-up *House of Assassins*, and latest entry *Destroyer of Worlds*. He is an avid gun user and advocate who shot on a competitive level for many years. Before becoming a full-time writer, he was a military contract accountant, and a small business accountant and manager. Correia lives in Utah with his wife and family.

Monalisa Foster won life's lottery when she escaped communism and became an unhyphenated American citizen. Her works tend to explore themes of freedom, liberty, and personal responsibility. Despite her degree in physics, she's worked in several fields including engineering and medicine. She and her husband (who is a writer-once-removed via their marriage) are living their happily ever after in Texas with their children, both human and canine. Her epic space opera, *Ravages of Honor*, is out now.

Daniel M. Hoyt is a systems architect for trajectory physics software, when not writing or wrangling royalty calculations. Dan has appeared in premier magazines like *Analog* and several anthologies, notably the recent *Stellaris: People of the Stars* (Baen), and Dr. Mike Brotherton's *Diamonds in the Sky* (funded by the National Science Foundation); and has edited *Fate Fantastic* and *Better Off Undead* for DAW. Having published in several genres, Dan returned to his science fiction roots with his debut space opera, *Ninth Euclid's Prince*, and has since become known for plausible science fiction tales with emotionally resonant characters. Catch up with him at danielmhoyt.com.

Sarah A. Hoyt has published over thirty novels with various publishers (and one indie) as well as a hundred short stories with magazines such as *Asimov's* and *Analog* (and a lot of anthologies). She prefers science fiction but has been instructed to give fair warning that no genre is safe from her. Well, except perhaps picture books and men's adventure. She also writes as Sarah D'Almeida and Elise Hyatt.

Sarah lives in Colorado with her husband and a varying number of cats. When not writing she can be found walking, reading, refinishing furniture or creating miles of fillet crochet.

Les Johnson is a husband, father, physicist, and author. *Publisher's Weekly* noted that "The spirit of Arthur C. Clarke and his contemporaries is alive and well . . ." when describing his 2018 novel, *Mission to Methone*. His 2018 nonfiction book, *Graphene: The Superstrong, Superthin, and Superversatile Material That Will Revolutionize the World*, was reviewed in the journal *Nature*, excerpted in *American Scientist* and on Salon.com. His latest anthology, *Stellaris: People of the Stars*, co-edited with Robert Hampson, was released by Baen Books in 2019.

Les was technical consultant for the movies *Europa Report* and *Lost in Space* and has appeared on the Discovery Channel series *Physics of the Impossible* in the "How to Build a Starship" episode. He has also appeared in three episodes of the Science Channel series *Exodus Earth* as well as several other television documentaries. Les was the featured "interstellar explorer" in the January 2013 issue of *National Geographic Magazine* and appeared again in the March 2019 issue for his work on solar sail space propulsion.

Les won the Watkins Prize for his popular science writing and was a nominee for the 2019 Prometheus Award for his novel, *Mission to Methone*.

By day, Les serves as Solar Sail Principal Investigator of NASA's first interplanetary solar sail space mission and leads research on various other advanced space propulsion technologies at the George C. Marshall Space Flight Center in Huntsville, Alabama. During his career at NASA, he served as the manager for the Space Science Programs and Projects Office, the In-Space Propulsion Technology Program, and the Interstellar Propulsion Research Project. Les thrice received NASA's Exceptional Achievement Medal, has 3 patents, and was selected for membership in Mensa.

A Webster Award winner and three-time Dragon Award finalist, **Chris Kennedy** is a Science Fiction/Fantasy/Young Adult author, speaker, and small-press publisher who has written over 25 books and published more than 100 others. Chris's stories include the "Occupied Seattle" military fiction duology, "The Theogony" and "Codex Regius" science fiction trilogies, stories in the "Four Horsemen" and "In Revolution Born" universes and the "War for Dominance" fantasy trilogy. Get his free book, *Shattered Crucible*, at his website, chriskennedypublishing.com.

Called "fantastic" and "a great speaker," he has coached hundreds of beginning authors and budding novelists on how to self-publish their stories at a variety of conferences, conventions and writing guild presentations. He is the author of the award-winning number 1 bestseller, *Self-Publishing for Profit: How to Get Your Book Out of Your Head and Into the Stores*, as well as the leadership training book, *Leadership from the Darkside*.

Chris lives in Virginia Beach, Virginia, with his wife, and is the holder of a doctorate in educational leadership and master's degrees in both business and public administration. Follow Chris on Facebook at facebook.com/ckpublishing.

Jody Lynn Nye lists her main career activity as "spoiling cats." She lives near Atlanta with three feline overlords, Athena, Minx, and Marmalade; and her husband, author and packager, Bill Fawcett. She has published more than 50 books, including collaborations with Anne McCaffrey and Robert Asprin, and over 165 short stories. Her latest books are *Rhythm of the Imperium* (Baen), *Moon Tracks* (with Travis S. Taylor, Baen), *Myth-Fits* (Ace), and *Once More, with Feeling*, a short book on revising manuscripts (WordFire). She teaches the annual DragonCon Two-Day Writers Workshop every Labor Day weekend in Atlanta, Georgia, and is a judge for the Writers of the Future Contest.

Vivienne Raper is a freelance journalist with a PhD in satellite engineering who somehow ended up writing about biomedical science for a living. Her fiction is unsurprisingly hard SF, but with a smattering of mil-SF and crime-thriller. Married with a medium-sized husband, small son and huge poodle, her hobbies include renovating a crumbling Victorian house and playing board games.

Brent M. Roeder is a neuroscience PhD candidate researching how to restore damaged memory function. A life-long geek, he enjoys world building and writing sci-fi and fantasy to relax from work. Very occasionally he even remembers to finish a story.

Catherine L. Smith earned a BS in Entomology, and a BS in Agronomy from the University of Wisconsin and subsequently an MS in Entomology from the University of Tennessee. She currently works as a Molecular Biologist tracking veterinary disease strains for autogenous vaccine production where she uses next-gen sequencing and metagenomic techniques to aid in diagnostics and novel pathogen discovery. Cathe has been a consultant on alien design for numerous science fiction authors, and finally begun writing her own stories.

A native Texan by birth (if not geography), **Christopher L. Smith** moved "home" as soon as he could.

Attending Texas A&M, he learned quickly that there was more to college than beer and football games. He relocated to San Antonio, attending SAC and UTSA, graduating in late 2000 with a BA in Literature. While there, he also met a wonderful lady who somehow found him to be funny, charming, and worth marrying. (She has since changed her mind on the funny and charming.)

Christopher began writing fiction in 2012. His short stories can be found in multiple anthologies, including John Ringo and Gary Poole's *Black Tide Rising*, Mike Williamson's *Forged in Blood*, Larry Correia and Kacey Ezell's *Noir Fatale*, and Tom Kratman's *Terra Nova*. He has co-written two novels, *Kraken Mare* with Jason Cordova, and *Gunpowder & Embers* with Kacey Ezell and John Ringo.

His cats allow his family and their dogs to reside with them outside of San Antonio.

Brad R. Torgersen is a multi-award-winning science fiction and fantasy writer whose book *A Star-Wheeled Sky* won the 2019 Dragon Award for Best Science Fiction Novel at the 33rd annual DragonCon fan convention in Atlanta, Georgia. A prolific short fiction author, Torgersen has published stories in numerous anthologies and magazines, to include several Best of Year editions. Brad is named in *Analog* magazine's Who's Who of top *Analog* authors, alongside venerable writers like Larry Niven, Lois McMaster Bujold, Orson Scott Card, and Robert A. Heinlein. Married for over 25 years, Brad is also a United States Army Reserve Chief Warrant Officer—with multiple deployments to his credit—and currently lives with his wife and daughter in the Mountain West, where they keep a small menagerie of dogs and cats.

International bestselling author of military sci-fi, space opera, and zombie apocalypse **Mark H. Wandrey** is also the only four-time DragonCon Dragon Award finalist!

His most successful works to date can be found in the Four Horsemen Universe (4HU), which he created and now shares with a slew of incredible authors, including his writing partner and publisher, Chris Kennedy. The first book in the series, *Cartwright's*

Cavaliers, was his second Dragon Award Finalist in 2017. With more than 40 titles available, and more every month, if you love Military Science Fiction, this is the series for you!

Living the full-time RV lifestyle as a modern-day nomad with his wife, Joy, and two Chihuahuas, Mark Wandrey has been writing science fiction since he was in grade school. He launched his professional career in 2004. Now, 15 years later, he has written more than 25 books and dozens of short stories.

Follow him on Facebook: facebook.com/mark. wandreyauthor.7; his website: worldmaker.us; or Patreon: patreon.com/MarkHWandrey.

David Weber was born in Cleveland a long, long time ago, and grew up in rural South Carolina. He was a bookworm from childhood, blessed with a father who collected autographed copies of every E.E. Smith hardcover and introduced him to Jack Williamson at the tender age of ten, and a mother who ran her own ad agency and encouraged him to write. From that start, with a love of history from a very early age and as a practitioner of RPGs before the world had ever heard of something called Dungeons & Dragons, it was inevitable he would fall into evil company and become a writer of science fiction himself. He sold his first novel to Jim Baen, his enabler at Baen Books, in 1989. Since that time, he has perpetrated 67 solo and collaborative novels (with 2 more delivered) and an unconscionable number of anthologies upon an innocent and unsuspecting public. He is perhaps best known for his character Honor Harrington, whom he hopes never to meet in a dark alley, given all the bones she has to pick with him. Fans should be warned never to press his "talk button," because if they do, they will never get him to shut up again.

Philip Wohlrab has spent time in the United States Coast Guard and has served for more than 13 years in the Virginia Army National Guard. Serving as a medic attached to an infantry company, he earned the title "Doc" the hard way while serving across two tours in Iraq. He came home and continued his education, earning a Master of Public Health degree in 2016. He currently works with Booz Allen Hamilton as an Adaptive Wargamer for the United States Air Force.